The Bridge
A Novel

Copyright © 2023 Gera Jones

All Rights Reserved

Geralogy, LLC
Muses Mills, Kentucky
geralogyllc@gmail.com

The Bridge – A Novel
Copyright© 2023 by Gera Jones
All Right Reserved

Printed on demand by Kindle Direct Printing
An Amazon.com company

ISBN# 9798391096771

Cover design by Gera Jones
Edited by Rebecca Herbert

With on-demand printing, this book has been expressly printed for you!
I hope you thoroughly enjoy your journey through these pages!

gerajones

This is a work of fiction. Unless otherwise indicated, all the names, characters, businesses, places, events and incidents in this book are either the **product of the author's imagination or used in a fictitious manner**. Any resemblance to actual persons, living or dead, or actual events is purely coincidental.

Dedication

To all those lost before their time.

If only you had found your purpose...

Acknowledgements

Thank you, God! You rested on my shoulders, casting glances on my fingers, as they cruised the keyboard. You continue to provide to me the right words! You know best!

To the Simon Kenton Memorial Bridge—my inspiration!

To Maysville, Kentucky—the setting for this novel. A unique river town!

To my favorite Maysville places and their people—Parc Café, Bradley's Boutique and Haberdashery, Kenton's Stories and Spirits, DeLite's, Sprinkles of Hope, McRobert's Furniture, Mason County Public Library, the Kentucky Gateway Museum Center, the random people along the streets, and any others I may have missed. You all contributed to my experiencing the specialness that only Maysville offers!

To my mother, Rebecca Herbert, for her editorial skills, enthusiasm, and encouragement—and—for pushing me to write a story set in her beloved hometown, Maysville, Kentucky. I never understood her passion and sincere love for this place until I set out on this story. Now, I too am embraced by its loving arms!

To my sister, Sherra, my faithful reader and critic! You are always there! Your viewpoint and insights are essential!

To the late Catherine Clark Pope, my grandmother. I will never forget and will always cherish the memories we made in the little white house on the corner of Florence Street (Maysville, KY). I once was asked, "If you had a hero, who would be yours?" My answer was, "Grandma Kentucky" (my special name for her). She was a woman of God and was built of steel. She had the same strength and fortitude as the bridge in this story. She was its human exemplification.

Forward

The Simon Kenton Memorial Bridge was born into service in 1931, just five years before the birth of my own mother. It is famed as one of the few historic suspension bridges remaining on the grand Ohio River, and its purpose was to connect the lives and livelihoods between Maysville, Kentucky and Aberdeen, Ohio and the many communities and cities beyond.

The bridge's namesake was Simon Kenton, a frontiersman and soldier who lived between 1755 and 1836. As an American explorer, he became known as the 'Father of Mason County,' home to Maysville, Kentucky.

While my other novels are set in fictious settings, Maysville, Kentucky is the setting for this novel, *The Bridge*. The characters and circumstances of this work are purely of my imagination; however, Maysville is a real place. There is no way to replicate the magic of this unique river town and the spirit that graces its streets, providing welcoming hugs to all that traverse. And, when visitors reluctantly prepare to leave this special place (and some don't!), Maysville reaches out with its humble hand, waves, and says, *"Now be sure and come back, y'all!"*

As this story wove itself, I was as drawn to the Simon Kenton Memorial Bridge as were my characters. Multiple visits to this majestic bridge, involved taking pictures (thus the cover of this book), and walking and sitting in its grandeur along the expansive Ohio River. Stately, steadfast, and confident, this magnificent structure exuded an energy that focused my story.

The Simon Kenton Memorial Bridge continues to stand with importance and purpose!

Author's Note

While this is a fictional work, this novel deals with the topic of suicide,
which is a particularly upsetting subject—to some and to everyone.
In no way am I endorsing suicide or making light of it in this work.
Suicide is not a subject people like to discuss--
this book hopes to bring awareness.
Suicide is real.
It happens.
And sometimes, it doesn't. It fails.
It is the failed attempts at suicide that we rejoice in,
but they are also the most troublesome.
Many times, failed attempts at suicide go unnoticed and unreported.
They are hidden, unobserved and unknown to loved
ones, friends, and professionals.

According to the American Foundation for Suicide Prevention (AFSP),
the following was true concerning suicide for the United States in 2022:
- the highest rate of suicides is among adults 25-34 years of age
- suicide is the 12th leading cause of death
- there were over 1.2 million suicide attempts
-13.48 out of 100,000 people died of suicide
- 130 people per day died of suicide
(That means someone died of suicide every 11 plus minutes in 2022)
-93% of adults surveyed in the United States believe suicide is preventable.

If you or someone you know is in emotional crisis
and/or is contemplating suicide,
please reach out to the 988 Suicide & Crisis Lifeline.
Just dial "988"
Confidential help is available 24 hours a day, 7 days a week.
Help save a life, even if it is your own!

https://988.ky.gov
https://www.afsp.org

Contents

Dedication
Acknowledgements
Author's Note
Chapter 1 – The Simon Kenton Memorial Bridge
Chapter 2 – Blazing Fury
Chapter 3 – A Woman's Scorn
Chapter 4 – Casting Call
Chapter 5 – Burned Bridges
Chapter 6 – The Duplex
Chapter 7 – Improvisions
Chapter 8 – The Real Why
Chapter 9 – The Kiss
Chapter 10 – The Meadows
Chapter 11 – Week Two
Chapter 12 – Back to Business
Chapter 13 – Communication
Chapter 14 – Thanksgiving
Chapter 15 – Things Are Moving
Chapter 16 – Mixed Messages
Chapter 17 – Getting in the Spirit
Chapter 18 – Home
Chapter 19 – Coming Clean
Chapter 20 – The Real Caroline
Chapter 21 – Piece of Cake
Chapter 22 – Christmas
Chapter 23 – Angels Sing

About the Author

CHAPTER 1 – THE SIMON KENTON MEMORIAL BRIDGE

Mark Meadows leaned over the counter that separated customers from the office assistant. He'd known Rhonda since Kindergarten, so she wasn't in a hurry to tell him to stand back like she would other customers. Her computer screens were conveniently hidden by the counter overhang, so Rhonda wasn't worried about what Mark could see. Mark, on the other hand, strained to see if Rhonda was really telling him was what she was seeing on those screens. Her fingers clicked with warp-speed on the keyboard, stopping to click the mouse here and there. The phone continued to blare its electronic noise going unanswered. When the ring quit, another call was right in line to take its place.

"Come on, Rhonda!" Mark said with urgency. "It's gotta be there!" Rhonda didn't look up at him, continuing to flip and scroll through screens. She worked quietly as Mark breathed down upon her, leaning over his folded arms that rested on the counter. Despite being tall, Mark saw only the bottom sections of the three screens before the woman. Finally, her fingers quit clicking.

She pushed back the keyboard and folded her hands on the desk. Slowly she looked up at Mark, a disturbing look on her face. The look was accompanied by a sigh. It was a deep sigh. Silence followed as her eyes scanned his face. He knew right then. She was trying to find a way to tell him. Easy. But there was nothing "easy" about the words that were about to come.

"It's just not there, Mark." Rhonda matted her lips together. She watched as he stood erect, with the palms of his hands resting on the counter. His face was blank. The words floated around him in the air, but they did not resonate with him. He looked at her silently. Speechless.

"Like I told you when you came in, I haven't seen Jake all week." Rhonda repeated her earlier words, hoping they would register with her friend. "The last time I saw him was Friday evening when we both left for the weekend. He told me to have a good weekend and he'd see me Monday, and he drove off in his car. Just like any other Friday." Rhonda looked into Mark's eyes to see if he was finally grasping her words. Maybe just a little. She went on, "Then Monday the calls began. Everyone was wanting to cash in their shares. I honestly don't know what he did with your money, Mark. Well, rather, your parents' money. It was deposited in the investment account the day you gave him the check, just like everyone else's, but I'm not seeing where he ever bought the shares with it. And now the money is gone. And so is Jake." She paused as Mark's eyes finally connected with hers.

"Gone," he said. "Just like...POOF!" His hands splayed to the sides. Mark was having difficulty understanding how four-hundred and fifty thousand dollars could just vanish. He searched her eyes for answers.

"The account is empty. I'm as baffled as you are Mark." Rhonda's tone was filled with a mix of sympathy, anxiety, and fear. "Like I said, you are not the only one! There are probably a hundred investors just like you out there! They're calling right now!" She tilted her head towards the ringing. "All I know is that the shares were never purchased, and the entire balance in the investment account appears to have been electronically transferred to another account. At a bank in another country. I have no way of knowing what or where that is. I'm afraid Jake's pulled a fast one on all of us!"

Rhonda stretched to look out the window behind Mark. Her brows pulled together as her mouth parted slightly. Mark turned to see what caught her attention. A dark car was parked in one of the empty spots out front, and three men in suits were exiting the vehicle. Probably the FBI. Several of the other investors had already reported their money missing. as well as the missing Jake Perry. Rhonda told him it was only a matter of time before the FBI and the SEC swooped down. She took another deep breath, this time bracing herself for what was about to walk through the door.

"Mark," she looked back at her friend, who wiped at a tear forming in the corner of his eye. "Look, you need to go report this to the police. Get on the list of investors. But right now, you've got to get out of here. The FBI is about to walk through the door, and you don't need to be here, okay? I expect I won't be here very long myself!"

Mark nodded, glancing out the window. "Okay. Thanks, Rhonda. I appreciate your help." Mark turned to leave, but paused, looking back at his long-time friend. She had dropped her face in her hands, bracing herself. "Prayers to you, Rhonda!" She never looked up. She just nodded her head in her hands.

As Mark exited the door of the building, one of the three men held the door for him waiting for him to clear the doorway. Each of them wore dark colored suits and mirrored sunglasses. It reminded him of a scene out a movie he'd seen years before. Apparently, they really did dress like that. He curtailed an inappropriate laugh, but sometimes when his nerves flared, a laugh was his nervous response.

As he pulled the truck door closed, he sat a moment and watched through the window of the investment office. The men were displaying badges to a now standing Rhonda Wheeler. The look on Rhonda's face imprinted instantly in Mark's mind. This wasn't going to be good for her, but he'd known her a long time. More than thirty years. There was no way she could have had anything to do with whatever scam Jake was pulling! She didn't even really know what happened. The only information she had was what she was pulled together from data on the computer. That and the fact that Jake was missing for three days now.

Then again, Mark knew Jake for as long as he'd known Rhonda. They'd all gone to school together, and Mark had even played sports with Jake in middle and high school. Mark trusted Jake and never would have thought him capable of some sort of scam like this. That trust was the main reason why Mark entrusted his parents' life savings to Jake. Mark knew Jake would do right by them. So much for what Mark knew. He suddenly felt nauseous.

Swallowing hard to keep the bile from rising, Mark's mind reeled with thoughts. As he backed out of the parking spot and pulled away, the investment office grew smaller in the rearview mirror, finally disappearing. And who knows… maybe this had nothing to do with Jake. Maybe this wasn't Jake's doing, and he was as much a victim as the rest of them. It was too soon to point fingers. The police, the FBI, and whoever else was involved in matters like this had investigating to do. But how long would that take? Mark had heard of instances where people absconded with large amounts of money and the investigation took years and years, especially if they escaped to other countries. His parents' money might never be recovered. The thought made Mark shiver.

Mark had been avoiding Beth's questions about whether he spoke to Jake about cashing in some of the shares. He told his eldest sister he hadn't been able to get ahold of Jake. Which was true, but Mark worried about how long he could stall telling her. How long it would be before the news of Jake's disappearance hit the newspapers and local T.V. In fact, he was shocked it hadn't already. Usually, the media gobbled up a good scandal or even just hints of one. Something was definitely off with this situation.

As Rhonda suggested, Mark drove over to the police station and made a report on his and his parents' investment gone missing. Mark explained to the officer taking the report that he had financial power of attorney for his ailing parents, so it was actually their money. Four hundred and fifty thousand. He told the officer how he had stopped at Perry Investments on Monday to inquire about cashing in a portion of the investment to cover unexpected costs for an addition for his parents on his sister's house but was told Jake Perry hadn't shown at the office. He recounted what he learned from Rhonda that morning: the money had never been invested in the shares and had presumably disappeared with Mr. Perry. The officer presented a grim expression to Mark once his finished scribbling on a form. He sat back in his desk chair, the chair tilting backwards.

"Mark, I gotta tell ya," Officer Keyser began, "We've been taking reports and statements for the last three days on this. There's a lot of people affected by this, and several of them are pretty influential folk, if ya know what I mean. I hate to tell ya, but the amount of money you're talking about is a drop in the bucket compared to some of these folks."

Mark watched Officer Keyser bounce slightly in the chair. "So, what are you telling me?"

"Look, there's gonna be all sorts of agencies involved in this." Officer Keyser quit bouncing and leaned forward on the desk. "The FBI got here this morning, and the Securities and Exchange people and Department of Justice folks are due at any time. Then there's the District Attorney, the Attorney General. Plus, the IRS is gonna have its nose in this, and a whole laundry list of those financial agencies that are going to descend like buzzards to try to pick this thing clean. And, if this Jake guy's left the country like some are saying? Who knows who else will get involved!" He paused looking a Mark for a few seconds. "All I'm saying is be prepared for this thing to go on for a long while."

Officer Keyser was not smiling. He was being frank. "Look. We got your information, and if we hear anything, we'll let ya know. That's about the best we can do right now."

Mark let out a sigh. This was not what he wanted to hear. As he rose from the chair opposite the officer, he felt his mood drop a little further. It began to swirl inside his bile-coated stomach. As he walked toward the exit, his feet became heavy, and each step being weighed down by an invisible a mass of concrete, dragging him down further and further. *How…just how was he going to explain any of this to his family?*

When he left the police department, he decided to stop and check on his guys at a few of the jobs they still had going on. Maybe it would take his mind off his current worries. He spent the rest of the afternoon, going from jobsite to jobsite, checking on the progress of the work. Most jobs were nearly complete. As soon as they were, his guys would be officially on seasonal unemployment. Mark had a few workers that, like himself, were part of the leaf and snow removal crew and worked in the fall and winter when called to duty.

At the last jobsite, Jared approached Mark as he climbed into the truck cab.

"Hey, man!" Jared threw his hand up. Mark paused closing the door, waiting to hear what his friend and colleague wanted. Jared was one of the few who worked off season. "Everything okay, Mark?" Jared asked.

"Yeah, I guess so," Mark replied. He shrugged his shoulders, trying to seem believable. "Why? Does something seem wrong?"

"No. Well…yeah," Jared said. "You seem a little off. You're not getting…"

"No, Jared. I'm fine," Mark lied. He felt the anxiety rising and tugging at his collar. Jared began working for Mark's landscaping company from the very start, and over years of laboring long days together, they had become good friends. Jared was well aware of Mark's bouts of depression. He could spot when Mark's mood was slipping and knew how the change in seasons tended to bring him further down.

"Well, you better get that light of yours going when you get home!" Jared patted Mark on the arm. "Ward it off, man!" Mark saluted in reply and closed his door.

Fifteen minutes later, Mark pulled in the driveway of his duplex. Located in one of the developments off Route 68, he owned the entire home but lived on the left side. Modern in style, he had done the landscaping the year before and used his home as one of his promotional pictures when bidding jobs. The month before, Mark rented the right-side apartment to a pleasant young family, so he was still getting used to seeing toys in the driveway and in the back yard. As one of his fall projects, Mark planned to fence the backyard to add the safety element for their children. And maybe for his own if that ever materialized. Waving to the young mother, who supervised her toddler on the trike-like toy, Mark unlocked his door and disappeared inside.

His keys hung limp in his hands, and Mark leaned against the closed front door and closed his eyes. He tried to take in a slow deep breath to calm his nerves, but his lungs seemed to reject the air. They were tense and tight. His whole body was tense. Silently, he shook his head. What was he going to do? How was he going to explain this to his parents and his siblings? That he lost every penny of his parents' money? *How could he be so stupid?* He had an MBA. He knew better than put everything in a 'sure thing' stock. Unfortunately, it really didn't matter. If he had put it in a conservative mutual fund, he'd be facing the same situation. The money never made it to *any* investment and now was gone!

Jennifer had been right. Mark hated to admit this to himself. She told him over and over that he was a bad judge of character. And he was too trusting. She certainly had proven that true when he found out she'd been cheating on him for over two years. He'd been oblivious. He believed her when she said she was too tired from shuttling the girls around after school, cleaning the house, doing the shopping and meal preparation. He never suspected a thing. Not even when she quit cooking, and the house showed lack of care. When Jennifer handed him the divorce papers, she might as well have handed him a bomb. His whole life imploded in a matter of seconds.

And it was happening again, only instead of happening in seconds, the implosion was in slow motion occurring over days. Taking his coat off, Mark hung it and his keys on the rack in the closet. He walked toward the bar countertop that separated the kitchen from the living room and sat on one of the chairs. Yep, days. At least with Jennifer, it had been quick. He shook his head. As he did, it felt light and aloof, like it was going to roll right off his neck. Though the tension squeezed his muscles and bones, his insides felt empty. Lifeless.

She had called him a 'screw-up.' Over and over. And Jennifer hadn't been the only one. Larry and Lynn were always asking Mark when he was going to pull his life together. His reply to his siblings was, "You don't understand." They weren't plagued with the issues Mark was. Beth sort of understood, but the only ones' who had ever fully 'gotten' Mark had been his dad and mom. Mark always assumed it was the psychiatrist in his dad. As far as his mom understanding him, Mark figured it was because she was just like him. She had her spells of darkness and disappeared for days and sometimes weeks from the family picture.

As he pondered his situation, his phone began to vibrate in his pocket. It was Beth. He knew it without even pulling it out. His sister had called at least a dozen times during the day and left at least four voicemails, none of which he listened to. He didn't need to. He knew what they said, and he didn't have any answers for his sister. Not yet. And maybe not for quite a long while, if ever. Mark dropped his face into his hands much the same way Rhonda had dropped hers earlier that day. He knew no good was to come from this.

***

Caroline drove the white Range Rover up and down streets in town. She drove slowly, peering into homes when she could, trying to get a glance of what a normal life looked like. *What was normal?* She kept asking herself this. It was a question she first posed to herself as a child, but here she was still searching for the answer. She knew she wasn't going to find the answer on the streets, but the driving was a distraction. It kept her moving. So, she didn't have to think.

She had been sure she discovered 'normal' on that sunny spring day when she sat on the bench built around the huge oak in front of Allie Young Hall. She'd had her binder open in her lap and was struggling to keep the pages flat in the soft breeze. It was last minute studying for her Macroeconomics final. She was going into the final with a "C" average, so passing the class depended solely on her performance on this last exam. As she moved to smooth a flapping page, it wasn't her hand that held the page, but rather Steven's.

The handsome fraternity boy had been in most of her general business classes, and he seemed to effortless sail through the course material and tests. He had slipped onto the bench beside her without her knowing and greeted her with that carefree and charismatic smile. He'd been paying her attention over the last few weeks of the semester, but she couldn't understand why someone like him wanted anything to do with someone like her. But she could not deny the tingle that travelled her spine down through her extremities when he was close and gave her his coveted smile. As his hand held the page down, Caroline had smiled back. Then his hand had moved over hers, and he leaned over and left a gentle, lingering kiss on her cheek!

"That's a good luck kiss," Steven had said. "You're going to ace this!"

A swell of confidence soared through Caroline, and she did 'ace' the exam. She had attributed her success completely to the kiss, and she thanked Steven with a kiss of her own. Which led to more kisses, and then dates, and before she knew it, Steven was showing her the Range Rover. It was his gift to her for their tenth wedding anniversary. Yes, on that day she believed whole-heartedly she knew what 'normal' was.

Flemingsburg was a quaint little town with some of the prettiest homes, some even historic. Her home was one of the prettiest, but it was outside town in one of the up-and-coming developments. The development lifestyle offered a little more land around the homes, and depending on how the property was landscaped, led to the appearance that those homes were more...well...grand. At least they tried. Caroline's home was among those trying to be grand. Prominent. Steven wouldn't see it any other way. It was part of the image that was so important for his business.

Providia Life and Casualty. Steven was the agent/broker, but Caroline had played a critical role in helping their branch of the company get established. As an accountant, she took care of the books during the start-up years, while also working in the business department of the university in nearby Morehead. She still worked at the university, but a few years earlier Steven had finally encouraged her to let go of the bookkeeping responsibilities at Providia. The business could afford its own bookkeeper, and he was afraid Caroline was working too much. He wanted her to stay fresh for entertaining and wining and dining clients. Unfortunately, after some cuts to the state budget passed down to the universities and community colleges, Caroline found herself working additional hours. Then, a 'realignment' of positions reassigned her as an advisor in the business education department where she worked with students on their schedules. During peak times, her days became even longer. Caroline was thankful she didn't still have the Providia responsibilities!

Caroline turned onto the road that passed the old courthouse and cruised down the hill to the new courthouse. She felt sorry for the older buildings that lined the hill. Many of them still occupied by businesses and were sorely dilapidated, just a shadow of their former glory. She never could understand why someone—the city even—hadn't restored these fading gems. At the bottom of the hill, the light was red. She waited patiently for it to turn so she could turn. She was in no hurry. She had nowhere to go. Not really.

The red glow illuminated another tear running down her cheek from the corner of her eye. Caroline quickly wiped it away. She didn't want to be seen crying. Although who was going to see? The Range Rover had tinted windows, and she was the only vehicle at the intersection. There was absolutely no one in sight on the sidewalks at this time of evening. Glancing again in the rearview mirror, she saw the blotches were beginning to clear from her face.

When the light changed to green, Caroline guided the Range Rover to the right, passing more of the historic buildings, then the schools, and then the last stoplight in town. Green, she drove right through. She didn't even think about it. Her only regret in leaving Flemingsburg was that she hadn't made more of an effort to become friends with some of the people in the houses she passed.

She'd put all over her energy, attention, and emotion into Steven, and Steven alone. She'd spent every available moment and thought on building up him and building up the business. She failed to make time to develop friends. Sure, she had plenty of acquaintances, but they were acquaintances of both her and Steven and mainly related to the business. But did she have any true friends? You know, the ones you could turn to in a crisis? Like the one Caroline found herself submerged in? No. Caroline had not developed any of those. Steven had been her world. And now he was not.

She headed along Route 11, not even realizing she was headed towards Maysville. She was just driving. Driving aimless around. Her mind empty. She had cried its contents out already, and her heart sat shriveled in her chest from dehydration. She wasn't even sure if it continued beat. But it must. She was still moving.

When she woke up that morning, she had no clue she was facing the longest day of her life. A day that would seem to have no end. She'd poured the rest of the coffee from the pot into her travel mug and then headed for the door to the garage. But as she passed Steven's office, the house phone began to ring. Rather than go back to the kitchen, she stepped into the office to grab the call. It was a Robocall. She replaced the handset as soon as the recorded message began playing. *Who Robocalls this early in the morning?* She reached for her coffee that she'd set on the desk, and as she did, her eyes landed on a document in an open file folder on Steven's desk.

It was her name in the document that caught her attention, and she paused to take a closer look. As she read through the paragraphs, her head jutted back when she realized she was looking at her life insurance policy. Her own life insurance policy, and it was open to the page that discussed payouts for accidents. *Accidents?* The notion caught her off guard. Why would Steven have the policy out? And looking at the accident section? She flipped the page over and scanned that text. It spelled out the payout policy for death by suicide. None. Zero. Then she flipped to the front of the policy and found what she was looking for on the third page. Caroline Reeves-White was worth $1,000,000. Dead.

A chill ran through Caroline. Confusion jumbled her insides. She restored the document to the state in which she found it, with a variety of thoughts swirling. She glanced around on the desk to see if Steven's policy was out as well, but the rest of the folders on the desk related to policies he'd been working on for others the night before. *Why...why would he have her policy out?* It simply stumped her. Maybe he was getting ready to revise them? Caroline picked up her coffee and headed out the door, glancing once again towards the office with a perplexed look.

As she backed the Range Rover out of the garage, she fully intended on heading to work. It was what she did every day during the week. And lately, sometimes on the weekend. But as she came to the stop sign at the end of her road, instead of turning towards Morehead, the Range Rover veered left. Before Caroline consciously grasped where she was going, she had pulled into a parking spot in front of Providia Life and Casualty, right next to a Mercedes. A pink Mercedes. There was only one pink Mercedes in town, and that belonged to Brandia Damron. The Mary Kay lady.

Not even eight in the morning and already Steven had a client. No wonder he'd been leaving early lately. Business was booming, just like he said. Caroline entered the office and was greeted by an empty reception area. Kathy, the office assistant/bookkeeper, usually arrived around eight-fifteen after she dropped her kids at school, so Caroline sat in one of the reception chairs, waiting for Steven to finish with his client.

Even in the reception area, Caroline could hear Steven's and Brandia's voices as they discussed business. Caroline initially paid no attention. She was thinking about her to-do list at work, but when she heard her name murmured, the voices suddenly seized her interest. She shot a look in the direction of the hallway that led back to Steven's office, and in an instant, she was on her feet halfway down the hall. Their voices were now completely audible through the closed door.

"I thought you were divorcing Caroline?" A tone of disgust was in Brandia's voice. "You've been telling me this for almost a year now! When's it going to happen, Steven?"

"Brandia, I told you it's going to take some time. There are too many things involved." *The frustration in Steven's tone indicated this was not their first discussion of the matter.* "Caroline's name is on just about everything. The house, the business, our investments. I'm slowly getting everything moved over to my name. But, if I slap her with divorce papers right now, she'll get half of everything. Maybe more."

Caroline's hand went to her mouth. Really? She'd get half? Or was Steven just saying this?

"Steven, I love you with my entire soul, but sweetie...you know I'm not getting any younger. We've been together for two years, and I am trying to be so patient. My childbearing years are fading fast. If you're wanting a Steven Junior, we're going to have to work quickly! But I am not going to have a baby with you unless you are completely and totally mine!"

"I know, I know, darling. We've been through this." The pause that followed indicated to Caroline that Steven was pacing. It was what he did when in a tough spot. "Look, my love…I've been looking into some other options, but I really can't discuss them right now. Can you be content with that for the moment?"

"What kinds of options?" Curiosity ruled Brandia.

"I told you. I can't discuss them. But one or the other might solve our issue. Permanently. I just to research them a little further…"

The conversation sounded like it was dwindling. Not wanting to get caught listening, Caroline turned abruptly and made her way quietly to the exit. Once outside, she realized she had at some point stopped breathing. As she closed the door on the Range Rover and started the engine, she gasped for air. She took several more gulps of air as she backed out and left the parking lot, careful to make no more noise than necessary. Fortunately, the vehicle was hybridized, sometimes emitting no noise at all.

As the oxygen flowed to her extremities, she felt tingling and numbness simultaneously. Inside her head, the conversation repeated over and over. *Divorce. Baby. Options. Two years!* Heading down the road, she felt angry and distraught and heartbroken and deceived and betrayed. The feelings churned together into a hard mass that collected at the base of her throat, half choking her. She managed to pull the Range Rover into the vacant parking lot of a convenience store long closed. The tears washed away any sign of makeup from her face in the first minute, and she found herself hyperventilating in between wails. Wails that she prayed no one heard.

She had no idea how long the Range Rover remained in the lot. But she became keenly aware it had been too long. If one of the town's police cars had patrolled by earlier, and they found her still there, they would investigate. She started the engine, and the car rolled back onto the road as Caroline continued to ingest and process what she'd heard.

She'd had suspicions Steven might have been seeing someone. The dinner meetings with clients, the working late at the office or the not being at home when Caroline got home from working late. And just what did he do on those Saturdays when she had advising orientations at work? Steven was always so vague about things. But she'd never had enough evidence to be sure. She had gut feelings. Intuitions. Suspicions without anything to back them up. Caroline had to admit—there was the possibility that she did not want to ask Steven. To confront him. Perhaps she was afraid of the answer and of destroying her ivory tower vision of their marriage and life. But now she knew. *Now she knew.*

She drove aimlessly for hours. She drove down roads she'd always wondered where they led. Many of them took her other roads to explore. And more. As the Range Rover kept moving, her thoughts knitted together all the stray scraps that had permeated her and Steven's life, but that she'd never paid attention to. With each turn, the scraps began to form a cloth, an underlying reality that Caroline was completely unaware. An underlying reality that turned Caroline's vision of life—of 'normal'—into a lie. Fiction.

As she drove along the dark highway, she passed dark fields that had been harvested and prepared for winter. She'd come across clusters of lights here and their where homes and barns huddled together. Otherwise, the October night sky was clear and dark. She headed towards Maysville, but she felt indifferent. At this point, it was just another place. As the Range Rover cruised smoothly down the highway, the road Caroline travelled internally was bumpy and full of holes. Her whole life was undergoing review. Every important decision made in her thirty years was summonsed in front of her. On trial. Before a jury and judge of one. The decisions she previously regarded as good decisions, she decided were in fact very bad ones. Her basic notions of good and bad were totally askew. And she realized at some point she had traded her soul for what she mistakenly thought to be 'the good life.' The truth was racing at her faster than her mind could process.

She'd been conned. Steven had used her. Caroline wondered now if he ever even loved her. Steven had kidnapped her and systematically cut her off from her family, and then her friends. He said and did things to hamper her establishing new friends. Without her recognizing what he was doing, he was locking her away in that ivory tower. But after what she heard, after hours of scouring her mind and soul, and after a day devoted to shedding some of the most unbearable emotions and grief, the only emotion that remained with her was anger.

It sat inside her quietly all day, waiting for its moment. When the clouds of thoughts and emotions started to part, anger reminded her of the first thing she saw that morning. Anger slapped the pages before her once again. Her life insurance policy. Opened to the page concerning accidental death payouts. Steven had said it himself. He was "researching other options." If an unfortunate accident befell her, not only would that son-of-a-bitch end up with everything they owned, but he'd walk away with a hefty million in addition. Anger would be damned if that happened!

As the lights of Maysville appeared in front of her, Caroline felt herself grow hot. How? How could she stop him? Then it occurred to her—she could be driving a time bomb right then. Was her car rigged? Brakes? Steering column? What do they do to cars to cause 'accidents'? The thought made her even angrier. She knew Steven. She knew him pretty well after ten-plus years. He was determined. She'd gotten to know him even better during the last twelve hours. He was beyond determined. She needed to outwit him. But the only way she could think to do so had a heavy cost. But at this point, what did she have to lose? She'd lost everyone and everything she loved in her life. *What was one more?*

As the Range Rover turned towards downtown Maysville, the brightly lit bridge crossing the Ohio River came into view. The lights twinkled in the night sky like dewy stars perched on the bridge, beckoning her. Whispering her name. Instantly, the idea filled Caroline. She couldn't keep Steven from everything, but she could keep him from the insurance payoff!

She drove around downtown Maysville, slowly cruising the one and two-way streets, as she formulated her plan and assessed her options. On the fourth trip around downtown, she passed the road that led downtown and headed for the road to the bridge. The Simon Kenton Memorial Bridge. The bridge was already famous in those parts, but was she about to make it a little more famous?

When the stoplight turned green, Caroline guided the Range Rover to the left and stomped the gas pedal. The thing she loved most about her Range Rover was its ability to accelerate in seconds. The sides of the two-lane bridge began to speed by as she approached the center of the bridge. She didn't even look down to see how fast she travelled. She kept her eye on her target: the side of the bridge. And as she made a sharp left turn into the side of the bridge—and hopefully through the side of the bridge and into the dark waters below—her headlights illuminated a man. A man standing on the upper railing grasping one of the suspension wires. As her headlights shone on him, he turned to look. Their eyes met. It was the last thing she saw.

CHAPTER 2 – BLAZING FURY

Mark heard a car accelerating on the bridge. Hopefully, it would pass quickly, and the driver would not notice him on the upper railing. The steel suspension wire he held onto was cold in his left hand, and it matched the cold and emptiness he felt inside as he mustered the courage to do what needed done. He stared down into the dark water below. The current of the river hidden by the night except for the reflection of a bridge light here and there. The whole sordid scandal aired on the six o'clock news. "Breaking news," the media called it, although it had been breaking over the last three days. As he listened to the report, Mark decided right then he could not face his family. He shut his phone off, stuck it in his back pocket and left the house.

If Beth and the others couldn't get him by phone, they would come knocking. Hopefully, his body would have washed down beyond Cincinnati or be nearly to Louisville by then. His hand loosened its grasp from the wire just as the speeding car approached. When the car made a sharp left turn toward the side of the bridge, its headlights shining on him, a startled Mark tightened his grasp on the wire out of instinct.

Turning his head, he saw a flash of a woman's face through the windshield and a glimpse of her eyes, as she came towards the side of the bridge. She abruptly swerved right, hitting the high curb, bouncing up on it. The driver's side back fender hit the railing on the bridge, sending the white vehicle careening towards the right side of the bridge. Mark felt the steel vibrate with his feet. The car again hit the curb and bounded up on the sidewalk. However, the Range Rover didn't bounce off the side of the bridge this time but rode partially up its side, sending it airborne backwards towards the center of the bridge. The vehicle landed on its hood and roof. The scene occurred in seconds, but in Mark's mind it took minutes to play out. Shaking his head, Mark witnessed every small detail of the crash but heard not a single sound until the car came to rest upside-down. Like there was a three-second delay on the noise that accompanied it. The sound couldn't keep pace with the speed of the events.

Mark turned around on the railing, still grasping the wire, taking in the whole scene. Everything became painfully still and quiet. Mark was comprehending what had just unveiled before him. A waffling metallic noise on the other side of the car interrupted the silence. Something fell off. The noise nudged Mark to remember at least one person was inside. He jumped down from the railing and hopped off the curb, moving urgently toward the car. The smell of gasoline permeated the air. Going around the side of the car to the driver's door and sinking to his knees, Mark tried to look in the car. The dark tint held the broken window glass together, shielded sight of anything within. He cupped his hands and peered into the corner of the windshield. He made out the shape of a figure in hanging limply from the driver's seat. He saw no further than the driver's seat, and there was no movement.

Going to the driver's door, he attempted to open the door. It started to open but the top of the door was stuck on the pavement. Mark pushed his shoulder against the side of the car attempting to tilt it enough to free the door top so the door could open. On the third try, he shifted the car just enough to push open the door with his foot. Dropping back on his knees, he stuck his head into the dark car looking for victims. The only person he saw was the driver. The woman. He reached into the dark car and fumbled around the base of the seat, which was now in the air. When he found the button for the seatbelt release, he positioned his body to help ease the woman down from the seat instead of letting her fall. He was aware she might have serious injuries and wanted to minimize any additional injury by removing her from the car.

As he struggled to gently extract her, Mark was aware the puddle of gasoline expanded, and the cloud of fumes intensified. With the woman in his arms, Mark scooted on his bottom to clear the doorway of the car. Outside the car, Mark laid the unconscious woman on the pavement and stood to look around for help. A couple of vehicles slowed as they approached from the Ohio side. Another was at a full stop from the Kentucky side. He smelled the smoke before he saw the flames. Acridness tinged the odor of molten plastic. Glancing towards the exposed underside of the car, flames peeped up from the engine compartment.

Mark motioned the other motorists to stay back, and he quickly scooped the woman into his arms and dashed away from the car. Clearing a good forty-something feet from the car, the explosion knocked Mark and the woman to the ground. Mark thought his back was ablaze, but as he rolled on his back, he realized it was the intense heat. He saw the driver from the Kentucky side coming towards them, braving the inferno. Mark rolled onto his knees and once again lifted the woman in his arms. With the help of the other man, Mark got on his feet, and they hurried away from the blistering flames.

Mark laid the limp woman on the sidewalk a safe distance from the blaze. He put two fingers besides her neck to check for a pulse. His fingers felt faint thumping in her vein.

"She's alive," Mark said looking up at the man who'd helped them to safety. Beyond the man, the lady in a car that pulled up next to the pickup had her cell phone to her ear and spoke unheard words.

"Thank you!" Mark said to the man. The man had beads of sweat on his forehead, and a reddish tint colored his skin.

"Were you both in the car?" the man asked. "What happened? It looks bad!"

Mark looked towards the white car—no longer white but recolored in blue, yellow, and orange flames. An occasional flash of green or purple shot out as a component or chemical caught fire. He looked down at the woman lying lifeless on the sidewalk. Thoughts flew through his mind. *What was she trying to do? Drive off the bridge? She was trying to drive off the bridge! That's it!*

"No, I was taking a walk on the bridge," Mark replied. "The car...the woman...she came flying over the bridge. It looked like she hit the curb and spun out of control." His hand gestured towards the various sides of the bridge the vehicle impacted.

"Well, she sure is lucky you were walking along!" the man said over the sound of an approaching siren.

Lucky indeed.

The police car approached the stopped cars, pulling to a stop the opposite lane. The officer climbed out of the patrol car and spoke into a radio fastened at his shoulder, pausing as the lady on the cell phone walked towards him. She pulled the phone away from her head, speaking more unheard words to the officer. He motioned her towards the car and truck, and she abruptly turned back. The officer strode towards the trio on the sidewalk. Mark recognized him as Officer Keyser from earlier that day. Beyond Officer Keyser, he watched the lady in the car back up, turn and head off the bridge. In the distance, more sirens sounded. Probably fire trucks and maybe an ambulance, Mark assumed.

Office Keyser first inquired who was driving the truck. The other man raised his hand, saying, "I am."

"I need ya to back up and move your vehicle off the bridge so that the fire department and ambulance will have access," Officer Keyser said. The man agreeably hurried towards his truck to clear the path.

"What happened here?" Office Keyser asked Mark. The officer looked at him a moment and then added, "Hey, you're the Mark guy from this morning..."

Mark nodded. The blaring sirens got louder. "I was just out for a walk, and this car came speeding over the bridge. It

29

looked like she hit the curb and lost control. The car bounced around a bit until it ended upside down." Mark motioned his hand towards the sides of the bridge, explaining what he saw. *Which he did see. And he had been walking on the bridge. At least, until he had climbed up on the railing.* He thought it best to leave that part out. Yes, this would be his story. He wasn't sure what the woman's story would be when she woke. *Well, if she woke.*

"Ya get her out of the car?" Officer Keyser asked. Another patrol car pulled behind his.

"Yes." Mark wiped at his forehead with the back of his hand. He felt something wet and dripping. "I smelled gasoline immediately after the car flipped. I rushed to get her out before the whole thing caught fire."

"Did she hit ya?" the office asked.

Mark looked at him, squinting his eyes and furrowing his brows. "No, why?"

"Ya look in bad a shape as she does!" Officer Keyser pointed to Mark's forehead. Mark raised the back of his hand. *Blood.*

"I must have gotten banged up when the car blew," Mark replied. "It knocked us both down as I was trying to get her away from the burning car."

"Any idea who the woman is?" the officer asked, looking impatiently in the direction of his colleague and for the other emergency vehicles.

"No," Mark replied. "And I'd say anything that told us who she is has burned up!" He pointed at the car. It was melting before their eyes, with only the thickest parts of metal resisting the heat.

The fire trucks arrived on the scene followed by the ambulance. The firefighters began assembling their gear and grabbing hoses to extinguish the blaze, and the EMTs came towards Mark and the unconscious woman rolling a gurney loaded with life-saving equipment. Mark stepped aside to allow the EMTs to go to work—blood pressure, checking her pupils, pulse and listening to her heart and breathing.

They worked quickly, as Officer Keyser retold them the information from Mark.

One of the EMTs, suddenly took interest in Mark and flashed a light in his eyes, checked out the cut on his head, and asked him if he hurt anywhere. Mark was so focused on rescuing and tending the woman, he hadn't given any thought to his own condition. He realized his head and shoulder hurt, along with a few other joints and spots on his body.

"Well, we're going to take you in with the woman," the EMT said. "That's a nasty cut on your head. You'll need stitches, and they'll probably want to check you over. Possible head trauma. Being thrown down in a blast can cause internal injuries."

Mark just nodded his head. It surprised him that he was now a victim as well. At least, no one was questioning his story about being out walking on the bridge.

***

The beeping urged Caroline's return to consciousness. She thought it was a dream, but as the fogginess parted, it was just beeping. Annoying beeping. Her eyelids fluttered but were too heavy to open. She rolled her head toward the beeping sound, quickly discovering that was a bad idea. Pain screamed around the inside of her scalp. Oh! Her head froze in its new position. The beeping continued, swirling inside her head with stabbing pangs the movement stirred. Caroline tried to move her arm, her right arm. Somehow fastened to her body, it did not budge. She reached over with her left hand, finding fingers and part of her right palm, but everything beyond was wrapped in something. Soft and cottony. Her left arm moved only so far before something began tugging on it. She attempted to open her eyes again, and this time her lids fluttered open like a new butterfly spreading its wet wings.

While a white haze covered the world, Caroline knew she hadn't made it to Heaven. The beeping was indication she had gone elsewhere, but that would be expected given her last actions. She let out a sigh, shifting her foot. Searching for a cool spot, her foot also seemed to be wrapped. The sore sensation in her right ankle finally registered with her. Her most distant extremity, the pain in her foot had a farther distance to travel. Caroline blinked hard a couple times, trying focus her eyes. A monitor showing different colored lights and lines was the source of the beeping. Next to the monitor, bags filled with clear liquids hung from hooks on a pole. Tubes hung down from the bags, and her eyes traced them from their source to their destination: an IV in her left arm. *Hospital.* She was in a hospital, not Hell. Though over the years she'd heard a few people refer to it being one and the same.

Caroline turned her head to look at her immobilized right arm. It laid partly covered by a white blanket and was wrapped in gauze and some sort of cotton dressing. The dressing began at the base of her hand and extended to just under her armpit. She noticed a strapping of sorts held her arm to her torso. She felt no pain under the dressed area, but her right shoulder ached. It ached as much as her head. She tried to shrug her shoulder, thinking it was just a kink, but the movement inflicted another stab of discomfort. It spread throughout her shoulder blade and down her right arm to her elbow. She let her shoulder sink back against the pillow. Next, she looked towards her legs and feet. Hidden under the blanket, she saw her right leg and foot was larger than the other. Another sigh rose from deep inside her and escaped her lips. *What had she done?*

The sigh mingled in the antiseptic-rich air reaching towards the man asleep in the chair beyond Caroline's feet. Propped on an upright arm, the man began to stir. He looked vaguely familiar, but Caroline could not place him. *And why was he asleep in her room? Or was it just her room?* She braved the pain, moving her head from side to side to see if she had a roommate. Only one bed. She was the only occupant. Other than the man. Caroline looked back at him, trying to remember how he figured into her life. Though slumped and sleeping in the chair, she could tell he was tall. At least six-foot. A square jawline reached up to angular ears, and a short haircut above. An area on his forehead had been shaved, showing a patch of skin, partly tanned, partly untanned, joined by a track of stiches.

The heavy wood-stained door opened blocking her view of the man, as a woman in scrubs wheeled in a computer on a cart. Guiding it towards the bed, the computer screen held the woman's attention. When she looked up, she practically jumped.

"Oh, wow!" she said. "You're finally awake! Welcome back!" The nurse had dark hair that hung in ringlets around her brown face and eyes. A perfect face that needed no make-up. Her pink lips parted in a smile. "Maybe we can solve the mystery!"

Caroline croaked out her response: "What mystery?"

"Why, the mystery of who you are!" the nurse continued to smile, adding a laugh. The man appeared from behind the opened door, wiping at sleepy eyes, and headed to the other side of the bed. He leaned against the window ledge, waiting for the mystery to be solved as well.

"Oh, good morning, Mr. Meadows!" the nurse greeted him. "Stayed all night again?"

The man nodded as he yawned.

"Who I am?" Caroline asked, looking from the nurse to the man. "What do you mean?"

"Honey, you came in with nothing," the nurse replied. "No ID, no phone, nothing." Caroline noticed her name badge read 'Rachelle.' Rachelle flattened her mouth and tilted her head. Her face held a sympathetic look.

"Everything burned up in the fire," the man added. He did not smile. A concerned expression occupied his face.

"Fire?" Caroline asked. *Fire? What fire?* She didn't remember a fire. The last thing she recalled was driving across the bridge as fast as she could and abruptly turning left, hoping the speed would propel the Range Rover through the side of the bridge. She looked again at the man, Mr. Meadows. The face was familiar. She'd seen it... *It was him!* She'd seen him on the bridge. He'd been on the railing. *The eyes.* It was the last thing she remembered.

Recognition must have shone in Caroline's eyes as her mouth dropped open. The man, Mr. Meadows, ever so slightly shook his head at her, conveying some hidden message. Caroline squinted her eyes at him, as Rachelle looked from one to other. The pain in Caroline's head intensified.

"Mr. Meadows is the one who saved you!" Rachelle smiled again, "You wouldn't be here if it weren't for this fella!" Rachelle nodded her head towards Mr. Meadows. "He's quite the hero around here!"

"Saved me?" Caroline struggled to find the meaning from the words. "From a fire?" She sensed something was a little off. Or maybe it was just her. She shook her head, not understanding. *Not a good move. The pain!* The Range Rover was supposed to submerge in river water after it went off the side. How could there be a fire?

"You were going over the Simon Kenton Bridge, and you somehow hit one of the curbs," the man, the hero, began explaining. "It sent your car into the side of the bridge, and then it bounced off the other side and ended up on its top. I barely pulled you out of the car before it burst into flames and exploded."

"Exploded?" Caroline's eyes grew wide. The insurance policy flashed through her mind. She saw the page opened to the accidental death clause. Its words were very clear. There was no misunderstanding them.

"Yes, the explosion threw us to the ground," Mr. Meadows answered. "That's how I got the gash on my head, and blistered up a bit, but at least you were okay." His eyes scanned her broken body lying in the bed. He grimaced, correcting, "Well, you are alive." He added, giving her an intent look, "You were lucky I was out walking that night and happen to be in the right place at the right time."

Caroline fretted her brows, and action that caused her to close her eyes briefly from the pain. *What had gone wrong?* Opening them, she saw the man was gently nodding his head. It was like he was speaking in code to her.

"God was certainly watching over you!" Rachelle chimed in as she clicked on the keyboard. "Now, let's get down to business! Can you tell me your name, sweetie?"

Instead of looking at Rachelle, Caroline's eyes focused on Mr. Meadows. "Caroline. Caroline Reeves-White."

Rachelle then rattled off additional questions: birth date, address, insurance, employer, marital status, family, emergency contact, and the rest of the usual demographic questions. The nurse seemed surprised that Caroline's memory was accurate.

"Usually after sustaining such a head trauma, the details are vague and fuzzy. You're doing really good, Caroline!" She then asked, "Do you need us to call your husband?"

"No!" Caroline was abrupt with her answer but offered no explanation. Deep inside she felt a spurt of emotion signaling tears. She mentally stomped the spurt like one would a spark or glowing ember in dry woods.

Rachelle shrugged. "Okay, but we will need to let the authorities know your identity. That's protocol."

"That's fine," Caroline responded in a softer tone.

Rachelle picked up two syringes filled with liquids, both clear. She injected one syringe directly into the IV tube port, the other she injected in one of the hanging bags of fluid.

"Caroline, I have just given you something for pain and a dose of antibiotics, which will take about 90 minutes to drip." Rachelle dropped the spent syringes in a red medical waste box hanging on the wall. Then her long dark fingers flew across the keyboard, typing more data into Caroline's record. When her fingers stopped, Rachelle looked back at Caroline. "I'll be ordering you a meal to be sent up. I'm sure you're starved not having eaten anything for four days!"

Caroline frowned. "Four days? I've been here for *four days*?"

"Oh, yes! You had some swelling on your brain. Cerebral edema. From the blow you took to your head, and the medications pretty much kept you knocked out while they got the swelling down and to keep you from feeling too much pain after the surgeries." Rachelle straightened Caroline's pillows and covers as she spoke. Caroline held her breath to tolerate the discomfort as Rachelle fluffed the pillows.

"Surgeries?" Caroline suddenly realized she was missing a four-day chunk out of her life. Life apparently paraded on without her knowledge. *And why was this strange man here and not her husband? Steven. Where was he? Did he know? Most likely not. Did he even care?* She sighed again, Steven's absence being the answer to all her ponderings but the first.

"Yep! They operated on your upper arm and your forearm," Rachelle said, returning to her computer. "The put plates and pins in your humerus, and you shattered your radius and ulna. They had to piece those babies back together like a puzzle. Said that the jagged bones cut through tendons, ligaments, muscle and nerves." Then she pointed toward Caroline's foot. "Now you're lucky down there. You only fractured your metatarsals and pulled the ligaments down there. But it'll still be a while before you're getting around real good." She followed the bad news with a bright smile, saying, "God must have important plans for you, saving you from that fire like that!"

Still processing all her injuries, Caroline gave the nurse a slight nod. Watching Rachelle roll her computer cart out the door, the nurse's comments about God swirled with the pain in Caroline's head. She was under the impression God had all but abandoned her because of her life choices. Especially her last choice. But, then again, that didn't happen. Instead, she laid as a crumpled mess in a hospital bed with a stranger keeping vigil over her. After the nurse closed the door, Caroline slowly turned her head toward Mr. Meadows, the hero.

"Why are you here?" Caroline's question was blunt. The image of him standing on the bridge railing flashed through her mind. He made her swerve. He caused her to abandon her plan. A trickle of resentment flowed through her veins. It tried to reignite the anger she held for Steven.

His arms still folded and continuing to lean against the window sill, the man looked at her for a minute. A long minute. Caroline had to look away from his gaze, his brown eyes seemingly forming a judgment of her.

"Well," he began with a sigh. "You don't save someone's life, a person with no name and no identity, and then walk off and leave them." He unfolded his arms, resting his palms on the window sill. "What if you'd woke up and had no idea who you were and what happened to you?"

"But I do know who I am!" Caroline replied curtly.

"Do you?" Mr. Meadows asked. He recaptured her eyes, a pale blue, with a faint circle of brown, and desperately trying to hide something. "Looked like to me you were running from someone you'd become, but not who you are." Yes, he judged her.

Caroline pondered his comment for a moment. She didn't like what he suggested, so she changed the direction their discussion. "Don't you have family? Responsibilities you need to take care of?"

"Nope," the man replied promptly. He looked straight at her. "Right now, my sole responsibility is to find out why you were on that bridge."

"Why were you on the bridge?" she asked curtly, adding, "On the railing of the bridge?"

Immediately Mr. Meadows' expression changed. A defensiveness peeked through his otherwise controlled demeanor. He looked away from her towards the floor. Thinking.

"Why did you swerve?" he finally asked. "Why didn't you keep going for the side?"

The defensiveness jumped from the man to Caroline. She bit down on her lips hard. Then winced, realizing even her lips hurt. She began to speak but stopped short allowing just a noise to slide off her lips. Caroline realized they were engaged in a fist fight with words but arrived at a stand-off.

"I don't think you want anyone to know *why you were on that bridge* any more than I want anyone to know *why I was on that bridge*." Mr. Meadows' statement was correct. He looked at Caroline frankly.

"No," she replied. "No, I don't." She looked guiltily down at her arm and hand lassoed to her body, then to the other arm hooked to tubes. He knew why she was on the bridge. He knew what she was doing. And she knew what he was doing. "So, that's why you are here? To preserve our secrets?" Caroline asked.

"Maybe. Partly," the man replied. "But I really did want to know you were okay." He nodded his head several times before adding, "But it would be good if we got our stories straight. It won't do any either of us any good if anyone knew the real reasons."

"No, it wouldn't," Caroline agreed. Psychiatrists and mental health practitioners would descend on them each like a swarm of fruit flies. She took a deep breath. Even her lungs hurt. Sore. Perhaps this was her punishment for even conceiving such a heinous crime. "So, what's our story? I am sure someone will be in asking me questions. It'd be best if I knew what you've been telling them for the past four days." She frowned at the last part of her comment. *Four days. Lost.* Then Steven reappeared in her thoughts. Had he been here? How would she know? A chill ran through her, as she began to wonder if the Range Rover's blaze might have other origins.

"Well, first off, my name is Mark. Mark Meadows." Mark picked up the chair, placing it closer to Caroline's bed and sat. "I was out for a walk, you know, just to clear my head about some things going on, and I heard a car accelerating on the bridge. It turned out to be yours." Caroline nodded as he continued. "You must have hit a curb. They are pretty high, and it sent your car out of control. You never saw me walking. Not on the sidewalk. Nowhere. You certainly did not see me on the railing. You lost consciousness as you bounced off the sides of the bridge, and then I pulled you out before the car burst into flames."

"Okay. Sounds simple enough. I never saw you," Caroline agreed. "Not until here in the hospital," she added. He nodded, with a quarter-smile appearing on his face.

"So, why were you on the bridge?" Mark asked.

Caroline frowned again. "Why was I really on the bridge? Or…what is my story of why I was on the bridge?"

Mark shrugged. He sat with his hands clasped between spread legs. He observed Caroline as she formulated her story.

"I…I had just found out that morning my husband was having an affair, so I was just driving around trying to decide what to do. I couldn't go home until I knew." Each word scrapped her throat on the way out, leaving behind a rawness. "I was upset. I'd never been over the bridge before. I thought that by being on the other side, I might have a different perspective on things. As I was driving, something happened to the steering. I lost control of the car." Then, she looked at Mark and asked, "Has Steven been here?"

"Who's Steven?" Mark shook his head questioningly.

"My husband." Caroline stared again into Mark's eyes. "Has he been here?" But, before the man spoke, she read the answer on his face.

"No. At least not while I've been here." Mark paused, thinking. "If he had, we would have known who you were."

Caroline nodded. She looked off thinking about this. A

strange look crept across her face. The fingers on her left hand played with the cotton blanket that covered her.

"Do you want me to call him for you?" he offered. He started to reach for his cell phone.

"No!" Caroline blurted. "No. I don't want to see him. I am done!" The anger she'd felt right before the accident resurfaced. Her tone carried a hint of sarcasm, "That bastard doesn't know that I know! About the affair! And apparently, I've been gone for four days! You'd think he'd be calling hospitals. The police. He hasn't had the decency to even look for me!" A red flush rushed to her cheeks and her neck. Instead of tears, fury flowed.

CHAPTER 3 – A WOMAN'S SCORN

As Mark buttoned his shirt and tucked the tails into his jeans, he considered Caroline's sharp words about her husband. Then he replayed the story she planned to recount to those that asked. It didn't make sense. The story and the emotions did not match. Mark had been there himself years before when he learned about his wife's 'indiscretions.' That's how Jennifer had referred to the affair. He felt the betrayal, the hurt, and the loss. He'd cried. Alone, so no one witnessed his weakness. He loved Jennifer. Up to that moment and even after. Reality had slapped him in the face. Just the thought of Jennifer triggered his mood to darken and the sadness to rise.

He returned his thoughts to Caroline. A distraught, sad person who believes all is lost thinks about suicide. Suicide is the perceived solution for a person who feels empty and worthless. That there is nothing to live for. Caroline's anger was real. Spontaneous. Yet, she showed no emotion—no hurt, no sadness—when discussing the affair. An angry person seeks revenge, not suicide. It didn't make sense.

Mark stopped in front of the mirror in the bathroom to comb his hair and run his electric razor over the stubble that grew during the night. Since he was a teen, the whole facial hair thing had intrigued him. How could these hairs keep growing, day after day. Though his head of hair was a dirty blond, the spikes that poked out of his chin and jawline were dark as coal, lending an odd look if they got any length at all. Mark was no candidate for a beard, not at any cost. After a quick slap of aftershave, Mark brushed his teeth and proclaimed himself ready.

Getting into his truck, his phone began to vibrate again. Ever since the media reported his heroism for saving the mysterious woman from the burning car, his phone lit up non-stop. Pulling it out of his belt clip, he saw Beth's name in the display. Again. She'd attempted to contact him for five days now, but Mark's only reply had been a brief text telling her he was 'avoiding his phone due to all the calls.' But that still hadn't kept her from trying. Or Larry or Lynn. And the neighbor lady mentioned the previous evening that all sorts of people had been knocking on his door throughout the day. It was the reason he was late to return home and left early. He wasn't in the mood to speak with anyone. Except Caroline. Oddly.

For some reason, he was drawn to her. He kept telling himself it was because no one knew who she was, and he wanted to be sure she was okay after 'witnessing' her horrific crash. Yet, a part of him couldn't help but feel responsible for the crash. Had she not seen him balancing on the top rail of the bridge, holding onto one of suspension wires, she might not have swerved, but instead taken them both over the edge of the bridge. End of story. But their eyes met, and the look of shock on her face remained with him. The rest was history.

Mark felt a tinge of annoyance with the woman for interrupting his plan, but he suspected his presence interrupted her plan as well. He faired the failed attempt far better than she had. He spent only one night in the hospital, mainly for observation of the head injury and to be sure he had no internal injuries. Mark had the gash on his head and multiple bruises on his body, not to mention a first degree burn on his back from the heat of the blazing car. His body had shielded Caroline from a burn, but she was otherwise a broken, bruised mess. Caroline was starting day six, and her second day awake. She was headed for some tough-going when the hospital decided to let loose of her. It sounded like the Steven character wouldn't be much help, but Mark hoped she had some good family and friends. She was going to need assistance, and a lot of it.

Mark paused to knock on the slightly ajar door.

"Come in," a muffled voice said.

Entering the room, Mark found Caroline sitting up in bed, the bed positioned upright. Instead of her hair being scattered on her pillow knotted and twisted, it had been combed and hung mostly straight but with a slight wave slightly above her shoulders. She was still plenty pale except for the bruises. They added patches of color to her otherwise flawless face. She looked up at him as he returned the door to its 'ajar' position.

The rolling table was hanging over her lap, and a tray of food was in front of her. She held a steaming Styrofoam cup, that she blew on each time before sipping. A fork laid on the plate, indicating she may have sampled the scrambled eggs. Mark recalled they were pretty good.

"Good morning," Mark said. "Do you mind if I sit?"

"Good morning," she replied, putting her cup down. "I was wondering if you would make an appearance today."

"Oh, really?" Mark raised a brow as he hung his coat on the back of his chair and sat.

"One of the nurses said you'd been keeping a vigil over me ever since you were released."

Mark nodded his head in a haphazard way, trying to act blasé about his attentiveness. "I wouldn't call it a *vigil*," he replied. The woman in the bed raised her brows doubtfully. It reminded Mark of the look his mother gave him when she didn't believe a word he said.

"So, what were your war wounds?" Caroline asked. "Besides the gash on your head?"

"Me?" Mark asked pointing his fingers towards his chest. "Oh, I just had mostly bruising. A minor concussion. They were mostly concerned about internal injuries, but they gave me an all clear." He didn't mention the burn. It was mostly healed and in the itching phase. "How are you doing this morning?"

"Oh, my head feels lightyears better." She picked up the fork with her left hand, holding it awkwardly. "The rest of me? Well, the pain is mostly gone in my foot, if I don't put weight on it. My arm is a different story." As she stabbed at link of sausage, tears welled in her eyes.

Mark tilted his head, wondering the cause of the tears. Had the doctors been through? Had they told her? A couple days before, the doctors' mistook him for 'Jane's' family and shared her entire prognosis with him. Mark never corrected them, saving them from a moment of embarrassment. He watched as she brought the whole link to her mouth and bit off the end. The chewing movement caused several tears to teeter out of her eyes and down her cheeks. As she stared at the link, Mark stared at her eyes. The wetness had enhanced the blue of her irises and brought out the brown ring that encircled them. It was the same color brown as her hair.

"What?" Caroline asked, noticing Mark stared at her.

"Your eyes..." he replied, sitting back in his chair. "I hadn't noticed the ring...the brown ring."

"Why would you? I've been in a drug induced coma for four days until yesterday." She bit another piece of the sausage. "This has maple in it. It's actually pretty good." She spoke while chewing.

"Yeah, the breakfast wasn't too bad," Mark agreed. "The coffee isn't exactly McDonalds or Starbucks." The comment brought a smile to Caroline's face. She continued to chew.

"I don't suppose," Caroline muttered between chews. "At some point you might be able to sneak some real coffee in to me?" She looked at him pleadingly.

"Of course, I haven't had any myself yet today," Mark replied. "So, if you don't mind me prying, why the tears?"

Caroline paused chewing and swallowed. She looked at the half link of sausage still on the fork, and then set it on the plate. Her shoulders slumped in a defeated way. She slowly looked towards Mark, rubbing her lips together, prepping them for what was to come out.

"So...um...the doctors were doing rounds this morning," she began. Mark nodded. He'd assumed right. "And, they told me I have multiple fractures in my foot with a pulled ligament, but in time that will heal. It'll just take a while. Especially for the ligament. And the swelling on my brain has gone down with the medications. I can tell. It's doesn't hurt hardly, and my thinking's not fuzzy," Caroline paused, considering her next words.

"And?" Mark knew she'd feel better if she voiced it, got the words out in the air instead of holding them inside.

Her eyes connected with Mark's. Once again, they began to glisten. He could tell she was holding back more tears. After a deep breath, she continued.

"The doctors' explained what they did during my surgeries. They told me how badly my arm was…crushed basically. It was much worse than what Nurse Rachelle let on. They told me I might require additional surgeries, and…and…" She lifted her left hand to wipe at her eyes. "And…I may never have full use of that arm." She nodded her head, as if she were trying to convince herself. Her mouth was mashed flat, and her reddened eyes scanned the room.

"I'm sorry," Mark said.

"Oh, it's nothing for you to be sorry about." Looking back at him, the corners of her lips upturned. "It was an accident, right?"

Mark nodded. She was playing the game. "Yes, a bad one. You're blessed to be alive."

"Thanks to you, Mr. Meadows!" she attempted to smile. "My guardian angel!"

"I don't know about that!" Mark laughed. "And it's Mark, not Mr. Meadows." Then he asked, "Did the docs say how long they plan to keep you?"

"A few more days," Caroline replied. "They want to make sure there is no infection before they cast my arm." She pointed to the bags on the pole. "They're dripping antibiotics to me like crazy and said I'll go home with pills to take."

"Home?" Mark asked, raising a brow. "Will your family and friends be there to help care for you?" She'd said little about her husband, none of it good. She'd mentioned nothing about family.

Caroline jerked at Mark's question. Looking at him, she became quiet. Her expression went blank.

"You realize that you're going to need help doing pretty much everything, right?" he continued.

"I...I hadn't thought about it," she finally said. "I guess I'll hire someone. Maybe my insurance will cover..." An urgency sprang to her face, interrupting her words. "Oh gosh! I bet my work doesn't know anything about this! I'm sure no one has called them!" Her head darted from side to side, looking for something. "Is there a phone in here?"

Mark leaned forward in his chair, pulling out his cell phone. He rose and took a couple steps towards the bed, handing his phone to her.

"Are you sure?" she seemed surprised he offered his phone.

"Call them," he encouraged. "They are probably wondering what's happened to you. "Or do you want me to call for you?"

Caroline reached for the phone with her good hand, the corner of her mouth upturned.

Continuing to stand, Mark said, "You make your call, and I'm going to go for some coffee!"

The woman nodded, holding his phone, dialing with her thumb.

***

Mark walked out of Starbucks with two 'venti' Pike Place coffees in a carrier and creamer and sugar on the side for Caroline. He pondered her comment about hiring someone to care for her. She completely avoided his comment about family and friends, and interestingly none of them had been to see her. He wondered if they even knew. Even if she wasn't status quo with her husband, Mark figured she would have immediately been calling parents, siblings, and friends. Instead, she called work, and he continued to be her only visitor. *How strange!* If he hadn't been making his daily visits, would she be completely alone? Broken up and alone?

But, then again, he'd been avoiding his family and friends. Who was he to judge? Perhaps she had unusual family dynamics. Or maybe she didn't have any family? But surely, she had friends. Who didn't have friends? The more he got to know Caroline, the more perplexing she became to him. He didn't want to barrage her with questions, not in her condition, and he certainly didn't want her doing the same. They both appeared to carry more than the one secret.

When Mark once again entered Caroline's room, she was just ending her call, setting the phone on the table. The breakfast tray was gone. Mark went towards her with the drinks and doled out the condiments for her coffee.

"I didn't know how you took your coffee. I should have asked before I left," he said.

"Light and sweet!" Caroline said with a cheerful tone, seeing the creamers and sugars before her. "Raw sugar! How did you know?" She tore open the packets with her teeth, two at a time. Mark helped her with the creamers.

"Uh, you just seem like a raw sugar kind of girl?" Mark jested. Really, it was just what they'd given him. In fact, he couldn't remember getting anything but raw sugar from Starbucks.

Caroline waited for Mark to pour the last creamer into her cup before she added the sugar. Stirring the mixture, she glanced at Mark. "By the way, when I got off with my work, you had a call. Hope you didn't mind me answering, but it was your sister, Beth. She said they've been trying to get ahold of you for days and have even been by your place, but you haven't been there. I told her you'd been here with me the whole time! She wants you to call her. It sounded important!" Caroline took a cautious sip.

"What did your work folks have to say?" Mark asked, skirting around Beth's call. He wondered what else, if anything, Caroline had told her. Or, what Beth may have said to Caroline.

"They were shocked!" Caroline put the coffee on the table to cool. "That's so much better," she referred to the coffee. "They had no idea what had happened to me, AND…they even called the house and spoke to Steven. Do you know that turd told them he thought I'd run off with someone?" Her cheeks quickly adopted the red flush that came with her anger. "The nerve! Anyway, I told my boss all about being in the accident and the coma, and no one knowing who I was because everything burned up. And I told her that Steven didn't even bother to report me missing! Or even come see me. Not that I would want him to…that two-timing jerk…" As she spoke, there was a knock at the door.

"Come in." Caroline said, pausing her discussion.

As the door pushed open, Officer Keyser and a female officer entered the room. Both were in full uniform, including hats, which Officer Keyser removed. The female office carried a black notebook and a pen.

"You Caroline Reeves-White?" Officer Keyser asked, then he looked towards Caroline's companion, seeming surprised to see Mark. Officer Keyser nodded towards Mark, who returned the nod.

"Yes," Caroline said.

"Pardon our interruption, but we were wondering if you could talk to us about the accident?" the female officer said. "I'm Officer Edwards and this is Office Keyser. Officer Keyser was the responding officer to the scene of the accident."

"Sure, I can tell you what I remember," Caroline offered.

Mark started towards the door to give their conversation privacy, "Excuse me." He sent a smile in Caroline's direction and nod of encouragement.

Mark drew the door closed but could still hear muffled voices as he leaned against the wall and nursed his coffee. It amazed him the beverage was still so hot, given the drive back to the hospital in the cold truck. The coffee must have been scalding as it came out of the pot. He was thankful for the ample cream added to his.

As the murmur of voices continued, he noticed a man exiting the elevator at the end of the hall. He was dressed in a grey wool suit, and his blond hair was pristinely combed, probably held in place with spray. Appearing lost and out-of-place, the man disappeared in the direction of the nurses' station. *Steven? Was this the husband finally making an appearance?* Mark gave a short snort, shaking his head.

As he did, the door opened, and the officers exited, thanking Caroline for her time. Officer Keyser paused, looking at Mark.

"It's Mark, isn't it?" the officer asked.

"Yep," Mark confirmed.

"I'm glad I ran into ya! I've been trying to call ya." Officer Keyser continued, "We got some additional intel on the Perry guy. It turns out he *has* left the country and has been doing some hopping around to throw his trail. INTERPOL is trying to locate him, but this guy's clever, unfortunately. It appears that he'd been planning this for some time. It may take a while to shake him out." Officer Keyser gave Mark a sympathetic look. "I'm really sorry! Turns out this guy took my grandparents for the ride as well! People are still coming out of the woodwork!"

"I'm sorry to hear about your grandparents," Mark replied, returning the sympathy. Jake Perry was the definition of scoundrel, taking advantage and robbing the elderly.

"Listen, I'll keep ya posted on developments," Officer Keyser said, giving Mark a pat on the shoulder. Mark simply nodded and watched the officers head down the corridor.

Stepping back inside Caroline's room, Mark headed for his chair. "How'd it go?"

"Oh, fine." She took a sip of her cooled coffee, and licking her lips, said, "I told them exactly what we discussed, but the guy officer seemed really interested when I mentioned the steering on the car. Then he started asking questions about Steven. I'm not sure what that was about. But I told them that Steven hadn't so much as called, and I told them what my boss said." Caroline sighed before continuing, "Boy, did their eyebrows go up on that! I still can't believe Steven told my boss that!" She looked down shaking her head.

"Did I hear my name mentioned?" The man in the grey suit stepped inside the open door to the room without knocking. He stopped a couple strides inside the room, looking at Caroline, and then his focus landed on Mark. His body pulled back slightly at the sight of him.

"Steven!" Caroline blurted out. "Yes, you heard your name!" Caroline's brows turned inward forming deep creases between her eyes. "How dare you show your face here!"

Mark rose from his chair, intending to give the couple privacy. As he took his first step towards the door, Caroline pointed at him.

"You! Sit!" she barked. Mark looked at her, and she pointed him back towards the chair. Mark raised his eyebrows, giving Caroline a doubtful look. "I need a witness to this conversation!" she spoke sharply. Mark returned to his chair and looked from Caroline to her husband. Prejudiced a bit from Caroline's comments, Mark immediately picked up on Steven's pretentious airs. The man snickered, indicating pleasure that Mark heeled to a woman's order. Mark expected Steven would have wanted the unknown man out of his wife's room. Did Steven need a witness as well?

"Darling, I just now heard about the accident..." Steven took steps towards Caroline's bedside.

"Stop!" Caroline put out her left hand. "Don't you come any further! I *know* Steven. *I know*!" Her tone was damning, and her eyes glared at him. The blue turned icy.

Steven threw his hands to the side and shook his head, feigning cluelessness. "*Know what*, my darling?"

"Don't you 'darling' me!" Caroline snapped. "You can save your 'darling' crap for Brandia!"

At the mention of Brandia's name, Steven's arms dropped to his sides, and he attempted to stand a little taller.

Caroline held the offense and put Steven on the defense. Steven attempted to intimidate Caroline with a looming stature to reclaim the offense. Mark found the body language intriguing. There was nothing intimidating about Steven's being.

"Brandia? Brandia Damron? What does she have to do with anything?" Steven replied.

"Oh, come on, Steven! I heard you and her in your office Wednesday morning!" Caroline rolled her eyes. "I heard everything you said!"

"It was just a client meeting..." Steven replied haughtily.

"Do you discuss 'Steven Juniors' with all your clients and refer to them as 'my love'?" One of her brows raised, and her mouth tightened.

Steven shifted to one side. The muscles tightened around his jaw, and his eyes narrowed. Then he spoke, "Caroline, you're taking what you heard out of context..."

"Shut up, Steven!" Caroline interrupted. "I know what I heard! You forget about the 'options'! So, Steven, *what are* the 'options' besides divorcing me? Huh?" Caroline punched him in the face with her words.

Steven's demeanor staggered. He swallowed hard but said nothing. Mark sensed Steven wanted to hear more about what Caroline knew. Caroline used her left arm to push herself more upright in the bed, while keeping her eyes on her husband, watching every twitch, every expression. She wasn't letting go of the offense anytime soon.

"Did you forget about leaving my life insurance policy open on your desk at home? To the page about 'Accidental Death'? Was this one of your so-called 'options'?" She raised her brows waiting for his response.

"I've no idea what you're talking about," Steven replied. His hands twitched.

"Sure, you do!" Caroline narrowed her eyes. A smug expression covered her face.

Mark felt increasingly uncomfortable about the

conversation but was captivated just the same. The seemingly fragile, broken woman in the bed had some fire of her own. He leaned back in the chair and took a sip of his coffee. While everything unveiling before him was real, it played out as one of the best stage productions he'd ever seen.

"Steven, you can be sure that I mentioned to the police that I lost control of the steering on the Range Rover. And I told them about the insurance policy." She paused letting the statement soak in. "A million dollars is a pretty big motive for attempted murder, don't you think?"

Mark flinched himself hearing Caroline's last statement. He saw Steven's whole body stiffen, and the man's eyes grew narrower. Had he underestimated his wife? Mark thought so. It suddenly hit Mark: he had been right. Something was off kilter with Caroline's story. Apparently, she'd fleshed it out a bit more for the officers, and even more-so for Steven.

"Well, isn't that something! For a man whose never been at a loss for words, you're awfully quiet!" Caroline paused, then went for the kill. "Oh, I was sure to mention your affair with Brandia, and that you had been discussing 'options' with her. Guess that makes her a co-conspirator, doesn't it?"

It wasn't a question. It was emphasis. Caroline tilted her head, looking at her husband, who remained speechless. Mark assumed his mind was scanning his client list for attorneys.

"Get out, Steven! Just get out! You'll be hearing from my attorney!" She motioned her left hand in a sweeping fashion, dismissing him. "Oh, and you might as well stop by the police station. They'll be wanting to speak with you! Save them a trip to Flemingsburg, why don't you!"

The man exhaled deeply and abruptly left the room. It looked like Steven wanted to run but struggled to hold back from doing so. As the man disappeared into the hallway, Mark heard his footsteps gradually hasten. The beep of the elevator indicated he was gone.

Mark took another sip of his coffee, replaying the scene. His eyes fell on Caroline as she leaned back against her pillows and looked toward the ceiling. The encounter drained her. He decided he'd let her speak when she was ready. In the meanwhile, his questions for her were stacking up.

A million dollars for an accidental death? Caroline didn't fabricate the episode on the bridge to look like an accident. What was her game plan? Where was her anger coming from? Why wasn't she crying? Upset? Like a normal woman who just learned her husband had another woman? Mark carried an intense sorrow for days, no weeks, after he learned about Jennifer and Todd. Where was Caroline's hurt? Broken heart? But then again, she'd just learned about the affair on Wednesday morning and crashed that evening. When did she have time to mourn the loss of her marriage? *No, there was nothing normal about this, but then again—what's normal?*

***

Caroline still stared at the ceiling when Mark excused himself, telling her he was going to go call his sister and run some errands. Before closing the door behind him, he asked her if she needed anything, but she shook her head. When she heard the click of the door, indicating it was closed, she lifted her head. She looked around the empty room. It exemplified her life. Empty. And she felt empty. Much as she tried, Caroline could not coax the tears. Perhaps there weren't any. Had she cried them all out as she drove around town?

She looked down at her body. The evening before, Caroline watched Nurse Amy change the dressing and wrap on her foot. A plastic splint had been woven in among the bandages to keep her foot at ninety degrees and from bending. Her foot was swollen and displayed all colors of the rainbow, but there were no wounds. All the damage was internal. Hidden. Nurse

Amy explained that Caroline may continue to use the wrap on her foot and go home with a 'boot' to stabilize her foot.

Caroline's arm was a different story. Nurse Amy removed the bandaging, cautioning Caroline about what she might see. "You'll need to get used to it. Your arm's at its worst right now. It will get better and better looking each day."

Caroline's arm was twice the size of her other arm. A four-to-five-inch track of staples held together the incision on her upper arm, while staples ran from her wrist to her elbow on her forearm. Like her foot, her arm was a palette of colors. Other than the incisions, Caroline saw none of the doctors' handiwork putting her arm back together. Again, hidden under swollen tissue and staples.

Nurse Amy inspected the incision, saying it was healing nicely. She applied an antiseptic liquid or wash to the wound, which stung. Caroline held her breath from the discomfort and figured if it made her feel that way, it couldn't be pleasant for the little bacteria that might linger in the area. Nurse Amy re-wrapped her arm, incorporating a plastic splint like the one used on Caroline's foot, only bigger, to hold her arm bent at the elbow. Eventually, Caroline's arm would be set in a cast. Once the nurse finished bandaging her arm, she gave Caroline a sling, reminding her to be cautious.

Caroline sighed. She was relieved that her arm was no longer tethered to her torso. How uncomfortable that had been. Like she had no arm at all. She shivered at the thought. The doctor's words reverberated. *She might not gain full function of her arm.* Time would tell. Caroline could not imagine how her life would change. She was right-handed. Everything she did was with her right hand and arm. At this moment, she was barely able to feed herself, never *mind* sign her name or write something. Typing one-handed? She guessed people managed. There were probably people out there who did it all the time. *Crazy! The loss of use of her arm made her sadder than the loss of Steven!*

Caroline picked up her coffee and sipped. Now room

temperature, it was more like an iced coffee. *Light and sweet*, she'd told him. Mark. He would remember that. She looked toward the empty chair. *What was up with this guy? Why did he keep coming back?* He felt guilty about something, that she could tell. Was that why he continued to occupy that chair? *Was he afraid I might tell what I really saw on the bridge?*

If she did that, then she'd give herself away. No. That couldn't happen. His faced flashed in her mind. She saw him balanced on the rail with his hand on the guide wire steadying himself, and he saw her gripping the steering wheel with both hands. Incredibly, her eyes connected with his. In a fraction of a second, their lives became inexplicably connected.

She knew why she was on the bridge, though she was now feeling quite silly for even conceiving the idea. Truthfully, the 'Steven thing' might work out even better now that she'd pointed to some suspicious behavior on his part. And, who knows what Steven was up to? Caroline put nothing past him. But at least now, if something happened to her, all fingers would point to Steven and Brandia. Caroline laughed to herself. Their greed made them the perfect pair. They deserved each other.

Caroline was astounded by the transformation of her perceptions of her life and of her husband from those few minutes in that hallway and during her random driving. It had been a lie. She'd been living that lie. She'd stayed so busy keeping up appearances and following Steven's directives. When had she stopped loving Steven?

She thought back on the years. Hard as she tried, Caroline could not pinpoint a specific instance. Perhaps, the love dwindled over time without her awareness. Maybe it hadn't been there at all. Was it possible she was in love with the *idea* of Steven and the life she could have and not actually in love with Steven? She didn't know. And now, it didn't matter. It was gone. But then again, was it ever really there? One thing Caroline knew well: she'd worked her butt off for Steven's success. She wasn't going to walk away without a fight and her share! She refused to let him come out unscathed.

Caroline took another long sip of her coffee, as her mind swung into action. As she set the cup on the table, she realized Mark left without his cell phone. That meant he'd be back. Caroline smiled. Of course, he would. In the meanwhile, she had a few calls to make…

CHAPTER 4 – CASTING CALL

Mark pressed the speed-dial button next to Beth's name on his house phone. He'd looked around for his cell phone but found it nowhere. He hoped he'd left it at the hospital in Caroline's room. Beth answered on the second ring, as if she'd been waiting anxiously for his call. She was.

"Well, it's about time, Mark!" she scolded. "You've had everyone worried to death about you! Where on Earth have you been?"

"I've been at the hospital." Mark contemplated making the call all night long, wondering what to say and how much to say. He tossed and turned as sleep evaded him. By morning, he decided he'd be vague about the whole financial situation, giving the same information that was reported in the news.

"Mark! How bad were you hurt? Did that woman hit you?" Beth asked. "And what were you doing on the bridge at that time of night?"

"No, they only kept me overnight," Mark said, adding, "She didn't hit me. I got hurt pulling her out of the car. In the blast. Just a cut on my head and a few bruises."

"Blast?" Beth's voice squalled.

"Yes, the car burst into flames and knocked us to the ground."

"How is the woman?" Beth asked. "Why are you there? Do you know her or something?"

"No, actually, no one knew who she was until day before yesterday when she woke."

"So, why are you there?" Beth asked again.

Mark paused before answering. Why *was* he there? Was he there to make sure the story stayed straight? Was he using it to hide from his family and avoid the financial fiasco? Was he feeling sorry for the woman because she was alone? Was it all the above? Really, he didn't know.

"I don't know, Beth," he finally replied. "I just feel compelled to be there for her. I can't explain it." And he couldn't.

"Okay…" Beth's tone carried reservation. "So, what's going on with getting Mom and Dad's money out? Did you get it?"

The expected question. Finally. The pit that had been hiding inside him, made itself known to Mark. A wave of nausea passed through him as he spoke, "I'm sure you've seen the reports on T.V."

"Uh-huh…"

"Well, the FBI shut down the office," Mark began. "I went to cash in the stock, and the FBI was there and walked out the woman who ran the office. You remember Rachel Wheeler from school? Her."

"Yeah, she was in between our grades," Beth replied. "She worked for that crook?"

"Yep. So, I went to the police station to try to find out what was going on," Mark continued. "They told me Jake left the country and apparently took a bunch of his clients' money with him." Mark then corrected himself, "Well, they said he transferred the money to foreign bank accounts. They're working with an international agency to try to find him."

"He didn't run with Mom and Dad's money, did he?" Beth asked.

"Honestly, Beth, I don't know," Mark lied. "They've apparently frozen all of his client accounts until they can figure out what's going on." Then he remembered Office Keyser's comment about his grandparents. "The cop said that even his grandparents invested with Jake and they're trying to figure things out!"

"Well, I hadn't heard any updates on the news, and then we couldn't get ahold of you…" Beth sighed. "Then they were talking about this accident, and how you saved this woman. We were all kind of freaked out when they said they discharged you, but then you weren't home. Dad especially. He was kind of worried about…well, you know."

Mark did know. His family didn't hesitate to remind him whenever they could. It was one of the reasons he tried to stay busy. It gave him an excuse to distance himself when he could.

"Look, Beth, I gotta go. I promised Caroline I'd be there today," Mark twisted the truth. He hadn't actually promised Caroline anything, but if it got him off the phone...

***

Mark headed off the elevator and down the corridor with a coffee in each hand. One was sweet and light, while his was light. Slightly past the nurses' station, a "Mr. Meadows?" chased after him. Changing directions, he backtracked to the nurses' station.

"Was someone calling my name?" He asked. He set the coffees on the counter as the radiating heat was too much for his hands.

"Yes! Me!" Rachelle waved her hand in the air as she came towards him. "I'm glad I caught you!"

"What's up?" Mark asked, curious why the nurse wanted to speak with him.

"I know you said you had no idea who Caroline was or anything about her when you both came into the hospital, but you've been spending a lot of time with her, and I was wondering..." Rachelle paused, looking around her and over her shoulder. "Has Caroline by any chance mentioned anything to you about any family or friends?" Her question was in a lower tone.

"No, actually," Mark said. "I met her husband yesterday. He came to see her, but that didn't go so well."

"Yes, I know he was here. He asked for her room number," Rachelle's rolling eyes revealed her opinion of the husband. "Caroline was quite upset after his visit and asked that he not be allowed back in."

"I'm not surprised," Mark curled his hands around the

coffees.

"Well, the reason I ask about the family or friends..." Rachelle again glanced around. "...is that the doctors are talking about releasing Caroline, but obviously she's going to need someone around to help her and provide some care. We can't release her to go home without knowing someone will be there to assist her. Clearly, the husband is not that person."

"Well, I've been curious why no one's come to visit her, and I asked her about family. Friends. But she just changed the subject. Avoided the question." Mark shrugged. "I asked her who was going to help her when she got out of the hospital, and she said something about hiring someone."

"That's the response I got. It was very vague," Rachelle said. "Do you think you might be able to see if she might open up to you and tell you more?" Rachelle scrunched her face in a pleading expression. "The doctors are talking about casting her arm later today and maybe releasing her tomorrow, but we have to know who's going to be there for her. If there's no one at her home to assist her, she will have to go to a rehabilitation facility. Caroline is dead set against that!"

"Yeah, I'll see what I can do. I'll let you know." Mark picked up the coffees as Rachelle thanked him.

Mark turned back into the corridor and headed for Caroline's room. Caroline's aloneness once again struck him as strange. Granted, he didn't have a lot of close friends, but he did have some. Surely there had been more than the husband in her life. Where were her friends? There had to be someone. And a family member somewhere. She was going to need them.

***

"Good morning," Mark announced himself as he strode through the open door, a cup in each hand.

Caroline's face broke into a smile as soon as her eyes

landed on him. She was upright in bed, several pillows behind her back, and her curly mass of hair had been combed with an elastic holding it in a bunchy ponytail. One little detail of care perked up Caroline's outward demeanor. Of course, Caroline hadn't combed her own hair into the ponytail. One of the aides had done it after her sponge bath, and it no doubt reinforced to Caroline how she needed help.

"Good morning!" Caroline's voice carried a chipper note. She felt refreshed. "Although, you barely scrapped by...it's almost afternoon!" she teased. Her inside demeanor perked up the afternoon before when Caroline made another call on Mark's phone.

"For you, ma'am," Mark placed her coffee on the table and rolled it to where Caroline could reach the coffee on her own. He then retrieved his chair, placing it to the side of her bed. A little closer this time. As he sat, Caroline sampled her coffee.

"It's perfect!" she said. "You remembered how I like it!" She knew he would. He was the type who liked to please others. And he certainly pleased her with the coffee and his presence.

"Of course! It's all about the simple pleasures in life." Mark took a sip of his own coffee, tasting the creaminess against the robust flavor of roasted beans. "Those are the ones that mean the most."

"Isn't that the truth!" she agreed. "Today I celebrate the fact that I have one arm and hand to pick up this delicious coffee!"

"You're in a good mood today," Mark said. "Your hair looks nice."

"Thanks! You noticed!" Caroline swung her ponytail like a young girl. "It feels better to be pulled together a little more. Not in so many pieces," she smiled. "Oh! You left your phone yesterday..."

"Yeah, I realized it when I went to call my sister."

"So, you called her. That's good," Caroline paused, recalling the urgency in his sister's voice. She wasn't sure what that was all about. "How did that go?"

Mark raised a brow, then it sank back into place. "It went fine. Beth is one of those that tends to over-react about things. Tends to think worst-case. When she found out I was alive and had just been here visiting you, she calmed down." Mark wasn't completely lying. "Everything is good."

"That's good." Caroline leaned forward and angled her good leg so that she sat upright on her own. "Speaking of calls…and I hope you don't mind that I used your phone…" Caroline watched Mark shake his head, getting permission after the fact. "But I put in a call to one of my old-time playmates, Emily Fields."

Mark shifted in the chair, interested to hear more. It was the first mention of a friend.

Caroline explained that she and Emily had been playmates back when they were younger girls and lived up a holler. Older by a couple years, Emily was the only youngster her age in the holler besides Caroline's brother, but he had no need for girls at the time. When the girls began school, they slowly drifted towards other friends, and then Emily's family moved out of the holler. By that time, the girls greeted each other in the hallway, but that was the extent of the friendship.

The call to Emily hadn't been to re-kindle their friendship, but rather to consult with Emily about divorce proceedings. Emily had grown into Attorney Fields and was the only one Caroline trusted to take care of the messy business ahead. Caroline told Mark how she recounted all the details for Emily, after which Emily readily agreed to represent Caroline.

"Emily used the word 'jugular' at one point! I admit I like the sound of it!" Caroline's words projected a confidence. "Emily said she would swing by to have me sign some paperwork." Caroline looked from her bandaged, disabled right arm to her left arm. A sigh came from deep inside her, scattering any confidence that had emerged.

The hopelessness returned, and with it a trace of sadness. Sadness for the loss of a segment of her life and sorrow for all the sacrifices made during those years.

"You'll be fine," Mark said. "Just sign the best you can. Bet no one will be able to forge it!" he chuckled, trying to lightened things. "You mentioned a brother…"

Caroline shot a look at Mark, studied him a few seconds, then answered. "Yeah, Adam. We don't talk. We aren't close. I haven't seen or talked to him in over ten years." She averted her eyes to hide any sadness or regret they might reveal.

"Oh. I'm sorry," Mark replied, tilting his head. "I hadn't heard you mention family. I assumed you didn't have any."

"Basically, I don't." Caroline clipped her words. She hoped Mark realized this was an uncomfortable subject. Anything about her past carried a distressing tone.

"Maybe you should reach out to them? You know, given your condition?"

"My family was not family to me when I was well and thriving. They certainly won't have anything to do with me in this condition!" Caroline said looking down at her covers. *Why did she mention her brother? Why had Mark zoomed right in on that detail?* The internal porthole to her feelings of emptiness was open. Her dad's last words rang in her head: *"You are dead to us!"* He uttered them the day she told her dad and mom that she and Steven were getting married. Had her dad known something she didn't? Caroline shivered and reached for her coffee. She wanted to wash down the tears before they had chance to spring.

"Yeah, I really don't want to talk about that, okay?" She tilted one corner of her mouth upward before taking a sip.

"Sure. No problem."

***

Mark promised Caroline he would be in her room when she got back. But it didn't mean he couldn't leave and run an errand or two, being back before she was. *Was she developing an attachment to him?* He was, after all, all she had. At least, as far as he could currently tell. The comment about her brother surprised him. It rolled off her tongue effortlessly, but her response afterward was entirely awkward. Family. A sore subject. Caroline had more wounds than she was willing to admit. Then again, so did he. Right now, her physical wounds provided her refuge from the hidden hurts.

At the Dollar Store, Mark selected a plain lined notebook, a pack of pens, and a word search book. At the end of the aisle, a display of adult coloring books caught his attention. He flipped through the different ones and settled on the one that had pages of flowers and garden-like scenes. Stepping back into the aisle, he pulled a pack of colored pencils and a pencil sharpener from the hangers and then headed to the register. As he looked at the pencil sharpener, he stopped. How would Caroline sharpen the pencils on her own? He remembered seeing a pack of colored pencils that twisted up like a mechanical pencil. That was a better option for her. Anything that would reinforce what she could do independently was good. Back to the aisle, Mark replaced the sharpener and first pack of pencils with the pencils that twisted.

When Caroline realized that she wouldn't be able to sign the legal documents, a look of defeat surfaced on her face. Immediately an idea came to Mark. It quickly turned into a plan, which he was gathering the tools for. After he paid for the writing and drawing instruments, he went through the drive through and got some tacos before heading back to the hospital. It was just a matter of implementing the plan.

Mark hoped that Caroline would have a better idea of what she would be capable of with her right arm once the cast was in place. Having a broken elbow as a young teen, Mark knew what living with a casted arm felt like and did not envy Caroline. He also remembered how much assistance he had needed doing basic life activities. But it was not impossible.

Caroline needed encouragement. Lots of it. The problem? Who'd be there to give that encouragement to her?

Along with her physical injuries, Caroline plunged into the divorce process. From experience, Mark knew a divorce could turn messy quickly. Caroline's break-up was already immersed in a cesspool. It amazed Mark how two people could go from loving each other, from being each other's best friend and world, to being enraged rivals inflicting emotional wounds, scars, and irreversible damage. That had been his story. His intuition told him Caroline's story would be similar. Mark took Steven as the type of guy who wasn't going to be nostalgic or sympathetic, but whose bottom line was the dollar.

Caroline not only had physical needs that required attention, but she had the emotional ones as well. She was in line not only for a host of emotions from the healing process for her arm and foot but also from the warfare that was sure to erupt during the divorce process. Mark hoped she'd be able to come up with someone to help her with these. She had to. While Caroline's hopefulness was quick-lived, Mark's was restored upon hearing about her brother. Regardless of whatever history they shared, Caroline needed to let her family know what happened. Of course, Mark realized he had to be careful how he encouraged this, or it might backfire on him. Caroline could well use his own good intentions and tell him he needed to come clean with his own family.

Caroline's bed was still empty when Mark returned to the hospital room. He saw that his chair was once again on the opposite side of the room, and a reclining chair now occupied the space next to the bed. He figured they must be getting ready to get Caroline up and out of the bed more. Mark laid his packages on the floor and put the bag of tacos on the rolling table. While he was hungry, he decided to wait for Caroline to return so he could offer her a reprieve from hospital food. Situating himself in the new chair, he reached for the television remote and found a program to occupy his mind—to keep him from overthinking things—until she returned.

***

A gurney took her out of the room, but Caroline returned in a wheelchair. Her chit-chat with Nurse Amy lifted Mark from the light doze he'd fallen into while watching the television.

"Look who's made himself comfortable!" Caroline teased. "Amy, I thought you said they brought the chair for me?"

"They did!" The nurse laughed along with her patient. "But I think men naturally gravitate towards recliners. They are like an extension of their bodies!"

"Or a charging station!" Caroline added. "He looks just like an earbud in its case!"

Mark wiped his eyes and raised up in the chair at the sound of the women's banter. "Okay, okay! I'm moving!" he defended as he began to rise out of the chair.

"Now that we've got some 'hardware' holding things in place, this girl's not going to be restricted to the bed!" Nurse Amy rolled the wheelchair towards the recliner and locked the wheels. The nurse referred to the hard casts on Caroline's arm and foot.

"Look, Mark! Kelly green!" Caroline held up her foot. Green fiberglass casting encircled her foot and ankle up to mid-calf. She wiggled her toes, the only part of her foot visible and free. "I'll have to wear a boot with it, but I'll be able to walk on it! Yay!"

"With assistance!" Nurse Amy added.

Mark stood back watching as the nurse spoke to her patient, going over the proper ways to stand and move with her casted ankle. Caroline's arm was also casted in the same green, and a halter of sorts fastened her bent arm to her torso. It wasn't as restrictive of the previous binding, but it didn't have the 'freedom' of a sling. The nurse coached

Caroline how to sit gently so she didn't jar her shoulder and arm.

"As if having a broken arm isn't enough," Caroline told Mark as she sat in the recliner. "While the doctor casted my arm, she told me that I also dislocated my shoulder and tore my rotator cuff!"

Mark shook his head in disbelief. It seemed like every time the doctors got near Caroline, they found another injury from the accident. Probably the reason why her arm was wrapped against her body—they didn't want her using or moving her shoulder.

"Now, you know you won't be able to get out of a chair like this without help." Amy said. It wasn't a question. "Anything that sits low and is cushiony will let you just sink into it. You'll need an extra set of hands around or you may be sitting a while!"

"So, upright chairs are going to be a better option?" Caroline asked.

"If you want to get up on your own," Amy replied, helping Caroline to get situated in the chair. "Now we don't want you reclining in this right now due to your arm and shoulder. Just sit in it in the upright position."

"Okay," Caroline agreed, managing a smile. She seemed overcome with the rules and restrictions. She let out a deep sigh as the nurse left the room in search of a tray of food.

"Speaking of food," Mark pointed to the bag on the table. "Would you be in the mood to go rogue in the food department?"

A hint of a smile came to Caroline's lips, and her eyes showed trace of pleasure. "What did you get?" She asked in an almost giddy voice.

"Tacos."

"Really? I haven't had a plain ol' taco in ages!" The smile was fully out on her face, but then a frown wiped it away. "How am I going to eat it? You really shouldn't have." Caroline was again reminded of her new-found limitations.

"With your hand and mouth." Mark reached into the bag and brought out a wrapped taco. He peeled away the wrapping on one end and handed it to Caroline. Cautiously, she took it with her left hand and slowly bit into the exposed taco. Parts of the shell fell into her lap. As she chewed, an expression of delight came to her face, quickly followed by another bite. This time a streak of taco sauce was left beyond the corner of her mouth. As Mark chewed on his own taco, his hunger finally satisfied, he picked up a napkin. Leaning towards Caroline, he gently dabbed the sauce off her face. Smiling, he captured her unusual eyes again. The brown ring around the blue.

"How is it?" he asked.

"Oh, my gosh!" Caroline spoke with another mouthful of taco. "I think I could live on these! It's been years!"

"Good. I'm glad you're liking the change!" Mark took the taco from her and peeled down more wrapper. He noticed that her lap was filling with crumbs of shell, meat and chopped tomatoes. "You'll need to change after this!" he laughed.

"Oh! I don't care! There's plenty more gowns!" she replied, looking down at the hospital gown. Caroline frowned as she finished the taco, searching out the remaining morsels with her face buried into the wrapper. The hospital gown was the only clothing she had. Everything she wore into the hospital had been cut off her and disposed of by the Emergency Room staff. After she downed another taco, she picked at the crumbs and morsels that fell in her lap. Mark tried to clean the remaining taco fallout from her gown, but the red streaks from the sauce claimed their place, and he felt awkward reach towards certain places.

Licking her lips, Caroline handed Mark the empty wrapper. "Thanks so much! What made you think of tacos?"

Mark rolled the wrapper into a ball and tossed it towards the trash can on the other side of the bed. So far, he'd made the basket with each emptied wrapper. Boyish pride showed each time, making Caroline laugh.

"I hadn't had them in ages myself. They drew me in!" Mark wasn't going to reveal to her he purchased the tacos because of the challenge they posed. The tacos were a lesson to Caroline of how desperately she needed someone to help her when she went home. He had learned the lesson himself years before. Telling a person something was abstract. Words. Showing a person something hits home. It's real. It causes that person to admit to their own limitations and needs.

"Oh, I almost forgot!" Mark changed the subject, turning and going for the bags on the floor. "I got a couple of things to help keep you busy during the day!" Moving the taco bag, Mark removed the Dollar Store items one by one from the yellow bags and placed them on the rolling table. He watched Caroline's reaction, as he laid out each item. Puzzlement filled her face.

"What's all this?" Her voice was apprehensive. She looked at him, waiting for his reply.

"When I was a kid, I broke my elbow," Mark began. "My mom got me word searches, and coloring books. This type of stuff…" He pointed to the collection on the table. "It helped me to develop dexterity in my right hand so I could write and do things."

"Right hand?"

"Yes, I'm left-handed and broke my left elbow, so I couldn't write, hold a fork, that sort of thing." He flexed his left hand. "For six weeks I was using my right hand, and I got pretty good with it. I still use it. Made me ambidextrous, I think they call it."

"Huh." Caroline contemplated the items before her. "So, if I color and do word searches with my left hand, I'll get more used to using it? What about writing?"

"That's what the notebook is about," Mark replied. "You can use it to practice writing. Start with the alphabet and numbers and your name. Before you know it, you'll be able to sign your name!" Mark made known his true purpose of the items before her.

"Ahh…" Caroline's mouth lingered open. A second later, a glisten came to her eyes. With a sniffle, she wiped the moisture from her eyes. No sooner had she done so, the glisten returned. Looking from the spread of booklets, pens and pencils to Mark, a tear rolled over the edge of her eye and fell to her cheek. It was the first display of emotion, other than pain or anger, that Mark witnessed from her.

"I'm sorry," Mark said. "I didn't mean to upset you."

"No, no…" The words lingered as Caroline swallowed hard, choking down tears and emotion. "This is…is really thoughtful." Another tear landed next to the first, causing them to cascade down her face. A flush of pink colored her cheeks as she swiped away the tears. Sniffling again, Caroline picked up the coloring book and flipped through the pages, checking out the illustrations. Halfway through the book, she raised her head.

"Why are you here?" Caroline asked. She tilted her head to the side, her eyes searching out Mark's.

He shifted feet, feeling uncomfortable from the intensity of her eyes. The brown rimmed blue had a magnetic quality. What could he say? He was hiding out from his family? Hiding from his own issues? Beyond that, he wasn't sure why he was there himself. Coming to see her, to share part of the day with her, was a compulsion he didn't understand himself.

"I don't know…" Mark began, looking away from her for 'his' chair. It was on the other side of the room. He stayed put, leaning against the window sill. "Umm…I'm on seasonal layoff so I really have nowhere else to be. Might as well being doing some good."

"No," she said. "Why are you really here? Why are you being so nice to me?" Another wayward tear escaped. She seemed not to notice.

Mark shrugged. "You seem so alone. Like someone who

could use a friend. I just want to help." Trying to shift the conversation, he added, "You know, they aren't going to let you go home unless you have someone there to tend to you."

Caroline cocked her mouth to the side, wiping her face again. "Yeah. I know. They keeping hounding me about that."

"Don't you have anyone?" Mark asked. "A neighbor? A friend? A cousin?"

"No. Sadly, no." Caroline looked down at her stained hospital gown. "I invested my life in Steven. Boy was that a bad decision," she admitted. "I never allowed myself to get close to anyone." A frown look took her face. "Well, Steven never let me get close to anyone. I see that now. Funny what it takes to see the truth!" She let go a sigh.

"Well, you've got to figure something out," Mark said frankly.

"I know." Caroline's countenance became contemplative. "Oh, I've so got to get out of here!" Caroline said, shaking her head. "Don't get me wrong. They've all been good to me, but I've just got to go."

"You said something about hiring a caretaker. Have you thought about calling the community college or that university you work at?" Mark asked.

Caroline tilted her head. "What do you mean? Why would I call them?"

"Don't they train nurses, LPNs, and those people who work in nursing homes?"

"Yeah, I guess," Caroline shrugged, immediately reminded of the soreness in her shoulder. "I'm not sure what you're getting at…"

"Maybe one or two of those in training want some work on the side assisting you as you recuperate," Mark suggested. "It would be a good deal for you. You might not have to pay as much as for a regular caregiver since they're not yet certified, and it would be a good deal for them. They would be able to practice what they are training to do, and then they could study in down time."

"Huh." Caroline thought for a moment. "That's not a bad idea at all. I don't suppose you could look up the number for the community college for me on that phone of yours? I know the number to the university."

Mark pulled his phone from his pocket and began tapping on the screen. In less than a minute, Mark went to the table, opened the notebook, and broke open the pack of pens. At the top of the page, he wrote the name and number of the head of the nursing department. It was a place to start. And it would force Caroline to start practicing her writing skills with purpose. Mark set the pen down on the notebook and glanced at Caroline. Where she'd been biting her lower lip, a smile sprung, and her intriguing eyes showed a glimmer of hope.

Mark returned a smile but couldn't help but wonder what went through Caroline's mind. He understood wanting out of the hospital, but returning to the home she shared with her husband? Was she thinking he would be gone? Gone to live with his new sweetheart? What if he'd moved the other woman in? Mark's mind reeled with scenarios and all the things that could go wrong. To be fair, he searched for good aspects of her return home, but the only thing he came up with was, she wouldn't be at the hospital. That was it.

CHAPTER 5 – BURNED BRIDGES

Caroline pressed the red button to end the call. The warmth of excitement flowed through her body. She was beginning to feel alive once again. And, how easy it had been. On the first call she made, she found two students getting ready to finish their certified nurse's aide training who were more than happy to help Caroline in her recouperation—at least until they found full-time jobs. She'd worry about that when it happened. She glanced down at the chicken scratches she made on the notebook. She surprised herself at how coherent the marks were. Names and phone numbers. Perfectly readable, not just by her, but by anyone.

She was glad she'd waited until morning to make the call. Caroline not only caught the nursing coordinator in her office, but the students were in class. The nursing coordinator was able to walk down the hall, make the announcement about the need to the girls clad in scrubs, and instantly two hands went up! Not even five minutes had elapsed before the nursing coordinator called Caroline back with the good news and the girls' information.

Caroline was to call each of the girls that afternoon, once they were out of class, with the details. The girls only had two more days of class, and then they were done with the program. The timing was perfect. They would be ready to work, just when Caroline was released from the hospital! Another wave of joy passed through Caroline's body bringing another smile to her face.

A knock at the door drew Caroline's attention. She looked up from the notebook expecting to see Mark, but instead it was Nurse Rachelle with a tray. Caroline's smile faded.

"Well, honey, I'm happy to see you too!" Rachelle teased. Caroline attempted a smile for the jovial nurse. "Don't you worry! I get that reaction from everyone when I've got one of these trays!" Rachelle laughed, waiting for Caroline to clear a spot on the rolling table for her breakfast.

"What's got you smiling so brightly this morning, Caroline?" The nurse pulled the tops off the plates and stacked them in the corner of the tray. She then opened the creamers and poured them in the steaming coffee, while Caroline held the sugars in her left hand and opened them with her teeth. "You keep doing that, you'll be needing a dentist!" Rachelle said as Caroline poured the contents in the cup.

"I know," Caroline replied meekly. When she got home, she wouldn't be scolded about everything she did. At least she was doing something for herself. "I am happy because I have employed the needed assistance for going home! I've got two different girls who are nurse's aides that will help with my recouperation at home! You can tell the doctors to start that discharge paperwork!" Caroline's tone was giddy. A big smile filled her face. "I'm going home!"

"Well, that is good news!" Rachelle joined Caroline's smile. "I will message the doctor's as soon as I get back to the nurses' station. Hopefully the girls can cook better that our cafeteria folks!"

A smile still on her face, Caroline picked up the fork and stabbed into the scrambled eggs. She hadn't thought to ask if either of the girls could cook. *Oh, well. She'd find out soon enough.* In the meanwhile, she dug at the food before her, wondering if this would be the last hospital breakfast she'd have to stomach. All in all, the food hadn't been bad, it just wasn't her cooking. *And everyone complained about hospital food, right?* She wondered how soon she'd be able to regain control of her own kitchen.

Her plan was to do everything as told. The doctors told her that she'd have appointments with both a physical therapist and an occupational therapist, but it wasn't clear to Caroline whether they'd be visiting her at home or if she'd have to go to their offices. One of the girls could run her there. Either way, she intended to do exactly as told. She wanted to heal as quickly as possible so she could return to work and get her new life started.

New life. *Ugh!* Caroline sensed that nothing would be as it was. Between those moments in the hallway at Steven's office and the Range Rover flipping on the bridge, she felt like she'd been thrown into a parallel universe. Perhaps she had.

It felt especially so when Emily strode through the door sporting a Redweld folder the afternoon before. After a brief and somewhat stiff greeting, the attorney pulled out a series of papers for Caroline to sign. Emily was all business, explaining she was in the throes of a huge class-action lawsuit. Caroline picked up one of the pens Mark brought and "signed" her name to each document presented to her. She didn't read any of them, and for all she knew she could have been signing away her life. *No, wait…*Caroline thought with a silent chuckle…*she'd already done that when she signed the marriage certificate!* These papers would reverse that pact, restoring what should have been. The fact that she lost ten years of her life was a minor detail. The fact she could have lost all her years, but didn't, was a major detail.

Caroline prayed heavily before going to sleep that night that Steven wouldn't make things too difficult. He wouldn't go down without some sort of fight, that she knew. Hopefully he wanted Brandia badly enough that he'd just want to be done and get on with his new life. After all, Brandia wasn't getting any younger. She'd said so herself! Caroline shuddered, remembering her words.

Caroline couldn't shake the feeling that God had reached out to her in that last second of consciousness in the Range Rover. Caroline was not religious by any means, but she and Steven attended the Christian church every Sunday. For appearances, of course. However, ten years of Sundays had left an impression on Caroline. Especially when the pastor read passages from the Bible on the self-righteous. Steven was the poster child. Caroline realized at one point she wasn't far from self-righteous given she lived the life of plenty with Steven. Guilty by association. Which is why Caroline was surprised to recall the strange sensation that ran through her as Mark's eyes met her eyes on the bridge. The look in his eyes were imprinted in her mind. She didn't recall swerving the Range Rover. The last thing she saw were Mark's eyes as he perched on the railing. Getting ready to jump?

Had God intervened in two imperfect people's lives when in crisis modes and pushed their pause buttons? Had God positioned them exactly to be in each other's way? Was that why Mark kept coming back? Was he trying to figure out that strange moment on the bridge?

She initially was angry with Mark—then 'the man'—for fowling her suicide attempt, meant as an action to thwart Steven's orchestrated 'accident.' Mark's simple presence, returning each day annoyed her. But as she came from under the stupor of pain killers and shock, she began to realize they'd been somehow thrust together. She shook her head at the thought. They had gotten their 'stories' aligned, but the next day Mark was back. The man that kept showing up was becoming the closest thing to a friend she had. And she didn't know why.

***

Before Mark slipped out of his jacket and took a seat in 'his' chair, which he once again positioned closer to the bed, Caroline bombarded him with her good news. First, she had signed the papers setting the divorce into motion, and second, she'd found and hired two girls sight-unseen to care for her once back home. Caroline barely got breaths in between her words, having to gasp for air once she finished spilling out the happenings.

"Have they said when they plan to release you?" Mark asked, leaning back in the chair. He propped one foot up on the frame of the bed.

"I told Rachelle to let the doctors know I am ready!" Caroline replied happily. "I suppose a day or so. They've been asking over and over about who I had at home to help me, so I'm guessing they want rid of me!" A hopeful smile returned to her face.

Mark nodded his head slowly, asking, "So what do you know about these girls—certified nurse's aides, you say?"

Caroline's smile lost its luster. "What do you mean?"

"You're going to just allow two total strangers you know nothing about into your home and entrust your life to them?" Mark's question turned Caroline's lack-luster smile into a frown. A crease formed between her brows as she processed Mark's statement.

Twisting her mouth, she looked down at her empty tray then sideways at Mark.

"What choice do I have?" she replied with a sigh. "I didn't know any of these girls in here or anyone else whose been caring for me," she justified. "I didn't know you," she added for impact.

Mark nodded. She was right. Everyone in her life following the moment she approached the bridge in the Range Rover were total strangers. Strangers with whom she'd quickly developed relationships. Relationships that were quite possibly several times more meaningful than any she'd left behind when stomping the gas pedal. And here she was, sharing things with him, a person she'd met only days ago. What did she really know about him? She didn't even know what he did for a living! She hadn't asked. But why would she? She was so focused on her mangled self and going home.

"I've gotta ask," Mark began. "When you get released from the hospital, are you going to your house? Your house with Steven?"

Caroline frowned again as she considered his question. Slowly, she responded, "Well...yes. Yes. Where else would

I go? It's not just Steven's house. It's my house, too." A perplexed look lingered on Caroline's face as she lifted her left hand to swipe a bunch of hair behind her ear.

"Aren't you concerned that Steven might be there?" Mark asked. He knew he was treading on sensitive ground. "The man that you accused of trying to stage an accident for you? You're okay with going to sleep in the same house?"

Caroline's mouth opened instantly, but no sound emerged. It hung open a moment before she snapped it shut. She sat quiet for a minute, again processing his words. Then she looked over at Mark, the sheen of tears forming in her eyes again. Mark watched her swallow hard, a lump formed in her throat. Had he said too much? But it had to be said.

"I…I have nowhere else to go, Mark," she finally admitted. "And the house is half mine. I can't afford to let him take it from me. I can't walk away from it. He might use it against me." A tremble accompanied her words. "I've no other option." Again, she wiped her face clear of tears with hand. "Besides, he wouldn't try anything now. Now that his intentions are in the open." The last part she said to convince herself.

Mark shook his head. "Well, maybe he won't be there," he offered. "Maybe he'll have moved in with what's her face."

"Maybe…" Caroline replied, her thoughts floating off.

Caroline's hesitation confirmed to Mark she hadn't thought things out fully. Her eyes trailed off, and the look of vulnerability returned to her face. Mark remained quiet, allowing Caroline to travel her thoughts but he continued to look at her. While he'd noticed her unusually colored eyes, he couldn't say he'd really taken a good look at the woman. At least not without the bruises and swelling and telltale signs of trauma.

Her hair was a mass of dark curls hanging just above her shoulders. Her complexion had shed the pallor that claimed her for the first several days in the hospital. While her complexion was fair, signs of life had returned to her cheeks.

A long, delicate nose led to lips, now a sweet pink. Her shoulders were narrow, leading a person to assume she was petite, but she was taller than she seemed. Of course, he'd only seen her either in the hospital bed, in the recliner, or moving from a wheel chair to one or the other. Not prime situations for determining stature. He could tell that she was on the thin side, with a narrow face and a slim arm. Probably a requirement of her husband. For appearances. Overall, Mark decided Caroline was a very attractive woman, even at her current worst. He couldn't understand what Steven would want with another woman when he was already married to such a beautiful one.

"Good morning, Mr. Meadows!" Rachelle said as she strode into the room. Mark looked up to see the nurse wheeling in her computer cart.

Rachelle rolled the cart to Caroline's bedside, and then picked up the empty tray. Disappearing into the hallway for a moment, the nurse returned empty-handed. "Caroline, I've got to get your vitals. And good news!" Caroline looked up as Rachelle continued, "The doctors have issued a discharge order for you for tomorrow morning! You're finally going home!"

Mark lowered his leg so the nurse could scoot by to access Caroline's good arm for the blood pressure cuff. As she wrapped the cuff around her patient's arm and began pumping the bulb to inflate the bladder, Rachelle addressed Caroline's lack of response to the news.

"Well, honey, I figured you'd be leaping for joy outta that bed!" Rachelle paused pumping and listened into the stethoscope. When she was done, she uttered "102 over 78" and released the air from the cuff. Over the sound of the Velcro ripping apart, the nurse asked, "So what's going on with you?"

Caroline came back from her far-off thoughts, replying, "I suppose the reality of going home has hit me."

***

"I have no money. I have no driver's license, no credit cards or bank cards. No clothes. No shoes. No keys to my house, even." Caroline rattled off the list while looking forward at the blank wall on the other side of the room. She took a deep breath and shot a pensive glance at Mark. "I don't have any clothes to go home in, and I don't know how I'm going to get there."

"I can get you some clothes and shoes…" Mark began.

"No, you shouldn't have to do that! I'm not your responsibility, and you've already done so much for me." Caroline nervously rubbed the fingers that hung out of her cast. "They'll probably let me borrow a pair of scrubs. And I can call a cab."

"Scrubs aren't going to keep you warm," Mark rebutted. "And how are you going to pay for a cab? Besides, they're not going to release you to go home in a cab. They want to know someone's there for you."

Caroline fell silent, continuing to rub her fingers. Shaking her head, she began to speak but then stopped and dropped her head in her hand. A clump of curls fell forward covering her face. At some point the lump in her throat sank to her sternum, and it began to burn. It burned like a bonfire inside her chest. Her hand moved from her face to cover the singeing feeling. Again, she shook her head. She screwed up. What had she been thinking? Driving off a bridge? Look what it accomplished: it rendered her an invalid. She looked her casted arm up and down. Had it been a moment of temporary insanity? The shock of her discovery in the hallway? Why couldn't she have driven a little longer? A little farther? A different direction? Why? Why had she even considered such a thing? But here she was, all broken up and alone. Alone. There wasn't anyone there for her. Not anymore. No one.

"What are you thinking about?" Mark asked.

Caroline pushed her hair back from her face, revealing bright red cheeks, hot from shame and embarrassment. She exhaled, hoping to shed the futility building inside her. Looking at Mark, she shook her head in reply. She couldn't share. She couldn't tell this stranger that she now wondered if her husband, her best friend, and love of her life, had ever actually been there for her.

"Look," Mark said sitting up straight. "I've got a meeting this afternoon, but I am going to stop and pick up some clothes for you to go home in."

Caroline began shaking her head again, but before she could speak, Mark continued.

"No, I'm going to get you clothes, and I am going to take you home when they release you."

"No. No, I can't ask you to do that!" Caroline raised her hand, as if it would stop him.

"You didn't ask. I've *offered*," Mark stood, stretching. "I'll make sure you get home. In the meanwhile, you make sure you've got those girls lined up to be there for you." He reached his cell phone over to her.

"No, I can't take your phone. You've already been so good to me!" Caroline protested.

"You need it to make calls." Mark set it on the table. "I'm not expecting any, so you use it. You need to get prepared." He nodded, casting a smile in her direction. "I'll be back tomorrow to take you home. Okay?"

Caroline just nodded. Why was he doing all of this? She watched him move toward the door, and before departing, he raised his hand in a wave. Caroline peeked a smile in response, showing appreciation. Once Mark was out of sight, Caroline dropped her head backward and silent tears spilled down her cheeks leaving wet marks on the pillows. She was officially at the lowest point in her life and felt it. Why did this man have to rescue her from the Range Rover? Why couldn't he have just let her burn up in it? She had been unconscious. She assumed she would never have felt it. It would have been so much easier. So much easier. She struggled to be angry with this man who kept returning... angry with him for 'saving' her...but she just didn't have the energy. He was being so nice, and he was the only one there.

***

Mark lifted Caroline into the passenger seat of his truck. She was dressed in the oversized sweatshirt and sweatpants he'd found, and a large fuzzy sock covered her casted foot that had been wrapped in a boot. The other fuzzy sock covered her good foot along with an adjustable sandal. Additionally, Mark assisted Caroline to put her good arm through a plush flannel jacket, letting the other side hang over her shoulder and casted arm. It wasn't a horribly cold day, but he didn't want her catching a chill. He gently guided the seatbelt around her, careful to avoid putting pressure on her arm, and searched for the buckle. Finally, snapping it in, he pulled back, realizing how close he'd been to her. Practically hugging her.

Glancing at her, he flashed a smile and raised a brow in encouragement. Caroline had her lips mashed together and looked miserable. She lifted her left hand to wave to Rachelle and Amy and thanked them for their care. As the nurses retreated into the hospital with the wheelchair, Mark closed the passenger door and then climbed into the driver's seat.

"Wow," Caroline said. "This is quite the truck." She looked around, seeing the leather seats and the second row of seating behind. "Heavy duty."

"Yeah, it's actually my work truck, but I take the placards off during the winter. I don't want the salt to collect around them."

"Work truck?" Caroline asked as Mark pulled away from the hospital. "What type of work do you do?" The truck was in pristine condition.

"I run a landscaping business," Mark replied swinging the truck onto the Double AA Highway. "Right now, we're pretty much shut down for the winter, except for some snow removal and taking care of downed branches and trees. That sort of thing."

"So, you mow lawns and shovel snow?" Caroline asked.

"Yes, we do some of that, but we do much more," Mark corrected, feeling slighted. "My business offers full-service landscape design services. We landscape around commercial buildings, new homes, revive landscapes for older homes and parks, and much more. Then of course, we maintain those landscapes."

"Oh. I'm sorry. I didn't mean to make it sound…" Caroline replied. "It must keep you very busy."

"It does. I've got a crew of 15, several trucks, backhoe, you name it. Everything needed to get the job done." Mark shifted subjects, "So, where are we headed? Which direction is home?"

"You're going to head to Flemingsburg, but you won't go all the way into town." Caroline's tone was flat. All the excitement she had shown for going home must have stayed in the hospital room. "I'm in a development this side of town. Just off Route 32."

"Okay, just tell me when," Mark said as he headed past the shopping centers.

Caroline looked out the passenger window as they passed stores and shoppers going about their daily activities. She kept her envy of their mobility and independence to herself. Would she eventually be able to engage in such daily tasks again?

"So, have you spoken to your work people?" Mark asked, generating conversation for the ride.

"Yeah." Caroline sighed. "Yesterday afternoon after you left. There's some paperwork I'm going to have to fill out. Family Leave Act stuff."

"What exactly do you do at the university?" Mark turned

right onto the road that led to Flemingsburg.

"I'm an advisor for business students." Caroline glanced at Mark. His right hand hung over the top of the steering wheel and his left grasped the bottom. He looked entirely too comfortable to be driving. "I help the students with their schedules and keep them on track with their programs."

"Been doing that a long time?" Mark asked. Out in the daylight, Caroline noticed how tan Mark was, even for early November. But she supposed that was to be expected since he worked outdoors all summer long.

"I've been at the university ever since I graduated from college. I began as an accountant in the Business Office, then moved to an advising position," she replied. "It was our safety net while Steven and I were getting our business going. I enjoy it, so I stayed. I really like working with the students."

"What is your business?" Mark asked.

"Providia Life and Casualty," she said with a lofty tone. "Insurance. Home. Car. Life. Disability. Annuities." Caroline gave a laugh, "That's another reason why I am still at the university. For our health insurance. It's cheaper through a larger employer! Ironic, isn't it?"

"Oh, I understand," Mark replied. "I wish I could offer insurance benefits for my workers, but it's cheaper for them to get it on their own. And many of them have wives who are teachers or nurses and get it through them." Mark added, "I used to be on Jennifer's insurance, but now I pay for my own. All out of pocket. Can't afford to get sick!"

"Who's Jennifer?" Caroline asked looking away from the passing landscapes towards Mark. The muscles in his squared jaw twitched at her question.

"Jennifer was my wife," he said, glancing out the driver's window.

"Oh." Caroline considered his words. Was. "Did she pass?"

Mark laughed. "No, I couldn't be that lucky. It was divorce. And not pretty at that."

"Oh." Caroline said no more. She was headed down a similar path. "I'm sorry." She didn't know what else to say.

"I'm not," Mark glanced at Caroline, catching her looking at him. "Ended up being the best thing when it was all over with a couple of exceptions."

Caroline never considered that he'd been married. She mulled over his words, wondering did they have children? He didn't mention any. No wonder he'd had time to come sit at her bedside. But she still didn't understand why he did. When she inquired about his repeated presence, his answers weren't fulfilling to her. Like there was something more. Something left unsaid. She might never know. Looking ahead, the turn into her subdivision approached.

"You're going to take a right just up there." She pointed to the road flanked by stone columns. 'Hiddendale' shone in bright gold lettering against the stone. Mark slowed to make the turn.

"Huh," he said. "I did a landscape job up through here."

"Really? Who was it for?"

"I don't know. Did it for the builder." Mark cruised up the slight rise in the road. "Now which one is yours?" His head turned left and right, looking at the homes, each one larger than the previous.

"I'm in the cul-de-sac. Just keep going."

The road ended circling around a small green area with a couple of low-lying shrubs surrounded by a thick layer of mulch. In warmer weather the shrubs were joined by flowers of all colors.

"The grey one is mine." Caroline pointed to the second house on the circle. A massive roof of grey dimensional shingles topped a grey-sided home trimmed in white with a section covered in faux stone. A wreath in fall colors hung on the black front door. A drive curved in front of the house, with another drive leading to a garage on the side. Mark pulled into the curved drive and stopped directly in front of the door.

"Well, here we are!" He tried to sound chipper, smiling at Caroline.

Caroline tried to smile but it ended up more of a sigh. She looked toward the house, looking for any signs of life. All seemed still and silent.

"Are you ready?" Mark asked, as he opened his door. Caroline just nodded.

Mark came around to the passenger side and opened the door. Caroline had already released the seat belt, but it tangled with the draped jacket and her casted arm. Reaching up, Mark freed her of the seatbelt.

"Ready?" he asked again. After a moment's hesitation, Caroline nodded again, and Mark's strong arms scooped her out of the passenger seat and lowered her to the ground. "Do you want to try to walk?"

Caroline nodded again. Gaining a foothold, she clung to Mark with her good arm and tested taking a step. Then another.

The front door wasn't far from the drive—about fifteen paces—and then a single step-up to the slate front porch. By the time Caroline reached the door, she was out of breath and her legs trembled from the sudden activity. Caroline continued to cling to Mark as he opened the storm door and tried the front door. Locked.

"Fortunately, we have keyless entry!" Caroline grinned. Mark steadied her with his arm around her back as she punched in the code with her left hand. Each time a key was depressed, a beep sounded. The sound was the same for each key. And, then Caroline reached for the door handle to open the door. Depressing the latch, the door did not move.

"Hmm. Let me try that again!" Caroline once again punched in the code, but the door didn't budge. Tilting her head slightly, she looked from the door to the keypad and back. Her brows assumed a frown and her lips were pursed. "That's odd," she looked sideways at Mark, and then pressed the buttons a third time. Thoughts began flowing through her mind. *Surely, Steven hadn't...*

Realizing she was eye-level with his shoulders, she looked up at Mark. He patiently steadied her and said nothing, but she could tell thoughts rolled through his head as well. And probably similar ones.

"Um..." Caroline began. "Do you think you could do me a favor?" Mark nodded, making a grunting noise. "Could you help me to that rocker? I need to sit."

With his assistance, Caroline lowered into the white rocker. Ironically, it was the first time she'd ever sat in it. Once she was seated, she looked at Mark with a flat mouth, and then asked, "There's a keypad on the garage around the corner just like this one, could you go see if it will open? I don't think I can make it that far myself."

"Sure," Mark shrugged. "What's the code?"

"7-2-2-7," Caroline told him.

Caroline watched Mark step off the porch and tread through the grass around the side of the house. After he was out of sight, she closed her eyes and crossed her fingers. *Please open! Please open!* Surely Steven hadn't locked her out of her own home! Opening her eyes, she watched the empty spot in the yard for Mark to reappear. When he did, he looked directly at her, a grim expression, and shook his head.

Caroline exhaled and as she did, her shoulders slumped. *That fink! No. That ass!* She felt her blood warming inside her veins. The glow slowly returned to her cheeks as Mark stopped beside her.

"It seems you're locked out," Mark stated the obvious. "What do you want to do?"

"I need to call my lawyer." Caroline's words were slow and deliberate.

Mark pulled out his phone and handed it to Caroline. Setting it on her leg, she began to search the contacts until she found Emily's number. Pressing call, Caroline lifted the phone to her ear, though the ringing sound echoed on the porch. After a brief wait, the receptionist connected Caroline with her lawyer, who instructed her to call the Sheriff's office. She told Caroline that Steven had no legal cause to lock her out of her home. Hanging up, Caroline looked up at Mark. Although the call hadn't been on speaker, he'd heard every word.

"Call the Sheriff," he prodded.

"Can you look up the number?" Caroline handed the phone to Mark. When he had the number, he passed the device back to Caroline so she could push the call button. After three rings, a deputy answered, and Caroline explained her predicament. The deputy told her he was headed over, and she clicked off the call. Leaning back in the rocker, she winced as her shoulder hit the slats that formed the back of the chair.

"How long do you think it will take him to get here?" Mark asked.

"Who knows. He said he'd be right over, but my experience is that could be anywhere from ten minutes to an hour or more." Another sigh escaped her parted lips, as pink as her flushed cheeks.

"I got to admit, this is pretty shitty." Mark got to the point. Caroline agreed, barely nodding her head. "What time is your aide supposed to be here?"

"Three-thirty." Caroline looked towards the door and then the keypad. "Hopefully, I'll be in by then!" Glancing back up at Mark, she continued, "I'm so sorry for this! I'm sure you've probably got somewhere to be! If you want to head off, I'll be okay!"

"No, no. I'm not going to leave you until I know you're inside, safe and sound."

Caroline looked defeated. "You are being way to kind to me. I don't deserve all this royal treatment."

"Ha!" Mark replied. "If this is 'royal treatment,' I really would hate to see how ol' Steven treated you!" Caroline heard the sarcasm in his voice, loud and clear. She leaned her head on her propped left hand, saying nothing. She wasn't about to admit to Mark that his comment hit home.

Ten minutes later, a sheriff's car pulled into the drive behind Mark's truck. The deputy emerged from the car straightening a hat on his head and a folded piece of paper in his hand. The deputy took the few steps up the sidewalk but stopped short of the porch.

"Hello!" Caroline greeted the deputy.

"Good afternoon," the deputy replied stiffly, looking from Caroline to Mark to the front door. "Are you Caroline White? The woman locked out of the house?"

"Yes," Caroline managed a smile for the officer. "It's actually Caroline Reeves-White, and it seems my husband has changed to keycode for the house, and I cannot get in."

"You don't have keys?" the deputy asked, scratching his head. The folded paper curled in his hand.

"No, I was in an accident and am just returning from the hospital. I don't have keys with me."

"What about your husband? Have you called him?" The deputy seemed full of questions. Caroline felt her impatience rise.

"No. I haven't. We are about to get a divorce, so I don't believe I will be calling him." Caroline replied with controlled words. *Why so many questions?* "Could you be so kind as to assist me to get into my house?"

"Do you have identification?" The deputy shifted feet, reaching to position his hat again.

"No sir. Unfortunately, my purse was in my vehicle when it exploded into flames. I will need to get a replacement driver's license." Caroline looked up at Mark, who stood back some allowing the two to converse. He had an arm crossed and rubbed his chin with the other.

"So, you say you've been in an accident?" The deputy continued his questioning, as he unfolded the white paper in his hand. "Would that be the same accident you accused a Steven White of orchestrating?" The deputy looked at the paper in his hand.

Caroline's eyes grew wide as she eyed the paper. "That's a possibility, yes." She looked at a frowning Mark and the back at the deputy. "Why do you ask? I just need in my house so I can recuperate." Caroline shook her head, confused.

"Well, ma'am, I'm afraid I cannot do that." The deputy adopted a serious look as he stepped up on the porch and handed the paper to Caroline. Still confused, Caroline looked down at the paper as the deputy continued speaking. "Caroline White, you are hereby being served with a Restraining Order stating that you must stay at least 500 feet away from Mr. Steven White and any of his property at all times for the duration of the order."

Caroline's mouth fell open as the words entering her ears confirmed the words on the paper. "What?!" Her look of disbelief followed the deputy as he stepped down from the porch. Mark's arms fell to his sides, and he took a step towards Caroline to glance at the paper.

"Yes, ma'am. Apparently, Mr. White fears for his safety as you have made false allegations against him. I am going to have to ask you to leave the premises." The deputy assumed the stature of his feet spread apart and his thumbs tucked into the belt of his trousers.

"That's ridiculous!" Mark said. "Officer, you can see by just looking at Caroline that the 'allegations' have merit, and you can see that she cannot possible be a threat to her husband!"

"And you are?" The deputy remained in place, shifting only his look in Mark's direction.

"Mark Meadows." Mark place a hand on his hip, glancing down at Caroline who sat frozen, staring at the paper in her trembling hand. "I'm a friend of Caroline's and brought her home from the hospital."

"I'm sorry, Mr. Meadows, but I am just serving a court order." Turning to Caroline, he said, "I'm afraid you'll need to leave the premises, Mrs. White. I will need to wait until you are gone."

Caroline looked up at the deputy. Her mouth still hung

open, and her eyes were wide. She moved her lips, but no sound emerged. The flush that filled her cheeks a short while before left the scene, leaving her as pale as the white paper. She felt herself lifting into the air, not realizing Mark once again scooped her into his arms. She continued to hold the paper, reading the words over and over.

Mark stepped down from the porch and headed to the truck. The deputy stepped aside and watched as Mark struggled with the door handle. Caroline's good arm was wedged against Mark's torso the paper still shaking. She was not able to reach out.

Finally, the deputy asked, "Do you need help?" just as the passenger door swung open.

"Apparently not!" Mark replied sharply without looking back at the deputy. Mark took his time to work the seatbelt around Caroline and buckle it, avoiding her bad arm. As he landed in the driver's seat and closed the door, he looked over at Caroline, fully focused on the paper.

"Here, let me see that," Mark said reaching for the paper. Beyond the passenger window, the deputy stood on the walk, with his hands on his hips waiting for their departure. Mark wasn't in any rush. The Restraining Order limited Caroline from contacting or being 'within 500 feet of his person or property.' Steven White claimed his wife was harassing him and trying to discredit his 'impeccable' reputation with false allegations that he was responsible for her accident by tampering with her car. Caroline sat quietly and watched Mark read the order. Reaching the bottom of the page, he handed the page back to Caroline.

"Don't worry about this. Restraining Orders are common in divorces," Mark said, trying to offer comfort. "Jennifer took one out against me. You'll just need to contact your lawyer, and she can write a response to it. Don't worry. It'll will work out." Mark watched Caroline shake her head, looking again at the paper. In the background the deputy stood with crossed arms, indicating growing impatience.

"What am I supposed to do in the meantime?" Caroline asked holding the paper to the side. She stared through the windshield. "Seriously, Steven? UGH!" Shaking the paper in her hand, the question was more for the air. To vent.

Mark saw the deputy start towards the truck, so he started the engine and shifted into drive, creeping slowly out of the circular drive. They didn't need the deputy coming up with something like obstruction of justice or trespassing. Mark headed straight back down the road, glancing a couple times towards Caroline as she continued to process the new information.

"Do you want my phone?" he asked, coming to the stop sign.

"For what?" Caroline asked, shaking her head again.

"To call your lawyer?"

"Yeah, I guess," Caroline took the phone extended to her. Another 'ugh!' filled the cab of the truck as the phone rang.

"Fields Law Office, this is Rachel," the voice answered.

"Hi Rachel. Is Emily in? This is Caroline Reeves-White."

"Oh, hello Caroline," Rachel greeted. "No, I'm sorry but Attorney Fields has left for court this afternoon, but I can get a message to her if necessary."

Caroline told the law assistant about the Restraining Order. "Let Emily know I have nowhere to go! I guess I'm headed to the homeless shelter in Morehead. She can reach me th..."

"No, tell her she can reach you on my phone," Mark interrupted. Caroline frowned at him.

"How?" she asked him, squinting her eyes.

"You're not going to a shelter," Mark replied.

"Um...I guess she can reach me at this number," Caroline repeated for Rachel. "Thanks."

Caroline ended the call and looked at Mark with her mouth open and her face contorted in confusion. "What do you mean, I'm not going to the shelter?" she asked. "Where else do I have to go? *I'm homeless!*"

"Do you honestly think a homeless shelter is going to take someone in your condition?" Mark asked as they continued to sit at the stop sign. Glancing in the rearview mirror, he saw the deputy's car approaching. Putting his blinker on, he pulled onto to the highway in the direction they'd come from.

"You're going the wrong way..." Caroline tried pointing in the other direction, the paper flopping in her hand. "Ugh!" She threw the paper down in her lap. "They have to. I'm homeless."

"Do you have any identification?" Mark slowed for a car that pulled out of a drive. The rearview mirror indicated the deputy decided to head the same direction.

"No." Her tone was hesitant. "But I'm going to get a new driver's license."

"The shelter won't take you without identification." Mark continued, "Is the shelter going to take you to get a driver's license?"

"I don't know. Maybe."

"Caroline, you cannot take care of yourself. A shelter is not going to take you in," Mark insisted.

"Well, then drop me off at the nearest bridge! Don't homeless people live under bridges?" Caroline quickly realized what she just said, adding, "No, forget that! That's what got me in this shape!" Caroline dropped her head in her hand as her elbow rested on the console between them. "Dear Lord!" she let out with a sigh.

"Religious?" Mark asked.

"Huh?" Caroline lifted her head enough to look at Mark.

"It sounded like you were getting ready to pray," he remarked.

"I should! It's probably the only thing I have left!" Her words were coated in sarcasm. "At this point, I doubt God or Jesus would listen to anything I have to say! I've burned my bridges even with them!"

Mark instantly broke out in laughter. He looked over at

Caroline, who continued to look at him with a scrunched-up face. It dawned on her why Mark laughed. With another sound of despair, she dropped her forehead back into her hand.

CHAPTER 6 – THE DUPLEX

Mark put the truck into park in front of the duplex. Unaware the truck had stopped, Caroline continued to cradle her head in her hand, propped up on the console. Somewhere around the Fleming-Mason-county line she'd quit debating Mark about the homeless shelter. When she did, the cab of the truck went silent. Absorbed in her thoughts and frustrations, she didn't even inquire where Mark was taking her. Mark walked around the truck, raising a hand to his neighbor who stood with a steaming drink as she watched her son navigate circles in their drive in a toddler toy. Waving back, the mother was suddenly intrigued by Mark's passenger, observing Mark open the door rather than watching her son.

The cold air rushing into the cab perked Caroline up. She began to raise her head, as Mark reached over her to release the seat belt. Still leaning on her arm, she looked up to see Mark's face only inches from her own. His warm breaths touched her skin, bringing her back to life.

"Where are we?" her voice croaked.

"Oh, you'll see here in a moment," Mark replied. "Do you want me to carry you? Or do you want to try to walk?" Regardless of her answer, Mark scooped her out of the seat, waiting to see if he should put her on her feet.

"I think I should try to walk."

Setting Caroline on the paved drive, he put his arm behind her lower back as she grasped his arm for support. Taking slow steps, Caroline began limping toward an orange door. A couple of awkward, wobbly steps winded her, and she stopped to rest and catch her breath.

"Do you need help?" the neighbor called. The toddler even stopped circling to look.

"No, but thanks, Christy," Mark called back. "We've got it! Just a little slow-going!"

With another stop to rest, they made it to the door. Not a fan of orange, Caroline was surprised at how pleasantly it contrasted the charcoal-colored siding. Mark produced a jumble of keys, one of which slipped into the lock and the door swung open.

The contemporary style of the home continued inside. Mark assisted Caroline to a low-lying couch in the middle of the room. Caroline twisted her head to take in the sparse features. Grey walls, modern straight-lined furniture, and touches of color in a painting on the wall and a throw over the back of a chair matching the charcoal couch. The coffee table was a slab of thick clear glass atop a black metal frame. The light-colored wooden floors had a whitewashed finish, and a simple woven rug in various hues of greys and blacks sat under the living room furniture.

Getting situated on the couch, Caroline found the cushions firm, and Mark told her to rest her casted foot on the table. As she raised her foot, he bent over to remove the walking boot and set it next to the table. The emerald-green cast was another nice contrast to the neutral room.

Mark then helped Caroline out of the flannel jacket which he hung in a closet with his own before making his way to the kitchen.

"Something hot to drink?" he asked as he leaned on a narrow bar that separated the two rooms.

"Sure." Caroline's attention turned to the kitchen. Two black stools stood beneath a butcher-block countertop. The bottom of the bar was painted the same olive green as the bottom cabinets in the kitchen. Well, the ones she could see. The top cabinets appeared to be a shade of grey slightly darker than the walls with textured glass doors, and the fixtures all appeared to be stainless. Glancing around, Caroline noticed there wasn't a speck of dust on any of the surfaces and the furnishings were in immaculate condition. Not what she expected from a man. Especially not Mark. Someone who spent so much time outside working in dirt.

"So, this is home?" she asked.

"Yep. Tea okay?" He held a kettle and with her nod of approval, he filled it with water. "I've got Earl Grey, English Breakfast, mint, chamomile, orange spice, and chai."

"Surprise me. Whatever you're having," she replied. She was curious which tea he would select. He'd contradicted many of her assumptions about him already. As he pulled mugs and tea from a cabinet, Caroline looked around the room again. In the corner of the living room sat a dining room table with six chairs. Its simple lines were made from a light wood. Maple? An oval bowl in the center of the table contained a few pieces of fruit. Against the far wall, an open staircase with black spindles led to a second floor. Its treads were the same whitewashed wood as the floor.

"So…" Caroline turned back towards Mark as he tended to the tea. "You've brought me to your home?" *Why would he do that?* Hadn't she been enough of a burden? She'd already called the aides and put the care plans on hold until she was able to get home. "Why?"

"Why not?" Mark lifted the kettle of boiling water and poured each cup. "I've got plenty of room." He dunked a teabag up and down in one of the mugs. A hint of mint reached Caroline. Interesting. "Besides, I'm pretty much free for the winter. I can at least help you out."

"That's very generous of you," Caroline replied, watching him dunk the other teabag. "But don't you seriously have better things to do than to take care of an invalid. A stranger?" Then after pause, she added, "You really don't want to take this on. Me. Steven. This whole mess." She shook her head again, thinking about the restraining order. That was just the beginning, she was sure. Her head ached just thinking about it.

Mark picked up the mugs and headed into the living room. "Sometimes a person just needs a friend to help them through tough times," he replied. He placed both mugs on the glass coffee table. "Those will need to cool a bit." Taking a seat next to her on the couch, "I appear to be the only friend you've got at the moment."

"I am basically a total stranger to you, Mark. Why do you care?" Caroline played with her fingers sticking out of the cast as Mark laid his arm along the back of the couch, brushing her shoulders as he did so.

"Because I've been alone before," he said facing her. "I know what it's like to be alone. No one to talk to. No one to listen. It isn't fun. No one should have to go through that."

"But you've got family…" Caroline began.

"So do you, even though you don't seem to be on speaking terms," Mark countered. "But, even if you were, sometimes family are not the ones you need to talk to. They can't listen objectively. And they have their own ideas of what a person should do.'

Caroline nodded. She understood. Mark seemed to have a good relationship with his family. Or at least he spoke to them. Caroline didn't even have that.

"What got you through?" she asked. She assumed he was speaking of his divorce.

"Time." He leaned forward, taking a sip of the tea, testing it to see if it had cooled enough. "A few friends. But friends get… well…they can only listen to so much. You know?"

"That's how you'll be with me…" Caroline looked down at her fingers. "I promise I'll get out of here as soon as I can get back into the house. I don't want to be a burden." When she looked up, Mark's face was close to hers as he leaned to pass her tea to her. "Oh! Thanks." She took the tea with her good hand and passed it under her nose before taking a sip.

"I put a little sugar in it. I hope it's not too much," Mark rested his mug on his thigh, and Caroline did the same.

"No, it's perfect." She looked up and smiled. "So, how long have you been divorced, if you don't mind my asking?"

"Over six years," Mark replied. His eyes suddenly had a far-off look. "The first couple of years were difficult. Hopefully, it will be different for you. You don't have children."

"You do?" Caroline was surprised. She studied Mark's face.

He bit his lower lip before replying.

"Yep. Two girls. Christa and Brittany. Christa's fourteen and Brittany is eleven." His jaw muscles tightened again. "I don't get to see them. Haven't for more than four years."

"You haven't? Why?" Caroline voice conveyed her shock.

"Eh. You know how it goes. Their mother had nothing good to say about me during the divorce. Filled their heads with a bunch of lies." He took another sip, wetting his mouth. "Jennifer said I was violent with her and that I was unbalanced. I got slapped with a restraining order."

"Oh, that's why you know about restraining orders," Caroline diverted her eyes.

"Yeah. Didn't get to see the girls until that all that got cleared up, and by then they didn't want to see me. Still don't."

"Were you?" Caroline asked. She scanned Mark from head to toe. For the first time, she noticed his physique was quite built, but from the days she'd gotten to know him, she couldn't picture him being rough or physical with someone. It didn't seem his temperament. He was too giving.

"What?" Mark looked toward her. His brown eyes glistened with water. "Violent? No." He paused. "Well, when someone comes at you with arms flailing trying to attack you...yes, you're going to try to calm the situation down. She had bruised wrists from where I tried to hold her off. No one was interested in seeing the bruises and scratches she left on me."

Caroline said nothing. She was fortunate. Steven had never raised a hand to her. He was always completely in control. He prided himself on that. Controlled. It was the words and the psychological games he played that caused the damage. Bruises, scratches, and scars not to be seen, but there just the same.

"She's remarried," Mark said wiping at his face.

"Your wife? I mean ex-wife?"

"Yeah. She married the guy she was seeing when we were married."

"That hurts," Caroline commented, bringing her tea to her

lips. *Steven and Brandia probably already picked out rings, just waiting for the divorce to be final.*

"That's when she pretty much left me alone." He sniffled before adding, "The girls call him 'Dad.'"

"Ouch!" No, Caroline did not have to worry about such things with Steven. Perhaps that made her lucky. But she wondered what other worries Steven might send her way. "Do you have pictures of your girls?" Again, she turned her head looking for photos.

"Not out." Mark leaned forward and pulled his wallet from his back pocket. Opening the bill fold he searched in one of the pockets, pulling out a worn photo. He handed it to Caroline. "That's from last Christmas."

The two girls stood arm-in-arm, both tall but one slightly taller. The shorter one looked just like Mark. Caroline assumed the taller girl looked like her mother. Both girls were stunning. Caroline could only imagine what Jennifer-the-ex-wife looked like. Caroline was plain in comparison. It was suddenly clear to Caroline that Mark's interest in her had to be solely a mercy mission. Based on what she saw in the photo, she didn't come with a football field of being Mark's type.

"They're simply gorgeous," she said, handing the photo back to Mark. "The little one looks like you."

Mark nodded his head as he slipped the photo back into it place. Instead of pocketing the bill fold, he tossed it on the table, and then sat back on the couch. He returned his arm around the back of the couch, this time fully touching Caroline's shoulders. She picked up her tea, resting between her legs, and took another sip.

"So..." Mark drew the word out. "What are you in the mood to eat for supper tonight? It's getting about that time."

"Anything but hospital food!" Caroline replied without looking at him. She felt him shift his body toward her and it made her feel a little uncomfortable. It heightened her sense of being an imposition. "Tacos are perfectly fine. I'm not picky."

"Oh, no. The tacos were a special treat," Mark replied. "The only take-out I generally do is coffee."

Seriously? Caroline had to look at him. A gentle smile complimented his brown eyes, which seemed to have easily let go the previous topic. "If you're suggesting that I whip something up…" She pointed to her arm and foot. She hated to use them as an excuse.

Mark laughed. "No," he shook his head. "I'm actually a pretty good cook. It's something I enjoy doing. I find it relaxing. Soothing. Challenging even."

"Oh." Caroline gave him a semi-smile, shaking her head. "Really? Is there anything you can't do?"

"What about a shrimp scampi? Do you eat shrimp?"

"Uh. I love shrimp!" Her reply brought a large smile out on Mark's face.

He moved forward on the couch, and then softly patted Caroline's leg a couple times as he rose. "I better thaw the shrimp!" he said heading toward the kitchen. "You want more tea?"

"No, I'm good." She added, "If I drink too much, I'll need to pee." This earned another laugh from Mark as he disappeared into an unseen part of the kitchen.

***

Mark served the Shrimp Scampi over risotto so it would be easier for Caroline to manage. After assisting her to sit at one end of the table and placing goblets of water and flatware by her and the seat next to her, he brought two steaming plates filled with risotto topped with shrimp and a lemony-garlicy-buttery sauce. Flecks of red pepper hid among the shrimp and chopped fresh parsley was scattered across the top. Wedges of lemon garnished the side of the plate. The aroma engulfed Caroline. Briefly, Caroline transported in her mind to a five-star restaurant. The only thing missing were the table linens, flowers or a candle, and a bottle of white wine.

Rather than sitting at the other end of the table, Mark sat

on the side next to Caroline. As he scooted towards the table his long leg bumped touched her knee. She expected him to say 'sorry' and move his leg, but his leg remained comfortably resting against hers. Seemingly oblivious, he indicated that she go ahead and sample the food. Caroline awkwardly picked up the fork and managed to scoop up a piece of shrimp with some of the saucy rice. The bite was a bit larger than she normally could handle, so as she chewed her hand went to her mouth in case pieces tried to escape. Finally, she swallowed. All the while, Mark watched for her reaction.

"OMG!" she said, her hand still flanking her mouth. "That is sooo good! Where did you learn to cook like that?" She looked at Mark, who still hadn't touched his plate, but a gentle smile filled his face.

"Good. I'm glad you like it," he said. He reached over and half-patted, half-rubbed her hand as she reached for her fork again. Picking his own fork up with his left hand, he began to enjoy the meal with her.

"Seriously. Where did you learn to cook?" Caroline asked again after her third bite. "I mean, I cook. I enjoy cooking and experiment with lots of different things, but I've never made a scampi this good!"

"I used to help my mom in the kitchen quite a bit," Mark replied after washing food down with some water. "In fact, cooking was something we did as a family a lot of the time. We all helped with some aspect of the meal."

"That's really nice." Caroline thought back to her mom's tiny kitchen. The experience was exactly the opposite. Her mom chased her children out of the kitchen, saying they didn't have the food to waste if one of the kids made a mistake. Caroline always wondered about her mother's concern. The meals in her home generally consisted of biscuits or cornbread, some sort of soup beans flavored with hunks of meat, and a vegetable, potatoes, or macaroni and cheese. It wasn't like her family could afford high-end ingredients to make gourmet meals. Caroline often thought the kids got ushered out because cooking was her mother's 'alone time.' She hadn't considered it until now, but perhaps cooking was how her mom 'relaxed' just as Mark said it did for him.

"What are you thinking about?" Mark asked. It amazed Caroline how in tune he seemed to be to her. She looked up from her plate and smiled.

"I was just thinking how lucky I am to be eating this delicious meal at a real table rather than hospital food off a tray." It wasn't a lie. She just didn't want to share what life pre-Steven had been like. She was beginning to get the idea that Mark's family may have been a little higher on the social ladder.

Changing the subject, she asked, "So, are you left-handed or right-handed?" She motioned to the fork in his left hand. Yet earlier she watched him chop onions and garlic with his right hand.

"I believe I told you that I'm ambidextrous. From a broken elbow." He focused on scooping up another bite. "I've just continued to use both hands since then. I always eat with my left." His left hand guided the fork to his mouth and then stopped. "Did you know the Europeans always hold the fork in their left?"

"Really?" Caroline glanced up from her almost empty plate. She knew she was full and should quit, but the lingering food on her plate called to her. It was the best meal she'd had since... well, she couldn't even remember. "Well, I may end up doing everything European style!" She smiled upon finishing the statement, but the sprinkle of sarcasm in her tone hung in the air.

When they finished the meal, Mark cleared the table. Then he assisted Caroline to the downstairs bathroom. Closing the door, she had the sink and towel bar to hold onto. As she struggled to get the sweat pants and cotton underwear down, she heard the clinking of dishes and water running in the kitchen. When she finished her business, she struggled again to pull up her underwear with the one hand and did the same with sweat pants. Then she sat on the toilet, waiting until she heard Mark finish with the dishes. She didn't want to interrupt him so he could help her hobble to her next location, whatever that might be.

She silently chuckled to herself, gently shaking her head. What a fix she was in. There she was, in the house of a man she barely knew, sitting on the lid of his toilet, clothed in oversize sweats and a pair of cotton granny panties that the man bought for her. Cotton panties. Not even a pair of decent women's underwear! And no bra. He hadn't even gotten her a bra! He was probably either embarrassed or was clueless. On the other hand, she probably couldn't wear a bra the way her shoulder continued to hurt and with her arm strapped to her body to immobilize it. She couldn't even walk out of the bathroom without assistance or something to hold onto.

Bracing herself with the sink, she pulled herself up off the toilet, and then turned toward the mirror hanging over the sink. Seeing her reflection for the first time in weeks, she surveyed her face in the mirror. No makeup. Pale skin. Tired eyes with a hint of dark circles. Lips thin and starting to chap. Curly hair hanging limp. Nope. Not a pretty picture. She looked away from the stranger in the mirror and turned on the water with her hand. Rolling the bar of soap in her hand, she then rubbed her fingers together in attempt to wash her hand. Once done, her hand still didn't feel clean. Leaning against the vanity, she opened the door to find Mark about to knock.

Helping her out of the bathroom, he asked her what she wanted to do. Hanging on to his arm, she just looked at him. He immediately realized it had been a silly question.

"Honestly, I am exhausted," she told him. "Can I just lay down? Maybe watch a little television to get my mind off things?"

"Sure!" he grinned. Before she could respond, he swept her up in his arms and headed toward the stairs.

"But..." Caroline motioned towards the couch.

"No, no. You're not sleeping on a couch." He continued up the stairs emerging into landing with doors. Another bathroom, bedrooms, and a closet. He continued into the room straight ahead, stopping at the side of a large bed. Mark set her on her feet and bent to peel back the covers. "I've got some jammies, but they'd probably be huge on you," he said.

"I'm fine in this. Just glad to not be in a hospital gown!"

Mark propped up several pillows for her and assisted her to get into the bed, situated as comfortable as possible. On the wall opposite the bed was a series of shelves over which a large screen television hung. Grabbing the remote, Mark clicked the screen on and walked around the other side of the bed. Sitting on the side of the bed, he began flipping through channels.

"Is there anything particular you want to watch?" he asked Caroline.

"I don't suppose there's something light-hearted, cheery and uplifting?" she asked.

He punched in some numbers on the keypad landing on the Hallmark channel. A scene with snow, Christmas lights and a woman bent down speaking to a child appeared on the screen. "Ask and you shall receive," he smiled.

Caroline gave him another of her perplexed looks as he laid down on top of the covers, propping his head on his arm. Caroline shook her head. Apparently, he was into the Hallmark Christmas scene. He knew the channel numbers, and easily got comfortable next to her. She settled back into the pillows, her shoulder reminding her it was still sore.

***

It sounded like a doorbell. Caroline lifted her head from the pillow. The bed next to her was empty. Mark was gone, and the television was off. Daylight shined through the wide slats of the white blinds that covered the windows. Voices carried up the stairs and through the open bedroom door. Caroline pushed herself into an upright position so she could hear more clearly.

"Larry!" Mark held the door open, allowing his older brother to enter. "What brings you out so early on a Saturday?" Mark closed the door, as his brother removed his coat and walked towards the couch and chairs.

"Well, I figured you might actually be home this early!" Larry replied, laying his coat over the back of the nearest chair. "I had to come see my hero brother!"

"Hero brother?" Mark headed back into the living room. "Where you getting that from?" Pausing behind the couch, he added, "I've got coffee brewing. Want some?"

Larry nodded his balding head, and Mark moved toward the kitchen.

"That's what the news is saying!" Larry replied. "It's all over the T.V. and the newspapers! Says you saved a woman from a fiery crash!"

Hero. Mark was being billed as a hero in the media. Great. Retrieving mugs from the cabinet, Mark asked, "You still take your coffee black?" Mark knew his brother wasn't there to congratulate him on any heroism.

"Yep, still do. Creature of habit." Larry remained standing, looking around the duplex. "Like what you've done with the place. Very modern. It's got that minimalist feel."

"That's me, Larry," Mark called from the kitchen glancing at his brother. Larry stood, waiting for Mark to join him. "No frills Mark."

"There's quite a bit of grey in here," Larry commented. "Is that really working for you?"

Mark approached his brother and handed him the mug with black coffee. Mark invited his brother to sit. "Grey is the new neutral. As you see, I've got some color in here. And I can add as much as I want." Mark took a sip of his own coffee, the cream coloring it the same as the dining table. "So, Larry, you're not here to talk about heroes or colors. Why don't you tell me why you're really here." Mark decided to take the upper hand with his brother. Mark sat on the couch, leaning forward, holding his coffee in both hands.

"No, you're right." Larry sighed. "We've been worried about

you Mark."

"We?"

"All of us. Me. Beth. Lynn. Dad especially." Larry blew on the dark liquid before taking a sip.

"None of us have been able to get ahold of you," he continued.

"Now that's not true. I spoke to Beth the other morning," Mark corrected. "I've been busy."

"Hiding is more like it." Larry was blunt. "You've done this before, if you remember."

His brother's words stung, but Mark didn't show it. He took another sip of his coffee and then set the mug on the table. He continued to sit forward on the couch and clasped his hands between his spread knees. "Call it what you like, Larry. I've been busy. Being a 'hero' requires one to make appearances and have speaking engagements, you know. Oh, and then there is my job. My company. Getting everything and everyone situated for winter."

"Beth said you were very vague about the money." Again, Larry was direct.

"I told Beth what I know." Mark spread his hands as he spoke. "The police and FBI are trying to find Jake. He's left the country, and they've frozen all the investor accounts while they investigate. INTERPOL is even involved trying to find him. That's all I know." Mark looked his brother in the eye as he spoke. Trying to convince him this was the truth. Which it mostly was. "Oh, one of the cops I spoke to did say that Jake apparently took off with a bunch of his clients' money, electronically transferring it to foreign accounts. His own grandparents are victims."

"Was Mom and Dad's money among the funds taken?" Larry rested his mug on the arm of the chair.

"That I don't know." Mark spoke definitively. "I had Jake invest the money just like we discussed. I don't know how he could get at it without requiring one of us to sign off on selling the shares off." Still Mark was bordering on the truth. He just wasn't telling Larry the money never was invested. That it had been sitting in the escrow account Jake cleaned out. "The cop, Officer Keyser was his name, told me it may take some time before it all gets figured out."

Larry looked at Mark with raised eyebrows—his doubtful look.

"Hey, Larry, if you don't believe me, check it out yourself. I am sure the cop would be happy to tell you what he knows!" Of course, Mark had gotten additional information from Jake's assistant Rhonda, but he doubted she was talking to anyone these days.

"Well, I might just do that," Larry said. Shifting he raised the coffee to his lips. After a long drink, he commented, "You always did make the best coffee! I should stop more often!"

"That's quite okay, Larry!"

"So..." Larry turned to his other purpose for visiting. "Dad is curious why you were on the bridge, Mark. We all are, in fact."

Mark sat up straight, resting his hands on his knees. "Why?"

"Well, given your history, Dad's concerned..." Larry's words trailed off.

"Have you ever been on the bridge, Larry?" Mark asked, turning the questions back on him.

"I've been across it."

"No, Larry. Have you ever walked the bridge, especially at night when all the lights are on?"

"No, can't say I have," Larry replied. "No need to."

"Well, I do it quite often actually," Mark said. "It's a great place to go think and ponder things. It's quite spectacular at night."

"Dad was concerned you were there to jump." Larry was a wealth of bluntness,

"What?" Mark feigned surprise. "Jump off the bridge? Why would I do that?"

"Dad thought maybe you were upset about something, or that you'd gone off your meds." Larry added, "Or that you'd been drinking again." With that comment, Larry casually looked around the room for signs of alcohol.

"Let Dad know—and the rest of you—that I'm fine. I'm taking my medication. I'm not drinking. No, I take that back… I did have a short drink with Jared when their baby was born. That's it. All is good." Mark look at his brother. Again, doubt displayed on Larry's face.

"You know, Larry," Mark clasped his hands again. "I want to share a little secret with you. Promise not to tell the others?" Mark tilted his head waiting for his brother's reply.

"Why not share with the others?" Larry asked. Curiosity filled his tone.

"Because you of all of them are the best to understand what I'm about to say." Mark smiled at his bother.

"Okay…" Larry agreed tentatively. He himself sat a little straighter and drained his cup in preparation.

"Well, this is kind of hard for me to say," Mark began. "But here goes!" He looked straight at his brother, capturing his eyes. "The last time that I tried…well, you know…I wasn't successful, obviously. Do you know why I wasn't successful?"

Larry shook his head, continuing to listen.

"Because I had interference. This may sound crazy, but I believe God was there and he intervened. He made it impossible for me to follow through. He made sure I failed. And he showed me that I have a greater purpose in life. And he was right. You, Dad, the others never have to worry about me every making another attempt. God's words were loud and clear to me. They still are, and He continues to show me a very different side of life."

Larry reached up and pinched the wetness from his eyes. "Um. I'm shocked, Mark. I never knew you were open to God."

"I wasn't." Mark smiled again at his brother. "But God performed a miracle in my life, and it's pretty hard to ignore and not open up to that."

"Maybe, I'll see you in church?" Larry asked.

"Larry, at some point, when I am ready, not only will I be in church, but I'd be honored if you'd baptize me." Mark reached over for his brother's hand. Larry not only took Mark's hand, but he stood, pulling Mark up off the couch, and wrapped his arms around his younger brother. For the first time in, many, many years, the two brothers hugged. Hugged like squabbling little boys making up for some inconsequential difference.

As Mark closed the door behind Larry and watched from the window as his brother departed, a warmth spread through his body. He felt good about his disclosure. And he knew Larry was happy he had finally won Mark over. Years of preaching and pleading finally paid off. Larry walked away that morning feeling successful. Mark just left out the details that God's intervention was on the bridge as Mark perched on the railing. The flash that shone itself on the bridge was not just the headlights of the Range Rover, it had been something much more. Much stronger. Life changing. A miracle for sure.

CHAPTER 7 – IMPROVISIONS

"Can I sit at the bar on one of the stools?" Caroline asked as they reached the first floor.

Mark shrugged. "Sure. Do you think you'll be comfortable enough?" He set her down and began leading her towards the kitchen.

"Mark, can I tell you a secret?" she asked gripping his arm taking delicate steps towards the bar. Not waiting for his answer, "I'm never comfortable these days. Something is aching or sore or paining me regardless of what I do."

When they got to the bar, she let go of Mark, pulled the stool out, and slid onto it, steadying herself with her hand on the counter. Mark hovered as she exerted her independence, just in case. Once she was safely seated, he moved around the counter and retrieved a mug for her, putting his brother's in the sink.

"I hear the coffee's really good in this joint," Caroline said with a playful smile. It was Mark's turn to flush with embarrassment. *Had she heard everything he and Larry discussed?*

"Oh, I don't know about that!" Instead of fixing Caroline's coffee, he placed the cup of steaming brew in front of her along with a bowl of sugar and creamer. Lastly, he offered her a spoon. "You can fix it to your liking." He stood back sipping his second cup as she briefly stared at the condiments and the spoon. Slowly she took the lid off the sugar, and then picked up the spoon. She stirred the two spoonful's of sugar in her coffee, then added a dash of cream. It ended up being more than a dash, as she still didn't have good control with her left hand, but it was coming along. The cream rose to the top, creating abstract swirls and designs in the dark liquid, ultimately lightening the brew on its own.

"You're trying to encourage my independence, aren't you?" She asked, bringing the mug to her lips. "Mm. It is pretty good…" she tilted her head, giving him a slight smile. He sipped his coffee and continued to watch her.

"You know," Caroline began, "you're going to burn out your cornea's if you keep staring at me like that. I'm not much to look at, and I can only imagine what my hair is doing this morning." She reached her hand to her head and attempted to tame her bedhead using her fingers as a comb.

"Oh, you're plenty to look at," Mark replied. Caroline frowned at him, as if she didn't believe him. One thing he'd quickly learned about the woman was that she was incredibly hard on herself. Any comments related to her appearance or her abilities, she discounted without hesitation. Like she'd been brainwashed into believing she wasn't as wonderful as she really was. Mark realized his work was cut out for him. But he was very much the same way. He didn't take a compliment any better.

"I don't think you're saying that as a good thing," she replied. "I must look like a horror! You know they have make-up, curling irons and straighteners, and hair products for a reason!"

"You think you're going to be twirling a curling iron?" Mark laughed.

"No, because I am sure you don't have one!" Her smile turned smug.

"You been going through my things?" Mark teased. Setting his cup on the counter, he leaned his hands on the edge. He was still in a pair of green and blue plaid pajama bottoms and a blue pajama top. The buttons were undone allowing the collar to fold over, a couple of chest hairs peeking out.

"Yep, I ransacked your room while you were talking to your brother," she teased back.

So, she had heard everything. Mark just smiled. He knew if she was around for any amount of time, she'd been hearing and learning about some of his less-desirable traits. Everyone had secrets of some sort. And he was pretty sure Caroline had plenty of her own when it came to her family and her past. She was just more skillful keeping them under wraps.

"So…what do you want to do today?" Mark asked. "This is your first full day of freedom!"

Caroline looked at him with her ringed blue eyes. The blue was paler than usual causing the brown ring to look darker. She held her mug in her hand close to her face, her elbow resting on the counter.

"Well, I'd love to go shopping," she spoke slowly. "I could use more clothes, a little make-up, and some other things to help make me feel human; however, I haven't a dime to my name." She took a sip, and hurried to swallow, another thought coming to mind. "Well, actually, I have plenty of money of my own! Money that Steven doesn't even know about, but I have no way to get to it!"

"What do you mean?" Mark furrowed his brows. He continued to lean on the counter,

"Oh, I've got this little account at the credit union in Morehead. Since I've worked at the university, I've had a little bit of money taken out each pay period and deposited in to the account. I've never told Steven about it, and as far as I know, he knows nothing about it. I've made a point to never show him my pay stubs. They're all online anyway." She smiled again, a hint of deviousness in the corners of her mouth.

"Caroline, if you're needing things, I can get them for you." Mark looked at her frankly. "You don't need to worry about dipping into your savings. At least not right now."

"I've also got to get garbage bags and duct tape," she said.

Mark gave her a look, but then quickly remembered his days with a cast. She had to cover her arm and leg casts, so they didn't get wet when showering. "I've got plenty of bags and tape. You forget…I'm a landscaper. We use bags galore." Caroline shrugged, seeming okay with that news.

"Are you seriously feeling up to shopping?" Mark asked, squinting his eyes at her.

"No, not really. But, if I continue to be swathed in sweats,

I'll want to..." She suddenly stopped. "Um...I'll just not be in a good mood." Mark stood straight. He knew what she was jokingly going to say, but suddenly she remembered what she'd heard.

"Well, we don't want you in a bad mood!" Mark said moving around the bar. "Let me go throw some clothes on, and we can run to Wal-Mart and see what we can find that will accommodate your casts."

**

Mark was sure that Caroline would request a hat and sunglasses to disguise herself, however she seemed okay with gracing the store with her untouched self. They first headed for the scooters at the entrance of the store, thinking this would be the perfect way for Caroline to navigate the store. Until they realized the forward control was on the right side and the backup control was on the left. Caroline could not comfortably cross over her left hand to use the right control and still steer. There weren't any basic wheel chairs around, and so Mark and Caroline found themselves staring at one of the kiddie carts that had the plastic seat behind the cart. Mark looked at Caroline. Looking back, she shrugged.

Mark retrieved the cart and helped Caroline get situated in a sideways position. She didn't look thrilled, and as they moved through the store, many heads gawked at the non-conventional use of the cart. But it served the purpose. Mark steered her around the clothing section so she could look at the various clothing options to see what would work for her. Pants were out. The legs were too narrow to accommodate her cast. Leggings would be too difficult for her to struggle with to get on. Many of the shirts and sweaters were more form fitting, again not allowing arm room for a cast. Even the athletic clothing was too clingy. Just not suitable for Carolines situation. And the woman's department didn't seem to have sweat shirts or sweat pants anywhere to be found. Sighs emerged from Caroline frequently. At one point, her head fell into her hand out of sheer frustration.

Until Mark steered her over into the men's section. First, he took her by a rack of flannel bottoms showing her how the legs were wide enough for her cast. Second, her took her by a rack of long-sleeved t-shirts explaining she could pair them with sweaters and sweatshirts and color to the pants.

"Remember," he told her. "It's only going to get colder. Then at some point, you should be back in your own clothes!" She nodded agreement. As they left the men's department, they passed the women's lingerie section.

"Wait!" she called to him. "I need a couple of bras. And some better underwear!" Mark had difficulty steering the cart around the closely clustered bra displays. Caroline ended up scanning the items from a distance, sending Mark to bring her one to inspect.

"Um…Caroline?" Mark began. She looked up at him, a lacy pink bra in her hand. She raised her eyebrows encouraging him to continue. "How are you going to get that on?"

Caroline looked down at the undergarment for a moment and then back up at Mark.

"Even if you get that on, is it going to be comfortable on your shoulder? Or will it dig in?" Mark asked. She looked back at the lacy pink garment, contemplating his words. "And I know you want the silky, pretty panties."

"You do?" she asked, looking abruptly back up at him.

He nodded. "But how long are they going to last with you tugging on them with one hand to pull them up?" He added, "Who are you trying to impress?" Her mouth fell open as she stared at him. "You've got a whole pack of the cotton ones. Do they fit okay?" Caroline nodded.

They both ignored the snickers from a couple of women who passed by hearing their conversation.

"We can get you some white undershirts to wear, if you're self-conscious," he offered. Caroline continued to stare at him, biting her lips and chewing on the chapped skin that was forming. She reached up and handed him the lacy pink bra, a pout forming on her face. Mark gave her a gentle smile, as he hung the bra back on the display hook.

Once again, Mark navigated the cart back to the men's section and left Caroline in the aisle as he grabbed a pack of white short-sleeved undershirts. Putting them in the cart with the other items selected, he started steering the cart toward the beauty products. There, he let Caroline take her time in selecting the things she thought she needed to 'make herself presentable.' Additionally, she picked out other products like shampoo and conditioner, a brush, deodorant, a toothbrush, and some women's hygiene products. When she asked for them to be put in the cart, she watched him to see if he blushed. Instead, completely straight-faced, he laid them next to the shampoo. Mark had made countless trips to the store for such things when married to Jennifer. Those types of things did not faze him.

"Do you think you've got everything you think you'll need?" he asked before steering her towards the checkout. As they joined a line, a little boy in front of them pointed to Caroline.

"Hey, Mommy!" The boy tugged on his mother's sleeve. "That lady's riding in the same buggy as me!" The mother looked up briefly, and seeing Caroline wrapped up in casts, gave her a brief but embarrassed smile. The little boy continued to stare.

***

Caroline sat in one of the chairs as Mark brought the bags in from the truck. On his second load, he paused by Caroline in the chair and handed her his cell phone. Taking the phone, she looked at him with curiosity.

"Wha..?" She then looked at the phone, seeing Emily's name in the display. Putting the phone to her ear, she spoke,

"Emily?"

"Hello there, Caroline!" the lawyer greeted. "I'm so sorry I didn't get back to you yesterday, and I didn't think you'd mind me calling on a Saturday. In fact, I figured you'd want an update."

"No, you're fine. I absolutely want an update," Caroline said. Mark paused before heading back out for the rest of the bags.

"First of all, where are you? Did you find a place to go?" Emily asked. Her concern seemed genuine.

"Yes, I am staying with a friend…" Caroline tilted her head trying to see Mark at the truck.

"Well, that good. I'm assuming you're using his phone?"

"Yes."

"I've got to ask, Caroline. We don't need any surprises when we're in court. Is this guy more than a friend? Is this something Steven might try to use against you?"

"No. No, no!" Caroline gave a laugh. "Actually, I just met Mark. Honestly, I barely know him. He's the one who pulled me out of the car and saved me from burning up." Her comment was met with silence on the other end. Was Emily making notes?

"Interesting." Emily cleared her throat and continued. "I am going to write a response to the Restraining Order and get it filed on Monday. It will be put on the docket for next available spot, which means you'll need to appear in court. And I think it's vitally important that the judge sees you in your condition. It will speak more than any words can."

Caroline nodded and then realized that Emily couldn't see nods. "Yes. That's no problem. I will be there. I am sure Mark can bring me." Mark popped back into the house with another armload of bags as she spoke the last words. He looked towards her before closing the front door.

"Also, I found out the insurance adjustor has been out to look at your Range Rover, and for some reason, the insurance company is hesitating on a payoff," Emily added.

"Seriously?" Caroline's eyes widened. "But that's Steven's company. The Range Rover was insured through Providia!"

"Well, something's up with the policy or the car. I'm going to make some calls come Monday and see what I can find out," Emily replied. "And, the divorce papers have been filed with the court, and copies sent to Steven's lawyer. Oh, and Caroline, whatever you do, don't talk to Steven, okay?"

"Oh, don't worry, Emily." Caroline let out a brief laugh. "Steven is the last person I would talk to, but I don't think he'll be contacting me. Besides, he has no clue where I am. I kind of like it that way."

"Me too. Okay, so I'll call next week when I know more!" Emily clicked off before Caroline could even respond. She looked at the phone for a moment before the sound of rustling plastic called her attention.

Mark pulled items out of the bags and tried to fold the clothes to keep them from wrinkling. The shampoo, conditioner, and bodywash stood upright on the table next to the other products Caroline selected. Seeing all the purchases stacked on the table, Caroline felt a pang of guilt. She went overboard. When they checked out, she tried to see what the total was, but Mark skillfully blocked the device and then quickly pocketed the receipt. She did make him promise to keep the receipts so she could pay him back. 'Uh-huh' had been his only response.

"What are you doing?" Caroline asked watching the man organizing things.

"I'm trying to see what all we got so I can clear out some drawer space," he replied. "And some space in the bathroom."

"Are you sure that's necessary?" Caroline pushed herself forward in the chair, trying to scoot to the edge. "I might not be here that long."

Mark glanced at her over his shoulder, eyebrows raised. "You'll be here longer than you think," he replied. "That was your lawyer?"

"Yes. She's working on things." Caroline pushed herself

up out of the chair. She smiled to herself and felt a small tingle of success. "Look! I got up on my own!" Getting up by herself was one thing but maneuvering around without aid or something to lean on proved something else. Using the furniture to steady her, she got halfway towards Mark but chickened out going across the empty area herself. She ended up leaning her bottom against the top of the couch.

"That's pretty good," Mark put the package of t-shirts on the top of a pile and turned towards Caroline. "I think you could get around on your own with a cane."

"A *cane*?" Caroline blurted out. A cane hadn't even occurred to her. "They are for *old* people!"

"Ha!" Mark laughed. "Steven's kept you couped up in that shallow world of his for too long!"

Caroline threw him a look but wasn't about to disagree. He wasn't wrong. Steven had messed with her thinking and viewpoints. The longer she was away from her husband, the more she could see how Steven had managed to poison her emotionally. She was in a 'withdrawal' of sorts and was just beginning to rediscover the world. The real world.

"Canes are for people who need assistance walking. Who need the extra support," Mark said walking towards her. "Right now, I am your *cane*, but wouldn't you like to try moving around without me?" He reached out his hand, rubbing her left arm.

Caroline glanced at his hand touching her upper arm and then looked back at him. "I don't know. I think you've done a pretty good job so far. You haven't let me fall!" she teased. "Maybe you're the one who wants to move around without me!"

"Here. Stay right there!" Mark withdrew his hand and motioned her not to move. He took off into the unseen part of the kitchen, and Caroline heard a door open and close. Mark came back through the kitchen carrying a red pole. When he cleared the bar area, Caroline saw that the bottom of the red pole was a rag mop.

"What? Are you planning to have me mop the floors for keep?" she asked, rolling her eyes at him. Actually, if she could mop, she would. Mark far exceeded 'above and beyond.' She was happy to do anything in repayment for his generosity.

"Here," he handed her the mop. "See if you can steady yourself by leaning on this while you walk. It'll tell us if a cane will work for you."

Eying him and her mouth mashed skeptically together, she took hold of the red pole. Mark helped her stand on both feet and stepped aside waiting for her to take a step. Caroline stood for a moment, not knowing which foot to move first. The first step was automatic and something she didn't think about when she leaned on Mark, but the pole was new. She didn't trust it like she trusted Mark. She closed her eyes for a moment, visualizing the pole was Mark's ample arm, ready to grab her if she tumbled. Instinctively, she moved her right booted foot forward, bringing her left foot up next to it. She wobbled slightly, but pausing she regained balance and repeated the process. A smile began to blossom on her budded lips, and she glanced over her shoulder at Mark. Slightly nodding, his hands were perched on his sides. He encouraged her to go further. When she made it to the table, she rested the mop handle against a pile of clothes so she could pull out a chair. Gently, she lowered herself into the chair. Mission accomplished. Hearing clapping behind her, she turned to see Mark coming towards her.

"So now you've turned into a physical therapist!" Caroline laughed. "Is there anything you can't do?"

"Oh, I'm no physical therapist. It's just called common sense," Mark replied, a bashful color coming to his cheeks. "I think my mom's cane is still hanging around at Beth's house. I'll see if we can get ahold of that for you to use. The mop works temporarily, but I don't think you'll want to use it in public." Mark teased, grabbing a stack of clothes. He headed for the stairs.

"Your mom's cane?" Caroline asked. "Doesn't she still need it?"

"Oh, no. Mom's not walked for a good some time now," he replied as he scaled the stairs.

***

Mark lined the three stacks of clothes up on the top of the dresser and began opening drawers assessing contents. Several of them had just an article or two inside that could condense into another drawer, or even be put aside for Goodwill. He began neatly filling the drawers with the items purchased for Caroline. As the drawers filled, so did his thoughts.

Having a woman around again felt so natural to him. Though he'd known Caroline for basically a week and a few days—the days when she was in the coma didn't count—she somehow seemed to fit into his life. Like she'd always been there. And he wasn't going to deny that it felt good to be needed again. To be useful. To have purpose. He was struggling not to get to attached, but his attraction to her was growing. Without his permission or control.

He hadn't allowed a woman in his life since the divorce. He didn't want to experience that kind of pain again, and not just any woman could weather his issues. Fortunately, Caroline was so focused on herself and getting well, and he was so busy helping her, that his depression and the dark mood hadn't shown its ugly self. Secretly, he still blamed himself for Jennifer leaving. He hadn't been the easiest to live with. And, while he fought for visitation with the girls, in the end he'd given up. Why would young girls want to spend time with a dad who became emotionally paralyzed for weeks at a time?

Mark knew Caroline overheard his conversation with Larry. He hoped she'd quickly forget aspects of the conversation. If it looked like she might stay in his life a while, he'd muster the courage to say something to her. If it looked like she'd be moving on, he'd have to focus on keeping himself together and not falling into the dark abyss.

Mark descended the stairs, but Caroline was nowhere in sight, nor was the mop. At the bottom of the steps, he scanned the room, but then heard rummaging in the kitchen. Rounding the bar, he found Caroline with the pantry door open and her head tilting this way and that. She hadn't heard him come up, so when he made the noise 'uh,' she jumped, lost her balance, fell into the pantry door, and began sliding towards the floor. Mark rushed to grab her before she hit the floor hard.

"Sorry!" he said, trying to right her into a standing position again. "I didn't mean to startle you!"

"No, I'm sorry!" She brushed her hair back from her face, now a shade of rose red. "I shouldn't have been snooping!"

"Snooping?" Mark asked, laughing. "Give a girl a mop, and she's going to clean up!"

"I've never seen a pantry so well stocked!" Caroline said, ignoring his humor attempt. "I've always heard you can tell a lot about a person based on what they keep in their refrigerator and pantry!"

"What does my pantry tell you about me?" Mark asked.

"It's a conundrum. You're a contradiction, Mark Meadows. Your pantry just leads to more questions." She shook her head. "So organized! You could feed a family for a month or better out of this closet." Continuing to shake her head in amazement, she looked up at Mark.

"A conundrum," he repeated leaning back against the counter. He was interested in her thoughts. He was obviously not what she expected, but then again, what was she expecting? "What am I contradicting?"

Caroline stepped back from the pantry and closed the door. The mop handle was propped against the bar counter, but she steadied herself by grasping the corner of the wall. She was slow to speak but looked him over. He'd crossed his arms as if he might need to deflect her comments.

"I don't know..." She let out an uncomfortable laugh. She began walking using the counter to keep her balance. "You're...well..." Finally making her way to a bar stool, she sat, putting the counter between them. "You're very... manly looking. And, when you said you were a landscaper, I just took you for being, you know, rough and tough. But you're not. Well, maybe you are rough and tough, but you're so much more." Caroline looked over her shoulder. "Like... your house is immaculately clean. Nothing is out of place. No shoes by the door, no clutter, no dust. And everything is organized just so-so. You've even got your coffee mug handles all pointing in the same direction!"

"And that makes me a contradiction?" Mark asked, arms still folded. He tilted his head, catching her eyes.

She nodded her head vigorously. "For me it does. I guess I expected you to be the stereotypical male slob who flops in front of the television watching football games with a bag of Cheetos leaving orange marks all over the furniture and beer cans stacking up on the table. And smelly socks. Smelly socks in every corner!"

Mark couldn't help but laugh. She'd just described more than half the males he knew, all the guys who worked for him, and his brother Larry. A smile still seated on his face, he watched her struggle with her words. She obviously didn't have conversations like this with Steven.

"You're opposite of all those things. You don't have Cheetos anywhere in the house, you're a gourmet cook, and a clean freak. You've got a kind heart, you're so patient, and you seem to somehow know what people need even when they don't. And you watch Hallmark! Not football!" Caroline's face scrunched up with blotches appearing just before the tears.

Mark pulled off a section of paper towel and handed it to Caroline to blot her eyes. "I'm sorry," he said. He suspected her tears had nothing to do with him being a contradiction, but rather were due to pent up emotions trying to find holes to get out.

"It's not you," she snuffled. "I mean, it's you. It's just I don't understand. I don't know why I'm here. I don't understand why you want to help me. I don't…" she stopped to blow her nose. "I don't know where I belong, or where I'm going. I don't know who I am anymore. I don't even recognize myself. It's like I don't exist. Like Caroline never made it off the bridge! And I hurt. I am so sore, and I hurt! I don't even have the money for the medicines they wanted me to have! Not that I could have gotten them because I don't exist! I have no identity!" She dropped her streaked face into her hand, sobbing softly.

Mark pulled off another piece of paper towel and went around the counter, stopping next to Caroline. He laid the paper towel on the counter next to her, trying to imagine how his pantry had such an effect on her. Mark rested his right hand on her back as she slumped forward on the counter. Gently he began rubbing, making small circles just like his mother had for him as a kid when he'd gotten upset over something. The circling motions had a soothing effect on him. He hoped it worked for Caroline as well.

After a few minutes, the sobs slowed, and Caroline sat a little straighter. Mark removed his hand and used it to lift her chin so he could see her face. The whites of her eyes matched the red blotches on her face. Oddly, the brown circles were a protective barrier to her irises, keeping the redness at bay. For a moment, she took his breath. He shook off the feeling.

"It's going to be okay." His statement was soft but firm. "You are going to be okay." His smile was tender, as were his eyes.

Caroline tried to smile, but her lips became contorted by the other emotions controlling her face. She nodded.

"Do you know what you need?" His words were still gentle, and his fingers still held her chin. Caroline shook her head.

"How about a shower to wash all the dirt and nasty

business away?" He doubted she'd had one the entire time in the hospital. Nice warm showers always lifted his mood and left him feeling much better about his world.

"Hold on. Let me get a few things." He left her on the bar stool and headed into the garage. When he returned with a roll of duct tape and garbage bags in hand, Caroline looked like a crumpled heap perched on the stool. A beaten human being. His heart sank. And he wondered, was that how he looked during one of his spells?

"Come on, missy!" Mark scooped her off the stool and headed upstairs.

***

He set her on the closed toilet seat and laid the plastic bags and roll of duct tape on the vanity. Caroline looked at the bags and duct tape, immediately envisioning a scene from a horror movie. Body. Bags. Duct tape. Caroline shivered. Then it hit her. How was she possibly going to cover her casts with the bags and secure them with duct tape, so they were waterproof? She had only one hand and there was no way she could reach to put the tape on the back of her shoulder.

"I…I can't do this." She looked up at Mark. "I can't…there's no…I won't be able to…"

"Tape up the bags?" Mark finished. "No, Caroline. You're going to need some help."

"You?" she asked nervously. She looked around the bathroom, as Mark knelt beside her. "I'm so sorry! I never thought this through…"

"I can assure you my intentions are completely honorable," he said in a formal, stiff voice, bringing a little humor to an otherwise tense situation. "If you'll let me…"

Caroline nodded, looking down. "Okay." After all, there was no telling who had seen her naked body when she was in the hospital. For four days, they poked, prodded, and even operated on her. She was the subject of a roomful of people.

And then there were the aides who gave her sponge baths and helped wipe her butt. It had been humiliating, but she had to accept it was part of life. Just like this was part of life. For now.

"Let's wrap your foot cast first," Mark said, starting to open a smaller trash bag. Caroline stood and began to slip her sweat pants and undies down, quickly sitting back on the toilet lid. Bending over to conceal as much of her as she could, she watched Mark go right to work fitting the bag over her foot and gathering it around her bare calf above the cast. He tore off an ample piece of duct tape and secured the opening against her skin, making sure there were no creases to allow water in. When he finished with her foot, he reached to pull off her sweat shirt, but found her trying to clutch it to her chest.

"Caroline, I've seen a naked woman before." He raised an eyebrow in her direction. "You're going to have to let go so I can get the bag on your cast and get it secured." He rose on his knees to get the sweatshirt over her head. "Besides, this is not going to be the only time we do this. At least not unless you plan to get really ripe and stinky." He scrunched up his nose.

Caroline sighed and reluctantly let go of the sweat shirt. After Mark got it over her head, he gently worked it down her cast and off her arm. The fuzzy interior of the sweatshirt stuck like Velcro to the fiberglass cast.

Caroline watched Mark focus on getting the bag fitted around the angle of the cast and then gathered around her armpit and shoulder leaving furry fragments.

"Here, hold this here," Mark indicated the top of her shoulder. Her fingers held the plastic in place as he taped around the opening in her armpit area and then up around her shoulder. When he stood to apply the duct tape to the opening around her shoulder, he paused.

"What?" Caroline sensed he saw something unexpected. "Is something wrong?" She looked up at him, seeing he was inspecting her upper back.

"Um. It's just your shoulder is really bruised back here. It looks like the 'coat of many colors.' I would have thought a bruise would have faded by now." He resumed applying the duct tape but did so gently. "No wonder you're still hurting."

"No one said anything about a bruise back there when I was in the hospital." Caroline strained to turn her neck, trying to see.

"Let me get the water started, and I'll get you a mirror so you can see."

Caroline watched as Mark adjusted the waterflow with the handles. The water came flowing out of an overhead rain shower head. While her shower at home was nice, Mark's shower had her shower beat. It was tiled in a multicolored slate, matching the blue slate floor throughout the bathroom. Beside the rain shower head, there was a wall-mounted shower head and a hand-held shower wand. The shower was deep enough that shower doors or a curtain were not necessary. The slate floor had no lip where the shower began but was slanted to allow the shower water to flow down the drain in the shower floor.

As the water heated and steam began to rise, Mark pulled out a mirror and positioned Caroline with her back to the vanity mirror so she could she the bruising. Both Caroline's eyebrows raised as she saw the brilliant yellows, greens, and purples. Some fading was around the edges, but the bruise looked quite fresh.

"Maybe it's just slow coming out?" Caroline suggested, looking at Mark in the mirror. She lowered the mirror, handing it back to Mark, noticing he was quite close. She was thankful that the bag covering her arm also covered some of the rest of her. Mark didn't appear to notice her at all. He kept his eyes on her face.

"Are you okay?" he asked.

Caroline wasn't sure if Mark was referring to the bruise on her back or the whole ordeal of revealing herself in front of a man she'd only known for…what…a week? Two weeks?

"Got to be, don't I?" she replied limping towards the shower, holding on to the walls.

"Test the water," he told her. "I think it's ready for you." He gathered up her clothes from the floor and began to leave the room. "I'll be out here if you need anything. Just holler."

Caroline stepped into the stream of warm water, letting it cascade through her hair onto her shoulders, and down her body. Once she was wet all over, she reached for the shampoo she'd purchased. She looked at the top, the flap open, but she began considering how she was going to squirt it into her hand. Studying it a moment she put it back on the rack but on its side, thinking it might run out into her hand. She waited a moment, then took her hand to apply pressure, a little came out, but it dripped directly on the floor and the shower water rinsed it quickly down the drain. Then, she looked at the body wash. It offered a similar struggle. She stood with the water splashing on her body, shaking her head. She felt the tears surging but tried to hold them back. The shower was supposed to make her feel better—to soothe her. So far, the shower experience had heightened her modesty and revealed to her just how dependent she was.

Once again, Mark Meadows had been right. There was not a whole lot she could completely do on her own. It seemed like with everything daily task she attempted to do, there was a least some small aspect that required someone else's assistance. She bit her lip, closed her eyes, and shook her head.

"Mark!"

Caroline's head hung in shame as he entered the bathroom. She clung to the grab-bar on the shower wall, not just to steady her, but for any internal strength the steel could offer.

"What's up?" he asked peeking around the corner of the shower. Caroline noticed he was taking special care to again look at her face and not her body.

"I can't do this." Water dripped from her eyebrows. "At least not alone. I can't open and pour shampoo with one hand. Or the body wash. It would be different if they had pumps on them, but they don't. I'm stuck." She finally said, "I need your help." She avoided his look.

Mark moved into the bathroom and reached towards the shelf the shampoo rested on. The top was already flipped open, so he squirted a dot in Caroline's outstretched hand. She began to rub it into her hair, missing spots, and held out her hand for more.

"Please tell me this will get easier!" she said as she tried to reach all sides of her head.

"Here. Come over here." Mark said, motioning her towards him. Shrugging, Caroline took a couple cautious steps. The bag on her casted foot was slick on the wet slate. Mark wet his hands, and then began massaging the shampoo into her hair and rubbing her scalp. "Is it okay if I scrub your scalp?" he asked. Caroline nodded. Once he scrubbed her head good, she stepped back under the rain shower to rinse, but strands of hair held onto the soap. Instinctively, Mark reached to help her rinse, getting the arms of his shirt soaked. Mark's grimaced quickly turned to a chuckle.

"Oops!" Caroline giggled. "I'm sorry!"

Pulling his hands back, he reached for the back of his shirt and pulled it over his head. Caroline paused rubbing her hair as Mark's broad chest was exposed. Tanned, it had the muscle tone that Steven's lacked. And hair. Curly tufts of hair flourished on a chest like Mark's, not like the random hairs that struggled to take hold on Steven's pale lifeless skin.

"If you don't mind, Caroline, I think this is just going to be easier."

Caroline just nodded, trying to extend the same courtesy of not looking.

Taking a step into the shower, Mark resumed rubbing her hair to rinse out shampoo. She just stood, letting the water rain down, as Marks large hands accomplished what her single thin hand labored to do.

While his shirt was no longer getting soaked, splashes of water hit his jeans. Caroline remained silent, holding back nervous giggles.

Mark repeated the process with the conditioner, and as he helped her rinse again. Caroline attempted to squeeze some body wash on the body puff they purchased, but as she struggled, she felt an arm reach around her offering assistance. Mark's wet arm grazed Caroline's bare skin, and she froze. The feel of his bare skin sent a tingle clear to her toes. She exhaled and took the body puff so she could scrub parts of her body she could reach.

"Let me get your back," Mark said taking her puff. He glided the soapy puff around her back, neck, shoulders and down around her hips and backside. With her sole hand she, took care of her front and other areas.

Once she was rinsed, Mark reached to shut off the water. Giving a large fluffy towel to Caroline, she began drying off. Mark also took a towel and tried to soak up the water that permeated his jeans. Getting nowhere, he turned to Caroline and helped her to finish drying areas she couldn't reach.

As he finished, he took the corner of her towel and brushed Caroline's face with two quick swipes. She laughed.

"Feel better?" he asked, looking down into her eyes.

"Better," she replied. Her head was still swirling with thoughts and ideas, but now they were mostly about Mark Meadows and why he continued to offer help.

CHAPTER 8 – THE REAL WHY

Found by her free foot, the cool spot was Caroline's first waking sensation. Yawning as she opened her eyes, she went to stretch her arms, a morning habit of many years, and the tinges of pain in her shoulder and upper casted arm reminded her it wasn't stretching. Her yawn turned into a sigh. At least she'd had thirty seconds of believing she was her normal self. Rolling on her left side to prop herself up, she remembered where she was. It didn't take long. The slate blue walls, the expansive bed covered with geometric-design comforter, and the wall unit filled with books and the television reminded her she was in Mark's room. Another sigh echoed through the room.

Caroline laid back down on the pillows, closing her eyes and shaking her head. It was coming back to her. The shower. The most awkward experience of her life. At least another of Mark's delicious creations followed—a salad of mixed greens topped with fresh basils, tomatoes, and seasoned scrambled eggs. Who would have thought? Scrambled eggs on a salad! A culinary delight! Oh, and the cheesy bread! During the meal, Mark kept stopping to watch Caroline, which in turn made her stop.

"What?" she had said. His constant glances made her a bit uncomfortable. Is he trying to *look* at me, she'd thought.

"You're awfully quiet," he had said.

"It's that good!" she had replied. It was. Caroline was thrilled she had food to fill her mouth providing her an excuse not to speak. The other truth was she was at a loss of what to say. Her main goal was getting through the meal, going to sleep, and starting another day.

Like the night before, Mark had done the dishes before he joined Caroline to watch a little television. Once again, he laid on his side, head propped on his arm as Caroline watched from the stack of pillows. Hallmark again. Who could resist a good Christmas romance? Apparently not Mark.

The thought made Caroline smile. Her foot once again went searching for a cool spot, and she rubbed her sleepy eyes. She yawned again, wondering what surprises the new day would present. As she pulled back the covers, her bare legs revealed. Well, except for the cast. She remembered she had slipped out of the drawstring pants to sleep. The pants laid at the bottom of the bed. After several attempts to sit up, she swung her feet to the floor and reached for the pants. Pulling a pant leg over her cast and over the other leg, she pushed herself up from the bed and pulled the pants the rest of the way up. Nothing was easy anymore. Things she used to do automatically, without a thought, now required attention and sometimes even strategizing. Ugh!

Without warning, Steven filled her head. How impatient he got when caught behind someone on a walker or in a wheelchair. Under his breath, he'd mumble something about their blatant disregard for the rest of society. The restaurant scene popped into her mind. They were seated in next to the family with the disabled child who made constant noises. Steven had voiced rude comments to the family and had complained to the manager. The family ended up having their meals wrapped to go and left. Caroline very much wanted to follow them, but Steven insisted she stay exactly where she was, explaining they had the right to be there and enjoy their dinner. Of course, she had done exactly as Steven wanted. She patiently listened to his non-ending justifications of how they had been wronged the rest of the evening.

Studying herself in the mirror over the dresser, Caroline could only imagine what Steven would have to say if he saw her right now. She knew exactly what words he would be mumbling. No make-up, hair hanging in a mass of unruly curls, dressed in a white men's t-shirt and drawstring lounging pants. All broken up. Caroline was now in a different set of shoes and eyes. She would forever view people with needs differently, and she was quickly learning not to take even the smallest of things for granted.

Spying the mop leaning against the nightstand, she took ahold of it and began hobbling towards the bedroom door. When she entered the hall, the smell of coffee met her. She made a quick stop in the bathroom, then exiting, the other open doorway in the hall awoke her curiosity. Instead of hobbling towards the stairs, she went towards the doorway.

Inside, walls of lavender contained two twin beds each outfitted with matching floral comforters in muted colors. Two white chests of drawers and a dresser matched the two nightstands, and an oval area rug accented all the colors in the room pulling all the elements together. Mark's daughters' room. Her heart sank. She felt like a horrible person. Here she luxuriated in Mark large king bed, while he slept in his children's room, in a small twin bed. That was just not right! No, she'd make sure they switched that night.

She immediately turned and used the mop to make her way to top of the stairs. Standing, looking down, she paused. The treads were wood and potentially slippery. Should she attempt going down on foot? Should she call for Mark? She pondered for a minute, and then a memory brought a smile to her face.

She, Adam, and Tory had a game of sliding down her Mamaw's stairs. In fact, they had made it a race, trying to see who got to the bottom first. Over and over, they sat three-across on the top step, and shoving off, their little bottoms bump-bump-bumped down each step. They laughed the entire way down. Of course, none of the three laughed the next day when they tried to sit. Bruised and sore bottoms reminded them of the 'fun' they'd had. But the very next time they went to Mamaw's, the three of them perched on the top step, ready to repeat the fun. Caroline hadn't thought of that in years.

Slowly, Caroline lowered herself to the floor and scooted to the top step. Then with the mop in hand, she carefully scooted to the lower step. She did this until she was halfway down the stairs, the smile evoked by childhood memories still on her face, she realized just how hard her Mamaw's steps must have been. As she readied herself for the next scoot, Mark stood at the bottom of the stairs, his mouth open in a broad smile and his hands on his hips. He was already dressed in jeans—a dry pair—and a quarter-button shirt.

"Just what do you think you're doing?" he asked, shaking his head.

Had he just used a 'daddy' voice on her? Caroline looked at him with a defiant child-like smile.

She shrugged, still smiling. "Improvising!" With that, she scooted to the next step.

"Do you know how hard those steps are?" Mark asked.

"Yep, I sure do!" Caroline replied. "Adam, Tory and I used to do this all the time on my Mamaw's stairs. We didn't have stairs at home." Then, she scooted down more steps until she sat on the third from the bottom. Holding out her hand to Mark, she signaled him to help her up. "But we didn't use as much care going down, if you know what I mean!"

"Plan on having something else bruised besides your shoulder?!" Mark said assisting her to stand. "There's coffee." Bending to pick up the mop, he asked, "You want your mop or me?"

"Oh, It's *my mop* now?" She reached out for the red handle. "I'd rather have you, but I suppose the mop is encouraging my independence." She took a step towards the beckoning aroma. Mark paused a moment making sure she was stable, and then headed for the kitchen.

By the time Caroline made it to the bar stool, Mark had her coffee poured and was stirring her favorites into the mix. He pushed it towards her and then came around and sat in the other bar stool. Setting his cup on the table, he offered for her to rest her casted foot on his leg.

"You don't have your boot on," he said as she raised her leg and extended her casted foot.

"No, it's upstairs. I forgot it." Caroline took a sip from her coffee. She had forgotten it on purpose. With it on, she felt like her foot was encased in a concrete block. She knew she wasn't supposed to be walking on the cast itself but figured a few times wouldn't hurt.

"Look at your little toes!" Mark began wiggling each one like in the 'this little piggy' game. "Your toe polish is flaking off."

Caroline looked at her toes. Sure enough. One of her little toes was missing polish altogether. She imagined her other foot was the same. "I guess I'll need to take that off. It'll be a while before I will be able to get them done!" She wouldn't trust herself with nail polish in her left hand, nor could she even reach with the arm cast. Again, the simplest things were unattainable. Of course, in her life before the bridge she would have gone and had a pedicure. But in life after the bridge, it would be a long time before she'd be able to afford to that luxury.

Sipping her coffee, she looked at Mark. He was staring at her cast with his left hand around it to keep it from sliding off his leg. In the bright morning sun coming through the large window over the sink, Caroline noticed some silver flecks in the closely cropped hairs around his ears. In fact, silver streaks shone throughout his brown hair. His hair had grown since the first day she laid eyes on him; however, the growth was disguised in forming curls that covered his stitched forehead. Caroline leaned forward and touched his hair by his head wound. Dark stiches still left a short track.

Mark looked up at her touch, and she quickly retracted her hand.

"You've still got your stitches…" she said, explaining her 'trespassing.'

"Yep. I'm supposed to go to my doctor to have them removed, but I'll just let Beth do it."

"Beth, your sister?"

"Yeah. She is a nurse," Mark touched his forehead. "Well, she was until Dad and Mom moved in with her. She retired to take care of Mom."

"Um. You mentioned your mom doesn't walk any longer…"

Caroline started.

Mark sat back against the back of the bar stool and raised his coffee mug. "Nope." Taking a sip, he rested the cup on her cast. "No, Mom's not walking. Not talking. Not eating. She's bedridden at this point, and barely recognizes any of us. Alzheimer's."

"Oh." Flattening her mouth, Caroline looked back at Mark. "I'm so sorry to hear that. You speak so fondly of your mom."

A smile broke across Mark's face. "Yeah, I try to. It's my way of keeping her real in my mind. I'm always thinking about the things we did together, the advice she shared with me. You know, trying to keep the good times alive. I even go over every Sunday for dinner and make a point to spend some time talking to her."

"That's really nice."

The smile fading from his face. Once again, the muscles of his jaw twitched. "Yeah, I guess. Although, I haven't been for a few weeks…"

"Not because of me, I hope!" Caroline felt another pang of guilt. "See, I knew you had other responsibilities that needed tending rather than coming to see me!" Not only did Mark's jaw twitch, but he avoided her look. Raising his cup and finishing the contents, he patted gently on her cast, which Caroline interpreted as a signal to remove her leg. Again, Mark Meadows presented as a paradox. He spoke lovingly of his family, yet he shut down at times when talking about them.

Mark rose and refilled his cup, offering to top off her mug. Mark had gone to his 'quiet' place. Caroline had witnessed him withdraw—emotionally pull inside himself—on several occasions. His emotional trips didn't last long, sometimes just minutes.

"Did I say something?" Caroline asked, tilting her head and raising her brows. Her brown rimmed blue eyes searched his face until they final caught hold of his gentle brown eyes. In the sunlight, they glowed with flecks of yellow. Like gold. A treasure chest. The pupils were key holes. She sensed that

THE BRIDGE - A NOVEL

a significant part of Mark Meadows was locked away in that treasure chest. The only problem? Where was the key?

He just shook his head.

"Forgive me if I am stepping where I shouldn't, but I get the feeling your avoiding your family for some reason. Is everything, okay?" She remembered his brother Larry's comments about how the family, his dad particularly, worried about him. That and something about money.

Mark set his cup on the counter and leaned on it with both hands. He looked at her, his mouth hiked to the side. Slowly, he nodded his head. Finally, he said, "You're right. I am."

Caroline was silent a moment, and when Mark didn't offer anything further, "You seem to be close to them, what could possibly be causing you to avoid them?" She might not have a key to unlock his golden box of secrets, but she could try to pick the lock. "Is it because of why you were on the bridge?"

Mark stood straight, removing his hands from the bar. His eyebrows turned inward, creating creases between his eyes, and the tension returned to his jaw. He walked out of the kitchen, into the living room and abruptly halted.

Turning on the bar stool, Caroline's eyes followed him. He stood, hands on his sides, his back to her. She wondered what thoughts flooded his mind. She'd thought and asked over and over, *why did he care so much about her?* Now, she had another thought—*why did she care? Why was she concerned about Mark Meadows and his life?*

Mark stood for several minutes, and just before he turned back to Caroline, his hand reached to wipe his face. His face was red, but Caroline didn't know if it was from anger or a more tender emotion. He opened his mouth, starting to speak, but only air sounded, he quickly snapped his mouth shut. Caroline remained quiet but tried to keep eye contact. He hastily turned his face, and strode over to the chair that faced her, letting his body collapse into the seat. Caroline stayed put, making no attempt to move.

Finally, Mark found his words. "Why do *you* think I was on

137

the bridge? I thought we discussed this." He looked directly at her, raising his eyebrows as if challenging her.

"We did have a discussion," Caroline began. "We discussed our 'stories' of why we were on the bridge. We didn't discuss why we were *really* on the bridge." Her words were slow and deliberate. "My perception was that you were going to jump. You were on the bridge to clear more than your mind. Why? What could be so awful to make you consider such a thing?"

Mark listened with a blank expression. His hands rested on his legs, and he rubbed the denim slowly. Another of his nervous ticks.

"I might ask you the same question," Mark replied, swallowing hard.

"It's not the same thing," Caroline protested. "I wasn't thinking straight…Well, maybe I was. I really was trying to keep Steven from cashing in on the insurance policy. A million dollars! I'd be damned if he did away with me and got the money. He couldn't touch the money if it was suicide. My life doesn't matter to anyone anymore. I am only a shadow of a person. I'm expendable. He was going to make it look like an accident. No one would ever miss me."

"I would have missed you," Mark replied.

"No, you wouldn't," Caroline shook her head. "You would never have known me. Nothing to miss. Besides, if you had jumped, you wouldn't have been around to save me."

Mark jerked at her words. Again, the muscles flexed in his jawline. "No, I guess not."

"So, what had you on the edge, Mark Meadows?" Caroline's words were pointed.

Mark took a deep breath and began. "Oddly enough, it was also because of money."

Caroline reached for the red mop handle and began to hobble towards the couch. "How so?" she asked as she lowered herself on the couch and put up her casted leg.

Mark explained how his mother's health was diminishing, and his father was no longer able to care for her himself due to his own issues. "They moved in with Beth, since she was a nurse, so Beth could help care for mom. Dad sold their house. It was the house all of us grew up in, but all of us had our own places, and Beth's house didn't have stairs, so it just made sense. Where I had the business degree, everyone decided that I would be the one to invest the money from the sale of the house." Mark shook his head and sighed. Leaning forward, he continued.

"The guy I took the money to was a friend of mine from high school. You know, someone I knew and felt I could trust with my parents' money. But apparently friendship means nothing, because Jake took off with our money and a bunch of other people's. He never even invested it like he was supposed to. After everything else that's happened over the years, it just drove home what a failure I am." Mark looked up at Caroline and asked, "How do you tell your aging parents and your brother and sisters you've lost the family inheritance? The money that's supposed to take care of our parents' medical needs? Gone! Right now, they think I just can't cash the investments in because everything's frozen due to the investigation."

"You didn't lose it, Mark! You were victimized by a scoundrel!" Caroline corrected. Mark's account brought out the same anger that the situation with Steven did. Greed made people do crazy things.

"Whatever. It's the lowest moment in my life," Mark clasped his hands, wringing them. "I still haven't been able to tell them the whole story."

"Why?" Caroline sat up. "You've done nothing wrong! You said it happened to others as well?"

"Yeah. Even Officer Keyser's grandparents," Mark shared. "Remember the officer that came to question you?"

Caroline nodded. As she replayed the scenario in her mind, she recognized that Mark was as hard on himself as she was on herself. *The lowest moment in his life. And he called himself a failure!* She looked at him. His head was bent towards his hands which were still clasped, but now he was flexing his fingers. Then it hit her. Her heart plunged inside her, aching for this man. She felt his pain. But his pain somehow went far deeper than an investment gone bad. She wanted nothing more than to get up and go wrap her arms around him, to comfort him. She looked down at her own self and sighed.

"You reported it, right?" she asked.

The top of Mark's head nodded.

"What have they said?"

Glancing up, he again swallowed hard. "Oh, Jake's hopping from country to country, and had some elaborate scheme for transferring the money so that no one knows where it is. Or where he is. They say it'll probably be years before they track him down and the money."

"Don't investment firms have some sort of fraud insurance? FDIC. Like banks?"

"No, unfortunately," Mark shook his head. Looking at Caroline, his eyes suddenly looked tired. "You basically sue. But who do you sue if they've off and disappeared? That's why I met with an attorney and joined a class action suit. That's about the best recourse."

***

Mark was relieved that night when Caroline mentioned she'd skip the shower and just wash up at the sink. After he carried her upstairs, he showed where the towels and washcloths were stored and brought her a fresh set of clothes. He laid them on the vanity next to the towel and cloth.

"Leave the clothes you are wearing on the floor," Mark said after making sure Caroline had everything she needed. "I'll get them after I take my shower. Holler if you need me."

Caroline thanked him and gave him a tired smile, and he closed the door behind him. Going down the stairs, Mark chuckled thinking how she'd come down the stairs that morning. Very creative. He'd initially had apprehensions about bringing her to his home, unsure what he was getting himself into. But a homeless shelter? He'd never met a person who literally had nowhere to go.

So far, her presence hadn't been bad at all. She wasn't demanding in anyway, and mostly kept to her thoughts. Like him, she had a lot to think about. Maybe even more. He'd even enjoyed having someone to cook for, though he felt his culinary skills were a bit rusty. He didn't prepare elaborate meals for just himself. But his solo meals were healthy. Yep, he rather enjoyed having her around. Except for the awkward moments helping tape her up.

That wasn't going to go away anytime soon. Depending on what the doctor said at her upcoming two-week checkup, she could be in the arm cast another six to eight weeks, maybe longer. It just depended on how her shattered bones healed. With only one hand, taping the bags on was not going to be something she could manage. It didn't really bother him to help her. He tried not to look at her in a naked state. However, he'd seen enough to conclude her husband was a fool. Caroline, on the other hand, seemed completely mortified to disrobe in front of him. He wanted to be respectful of her privacy. He was glad, though, she decided to skip the night. Hopefully, she would alternate.

As he picked up the dish soap to clean up the dishes, an idea occurred to him. He could get dixie cups and pre-fill one each with her shampoo, conditioner, and body wash, so he wouldn't have to be there to squirt the products in her hand. Surely, she'd be able to clean all her parts with the one hand. She'd learn.

Her curiosity about his being on the bridge had taken him off-guard. Her questions triggered the anxiety to rise to his throat. At first, he felt like he was going to choke, but once he began talking, it got easier. Caroline was a good listener and was compassionate. And her questions helped him think about the situation from a different perspective. Yes, talking about it seemed to lessen the burden, the weight he'd felt pressing down on him. Over the years, he'd somehow accepted that, when things went wrong in his life, he was the sole reason. And the depression followed. That someone else might be responsible didn't occurred to him. Caroline helped him discover that. He was just thankful he didn't have to go into further details with her about his condition.

As he put the last pan away, he heard Caroline moving around upstairs. Turning out the lights downstairs, Mark climbed the stairs and went straight into his room. Caroline was balancing on one foot at the side of the bed and had a pillow in her hand. Mark passed through the room to the chest of drawers.

"Oh, hey!" Caroline said glancing up. Mark began searching for nightclothes, glancing over his shoulder.

"Did everything work out okay?" he asked. He noticed she seemed to be paused, not getting into the bed.

"Yeah. But I had a hard time wringing out the washcloth with my one hand," she said. "I got some water on the floor but tried to wipe it up best I could."

"That's not a problem. I'll get it," he said, closing the drawer and heading back towards the door.

"Umm, Mark?" Caroline asked, still holding the pillow awkwardly.

Mark stopped and looked at her. "Yeah?"

"Why do you have me sleeping in here?" she asked. "I'd be perfectly comfortable in the other room."

"Uh…Well, there's no television in there." He started towards the door again. "And I figured you need the extra room, so you'll be comfortable."

"The thing is, I hate that I'm putting you out of your own room."

"It's no inconvenience," Mark said over his shoulder. "I'm perfectly fine in the girls' room. I'm just sleeping." Closing the bathroom door, Mark wondered what prompted her concern about where he slept. He wasn't about to tell her that neither of the girls had ever slept in their room.

***

The next several days were uneventful. Mark shared his computer with Caroline so she could electronically sign the Family Leave paperwork for her job. He had a feeling she'd be off far longer than the 12 weeks allowed. Caroline hadn't heard anything from her lawyer, who was also now his lawyer. He was tempted to call but knew they'd let him know if there were any updates. Same for Caroline. He had to be patient and wait. When he wasn't encouraging Caroline to get up and walk, he was on his computer researching plants, soils, fertilizers, and checking out new vendors and pricing. In the landscaping industry, new products constantly appeared on the market, so during winter down time Mark updated himself on the latest innovations.

When Caroline wasn't walking laps back and forth in the living room with the mop, she occupied a chair at one end of the dining room table. Spread out before her were the coloring book, the word search books, and the spiral notebook. She went from attempting to color a floral scene in the coloring book, to practicing shaping letters and words with her left hand, back to coloring.

Sitting at the other end of the table with his laptop, Mark found himself pausing and looking towards Caroline. He'd catch her totally unaware and study her face. He'd noticed how she unconsciously pushed her hair behind her ear or ran her tongue along her lips when concentrating. A couple of times, she'd looked up and caught him staring. She smiled at him, and saying nothing, returned to her coloring or writing. He was pretty sure she was stealing glances at him as well. At least she had quit asking why he was taking care of her. He was growing frustrated with not being able to put his feelings into words.

Mark's idea of filling dixie cups worked out well. Other than having to get Caroline taped up, Caroline's shower time became more independent. She squeezed out the contents from the paper cups with her single hand. He cleaned up the kitchen while she cleaned up herself. Afterward, he showered and then they watched television until she fell asleep, at which point he retired to the first twin bed in the girls' room. In a week's time, Mark was astonished how the two fell into a routine.

On Friday evening, a week after Caroline came home with him, Mark was cleaning the dishes from a spaghetti and meatball super when his phone began vibrating in his back pocket. Pulling it out, he answered without looking at who was calling.

"Hello, little brother!" Beth's voice was loud and clear. Mark continued to rinse dishes as he cradled the phone to his ear.

"What do you want, Beth?" he asked over the sound of running water and clanking pots.

"Boy you're right to the point!" his sister sounded slightly offended. "Well, I was calling to find out if you're coming for dinner on Sunday. We've not seen you for over…has it been a month?

"Three weeks, Beth." Mark stacked the flatware upright in the drainer.

"Are you doing dishes?" his perceptive sister asked.

"Yes, I am."

"Cooking again? You wouldn't have to cook if you stopped by!" Beth taunted him. "So, we going to see you Sunday?"

"About that…" Mark began. "I need to, but it's just…well, I've got a houseguest."

"A houseguest?" Beth asked. "Larry didn't say anything about a houseguest after he came to talk to you?" After a pause, "Please tell me it's not that woman from the bridge!"

"Because I didn't tell Larry I had a houseguest. And, yes, her name is Caroline."

"Mark!" his sister scolded. "You don't know anything about that woman!"

"Not at first. Didn't even know her name!" he countered. "But after spending time with her at the hospital and a week here at the house, we're getting to know each other quite well."

"Just *how* well?"

"Beth!" he pushed back. "It's not like that. The poor woman… well, she can't hardly do anything for herself."

"But isn't she married?" Beth asked. "Why isn't she with her husband. Why isn't he taking care of her?"

"Well, because he's locked her out of their home and because he may have had something to do with her accident."

"You sure you want to be involved in something like that? You've got your own problems, Mark." Then she added, "I can't believe you're messing around with a married woman. That's a new low, Mark."

"Yes. You're absolutely right, Beth," Mark said, agitation in his tone. "I've got my own problems, but I guess that makes me an expert in helping someone else with theirs, doesn't it now?" He ignored the rest of her comment.

His sister shifted the subject. "Well, will you be here Sunday?"

"I can't exactly just leave Caroline by herself." Mark paused, drying his hands. "Hey, by the way, do you still have the cane Mom used?"

"Yes, it's in the closet. Why? And why can't you leave a grown woman by herself?"

"Well, I guess if I come on Sunday, you'll see. She'll be coming with me." As soon as he spoke the words, he heard a 'thud' from upstairs followed by a muffled cry. "Uh…I gotta go, Beth!"

CHAPTER 9 – THE KISS

"Are you alright? Caroline!" Mark shouted through the bathroom door. He almost burst right into the bathroom when he topped the stairs but remembered his manners at the last minute. Tilting his ear to the door, the only sound he heard was the running water and a moan.

"Caroline?" With no answer, Mark opened the door and entered the steamy room. To his left the shower looked empty at first. Until he looked at the floor. He immediately cut off the water and went to Caroline who laid at the back of the shower floor, her back propped against the shower wall. She gasped for air.

Without thinking, Mark bent down and lifted Caroline off the shower floor. Grabbing the towel from the vanity on the way out, he carried the dripping woman to the bedroom. He sat Caroline on the edge of the bed and draped the towel around her shoulders while she struggled to breathe. Caroline gripped the towel around her body, but the garbage bag caused it to slip off. Mark again reached the towel around her and took his hand to push dripping strands of hair from her face. His own heart was racing.

"Did you slip and fall?" he asked, his face close to hers.

Struggling to breathe, she gave a quick nod.

"Okay, I think you've just winded yourself. Try to relax if you can." His left hand went to her back began gently rubbing circles. The repetitive motions soothed him as well as Caroline. Finally, her diaphragm muscles loosened allowing her real whiffs of air, which she gulped. "See? You're alright!" He took his own deep breath of relief.

Caroline burst into tears. Mark couldn't tell the shower drops from the tears on her face. He wrapped his arms around her and drew her to him, hugging her, but careful about her casted arm. Instinctively she gripped him with her left arm and buried her face in the corner of his arm and chest. She wept. He felt her body let loose sporadic soft heaves.

"It's okay. Are you hurting anywhere?" he asked. Her buried head gave several short shakes. "Shh," he soothed. He continued to hold her close, his hand still offering comforting circles.

After several minutes, Caroline's sobs lessened. Mark's shoulder was completely soaked, a combination of salty tears and strands of wet hair. The rest of Caroline's wet body air dried. Coming from under her emotional collapse, she began to pull away from Mark. Mark found himself wanting to hold her but relinquished his gentle grasp. Caroline looked down and away and bit her lips, thwarting Mark's attempt to see her face. He wanted to make sure she was okay.

"Tell me what happened," Mark said taking his hand and cupping it around the side of her cheek. Her skin was soft in his rough hand. Caroline looked up at him for a moment, and then realized the towel had fallen loose around her. She tugged at it to recover herself, but the towel was caught. She turned her head to see what it was hung on and seeing she was sitting on part that slipped off, she shifted to free it. Mark pretended not to notice.

"I…uh…" Caroline glanced at Mark only for a second. "I must have gotten some conditioner on the floor when I squeezed it out of the cup, and it made the floor slick. I went down, but then I couldn't breathe." Her words were still short of air.

"Did you hit your head?" Mark asked. He eyes surveyed the wet clumps for any sign of a lump or bump. Instinctively, his hands went to her head, and he began feeling for any signs of trauma. Satisfied her head was clear of injury, he dropped his hands. She didn't need another bump to her head after all the swelling from the accident.

"No, I don't think so," she replied. "I went down so fast. I tried to grab the grab bar. My hand was slick." Pausing to take another breath, she added, "My feet went out from under me."

"Did you hit the wall with your shoulder or arm?" Mark

reached for her shoulder but withdrew his hand as Caroline shook her head.

"No, I fell mainly on my...my butt. Then when I couldn't breathe, I leaned against the wall."

"Here, let me help get this tape off you," Mark lowered the part of the towel that covered the tape on her shoulder, and began to peel the duct tape from her skin. As he pulled, the tape unwillingly let go of her skin. Caroline grimaced. "I'm sorry! I don't mean to hurt you."

"That's okay, it hurts worse when I take it off." Caroline lifted her bagged arm so Mark could reach the tape under her arm. The tape left a pink irritation on her skin. "I might need some lotion for that. Good thing, I'm not doing this every night!" She gave a quick nervous laugh.

Mark nodded as he worked the bag off Caroline's arm, again trying to avoid looking at her, but his eyes lingered this time taking in the beauty she eagerly tried to hide. The bag freed, he crumpled it up and dropped it on the floor. He then bent over towards her leg and started to work the tape off her calf. Her skin was less tender on her leg as she didn't wince as much as Mark peeled if from her skin. Crumpling that bag, Mark tossed it on the floor next to the other.

"Thank you," Caroline said. She tilted her head, giving him a hint of a smile.

"You are most welcome!" Mark said, patting her bare thigh. "You gave me quite the scare!" That was an understatement. He imagined the worst as he took the stairs two steps at a time. He rose from the bed, bending to pick up the trash bags, and started for the door. "I'll get your clothes."

While he was gone, Caroline slipped the towel from around her and started to rub dry her hair. The towel dangled in front of her as she used the one hand to work the towel around her head. When she lowered the towel, she looked up to see Mark standing in the doorway, his head turned aside, holding her clothes to his chest.

"It's okay," she said. "You can come in." Caroline held the

towel up across her front.

Mark walked towards her. "Do you need help? Or do you have this?" Mark set the garments on the bed next to her, and then went towards his chest of drawers for his own clothes. He rummaged for a clean pair of pajamas, finding none. He didn't usually wear them a lot, except in the very cold months. He settled on the pair he'd worn the night before, realizing a load of laundry was in order.

As he turned, saying, "I'm going to go show…" he abruptly stopped, watching Caroline slide up the pair of the cotton 'granny panties' with her one hand. The white t-shirt was already on. As she got them in place, she turned and met eyes with Mark. Silence passed between them. Momentarily paralyzed, Mark fumbled for words.

"Um… uh…shower. I'm going to take one now," he mumbled as he feet once again moved. As he neared the doorway, he stopped and half-turning, he looked back at Caroline. She folded back the covers and stacked the pillows. "Um…you know…" he began. Caroline looked up at him as she fluffed a pillow. "Steven's an idiot," Mark finished.

"Yes, I know," Caroline replied, a confused expression filling her face. "Why do you say that? You don't even know him."

"I don't need to know him." Mark's eyes travelled over her. "Any man who would walk away from someone like you is an idiot." Not waiting for her response, Mark left the room feeling the flush of embarrassment finding his face. And other places. Nothing a cold shower wouldn't cure.

***

Caroline sat propped against the pillows under the covers, as her thumb pressed the channel button. Cycling channels. She wasn't looking for anything particular. It was just motion. Helping her to process. While shaken from her fall in the shower, she was even more dazed by Mark's comment. She didn't want to read meaning into it. After all, Steven really was an idiot. There was no denying that. Anyone could see it, and now she could also. But was there an inferred message in Mark Meadow's words? He was, after all, tripping over his tongue. Caroline sighed.

While she had quit asking Mark directly, during the last week Caroline continued questioning herself why such a handsome, attractive man like Mark wanted to help her. He'd taken her, a complete stranger, into his home. *Who does that?* And not just a stranger, but a homeless, homely stranger. All banged up. Her life a total mess. Guilt about the burden she placed on him filled her. He clothed her. He fed her. He sheltered her. He helped her with everything she couldn't do for herself. And he was a perfect gentleman while doing it. She couldn't help but wonder if God hadn't sent her a 'guardian angel' of sorts. If that was who Mark Meadows was, she wished he hadn't been so darn cute! It wasn't solely Mark's looks: it was his whole demeanor. Kind. Gentle. Her pangs of pain were quickly being replaced with flutters and tingling sensations that had nothing to do with her injuries or the healing process.

And the way he held her after her fall—she could hear, maybe even feel, his heart beating as her face nuzzled against him. When her tears subsided, she found herself trying to think of something sad to keep them coming, just so she could feel the security and warmth of his arms around her. Crazy! She wondered if she hadn't even inadvertently tried to tease him as she put on the underclothes. She thought about him watching her as she dressed. It now embarrassed her. It hadn't when she did it, but in retrospect she wanted to hide her face under the covers.

She sighed again, landing on the Hallmark channel. She had to put such thoughts out of her head. She needed to focus on healing, getting her identity restored (well, at least her driver's license), going home (wherever that would be), and ridding her life of Steven White! She needed a normal life again! She looked towards the bedroom door, thinking she'd heard the water shut off.

Normal life. Yeah, she wasn't so sure what normal was going to look like or how quickly it might come. The idea of going home and no longer being such a burden to the man in the other room wasn't as realistic as it sounded. The truth was, she really did need Mark, more than she wished to admit. The bigger problem? She was starting to need him for reasons other than her injuries and rehabilitation! But the last thing she wanted was him thinking she was taking advantage. No. That could not happen!

When the bathroom door opened, Caroline stared intently at the television screen. Mark entered the room with an armload of clothes, hers and his, and he stooped at the foot of the bed to pick up her towel.

"Hey, what're you watching?" he asked. Going to the closet, he tossed the articles into an unseen basket. Caroline looked away from the screen and noticed Mark wore a white t-shirt and had on the same lounge pants as what she left at the foot of the bed.

"Hallmark," she replied. She smiled. "Huh. Twins!" She pointed to Mark and the pants laying on the bed.

"Yeah, I guess so," he nodded. "Except…" He interjected a devilish grin. "Except you don't have yours on!" He crawled onto the other side of the bed and assumed his usual position: laying catty-corner with his head propped on his elbow and hand.

Caroline squinted her eyes at him. "Maybe you should even the score!" she joked. Well, sort of.

"Oh," Mark shot back. "Trust me, you don't want me doing that! There's nothing to be seen there!"

"Bashful!"

"No…" Mark drew the word out. "Hey, right now I can say I've got a beautiful woman in my bed. The last thing I want to do is send her running down the street." He winked and then looked at the screen. "So, what's this movie about?"

Caroline looked at him a moment. He was teasing, right? Now he had her pondering whether he'd suffered some awful accident? Maybe one of his legs wasn't real? Mark looked back at her with a raised eyebrow.

"Oh!" she said slowly. "I really have no idea. I've been caught in my thoughts…"

"Really?" he smiled. "What thoughts caught you?"

Caroline shrugged. "I don't know. Just stuff. Life stuff." Her head bobbed in attempt to nod. "You know, I've really enjoyed getting to know you…and to become friends." She snapped her mouth closed, wondering how those words spilled out.

A smile still focused her way, Mark blinked slowly. "Likewise. And I'm glad you brought that up! Would you like an opportunity to get to know me better?"

Caroline's eye grew wide, and her mouth dropped open, speechless. Her hand clutched the covers as she stared back at Mark. So forward! She'd hoped for something more…romantic.

"Beth usually has dinner on Sundays at her house, and she asked if we were coming," he continued. If he noticed her response, he didn't let on. "You'd get to meet my overbearing family, who will no doubt tell you more than you ever want to know about my life."

"Dinner?" she asked, feeling her muscles relaxing. Feeling a little disappointed. Feeling foolish.

"Yeah, they do it early afternoon. After church," Mark said glancing back at the television. The two characters were about to exchange a kiss. Looking back at Caroline, "If nothing else, it would give you a chance to get out and see something other than my ugly mug." He raised both his brows, waiting for her input.

"You're far from ugly, Mark. I'm the ugly one, and I'm surprised you'd even want your family to see this mess…" she moved her hand motioning towards herself. Her eyes busy surveying her broken body, she didn't realize Mark had crawled up next to her.

As the rough skin of his hand once again cupped her face, Caroline looked abruptly at Mark, directly into his soft brown eyes, less than two inches from hers. His lips began moving, whispering.

"The most beautiful mess I've ever laid eyes on..." he said in almost a whisper, and before she uttered a sound, he covered her lips with his. As he kissed her, her free arm hooked around his neck, drawing Mark Meadows closer, and she kissed him back. Deeply and intensely. Caroline closed her eyes, believing it was just a dream.

***

Laying on his stomach, with his arms hidden under the pillow, and his head turned to the side, Mark opened his eyes. The first thing he saw were her red lips. Then he saw her chest and casted arm rise and fall in an easy rhythm. Caroline slept peacefully and soundly with curly strands of her brown hair spread chaotically across her pillow. Her bare left arm rested on top the covers. He followed it to where it joined the rest of her, hidden by the white t-shirt. The white t-shirt his hand had accidently brushed in a certain area, pausing briefly. She had vigorously returned his kiss and her body trembled briefly when his hand lingered. Then there was his own body's reaction. He had a good idea she would not have pushed him away, but it was too soon. All they could experience at present was a kiss. Caroline was still encased in fiberglass and recovering from both physical and emotional wounds. He couldn't add another level of complication to that. However, he was afraid he already had with the kiss.

It was spontaneous. He hadn't planned to kiss her, and he certainly did not expect her to respond as she had to the kiss. But he was glad she did. On a scale of zero to ten, the kiss had been a fifty. And it took everything within him to keep it to just a kiss. After their lips parted, the sweetness lingered between them as they simply kept each other close. Mark propped his pillow next to her, and they watched the Christmas movie. He remembered nothing about the movie but could recall every stroke of her fingers as she played with the curls forming on his head. He was overdue for a haircut but was now thinking twice. She might like the smooth feel of his cut hair, but should he chance it?

Raising his head and freeing his arms from under the pillow, Mark crept towards the edge of the bed careful not to wake Caroline. It had been a long time since he'd had that worry, but he was surprised how quickly that knowledge and skill returned to him. His bare feet were soundless on the floor, and he paused in the doorway for a minute to be sure he hadn't disturbed her. After her fall, she needed the rest.

Downstairs, he started the morning by measuring coffee and water into the coffeemaker. While it began puffing out its aroma, Mark retrieved a glass and poured it full of water, and then pulled out the plastic basket from the pantry. He placed the basket on the bar counter, and took pill bottles out one by one, carefully lining up the morning's dosage in straight line. Some of the bottles he didn't worry with until evening after the dishes were done. Some bottles opened only in the morning as he waited for coffee. Then there were the bottles he frequented twice a day. Once the morning line-up was complete, Mark took the pills two at a time followed by a gulp of water. Twelve pills, six gulps of water. Then he finished off anything that remained in the glass.

It was a ritual begun when he was a teen, and not one that he'd adhered to all his life. He regretted those times when he had been lax. His dad had even brought him a pill container so Mark could organize his morning and evening medications ahead of time, but Mark often forgot about the box and eventually learned that being sporadic with the medications had a worse effect than not taking them at all. Taking them out one by one was a conscious action and counting them in the line-up assured Mark missed none. He tucked the basket back on the shelf in the pantry and thought about how Caroline had stood with the pantry door open. He was thankful she hadn't commented on the basket and was hopeful she hadn't even noticed it. He wasn't ready to travel down that road of explanation just yet.

By the time Mark heard Caroline 'bumping' down the stairs, he was in his spot in front of his computer at the head of the table, already on his second cup of coffee. His lips grew into a smile with each thump, and after several thumps, he rose from the table and went to the foot of the stairs. He knew she was nearing the bottom. Still amused, he waited on her at the foot of the stairs. Smiling at him in return, when her bottom reached the third step Caroline held out her hand to Mark so he could help her rise into a standing position. Then, with her mop, she wobbled to the table as Mark fetched her a steaming cup of the brew.

"Sorry I slept so late!" she said as she lowered herself into a chair. "That was probably the best night sleep I've had since the…accident. I feel so rested!" She raised the cup with her left hand, blowing on it.

"I slept pretty well myself," Mark replied, returning to the computer. He glanced over the computer screen at Caroline. She took small sips as she stared out the window, mesmerized. He returned to the computer scrolling down the current page.

"So, it sounds like we've got tomorrow planned. Dinner with your family," Caroline said, still staring out the window. "So, what's the plan for today?"

Mark glanced out the window to see what held Caroline's attention. Nothing except the neighboring house and yards. He realized it was the sunlight she was taking in. The November morning's rays crept through the glass window illuminating the entire area they sat. The natural light was a definite mood lifter. It worked on Caroline just as it did him.

"I thought I'd put you to work with the mop," Mark teased. "It's about time to clean house."

"Ha!" She looked at him sideways. "To clean house would be getting rid of me! Besides, when I do my laps here in the living room, I'm basically dust mopping!"

"You're missing some spots!" his teasing continued. "No, seriously. I've got to do some laundry and cleaning. But thought maybe we could go for a ride. Maybe go to the grocery or something."

"Well, if we go to the grocery store, I'm staying in the truck!" Caroline gave Mark her frank, flat-mouthed look. "After the fall in the shower last night, I don't think my body can take being contorted by a shopping cart!"

"Are you sore?" Mark asked. His insides began tensing. Would her reference to the night before lead to the topic of the kiss?

"Oh, yeah! I looked in the mirror before I got dressed, and there's plenty of bruising coming out on my bottom!" She shifted in the chair. "By tonight, I'll probably need to eat standing up!" She let out a short laugh, and then brushed Mark's eyes with her own. "Thanks for rescuing me yet another time!" Mark noticed her eyelashes for the first time. He was normally so focused on her unusual eyes, that he'd not realized how long and thick they were. Jennifer had complained incessantly how women were cheated. She had insisted over and over that guys got the long eyelashes and women were given the short ones! Right beside him, Caroline proved her wrong! Caroline needed no make-up, no mascara. She was perfect just as she was.

The jingle on the phone, interrupted his thoughts. He swung around, looking for the ringing device. Still plugged in to charger on the kitchen counter, Mark jumped up to grab the call.

"Hello?"

"Good morning," the male voice said. "Is this Mark Meadows?"

"Uh…yes, it is. Who's calling?"

"Mr. Meadows, this is Officer Keyser," the caller identified himself. Officer Keyser! Mark's nerves went into sudden overdrive. Did the officer have good news or bad news?

"What can I do for you, Officer Keyser?"

"I apologize for calling, but the hospital said I might be able to reach Caroline Reeves-White at this number?"

"Yes, she is here. Hold on a moment," Mark replied, glancing at Caroline as he stepped back towards the dining area. His heart sank slightly learning the officer wished to speak to Caroline. Hearing Keyser's voice, Mark hoped the officer had news about the investment scandal. He handed the phone to Caroline, as he grabbed his cup for a refill.

"Hello? This is Caroline." She held the phone to her ear. Listening, her eyes were drawn back to the window and the sunlight.

"This is Officer Keyser. My partner and I spoke to ya when ya were in the hospital?" Officer Keyser phrased the statement as a question.

"Yes, I remember."

"I apologize for the intrusion, but I wanted to update ya regarding ya accident a couple weeks ago," the officer began.

"Okay..."

"Mrs. White, we've been contacted by the insurance adjustor from Providia Life and Casualty. During his inspection of ya vehicle...what was left of it...it appears he identified some irregularities with ya vehicle that could have led to the crash."

Caroline's eyebrows raised. "What type of irregularities?" She glanced at Mark as he returned with his cup and the coffee pot. He topped off her cup while she talked.

"While most of the car was burned beyond recognition, he found that on each of the vehicle's wheels, the lug nuts had been loosened, and some were missing altogether."

"Oh..." Caroline frowned and glanced up at Mark. "That's bad!"

Mark perked up, turning his head to try to tune into the voice on the other end. All he heard was Officer Keyser's mummering. *If only he'd thought to put it on speaker.* But then, he wouldn't want to invade Caroline's privacy. *It was her business, after all.*

"Unfortunately, that is not all he discovered." Officer Keyser continued, "he also found that the bolt on the steering column had been loosened, the airbags had been disabled, and there was a puncture in ya fuel line. Because there were multiple irregularities found he contacted us. We've had our own investigator go over the remains of ya car, and he determined that the alterations to ya vehicle appear to be intentional and not from normal wear and tear."

"The Range Rover was practically brand new. I'd only had it about a month!" Caroline said. "There couldn't have been 'wear and tear'!"

"Well, I just wanted to let ya know. Of course, our investigator submitted his findings to the adjustor, and it was included in the adjustor's report to ya insurance company. I understand ya husband is an insurance agent for this company?"

"Yes, that's correct."

"And I believe I recall you mentioning that ya and ya husband were not on good terms presently?" Officer Keyser asked.

"No, we're not. I have filed for divorce after learning he's been cheating on me," Caroline replied. "I learned about the affair the day of my accident. I overheard him talking to the other woman about him leaving me. Not by divorce, but that he was exploring 'other options.' And that same morning I found he had pulled out a copy of my life insurance policy, and it was opened to the section on 'accidental death'!"

"I see," Officer Keyser paused. "Well, thank you for that information." Then he continued, "Under the circumstances, we are labeling the accident as 'suspicious' and will be investigating the situation further. I just wanted to let ya know about our current findings. If ya think of anything else, just contact me at here at the station."

"I understand. I certainly will," Caroline shot a concerned look at Mark. "Thank you, Officer." When she clicked off the call, she set the phone on the table and stared at it. She sat silent a moment, biting on her lips. She was exceptionally quiet and still. And she grew pale. Mark swore he saw thoughts churning through her eyes.

"Do you mind if I ask?" Mark asked. "I know it's not really any of my business, but I did hear part of that conversation."

Slowly Caroline reached for the phone and slid it away from her. Like it was responsible for the bad news. Mark knew it was bad. She had said so. She shook her head and shivered, moving her eyes from the phone to Mark.

"It seems..." she began in a low voice, almost a whisper. "My suspicion now has a factual basis." Sipping her coffee, she recounted Officer Keyser's words for Mark.

Mark sat stunned. This type of thing didn't happen in real life. Or did it? Apparently so. Anger began to rise within him, but he pushed back. He instantly felt a dislike for Steven when he first encountered him at the hospital. There was something about his demeanor. But this? However, this was not his fight. His concern. Or was it? Had the crash been caused by Caroline's abandoned suicide attempt? Or by tampering? When she jerked the car, had the tampering caused her to lose control? Had the tampering caused the fire? He once again felt the singeing heat from the blaze. Instead, it was the anger trying to surface any way it could, causing him to flush.

"He was trying to kill me," she finished. Her voice was flat, but her eyes darted back and forth, fighting off the glossiness trying to surface. "He bought that car for me with the intention it would be my death trap." She shook her head again. "It almost was." Her voice choked.

The glossiness gave way to waterfalls. Not a single tear, but streams of water ran down both sides of a colorless face. Caroline's eyes became increasingly red as silent cries shook her body.

Mark jumped up from the table and went to Caroline's side. Taking her limp hand in his, he gently tugged. No response. Caroline faced forward with her red eyes engaged with some unseen force. Mark stooped and putting his arms under her knees and behind her back, took her from the chair to the couch. His held her close, her head resting on his shoulder. He felt her body vibrate as her cries continued, now becoming more audible.

"Shhh…" Mark told her softly, an attempt to calm her. Her back against the couch, he couldn't rub circles. Instead, his hand rubbed her thigh, moving back and forward, emulating the soothing motion, stopping only when Caroline let out a wail. Pitiful and off key, it reverberated among the high ceiling. As the wail left Caroline's lips, so did pent up emotions--anger, betrayal, pain, sorrow. Everything she had been holding inside while trying to be strong. It came out in such a rush that Mark's bones vibrated. Tilting his head, he kissed the top of Caroline's and then rest his head on hers, letting her know she was safe. She wasn't alone. Letting her know it was okay to let it out. Purge the bad feelings and thoughts from her body.

***

As her shoulders touched the stacked pillows, Caroline looked up at Mark with puffy eyes while he spread the covers over her. He then took his hands and tucked the covers into the creases around her body. Just like her mother had when she was a small girl. Had Mark's mother done this for him as well? And had he tucked in his own daughters the same way?

The television was dark. Caroline told him she wanted to be with her thoughts tonight. And get some sleep. She was exhausted from crying. She was done crying. She was cried out. She figured she shed at least five pounds of tears into the couch. A chuckle snuck out.

"What's funny?" Mark asked, turning up a side of his mouth. He was getting ready to take his own shower, though he pretty much had one while helping Caroline. She wondered why he didn't just go ahead and shower with her. After all, he'd seen her in entirety, and her sense of modesty was pretty much non-existent these days. But maybe he was the modest one? Or was there something he didn't want her to see?

"Oh, nothing. Just something silly running through my head." She managed a smile back at the man who took such good care of her. "Mark?"

"Yeah?" His eyebrows raised as he gave her a full smile.

"Thank you for everything." Caroline gave him her most appreciative look. "You've been perfectly wonderful to me. And put up with so much. I'll never be able to repay you for what you've done."

"Caroline," Mark mirrored her appreciation. "You already have." He bent over and touched his lips to her forehead, leaving a wet imprint. Then he was gone, and Caroline heard the water hitting the shower walls.

You already have. The words stayed with Caroline. How had she repaid him? He pulled her from the burning wreckage. He sat for four days with her as she lay unconscious in the hospital while no one knew her name. He continued to be there day after day to keep her company among the bleak hospital walls. When no one else came. Because there was no one else *to come.* He took her home when there was no one else to do so. Then he offered his own home when she was locked out of hers. And since she stepped inside Mark's world, he'd cooked for her and fed her, clothed her, bathed her, befriended her. He attended to her every need. How had she already repaid him?

She had only been in his world for...what...a week? A little over? That week and the time in the hospital felt like the only days on earth she knew. Thoughts of what existed before waking from the accident seemed foreign and unreal to her. They might as well have been an episode of some television show. Segments from someone else's life. The whole mess with Steven was surely a concoction of a writer's imagination. So cliched—the cheating husband trying to kill the wife for the insurance so he could live happily-ever-after with the mistress! Not very original, for sure.

Even when she woke in the hospital and told Nurse Rachelle her name, she felt like she was reciting someone else's name. She had an innate feeling that it wasn't hers. That it didn't belong to her. She was not that person. Opening her eyes in the hospital bed, she'd been born into a new world. She was having to learn everything all over again: how to walk, how to eat, how to write, how to dress and perform routine daily tasks. That was her new reality. Her new life.

The tears and the emotional release felt like the exhalation of what remained of Caroline's previous life, of the person who had occupied the body she now filled. Caroline knew it sounded silly. Yet revisiting some of the remaining memories of that person, Caroline was astonished at how that woman did the things she did and thought the things she thought. Who was that person? Why would she put up with what she did? That person was now gone.

Caroline considered that Steven was successful in his attempt to kill off his wife. That woman perished among the flames of the Range Rover. The woman Mark pulled out of the wreckage emerged a different being altogether. Thoughts of Steven did nothing to stir her. He meant nothing to her. There was no love. No hate even. Nothing. Just factual memories left by the former occupant of the broken body.

Of course, Caroline was left to tie up all the loose ends left behind: to legally sever any ties to that woman's husband. Then there was the splitting of the assets. There was the house, its contents, and the business. And of course, all of Caroline's personal belongings. Caroline would make sure that woman got what was due her. She refused to let the conniving husband live happily-ever-after. Caroline vowed she would see the end of his fairy tale, just as he had ended his wife's.

Kentucky law provided for a divorce to become legal in 30 days, provided there were no children, and the divorce was mutual and uncontested. With what Steven faced, surely the man wouldn't be stupid enough to contest the divorce decree. She couldn't wait to tell Emily about Officer Keyser's call, though she hoped it would not interfere with the progress of the divorce. Fingers's crossed: three weeks to go!

CHAPTER 10 – THE MEADOWS

Beth's house was in a small neighborhood located off Route 68 just outside Maysville. The one-story home sprawled yellow brick and white trim on a large plot. The manicured lawn was brown from the cold weather, and the shrubbery sat close to the house as if seeking shelter from the gusting winds that swept across the rolling landscape. The house sat back from the road with a paved driveway leading to the side of the house to a two-car garage. A fence shielded the backyard from view of the driveway, and concrete sidewalks led each to the front door and the gate in the fence.

Mark helped Caroline out of the truck and leaning on him (she'd left the mop back at Mark's duplex), they made their way around to the front of the house. Confronted with two steps up to the front porch, she navigated them with some difficulty but smiled with pride at her accomplishment. Mark smiled back, but his smile was filled with nervousness. The night before, Caroline finally convinced Mark to tell his family the *complete* story about the investment situation. He'd been on edge ever since. He'd even taken an extra nerve pill.

"Well, hello strangers!" Beth greeted as she whipped the front door open, the fall wreath flopping as she did so. She reached over and gave Mark a big hug. She was almost as tall as her brother and built very much the same. "Y'all get on in here and out of that cold!" Her long dark ponytail swinging, she stepped aside for Mark to assist Caroline with the last step-up into the house.

"Beth, this is Caroline," Mark introduced, as he slid the flannel jacket from Caroline's shoulders.

"Oh, honey! That looks perfectly miserable!" Beth squinted her face as soon as she saw the sling and green cast protruding from her sleeve and the boot on Caroline's foot.

"Hello, nice to meet you," Caroline said, balancing herself

as Mark hung their coats in the closet. "It's not the most comfortable for sure!" She attempted a smile for Mark's sister, who looked her over from head to toe.

Beth shook her head at what she saw and mumbled, "Uh-uh-uh!" She flung her arms around Caroline and gave her a gentle hug, swaddling her with the scent of lilacs, adding, "You poor girl!" Then, perking up, said, "Well, y'all come on in! Everyone but Larry is already here. He got tied up at church."

Caroline clung to Mark's arm as they followed Beth down a hallway and into a family room with a large fire place made of the same yellow brick as the house. Flames lapped up around a stack of logs, throwing off a soothing heat. Family members chatted comfortably from chair to chair to couch.

"Papaw! She's just a friend!" A blushing teenage boy said to an older man, who had a devious smile.

"Oh, she's more than a friend, Kevin!" ribbed a young lady about the same age as the boy. She winked at the older man.

"Hey, y'all!" Beth interjected. "Looks who's here!" She raised her arms towards Mark and Caroline, "Speaking of friends, this here is Mark's friend, Caroline!"

Still holding onto Mark's arm, Caroline smiled and glanced at Beth and then at the new faces in the room. "Hello," she said. A timidness rang in her tone.

Mark put his arm around Caroline's back. "Caroline, that young fellow there is Kevin, my nephew, my sister Lynn's boy. And the two giving him a hard time are Lizzy, Larry's daughter, and my dad, Dennis Meadows."

"Nice to meet you." Caroline raised her good hand.

Two other faces came up behind Beth. Both were women wearing matching aprons They were older than Caroline but younger than Beth. Pushing past Beth, each energetically extended a hand at the same time.

"I'm Lynn, Mark's sister." Lynn was skinny and tall with the same blue eyes as her father and dark curly hair like Mark's, but shoulder-length.

"I'm Becky, Larry's wife and Lizzy's mom!" Shorter and a bit plumper, her blond hair was pulled back and twisted up on the back of her head. She was an older version of her daughter.

The two women's hands slowly dropped upon seeing the cast, but Caroline reached out with her left hand and grasped each lady's hand. "Nice to meet you!" Caroline replied.

"So, you are the lucky gal that Mark rescued from the bridge!" Lynn said eying her casts.

Becky also took in Caroline's condition. "God certainly took you under his wing!"

"Yes, it appears to be the case!" Caroline smiled again politely. "But I think he came disguised as Mark Meadows." She glanced up at Mark, the smile still broad on her lips. His cheeks were a faint shade of pink. Mark rolled his eyes at his sisters but gave Caroline a quick wink.

"Well, we're putting the finishing touches on the food! We'd better get back at it!" The two women disappeared out the doorway.

Beth leaned toward Caroline. "I got the meal started while they were at church, but they're finishing up. That's how we do it. Gives ol' Beth a little rest from the kitchen!" Then she turned to Mark, "Don't you think there's someone you ought to go see?"

Mark turned a darker shade of pink. He looked around the room, and then addressed Beth, "Well, I'm leaving Caroline in your care!" At that, he rubbed Caroline softly on the back where his hand rested and then let go, heading out the same door as the women.

"You come on over here, Caroline," Beth took Mark's place at her side, leading her towards the fire. "This chair's a good sturdy one. Easy to get out of. And close to the warmth!" She helped Caroline ease into the chair. "So, tell us…what all injuries did you end up with?"

Caroline assumed it was the nurse in Beth causing her to inquire. She briefly summarized her injuries, starting with her head and working down to her foot, as Beth, Lizzy, Kevin, and Mark's dad listened with interest. "I go back to the doctor on

Thursday to have the staples removed from my arm. I guess they'll cut the cast off and then re-cast it. I don't know what they'll do about my foot."

"Oh, they'll leave that foot alone, I'm sure!" Beth replied. "But they'll definitely check out your arm. They'll probably take pictures to see how it's healing and make sure everything is still in place. Did they say if you'd have to have additional surgeries?" Beth took a seat next to her father on the couch.

"Maybe," Caroline replied. "It'll just depend." As her shoulders slumped a bit, she admitted, "They did tell me I may not get full use of my arm back." She mashed her lips together.

"You must be in a lot of pain!" Lizzy remarked. Her eyes were large with awe.

"Some," Caroline replied. "Mostly from my foot. I guess because I've been walking on it. And my shoulder stays sore from where I dislocated it." Caroline wasn't ready to admit she felt no pain in her lower arm and had no feeling or movement in her fingers.

"Well, you are just blessed that you are alive," Dennis Meadows said. Caroline nodded at Mark's dad. She took a good look at the man. Mark resembled his father, but the older man but was thinner. While Mark's dark curling hair showed streaks of silver, Dennis Meadows' straight silver hair showed streaks of white. He had the same smile as Mark, but his eyes were as blue as the sky. The same color as Beth's eyes. His hand rested on a pant leg, and it was weathered with age not manual labor.

"I'm here!" A voice boomed from the front of the house as a draft of cold air swung down the hall into the room and brought another hint of lilac Caroline's way. A minute later another Meadows entered the family room. Larry wore dress slacks and a button-down shirt and tie. He'd left his jacket in the closet with the other coats. His head shaved and shiny, he was thin like his father. "Where's the food?" he asked first, then "I thought Mark was coming?" He looked at Beth.

"He did," Beth replied. "He's with mom." Then she pointed

towards Caroline. "Larry, this here's Caroline! The young lady that Mark saved from the fiery inferno!"

Larry followed Beth's hand. As his eyes landed on Caroline, his eyebrows raised in unison, and a serious expression fell on his face. "The miracle," he said slowly as he moved toward her. Larry looked upward briefly and then back at Caroline.

Caroline supposed he was looking toward Heaven. Larry thought he was the only one present who understood the meaning of the words. However, she'd heard Larry's every word during his visit to Mark. Mark had not mentioned Caroline as having to do with the miracle in his life, but Larry somehow recognized she was part of that extraordinary event.

"It's nice to meet you, Caroline," Larry said extending his hand. Caroline reached out her own. Larry clasped both his hands around her one. Looking up from their hands, Caroline met Larry's eyes, deep brown eyes that communicated beyond words, and she nodded. She knew he had an idea about the real events on the bridge. "You are indeed a special person!" he said.

"Oh, I don't know about that!" she replied humbly. "It's nice to meet you as well!"

As his hands let go of hers, he turned and addressed the others in the room, "Let's eat people! I'm starved!"

**

"Beth, let Caroline sit in my chair," Mark said as he entered the dining room.

Beth turned and pulled out the chair adjacent to the one she was going to seat Caroline in. With her assistance, Caroline lowered into the chair at a well-appointed table. Mark joined them in time to help scoot Caroline in towards the table, and he then slid into the chair to Caroline's left.

After everyone was seated and settled, Larry announced, "Let's us pray." With hands joined around the table, Caroline breaking the chain with her casted right hand, Mark's brother said the blessing for the meal.

"Dear Lord, we thank you for yet another wonderous meal and for those who have prepared this treat. We shall use it to nourish not only our bodies and minds, but also our spirits in that You may thrive within each and every one of us seated here today. We thank You for bringing our most loved family together around this table, and we humbling recognize the miracles You have worked in our lives. May the bounty before us help us to do many deeds in Your honor. In your name, Lord Jesus Christ. Amen."

Amens flew around the table as heads raised, and hands parted. Except for Mark's. He continued to clasp Caroline's hand as they waited for the procession of bowls and plates to come their way. Caroline noticed that each dish started with Mark's dad, seated at the head of the table, and he passed each dish to the left. When the first bowl approached them, Mark reached over Caroline to take it. Still heaped with mash potatoes, Mark served a dollop on Caroline's plate and then his, before passing the bowl to his nephew. With each dish, Mark looked at Caroline and she either nodded or shook her head, depending on the contents. Nothing missed Mark's plate. Then, as everyone became quiet as they dug into the mounds on their plates, Caroline sat back to allow Mark to cut her pork tenderloin into bite-size pieces. Glancing to her left, she noticed Beth, chewing her food, watched as her brother took care of Caroline's needs before digging into his own plate. A small smile crept on Beth's face. Beth winked at Caroline and returned her attention to her own plate. None of the others around the table seemed to notice, busy with their meals.

Caroline mouthed "thank you" to Mark followed by a smile, as he handed her the fork. He gave her a quick pat on the arm and a weak smile. She knew he dreaded the conversation to come after the meal and was surprised he'd filled his plate so full. She figured his appetite waned from nerves and anxiety. Picking up his own fork with his left hand, he immediately went for the mashed potatoes and gravy. Caroline did the same, and as the creamy texture of the potatoes coated the inside of her mouth, she decided they were the best she'd ever tasted. She was the first to speak.

"Who made the mashed potatoes?" she asked, looking around the table. "They are wonderful!"

"That would be me," Lynn raised her fork in the air.

"You'll have to teach me how you do it!" Caroline continued. "I can never get the lumps out of mine!"

"Well, when you're all healed up, we'll just march you into that kitchen and show you how it's done!" Lynn replied, nodding her head.

"Thanks!" Caroline poked a piece of the pork and began to savory the juicy meat. The spicing was just as she liked. Plenty of black pepper forming a crust on the outside.

"I hope you're okay with the pork tenderloin, Caroline," Beth added. "I didn't even think to ask Mark if you had any food preferences."

"No, I pretty much eat anything. Just not a lot of junk food," she replied. "Of course, there's no chance of getting anything junky at Mark's. He's such a clean eater." She smiled at Mark as he enjoyed a mouthful. "And he's such a great cook!"

"Mark learned to cook from Mom!" Lynn replied. "When Beth and I were busy chasing boys, Mark was right at her side, learning everything she knew!"

"Because he was the baby of the family!" Larry joined in, flashing a teasing smile at Mark. "And Mom's favorite!"

"Now, you all!" Dennis Meadows interjected. "Don't get this started again. Like a bunch of children, I swear! All of you were Mom's favorites in your own right!" Pinching off a piece of cornbread, he added, "mine too!"

"Did you have a nice visit with Mom, Mark?" Beth asked.

After he swallowed his food followed by a sip of water, he replied. "Yep. She seems to be in a good mood today. Very lucid." Then he turned towards Caroline. "Mom wants to meet you. I'll take you in after we eat."

Caroline motioned her hand and fork towards herself, surprised. *Me?* She looked back at him.

"Of course, you, Caroline!" Beth said before Mark could. "While Mom can't walk or move around, and she can't speak or eat, she still has her moments where she's still with us. She recognizes us and seems to know what's going on. She comes and goes on us, but fortunately at this point she still here with us plenty." Looking back at her plate, Beth devilishly added, "She wants to meet the woman who has Mark's heart!"

"Now, Beth…" Mark looked up, giving his sister a scornful look. It only caused Beth to chuckle. Smiles also rode Lynn and Larry's faces at the exchange.

Caroline just shook her head. The banter back and forth reminded of when she was younger, sitting at the table with Adam and Tory. The teasing and taunting was endless. Apparently, it truly was endless because the Meadows children were doing it into middle age.

"So, Mark," Larry began, as he lifted a forkful of peas and onions to his mouth. A pea dropped off into his potatoes sinking partly in the gravy. "Do you have an update for us on this investor character? What's going on with that?"

"Yes, have you heard any further?" Dennis Meadows asked, plunging his fork back into the potatoes. "The news has been quiet on the subject."

Caroline never imagined his family would bring up such a discussion at the dinner table. She momentarily felt numbness in her body, as she glanced at Mark. He sat his fork down beside his plate and finished chewing his food slowly, looking toward his plate. As he swallowed, he glanced back at Caroline, and sat a little straighter in his chair. She felt like she, too, should stop eating, but she didn't want to be perceived as knowing more about family affairs than the family did. She noticed Mark looked around at all the faces, stopping briefly on each one. As if he were sizing them up.

"Well?" Lynn asked, her head tilted and a note of impatience.

With both hands, Mark pushed his plate forward, clearing a spot to rest his folded hands. He exhaled slowly, before he spoke.

"It's gone." Mark nodded his head almost imperceptibly. He looked around at his family and their reactions. As his words reached ears and were processed, a few mouths hung open, a couple of frowns appeared, along with raised eyebrows. Even the teens appeared tuned into the depth of the conversation. Dennis Meadows continued to hold his fork and kept chewing his pork, looking at his son. Contemplating. Caroline set down her fork and her hand instinctively went to Mark's clutched hands, resting hers on top. Mark glanced down at her hand, and quickly took it within his. She could feel his tension and the pulse of his blood flowing through his fingers.

"Gone? What do you mean gone?" Larry finally asked. "I thought you said they had just frozen the investor accounts."

Mark took a deep breath, clutching his and Caroline's hand firmly. He looked directly at Larry. "Just what I said. It's gone." The faces around the table were still having trouble with the words. Mark then looked to his dad. "I have learned that, while I gave Jake the check to invest in what we had agreed upon, he deposited the check in an escrow account. The account that he makes the investment purchases from. However, Jake never made the investment." Shocked and alarmed looks exchanged around the table. Caroline noticed that both Dennis Meadows and Larry kept their eyes dedicated on Mark. "Apparently, we were not the only ones he did this to. On the Friday he went missing, so did all the money in the escrow account. It was transferred to a foreign bank account, and transferred again, and again. Apparently, Jake got on a plane and flew out of the country, and they currently have no clue where his is." Mark scanned the faces around him, and then rested his eyes on his father. Dennis Meadows showed no reaction. He finally swallowed his pork.

Caroline felt Mark's hand tremble and gently squeezed his fingers, her way of offering support and encouragement. She looked from Mark's dad to his brother. Larry's face was thick with concern, and he continuously re-wetted his lips. His eyes were fixated on Mark.

Mark sat silent. Caroline saw his jawline twitch. He collected his thoughts before going on. The meal was forgotten, and Mark commanded total attention in the room.

"So, what was all this business about investment accounts being frozen?" Larry asked. He sat back in his chair and folded his arms, studying Mark.

"The investment accounts were frozen," Mark replied to his brother. "They still are as far as I know. We just didn't have an investment account, apparently." Mark swallowed hard. He reached for his water and taking a long sip. He almost emptied his glass.

"So, you lied." Larry shot him a disapproving look. "You led us on!"

"It's more like I didn't tell the whole truth." Mark's hands trembled visibly. Caroline used her thumb to rub his palm, hoping to calm him. "I...I guess I wanted to protect everyone. Until I knew more."

"So, I'm confused," Beth said. She seemed to be the least unnerved by the news. "How did you find out that the money was never invested?"

"I stopped by the office the Monday after Jake apparently went missing. I was there to inquire about taking some of the money out of the investment for the addition to the house, like we discussed." Mark looked sideways at his eldest sister. "Rhonda was there. Jake's assistant. She looked up the investment account and found there wasn't one. But she saw where the check had been deposited in the escrow account. When she came in that morning, she immediately noticed all the funds were gone from the escrow account. Transferred. Gone. Wired on Friday to some foreign bank. And when she couldn't get ahold of Jake, she got nervous and notified the main office, and they told her to contact the police. With the amount of money involved, the FBI was called in. They took over the investigation. And now where Jake left the country and has been hopping from place to place, INTERPOL is involved." Mark looked back at his father. Dennis Meadows sat back in his chair with legs crossed. His hands were folded in his lap with fingers interlocked. He quietly listened to his youngest son.

"Jake had a three-day lead on the authorities, and somewhere in his jumping from country to country, he assumed a fake identity. They've lost his trail." Mark looked down at his hands.

"The money?" Dennis Meadows asked. Caroline noticed the patriarch of the family showed no emotion. No anger. No sympathy. No worry. Just a blank expression.

"As I said, Officer Keyser told me the money was transferred and transferred again. To multiple bank accounts in various countries. Jake had it all planned out so they'd have difficulty tracing it. Keyser said it could be years before they have any answers. That's all I know." Mark look down at his hands. "I am so sorry I failed you all!"

Mark's usually squared confident shoulders slumped forward along with his head. He sat shaking his head from side to side. Exhales and sighs filled the room.

"Wow!" Kevin was the first to speak. "Who knew that little ol' Maysville would be the scene for all this action! First a rescue from a crash and now international espionage! I wonder when they'll make the movie!"

"Kevin! Shhh!" Lynn put her hand on her son, squelching him. "This is serious business! That was Mom and Dad's life savings! Their retirement! Now what are they going to do?" She shot an annoyed look at Mark. He didn't see it, but Caroline did. She desperately wanted to say something in Mark's defense, but knew she was invisible in the matter. At his sister's comment, Mark let go of Caroline's hand and covered his bowed face with his hands, his fingers outstretched. She suspected he was fighting back tears, from the shade of red of his cheeks and ears.

"Well, that's not entirely true, Lynn, dear." Dennis Meadows' voice brought all but Mark's eyes upon him. The older man hung one arm over the back of the chair. He rested his other hand on his crossed leg. Straight-faced, he looked at Lynn, who's expression turned confused, and then to Larry and Beth, with his gaze finally resting on Mark. "The money we're discussing is only the money from the sale of the house. The homestead. Do you think your mother and I would be so foolish as to hand over everything we have to one investor?" The comment earned Mark's attention. Shielding his face from his brother and sisters, he looked at his father. Caroline rested her hand on Mark's back just as he had many times on her.

"No, no!" their father continued. "Certainly, it's a hit! But I suspected there are many others that will fare far worse in this situation than we will! No, folks, your mother and I have investments with several brokerage firms, and we've got CDs at a number of banks. I've got it all recorded in a file. Beth knows where it is, just in case." As Dennis Meadows looked at Mark, he added, "the only thing that truly troubles me is that Mark felt he couldn't come to us and share the news. He felt he would be judged by us, and he has been. He is being judged right this moment. That is not right, and it is not in keeping with the Christian ethic of this family. Each of you rightly owe him apology. Me included."

Mark leaned back, taking Caroline's hand in his under the table. His eyes were as red as his cheeks and ears, and tiny beads of wetness lingered on the sides of his face. His shoulders still slumped, and despite his size, Caroline got a good idea of what the young Mark looked like. In fact, after Dennis Meadows' comments, all the siblings had reduced to their younger selves.

"Mark, my son. I am very sorry that I was not more forthright with you about our financial standing, and that you worried over this situation. This could have happened to anyone. And it did. Many apparently. There is nothing you did wrong, and there was no way you could have known or prevented it. There are just evil, greedy people in the world doing the biddings of the devil." The older man rose slowly from his chair and walked around the table, stopping next to Mark. He laid an aged hand on Mark's shoulder, letting it rest a few seconds, and turned to the others. "The rest of you can make that apology on your own time after you give this some reflection." Dennis Meadows left the room.

He left behind a quiet. Looks bounced from one to the other and towards Mark. He avoided eye contact by focusing on his half-eaten plate. Caroline sat, also quiet, clueless of what to do.

"Well!" Beth was the first to speak and move. "I guess that concludes this meal!" Looking at Larry and Lynn as she pushed her chair back, she said, "Why don't you two help me clear the table!" At that she picked up her own plate reached for the plate of pork loin. She motioned her head towards the others as she swung her ponytail and headed for the kitchen. The two teens made a dash for the family room.

As the dining room table began to clear, Mark turned to Caroline. "How about we go see Mom for a minute?" His voice was a whisper. Caroline nodded. Anything to escape the tension that lingered in the room.

Leaning on Mark, Caroline walked with him towards a room off the side of the house. It must have originally been a sunroom or finished porch. Windows encircled the room allowing the light to pour in, despite it being an overcast grey day. Off to the side of the room, Mark's mother laid in a hospital bed covered with blankets and a handstitched quilt. The quilt was constructed from many scraps of fabric of all colors and shapes. *Maybe one she had made? Or perhaps by her mother?* Her thick, curly white hair blended with the white pillows behind her, and her face was pale in comparison to the lively quilt. As they approached, the older woman stared straight ahead with her arms resting at her sides on top of the quilt. Caroline noticed that one of her fingers ever-so-slightly rubbed the quilt, touching the puckers created by the stitches. It was her only movement.

"Hi, Ma," Mark said. He reached and touched her arm. Slowly her brown eyes moved until they rested on Mark. "Ma, I brought Caroline with me. She's the girl I told you about. I want you to meet her." Again, the woman's eyes moved, searching for Caroline. Caroline smiled and wondered if the woman was smiling on the inside. "Caroline, this is Joy Meadows, my mother.

"Mrs. Meadows," Caroline began. Without thinking, she reached for Joy Meadow's hand and gently brushed it. "It's so nice to meet you. Mark talks about you all the time!" Caroline wasn't totally sure, but she thought she saw a flicker in the woman's eyes. Then Caroline laid her hand on the woman's. "You have done an amazing job raising Mark. He is the kindest, most thoughtful man I've even known! I know you had an important hand in that! He's been taking good care of me!"

Joy Meadow's blinked. Her eyes moved back to Mark. Yes, Caroline was right. A smile tried to find its way out. As Mark's mother looked at her son, a glimmer surfaced. Was she telling him she was proud? A definite and obviously special connection spanned the two.

As Caroline witnessed the tender interaction between mother and son, she suddenly felt so alone. Would she ever know the bond between a mother and child? The type of bond that was so explicitly right before her? Steven had been adamantly against children. He'd robbed her of ten of her most fertile years. Being 30, she still had time, but it was running thin. Would she ever be lucky enough to experience the type of love shared only by mother and child?

"Well, Ma. We're going to head off." Mark took his hand and softly rubbed it against his mother's cheek. Her eyes closed, and when they opened, they seemed to smile. "We'll be back to see you, okay?" Mark leaned over the bedrails and kissed his mother's cheek. Again, her eyes closed, this time remaining closed. Was she savoring the moment?

Mark led Caroline back into the living room. It was a more formal room appointed with a large sofa and love seat situated around a coffee table, several wingback chairs with end tables, and a large tapestry rug defining the sitting area. All were place before a large bay window framed with corded drapes. Dennis Meadows sat in one of the wingback chairs, his elbows propped upright on the chair arms and his hands touching, forming a triangle. He stared at the triangle as if in deep contemplation.

"Hey, Dad." Mark had no trouble interrupting his father's thoughts. "Mom's really alert today. She looked at Caroline."

His father tilted his head looking up at his son. "Yes, it's one of her better days. She knew you were coming." He watched Mark assist Caroline to sit in a chair. As Caroline leaned back against the cushioned back, she noticed a faint smile on the older man's kind face. She wondered what the father thought about his son helping a woman in her condition. Had Dennis Meadows assisted his wife, Joy, in the same manner Mark was assisting her?

"You okay?" Mark asked Caroline.

She looked up at him and smiled. "I'm great! Thank you!"

"I'm going to hunt down that cane!" he said, looking at the wall beyond which the rest of the family convened. He let out a sigh. Caroline could tell Mark dreaded facing his siblings. "I'll be back." He patted the top of the chair as he turned, casting a glance in his dad's direction before leaving.

Dennis Meadows eyes followed his son until out of sight. Then he focused on Caroline, providing her a warm smile to curb the usual awkwardness of being left alone with a stranger. What the man didn't know was that Caroline was over the awkwardness. She pretty much rolled with each situation. Most everyone was a stranger to her. Not just in the new life she'd been thrust into, but also in her old life. Probably more so in her old life. *People she thought she knew? Well, she didn't know them at all!*

"Cane?" Mark's father asked. His hands continued to form the contemplative triangle in the air.

"Yes, he spoke to Beth about borrowing your wife's cane for me," Caroline replied, returning the smile. "Since she's not currently using it."

"That's very nice!" The man nodded his head. "I'm sure you'll put it to good use! Although Mark seems to enjoy the role of being your 'cane' himself!" The older man chuckled softly.

Caroline laughed. "Yes, he does. Except at home, he's had me using…get this…a mop! He says he encouraging my independence!" She laughed again. The mention of the mop brought raised eyebrows from Mark's father. "Seriously, Mark's really taken very good care of me. I'm not sure why, but I am forever grateful!"

"Blessed!" the man said slowly, nodding.

Caroline upturned her lips and studied the man for a moment. "Yes, blessed indeed," she said. "I don't know what I will do without him when it comes time to go! But right now, there are so many unknowns in my future. I must see what happens with my arm." She motioned her head towards the sling holding her casted arm taut to her body.

"Well, we never know what the future holds, that's for sure!" Dennis Meadows finally dropped his hands to the arms of the chair. "It's important to live each day to the fullest."

Caroline nodded. "I am learning that. That is one of the important lessons I am learning."

"What is the most important lesson?" Dennis Meadows looked intently at her.

"Huh." The question was unexpected. The bridge flashed in Caroline's mind. Tilting her head, she looked at Mark's dad, into his blue eyes. "That life is precious. It's a gift from God. And… God is truly in control." Her reply surprised herself. It echoed between her own ears. The words didn't flow from Caroline because she thought them appropriate to use among believers. The words came from deep within Caroline. They were words she now believed. It was her new truth.

Dennis Meadows nodded and smiled. "Truly so. It is a lesson that I wish my son would learn. Perhaps you can teach this to him?"

"Mark?" Caroline was confused. "Why do you say that? Because he doesn't go to church?"

"No, no." Dennis replied in a low voice. "Ever since Mark

was a young boy, he's had difficulty understanding the value and worth of his own life. If he were to recognize his life as a precious gift from God Almighty, he might treat it differently. For Mark to understand that he is not the one in control, but that God is at the steering wheel, might free him from his burdens."

Caroline frowned slightly. "I'm not sure what you mean? Burdens?"

"It is not something Mark shares freely, or even wants to admit to himself at times, but because you are within his household, it something you should be aware of. You might even be able to help him," Dennis continued, his voice low.

Caroline shook her head. *Help Mark?* Of anyone she knew, Mark seemed to be the most tied together individual. Well, except for the bridge thing. What could his dad be speaking of?

"Mark has a diagnosed major depressive disorder. It surfaced when he was a just a kid and has unfortunately followed him through adulthood. He is on a strict regimen of medications that help to keep it under control. Provided he *takes* them."

"I would never have guessed…" Caroline replied. She didn't recall seeing him taking pills of any kind. But it might explain…

"Caroline, if you don't mind my asking," Mark's father leaned forward, speaking in a lower tone. "Do you know why Mark was really on the bridge that night?"

Caroline's eyes grew wide, and then they narrowed as she shook her head. "No," she lied. "I don't even recall seeing him. He said he was out for a walk. He told me he did that frequently. He said he thought more clearly when he walked along the bridge under the night stars. It helped him put things in perspective. I am fortunate he did that…that he was walking that night. Otherwise, I might not be here to even address your question." She gave him a quick smile when she finished.

Mark's dad leaned back in the chair, and his hands went back to their perched position forming a triangle.

"Well, that is comforting to know," he said with a quick

smile. He focused his blue eyes on hers. They projected a coolness. She knew he didn't believe a word.

CHAPTER 11 – WEEK TWO

"Good morning, Caroline!" Emily's tone was cheerful. Caroline hoped she had good news. "I'm so glad you called. You were on this morning's list."

"Okay. So, what's going on?" Caroline asked. She had the notebook before her and a pen laying close so she could record notes after the call.

"Well, first off, we've heard back from Steven's attorney, and they do not plan to contest the divorce. They are agreeing to the terms of our petition: the 50-50 split of personal assets and that Steven buy you out of the business for 25% of the current value. Normally for an uncontested divorce, you wouldn't need to appear before the District Court Judge, but because of the restraining order, you've got to appear. The court date is the Friday right after Thanksgiving. Nine in the morning. Jot it down. Ironically, that's when the divorce is final! The judge may sign off on those papers at the same time."

"That's wonderful news!" Caroline replied. She felt a giddiness rising inside her.

"Also, the judge has signed an order for you to be able to enter the house and remove your personal items. Do not take any furniture. You can make notation of various shared items in the house that you want. Apparently, Steven is not concerned with much of the content of the house except for his office." Emily paused. Caroline could hear her flipping pages. "Oh, and when you go to the house, you need to let the Sheriff's office know the date and time. They will send out a deputy to ensure that you have no problems, or you don't take anything you're not supposed to."

"Problems? What problems would I have?" Caroline asked.

"You know, Steven showing up and giving you a difficult time. That sort of thing," the lawyer explained. "But in your case, I think Steven is going to want to stay as far away as possible. And he may not even have a choice!"

"What do you mean?" Caroline laid the phone on the table and pressed the speaker button. "I'm putting you on speaker, Emily." She took the pen and shoved it down into her cast, trying to calm an itch on her calf.

"That's fine. The police are moving quickly on the findings from the car. They've already brought Steven in for questioning, but of course he had his lawyer with him, so they got little information." More rustling papers. "Also, the deputies have been out to Brandia's house to question her. That was a smarter move on their part. They caught her first thing in the morning and no lawyer present. Of course, that woman doesn't know what 'don't talk to the police' means! She admitted to the affair and said that she and Steven planned to marry 'as soon as Caroline was out of the picture'! Yep, those exact words!" An involuntary 'ugh' escaped Emily.

"Well, that's good, isn't it?" Caroline asked, feeling a spike of encouragement.

"Yeah, for the county's case. It really doesn't mean much in terms of the divorce. Totally separate matter. We want to keep the divorce proceedings as quick and clean as possible," Emily replied. "But in terms of the county's case, the Sheriff's department has been out talking to mechanics in the area trying to find out if any of them may have worked on the Range Rover. Of course, if any of them had, you know they said 'no'! But you will never guess what they did find?"

"What's that?" Caroline's interest piqued.

"One of the mechanics they approached over in Ewing turns out to be Brandia's half-brother."

"No way!" Caroline gasped, her hand going to her mouth. Just as she did, the front door opened, and Mark came in with two brown paper grocery sacks. Quietly, he closed the door and made his way to the counter where he deposited the groceries. Pausing, he listened to find out what Caroline's 'no way!' referred to.

"Yes!" Emily's voice took on a gossipy tone. "And he's already done time for things like turning back odometers, you name it! That's no coincidence!"

"No, it's not," Caroline said with a hint of a laugh. "That's just plain stupid!" She looked up at Mark as he stepped quietly back towards the door to haul more bags in.

"Exactly!" Emily did laugh. "But here's the bad news out of the whole deal…"

Caroline braced herself. She knew it wouldn't be all roses, as they say.

"Because of the tampering with the car," Emily began, "Providia may not honor the insurance policy on the Range Rover. No replacement. Especially if they find out Steven had something to do with the tampering that caused the accident."

Caroline exhaled. She figured she would somehow get the short end. "I suppose I'm not surprised," Caroline sighed. "Do I have any recourse? Could I sue Steven for a car?"

"Honestly, Caroline? The county attorney is all over this. If this investigation goes the way I think it will go, I don't think there will be anyone to sue. Attempted murder, insurance fraud, and whatever else they tack on. It'll put Steven away for several years. He'll lose the business, which I'm sure he will anyway. Providia is certainly not going to let him continue as an agent!"

"So much for 25% of the business!" Caroline said.

"My best advice is, get in the house, and get what you can while you're there. We'll see what the house brings when it's sold. Get whatever you can get! That's our game plan. And pray this divorce goes through without any hiccups. Hopefully the judge won't want to delay things. So far, they haven't filed criminal charges against Steven, but when they do…" Emily was frank. There were no sugar or sweeteners added to her words. "Oh, and just to prepare you, you may be called as a material witness for the criminal case, since you were the one he was…"

"Thanks, Emily. I'll keep my fingers crossed, and I'll even give praying a shot!" Sitting a little taller in the chair, Caroline's shoulder reminded her it wasn't quite ready for perfect posture. "Just keep me posted on any developments!"

"Will do!" Emily adding after a pause, "Caroline, I'm truly sorry you're going through all of this. No one deserves it, especially not you!"

"Thanks, Emily. That means a lot!" Caroline winced as she shut the phone off.

A blast of cold air followed Mark inside with three more grocery sacks, one in each arm and one dangling from a hand. He used his foot to close the front door. Ordinarily Caroline would have jumped up to help, but how? She sat in the chair and watched him struggle to keep the third bag in hand until he got to the bar counter. All three bags successfully landed on the counter, and Mark turned unbuttoning the navy wool peacoat dusted with white flurries.

"Why such a sour expression?" he asked heading to the closet to hang his coat. On his return to the kitchen, he stopped by the table with his hands on his sides. "I heard part of that. Wasn't it good news?"

"Some of it," Caroline replied. Her mood dipped towards the end of the call, and apparently her face showed it. "I have a feeling I'm barely going to escape from all of this. But I guess that's what most important. Being free. Moving on."

"It certainly isn't worth World War III. I got into that, and there was no winner there!" Mark attempted a smile for Caroline, but it was slow to surface. His sullen mood from the family dinner persisted. "I'd better get the food put away. I've got several frozen things."

Caroline pushed herself up from the table and started towards the kitchen using the cane decorated in a floral design. Caroline gladly traded the red-handled mop for Mark's mother's cane. After two days with the cane, Mark threatened to rig the cane with a dustmop on the bottom. He claimed he could see dust accumulating on the floor now that Caroline no longer used the mop!

"Oh, you're fine at the table." Mark raised his hand, waving her back. "I can get all of this!"

"No, it's okay." Caroline continued towards the kitchen. "I need to get up. I want to feel useful." As she entered the kitchen, she saw Mark grab a large white bag and quickly shove it into the pantry.

"Let me help!" she said reaching into one of the bags. She began pulling items out one by one. Carrots, celery, broccoli, onions, kale, apples, lemons, gluten free pasta, garlic, almond milk. When she finished with one bag, she began emptying the next. Mark took the items and stored them in their place.

"Oh, here's the frozen stuff!" She pulled out a package of frozen raw shrimp, followed by salmon, and a bag of boneless chicken breasts. Abandoning the other items, Mark gathered up the frozen items and disappeared through the door to the garage and the freezer. When he returned, Caroline had the rest of the bags emptied and was attempting to fold the paper sacks back into their original flat form.

"Looks like we've got some good eating ahead of us. What's on the menu tonight?" Caroline smiled at Mark. He seemed a bit distracted, and as he placed items in the pantry, he kept glancing down. Caroline assumed he was looking at the bag of prescriptions he whisked out of view.

"Huh? Um. Yeah." Mark replied. He hadn't heard a thing she said.

"I think we should have whatever is in that mysterious white bag!" Caroline said, teasing, trying to lighten his mood.

"What?" He stopped and looked at her. His brows furrowed, and he shook his head in confusion.

"For dinner!" she said, chuckling. "We should fry up whatever it is your hiding in the white bag!"

Mark opened his mouth but there were no words. His lips snapped shut, and as the air exhaled from his body, his shoulders deflated into a slump. He reached into the pantry bringing out the white bag and held it up between them. Caroline met his eyes and raised her brows.

"You know?" he asked.

"You think I didn't?" she asked in return.

"How?"

"Oh, I put it together." She reached out her hand and placed in on Mark's arm. She felt a slight tremble.

Mark laid the bag on the counter, facing her. "My dad." He scowled.

"Mm…not entirely." Caroline wiggled her head and shoulders. Her attempts to allay his brooding seemed to have an opposite effect.

"Mark, it's not a bad thing," she said. "I mostly figured it out after your brother was here." Then she added, "But your dad was pretty blatant. Besides, why are you hiding it?"

Mark rubbed the side of his head, and then his hand covered his mouth and chin. His fingers squished his mouth into a contortion, and then his hand dropped to his side. He looked at the remaining groceries on the counter and the unopened white bag. Instead of going for the bag, he turned and reached back into the pantry, pulling out the basket of pill bottles. He laid them on the counter next to the bag.

"There's the real Mark Meadows." Mark pointed to the basket of bottles. "A pill-head!"

"No." Caroline took a step closer to him. She reached her hand up to his face, placing her palm along his stubbly cheek. "No. This is Mark Meadows."

"So." Mark stood still. He did not reach for Caroline, but she kept her hand curled against his cheek. "Did you hear everything Larry said?"

Caroline nodded. Mark exhaled and looked away, leaning a hand on the counter as if to steady himself. Caroline could see the color rising to his cheeks.

"Mark…" Caroline said, touching his arm again. He tried to shake off her hand. He took a shallow breath, as if the air had been knocked out of him. "Mark, I didn't mean to pry. I'm not judging you in any way. You are my friend, regardless. This changes nothing."

"But you know…" His voice wavered. "Not just about the

meds..." His fingers played with his upper lip. Another of his nervous ticks.

"That you've had other low moments in your life?" Caroline said. It wasn't a question. "Of course, and I didn't have to be told. I pretty much assumed that the stunt on the bridge probably wasn't a first."

"Dad asked you about the bridge, didn't he? He wanted to know if I was..."

"Yes. And he got the only answer I know to give. And at some point, I want you to take me on a walk across the bridge to see those night stars, Mark."

He looked up from the basket of bottles. He looked at her from head to toe. And then he took a deep breath and shook his head.

"You are my miracle, Caroline." His words sounded desperate. Breathless.

"I know." She looked into his eyes. "You are mine." She tilted her head slightly one way, then the other. "I believe two stars collided on that bridge, and here we are. Divine intervention. Inexplicably connected. Like you, I felt God's presence on the bridge. Our lives are forever changed." Caroline looked away, feeling moisture flowing to her eyes. "In fact, I don't even feel like the same person I was."

Mark lifted her chin with his fingers in his 'Mark Meadows way,' and he studied her as his breaths slowed and his anxiety waned. She said nothing. She returned his gaze as he sought refuge in her eyes. Then he leaned down laying his lips on hers. A slow, gentle kiss. When their lips parted, they regarded each other for a moment. Caroline swore she saw stars among the clouds in his eyes, and wondered, did he see stars in hers?

"Let's get the rest of these groceries away!" Caroline said. "I want to know what masterpiece you're planning for tonight! And I want to help!" Cooking always helped to raise his spirits. She knew this.

***

Thursday's two-week follow-up with the doctor took longer than Mark expected. He wanted to accompany Caroline in the exam room, and although she asked for him to come with her, they were told the rooms were small and they'd needed room to move around. Mark landed in the waiting area, arms crossed and slumped in chair watching a home improvement show on the flat screen television hanging on the wall. The sound was turned low, but the show explained itself. And when it came to the backyard landscaping, Mark began turning his head slowly back and forth. He knew it was television, but he still counted the mistakes made. The wrong types of shrubs for the soil and climate, paving stones with gravel and no landscaping fabric beneath. The list went on. The next show was basically the same with a different cast of characters.

After a while, the flat screen lost his attention, and his thoughts took over. The first thing he wanted to do the next time he saw Larry was strangle him! That booming voice that carried! Great for a minister talking to a congregation, but not so great when talking about sensitive personal matters! Seriously, there'd be no strangling, but he'd remind Larry that he needed to tone it down when talking one on one. And his dad was no better. Retired no more than four years from psychiatric practice, and his dad apparently had forgotten everything he knew about patient confidentially. Mark couldn't get over how his dad discussed his 'affliction' with Caroline. While she might not be a stranger to Mark, she was a complete stranger to his dad!

Mark knew that if Caroline spent much more time at the house and around him, she would have eventually figured it out, or he would have discussed it with her, but it would have been on his terms. He would have shared what he wanted to, the way he wanted to. His brother and dad portrayed him as emotionally broken. As something even super glue couldn't fix.

He was surprised by Caroline's response. She took it in

stride. Perhaps knowing Mark was as broken on the inside as she was on the outside evened things out between them. They both had challenges. One more thing in common. The parallels in their lives were stacking up. Except for the family thing. Caroline was still close-lipped about her upbringing. And after the dinner on Sunday, Mark wished he'd been as close-lipped about his own family.

But he did come clean about the whole money thing. That relieved a huge pocket of anxiety he'd been toting around with him. Dwelling on. Losing sleep over. Caroline had been right. It hadn't been his fault. It wasn't his doing. How could he know that the man he knew since childhood and trusted would pull such a disappearing trick? Mark learned a valuable lesson: when it comes to money, trust no one. He was both relieved and thankful that his parents had other financial means. However, he was curious about his dad initially making such a big deal about the proceeds from the sale of the house being all that his parent's had. And why his dad made such a big deal about entrusting Mark to make the right investment decisions? His father, the psychiatrist, knowingly put enormous pressure on Mark, the same son he claimed to be emotionally fragile to Caroline.

Caroline's bringing the hidden medications to light did allow Mark to breathe a little lighter. One more secret and source of anxiety freed. That evening after her 'confrontation' about the white bag, he and Caroline enjoyed lemony chicken breasts over quinoa with a side of steamed broccoli. Caroline prepared the broccoli and the quinoa herself, feeling quite accomplished. 'Useful,' she had said.

Conversation over that meal was more relaxed than usual, and Caroline pronounced Mark's family as 'passive-aggressive' with him. She wasn't wrong. He hadn't realized it until she said it, but sometimes it takes an outsider to recognize the obvious. Caroline perceived his dad and his siblings viewing Mark as delicate and fragile, and their words and actions seemed to reinforce him as incapable, driving home Mark's sense of being a damaged person.

Perhaps that is what drew him to Caroline. She had such a fresh perspective of him and seemed to accept him as is. She didn't view him as damaged or fragile. She'd seen him at his worst, though just for a fraction of a second. She asked about it, but she didn't dwell. She was also dealing with her circumstances way better than he expected. He'd anticipated a lot of crying and mourning the loss of her husband. And pain. He expected moaning from the pain of her injuries and the hurt of a life lost. But instead, she plowed forward. She accepted the things placed in front of her and was trying to make the best of a bad situation. It was admirable.

And what drew her to him? Obviously, she had nowhere to go and no one to go to. She was with him by default. He was there. He knew that. And, when he went after the cane on Sunday, his sisters and brother plainly told him he was setting himself up for a fall: 'that woman' was taking advantage of him. *Using him.* But there was more to it. 'Inexplicably connected,' Caroline had said. That is how it felt. They were intended to find each other and be together. When it came time that Caroline finally had somewhere to go, a life to return to, Mark held the idea that she'd face the greatest dilemma in her life. To go or not to go. He already hoped it was the latter.

The door to the patient rooms opened, and Caroline came through the door with the assistance of the nurse who'd taken her back. The cane in hand, she limped forward as Mark jumped up going to her aid. Mark reached Caroline's side as she stood at the window waiting for an appointment card. The woman at the computer scribbled a date and time on a card and pushed it through the hole at the bottom of the plexiglass barrier.

"Four weeks from today, unless you have any problems," the woman said.

"Okay, thanks." Caroline took the card and handed it to Mark, who dropped it in the breast pocket of his shirt.

"So, how'd it go?" Mark asked as they headed for the door.

"Let's just go to the truck." Caroline's expression was flat. She limped through the door that Mark held open and once at the truck, waited for him to open the door and help her in. He belted her into her seat and crawled up into the driver's seat and paused with his left arm resting on the steering wheel and his body turned toward her. She looked out the windshield, her face emotionless. "Can we just drive?" she finally said, still not looking at him.

Mark started the truck and pulled out of the parking lot. "Where to? Home?" Glancing at her, she shook her head. The only thing that moved, beside her eyes. They darted back and forth, as if searching for something.

"What happened? What did they tell you?" Mark asked approaching a red light. "You were in there a long time."

Caroline shook her head again. Mark studied her until the light changed. Purple casting poked out of the sling, traded for the green. The tip of her boot was hidden by the dashboard. He couldn't tell if she'd had a color change there also. Caroline looked out the side window, not ready to discuss her visit. Mark's hopes for good news shifted down a couple notches. He turned the truck to the right and headed towards downtown instead of towards the house. She still said nothing.

Caroline's silence continued as Mark went into a local coffee shop and emerged with two tall steamy paper cups. She briefly glanced at them when he slid them in the cup holders. Going around the block, he pulled into the vacant lot at the newspaper office. It was not far from the fountain situated in a small park-like area.

"What are we doing?" she asked as Mark helped her down out of the truck. "Where are we going?" Her usual beaming smile was missing.

"It's a balmy November day. We may not get many more of these." Mark picked up the two cups from the hood of the truck. "I thought we'd enjoy the fresh air." He began walking toward the fountain. Caroline leaned on her cane and watched Mark walk away from her. Almost to the bricked walkway,

Mark stopped and waved her to follow. "Come on!"

Caroline rolled her eyes and exhaled long and slow. She moved the cane and took small steps towards Mark, who waited with steaming cups. Once she arrived where he stood, Mark turned and walked slowly so Caroline walked beside him. When they got to the concrete steps that led down to the tunnel under the train tracks, she stopped and looked anxiously at the descending concrete. Searching for a railing, her eyes landed on Mark. He simply raised his eyebrows encouraging her to attempt the stairs on her own. Sighing again, she stepped down with her booted foot, bracing herself with the cane, following with her good foot. She repeated the actions until she arrived at the hollow that went through the tunnel. Following Mark to the other side, she paused looking at the tiles that covered the tunnel walls. Handprints. Each tile had the impression of a hand. Some large. Some small. A few tiles were missing, revealing painted concrete beneath. On the other side of the flood wall, an asphalt path ran along the river surrounded by grassy areas contained by short concrete walls.

Mark waited for Caroline to catch up with him, and they headed toward a section of a short concrete retaining wall. Caroline sat on the knee-high wall close to Mark, leaning the cane against the wall, and he handed her a coffee. She blew into the hole in lid and took a cautious sip. The coffee had cream, but no sugar. Her nose scrunched up as she held the cup towards Mark.

"This one's yours," she said, her tongue working inside her mouth to counteract the bitter taste.

"Sorry." Mark exchanged cups. "They've marked them wrong." He was grateful she found the mistake. The thought of taking a gulp of sweet coffee? It wouldn't have been good. After four years of no sugar, it would have been sickeningly sweet.

Caroline sampled the exchanged cup and nodded approval. Mark leaned close and extended his arm behind her as he raised his cup to his lips. The hot coffee was a nice compliment to the sunny, but slightly breezy November day. He looked out over the river towards Ohio side, then to the right toward the bridge extending between the two shores. A towboat was approaching the bridge with a series of barges.

"Look." He held up his cup motioning in the direction of the bridge. "There are barges."

Studying the designs on the burgundy and pink paper coffee cup, Caroline looked in the direction of his hand. She saw the bridge first, then dropping her eyes to the waters, spotted the towboat making slow progress. They both watched as the boat guided six barges full of coal down the middle of the Ohio River. The water was surprisingly clear despite the rain the day before. Usually after a good rain, the water ran muddy. Instead, the water reflected the blue cloudless sky.

"It looks like the coal is floating in the water," Caroline observed. Her voice was still flat.

"Yep. They're loaded down."

"I've never seen barges before." Caroline pointed. "There's someone walking around out there."

"Probably checking to make sure the connections between the barges are secure," Mark replied. "It's not a pretty story if one breaks loose!"

"What happens?" Caroline asked, glancing at the man beside her.

"Hopefully it floats downstream where they can catch up with it and get it re-connected. But most of the time they end up following the current and crash into the shore or get caught on a bridge."

"Huh," she replied. "The boat's pretty big."

"Uh-huh. And the workers live on the boat."

"Live on the boat?" Finally, some life surfaced in her voice.

Mark nodded. "Yep. Some of the guys are on the river for a month or more at a time. They ride all the way down the Ohio to the Mississippi and to the Gulf of Mexico. Then they come back."

"Huh." She sipped her coffee and fell quiet again. Her eyes followed the towboat and its cargo.

Mark held his head back allowing his face to soak in the sunshine. When the back of his neck began to ache, his head resumed an upright up-right position, and he took a deep breath of the clean air. He was curious if Caroline was going to tell him about her appointment, but he didn't want to ask again. Clearly, thoughts swirling inside her head.

"It's nice to feel the sunshine," he said. "I miss that in the winter months."

Caroline looked at him a moment, then back at the floating barges. She sipped her coffee slowly and watched as the barges and towboat disappeared one-by-one behind the trees lining the bank of the river. Looking towards the bridge, she studied it for a minute.

"Do you also like to come sit in the shadow of the bridge?" she asked Mark, glancing at him and then back up at 'the spot.' The spot he had stood, and she had swerved.

"We're not in the shadow. The shadow is on the other side." he replied, looking at Caroline.

"You know what I mean..." Caroline's tone became flat again. "The shadow of *that night*." She looked out over the river towards the far shore, contemplating, then turned towards Mark. "Why didn't you go ahead and jump?"

"Huh?" Mark startled with her question. "What do you mean?"

"You were up there, standing on the railing, obviously ready to leap and plunge into the water below. Ending it all." She continued to keep her eyes fixed on him. "Why didn't you? Why did you change your mind and come after me?"

Struck by her comment, Mark looked at her. Anger clung to her words and filled her face.

"I..." His mouth hung open, stunned by her question. "I couldn't let someone in need suffer. I had to."

"Why?" she asked. "It's not like you would have had a guilty conscious or anything. You would have been dead. And so would've I." Forgetting, she tried to shrug her shoulders and winced from a streak of pain. "I could've burned up in the car.

I wouldn't have felt a thing. Unconscious. Everything would have been taken care of. No worries."

Mark sat with his lips parted, and one eye squinted towards her. What was she saying? And why? Why was she suddenly thinking this way?

"What...Why...What's going on, Caroline?" Mark asked. "Just the other night...stars colliding...you talked about God intervening. What's this all about?" Mark turned, facing her. He put his hand on her shoulder to get her attention as she looked away out over the water. She shrank from his touch, scooting on the wall.

A lone tear sat on her eyelashes. It seemed undecided about where to go. Caroline looked down river, hiding her face from Mark. Her mouth trembled, and she tried to keep her face from scrunching up. She shook her head. Mark's mouth continued hanging open, dumbfounded. He slid over to her.

"Caroline!" As he wrapped his arms around her, she tried to fight them off. Mark saw the pain on her face as she tried to raise her right arm and shoulder. Her coffee fell to the ground, the lid flew off, and coffee splashed her leg. His arms around her, she finally quit wrestling with him. "Caroline, what on earth did they say to you? Tell me!"

Somewhere through the struggle the tear flung off, but it was quickly replaced by an army of others. Caroline began to weep softly. Mark tried to hold her, but the support of her bones was gone. Her body went limp in his arms, and her torso flopped over his arms. He righted her and leaned her against his body. Holding her, Mark gently rocked her body, trying to calm her.

"Everything okay?" a passerby inquired. "You need me to go for help?" Mark shook his head and thanked him. The man headed on towards the bridge, glancing backwards several times. Mark briefly wondered if the man was one of the homeless people said to be living under the bridge. Then it hit Mark. The bridge. It drew all sorts of people who were lost, alone, homeless, or trying to find themselves or their way.

CHAPTER 12 – BACK TO BUSINESS

Caroline managed to flop over on her belly during the night, laying on her casted arm. The sling was tangled around her arm, but not holding it. The straps holding the sling and her arm to her body came undone, laying this way and that. The remnants of a dream spun in her head. She wondered if it was the culprit, causing her to flip. Maneuvering her good arm beneath her body, she used it to roll onto her side and then her back. As her shoulder landed against the mattress, she felt the pain. The stabbing pricks radiated towards her neck, down towards her shoulder blade, and just below her shoulder. Further down her arm, she felt nothing.

She laid on her back and focused on the ceiling, waiting for the pangs to subside. When she blinked, she felt soreness in her eyes. Reaching with her hand, she felt the puffiness from the crying. She needed a cold wet washcloth but felt no motivation to move to get one. The details of the afternoon before tried to creep back into her thoughts, but she pictured a door closing. More like slamming. Shutting the details out. Sighing, she looked towards the other side of the bed and shook her head. The covers were neatly in place. Mark slept in the other room.

Probably a good thing. With her thrashing in her sleep, she might have beat him with her cast. And, with the words that flew from her mouth afternoon before, he probably wanted nothing more to do with her. She wouldn't blame him. He was probably downstairs trying to figure out how he could get rid of her. Nope. She shut the thoughts off. They were twisting the knob of that closed door.

Movement sounded from the floor below. She smelled coffee. Normally, the aroma of roasted beans enticed her into action, but not today. She closed her eyes, tried to clear her mind, and imagined her body sinking flat into the mattress.

Disappearing into nothingness.

Then she heard the rattle. The rattle of a spoon? A fork? A dish? It got closer. When she felt the bed move, she opened her eyes looking straight up at the ceiling again. Movement in her periphery, made her looked to the left. A tray filled with plates of cut fruit and toast, cups, and a carafe of coffee laid on the bed. The bed shook again as Mark sat on the edge, with one leg bent and the other hanging over the edge to the floor. Without saying a word or even looking at her, he smiled and poured the coffee.

Caroline leaned up on her left arm, and watched Mark add the right amounts of cream and sugar to her coffee. She shook her head. How did he get to know her so well? She sighed, earning a look from him. Still saying nothing, he picked up a blueberry and popped it into his mouth. He picked up his cup and glanced at her over the edge, as he took a sip.

She pushed herself into a sitting position, bent her own leg for balance, and then stole her own blueberry. It was the perfect blend of tart and sweet. As she chewed it, she looked at him with raised eyebrows. Her head felt foggy, almost like she had a hangover. But how could she?

"Not talking to me?" she finally asked.

"No."

"'No,' you are *not* talking to me? Or 'no,' you *are* talking to me?"

"Of course, I'm talking to you." Not looking at her, he picked up a piece of buttered whole wheat toast. "Get some toast while it's still warm." His voice and mood were subdued.

Caroline hesitantly reached for a triangle of toast and bit off the end. Chewing, she noticed Mark's curling hair stuck out in all directions. He still had on his pajama pants and wore a white t-shirt. His feet were bare, and she noticed his second toe was longer than the rest. Little tufts of hair grew on each toe. Curly like his head. Mark Meadows was looking quite cute. Swallowing the toast, she sighed. She really screwed things up.

She realized he wasn't feeling too cute after what she said to him the day before. She wouldn't blame him if he never forgave her for the hurtful words that flew out of her. Why was she so hurtful to the only person who cared about her?

"Toast not any good?" Mark asked.

"No, it's great," she replied, putting it on the tray to get some coffee. Taking a sip, and then another sip, she set the cup down. "I'm sorry." She dropped her hand in her lap and looked at Mark, her mouth straight and her eyes sad. Did he see her remorse?

"Why are you sorry?" Mark picked up a square of honeydew and reached it towards her lips. She took it gently with her teeth. Chewing, her eyes grew wide for a moment. The melon was the perfect state of ripeness. But the sweetness was short-lived, returning her to the gravity of the conversation.

"Because I flipped out on you yesterday," she said after she swallowed the melon. She tried to swallow the guilt that clung in her throat, but it stayed put.

"You're allowed." He got his own honeydew.

"No, I had no right saying the things I did to you. They were mean and hurtful."

"Um…you…uh…so you really didn't really mean what you said?" Mark glanced quickly at her then back to his cup.

"No!" Her expression turned regretful. She set her cup back on the tray. With brows turned inward, she shook her head. "No. No. I didn't mean that. Or the other thing…well…things I said. I was angry. So angry on the inside. Not at you, but I guess I took it out on you. I'm so sorry!" She felt Mark's eyes on her, and she looked up to meet them. Shrugging, she added, "I was so wrapped up in myself. What they told me. How does that saying go? You hurt those that are closest to you? I shouldn't have done that. I'm grateful you were there to pull me out of the car. I'm grateful you're here right now." She tried to pull on a smile, but it resisted. "I should have told you what was going on. I acted like a child."

"You acted like someone who was having a hard time with information," Mark said as he chewed the melon.

Caroline slumped her shoulders and mashing her lips together. "I don't know why I was so surprised. They told me as much when I was in the hospital," she began. "But I suppose experiencing it for myself and then hearing confirmation. It suddenly became real."

"What do you mean? What did they tell you?" Mark held the toast in mid-air.

"My arm and hand are dead." Her flat mouth bent down.

"They told you that?" Mark's eyes grew wide.

"For practical purposes." She looked down at the fingertips poking out from the purple cast. "When they removed the cast, the doctor asked me what kind of pain I'd been having. So, I told him about my shoulder being sore and about the sharp pains when I tried to move it. And I told him I wasn't having any pain in my lower arm and hand. He took this prick tip object and started sticking my arm. I felt nothing. I've been feeling nothing. My fingers have been totally numb since I came home." She rubbed the fingertips. Her good fingers felt them, but her casted fingers had no sense of anything touching them. An odd feeling. Like she was rubbing someone else's fingers. "In the hospital, I thought it was all the pain meds, but after I left and wasn't on anything, the feeling never came back. And I can't even wiggle them. I can wiggle my toes, but not my fingers. They don't move. Nor did my hand when the cast was off."

"Do they know what's causing it?" Mark set the toast back on the plate and dropped his hands in his lap.

Caroline nodded. "Nerve damage. Extensive nerve damage." She began to lift her casted arm, still free from the sling, wincing from pangs in her shoulder. His eyes followed her hand as it moved along the underside of her hidden forearm. "I didn't know that I had staples along through here too. I only saw the ones on the top of my forearm and on my upper arm. Apparently, when the bones shattered, they also cut right through my skin down here. Through the muscle, the tendons, and the nerves. And in my upper arm, one of the major tendons. I forget what they called it. It ripped off, and they re-attached it with a *screw* to my elbow. Plus, it's got tears further on up that they stitched up. That's why they don't want me moving my shoulder. They're afraid it'll come loose." She picked up the sling from the bedcovers, flopping it back down.

Mark shook his head. He listened but did not look directly at her. His eyes were focused on the bed, the pillow, the wall, or something beyond. But not on her. He wet and re-wet his lips.

"They took x-rays and said things are healing, but slowly. The doctor told me it could be six months before my shoulder and the tendon heal so I can move it. But my lower arm…" Caroline looked back down at the purple cast. Moisture crept back into her eyes. She wiped at them with her good hand, sniffling. "With the amount of damage, he said it was 'improbable' that I would get use back. He said that nerves do repair themselves over time, but it could take years." She looked off, trying to remember what else the doctor had told her. There had been so much, and as the doctor had spoken, the words swirled in her head. But she wanted to keep talking. It held the tears at bay. She'd cried enough the day before. "Oh yeah, the muscles. He said that even if the nerves healed 100% percent, which they won't, I'll never have the flexibility with my arm that I had. The pieces of bone cut my arm muscles crossways. Even though he stitched them up, he told me that they'll never be able to stretch like they used to and could even rip again if I put too much force on them. That just adds to the nerve damage."

Mark turned his head, eying the green cast on her foot. "What did the doc say about your foot?"

Following Mark's eyes, she wiggled her toes. The chipped and missing nail polish gave them a 'shabby chic' look. "My foot is healing right on track! Four more weeks, and the cast will come off, and then I'll just have to deal with the boot for a few more weeks!" Smiling, she added, "That was the good news."

"I knew the report wasn't good," Mark said. He reached over

and rubbed her shin. Caroline notice the soft blanket of hair cover now stuck up in all directions. What she'd give for a good shave. Perhaps she'd borrow a razor and some shaving cream and prop her legs up on a chair. She could wipe them off with a wet cloth. She'd have to practice reaching the far side of her right leg.

She shook her head. "No. Not good." She wiped at her eyes again, catching the wetness before drops formed. Sniffling again, she reached for her toast and took a bite. The butter turned white again, but it helped the crunchy bread slide down.

"I was hoping I'd be able to get out of your hair and back on my own. Where-ever and whenever that will be," Caroline said between chewing on another bite. "I'm not sure how I'm going to manage with only one arm."

"Caroline, there's no time limit on you being here. You stay as long as you need to. As long as you want." Mark clasped his hands around his bent leg, his knee upright and his bare foot on the bed. "I am truthfully enjoying your company," he added.

"That is really, really nice of you." She entertained her thoughts quietly, then said, "I guess I need to go see if I can get my driver's license. Or a copy of it. I'm sure I'll need it for when I go to the credit union."

"Credit union? Why do you need to go there?" Curiosity marked his face.

"So, I can get some money to help pay you back for all the food and lodging, not to mention driving me around to appointments." Her eyebrows arched with her words. "Also, I think I'm going to call my boss and see if there is any way I might be able to work remotely." She raised her coffee and paused looking into the cup. While sitting undisturbed, the cream had begun to form a skin on top. She gave the cup a swirl, causing the skin to disappear in the mini tidal wave in the cup. "I'd have to get my computer from my office and all. And I'll need a phone. I can use one hand to type! All I would need is to load Zoom so I could have video conferences with the students."

"You also need to go get your things from the house," Mark added.

Caroline shivered slightly at his words. Thinking about and making plans for moving forward with work and establishing new living arrangements inspired her, but the idea of going back to her house—the mere suggestion of it—instantly thickened the air inside her. She breathed out so she could replace stale air with fresh.

"I don't know where I'd put them," she replied glancing up quickly. "I'd have to get a storage unit or something."

"Not at all. I've got the garage. I rarely park in it. You could put what you're not using in there."

"Mark..." Caroline glanced at him sideways. "Next thing you know, your family is going to be pulling you aside saying, 'that crazy one-armed woman is taking over'!" She said it in jest, but they probably already had!

Mark poured more coffee from the carafe into both his and Caroline's cups. Caroline reached for a spoon to stir hers, as Mark picked up his.

She extending her hand to Mark, leaning over the tray between them. He looked up at her and reached for her hand. He bent his head and kissed her fingers. As he raised his head, he looked at her hand for a moment, and then frowned slightly.

"What's wrong?" she asked. "Are we okay?" She felt an instant pit in her stomach, thinking she'd done something else to jeopardize their friendship. Maybe a growing relationship.

"Your rings..."

"Rings?" She looked confused.

"Did you have wedding rings?"

Caroline glanced down at her hand. "Yes. Yes, I did." Her fingers were absent any adornment. "I had an engagement ring and a wedding ring. And an anniversary ring."

"Did you take them off?"

"Nope." She shook her head holding her bare hand up. "Last

time I saw them was on my hand before the bridge." She looked at Mark, a slight smile on her face, and gave a carefree shrug with her good shoulder. "Oh well. They probably took them off in the ER at the hospital. It's not like I need them! Maybe it's Karma!" In fact, she was quite happy they hadn't made the way into her new life. She hoped she never saw them again. They were meaningless to her. Apparently, they had been for the last ten years. She just didn't realize it.

***

Over the next couple of days, Mark watched Caroline swing into action with renewed energy. He secretly wished he was able to recover from an emotional trauma as quickly as she did. Once the air was cleaned between them, and after they cleaned the tray and finished the coffee, Caroline was on the phone with her boss, ironing out the details of a remote work arrangement. As Caroline struggled to make a list of things she needed from her office, Mark moved the dust mop over the downstairs floor. Passing by the dining room table, he took covert peeks as she awkwardly held the pen forming letters and words on a page of the spiral notebook. For no more practice than she'd had, he thought she did quite well. Once she finished her list, she was back on the phone with her credit union, ordering a new debit card, checking her balance, and changing her address to Mark's. When she ended the call, she carefully penned more notes on the paper.

While Mark cleaned the downstairs bathroom, Caroline offered to gather and sort the laundry. He was glad to see her moving around more and didn't mind the help. After creating piles of whites, darks, and towels, she pulled the covers off the bed in Mark's room and pulled off the sheets. She also shook the pillows out of the pillow cases, created another pile on the floor with the sheets, and went in search of a clean set for the bed.

Entering the upstairs bathroom, she found Mark cleaning the walk-in shower walls. He rubbed the mesh covered side of a windshield washer wand over the large slate tiles on the wall, followed by spraying the wall off with the hand-held shower head. A bucket filled with sudsy water sat on the shower floor by his bare feet. She laughed seeing his jeans rolled up a couple turns to his ankle to keep them from getting wet. The smell of bleach filled the room.

"I've never seen anyone use one of those to clean a shower!" She continued to laugh. "You're quite the sight!"

Mark shrugged, indifferent to the pleasure she found with his cleaning habit. "Hey. It works." Then he added, "I normally do this naked, but with you here..."

"Oh, please! Don't do anything special on my account!" she teased. Shaking her head, she watched as he used the rubber side to squeegee the water off the wall. He paused with every swipe, looking at her and raising his eyebrows, attempting to convince her it was the best way.

"Look at that!" he said, smiling with pride. "No water spots! Completely streak free! See? See?" He pointed with each swipe.

"Mark! You'd couldn't see a water spot on slate tile if you tried!" She continued to laugh. "Hey, where are the clean sheets for your bed?"

"The closet in the hallway," he pointed. Dipping the wand in the bucket, he turned to scrubbing the shower floor. "The only bad part about this is it doesn't get the corners very well." He stood, reaching for his pocket. "That's what this is for!" He held up a toothbrush, showing his pearly whites.

"You're so goofy!" She headed towards the short hallway. "And I'm hiding my toothbrush. I'm beginning to see you're a little OCD on the cleanliness thing!"

Mark heard her tug on one of the two doors opposite the bathroom a couple times. It didn't budge. "The other door," he said.

"Oh! Here we go!" The door to the left revealed linens of all sorts, toiletries, and cleaning supplies. "Found them." She had no problem differentiating his sheets from the ones that went in the flowery bedroom. "Hey, what's behind the locked door? How did I never notice these doors?" she called to Mark.

"Because I've always had the towels out." Mark peeked out of the shower. "That's just another room. It's not finished all the way."

"Oh, wow! This place has all sorts of space!"

Mark watched her pull a set of charcoal grey sheets from the shelf and search for pillow cases. Satisfied that she found what she needed, he returned to the shower floor. "Let me know if you need help!"

He expected her to question the unfinished room, but she hadn't. Not that there was anything really to it. He simply hadn't determined its purpose, and decided the paint and flooring could be done once the space had a need. He didn't exactly want to tell her that his visions for the room was a nursery. To become a baby's room someday. When he met the right woman. Until then, it sat dormant, waiting to blossom.

By the time he emerged from the bathroom, Caroline managed to stretch the fitted sheet on the mattress after several tries, spread and tucked the flat sheet, replaced the comforter, and stood looking puzzled at the pillows and pillowcases. He folded his arms and leaned against the doorway, watching to see how she tackled that challenge. She raised her knee and placed it on the pillow holding it from sliding as she used her one hand to open the pillowcase and guide it on the pillow. She went back and forth from side to side inching the case onto the pillow. Once it was a third of the way on, she picked up the pillow and bent down, taking one side of the pillowcase in her teeth. Shaking the other side with her hand, she encouraged the pillow to slide into the case. Crooked, she flipped the pillow and grabbed the other side with her teeth, giving another shake. After several attempts, only an inch or so of the pillow was still visible, and the corners of the pillow case poked up like horns. She sighed.

"Need help?" Mark asked. She turned and eyed him realizing he delighted in her struggle.

"Oh, sure! Just stand there!" She plopped on the edge of the bed. Another sigh exited her. Mark went over and picked up the pillow and straightened the case and shook the pillow the rest of the way in. He did the same with the others.

"You're getting there! You get an 'A' for effort!" he smiled at her. "Don't dwell on what you can't do. Be glad for what you can do!" He pointed towards the bed and the piles of clothes on the floor. "I'll get the bed in the other room!"

Downstairs, she loaded one of the piles from the laundry basket Mark carried downstairs. One by one she put the clothes in the washer tub. Then she measured detergent in the cap, pouring it in over the clothes and turning on the machine. That she could do. It took a little longer than usual, but she got it done.

"Apparently, laundry is my thing!" She smiled at Mark as she came out of the laundry room. He held the basket full of the towels and sheets. "Though I don't know how well I will do folding things!" She moved to the side so Mark could set the basket on the dryer.

"You know, Miss Caroline," Mark approached her as she leaned against the counter. "I rather like doing domestic things with you." He stepped close to her and put his arms around her.

"You do?" she asked, raising her brows, putting her arm around his.

"Yes, I do. It makes me feel …" he paused, smiling at her. "Domestic!" he finished.

She broke out laughing. "You are so gifted with your words!" Then, she looked at him, her expression turning serious. "I could never have gone home. I don't know what I was thinking. Even with those hired aides…those girls…I couldn't have taken care of myself. It would have been a disaster!"

"No. I don't think you realized how much help you were going to need." Mark pulled her towards him. She rested her face against his chest and hugged him with her one arm. He felt her sigh again, and her casted arm pressed against his stomach.

"Thank you, again!" She nuzzled her head against him. "Thank you for pushing me also. For helping me realize what I can do! I have a feeling that I'll be learning to do a lot of things differently." She glanced down at the purple cast hiding in the sling.

***

On Monday, Mark helped Caroline into the truck, and they drove to Flemingsburg. Caroline was intent on getting a copy of her driver's license or a new one. She was desperate to have her identification back. She didn't necessarily want that identity, but it would do for the moment. The best Mark could figure, she didn't feel like a real person without it.

As Caroline limped towards the counter at the clerk's office, a woman turned and watched Caroline with wide-eyes and a dropped jaw.

"Caroline?" the woman asked. "Is that you?"

"Hi, Lisa," Caroline puffed, out of breath from the trek from the truck across the street. "Yes, it's me! I know…you barely recognize me! All mangled up!" Caroline did her best to apply some make-up and fix her hair before heading out into public, but Mark gathered by her reaction in the mirror, the results were not what she expected. The old Caroline did not emerge. She'd made a sour face into the mirror, but Mark thought she looked stunning as she was.

"No! It's not that!" The woman scanned Caroline's condition. "Well, I guess it is that, but you look so much younger! Like you did when we were in high school!"

"Oh, Lisa! That's so nice of you to say!" Caroline blushed a bit. "I'll take any kind lies to help me feel better about myself!" She glanced humbly down at her casts.

"Oh, no lie! You do!" Tilting her head slightly, Lisa asked, "How can I help you today?"

"I am needing a copy of my driver's license. As you may have heard, I was in an accident and everything I had burned up in the car."

"Yes! You are so fortunate to be alive! Look at you!" the

woman replied. "Normally, I have to have identification," she inserted a nervous laugh. "But I can vouch for you! Known you all our lives!" Lisa moved to the computer and began clicking on the keyboard, studying the screen. "Do you just want a copy of the license you had, or do you want to take a new picture?"

"A copy would be just fine. I'll probably be back in within the next month to change the name anyway. I'll do a new picture then. When I'm more presentable."

"Oh, you look great!" the woman replied smiling at Caroline, taking notice of Mark who stood next to Caroline. Mark gave a quick smile. Lisa's eyes passed between the two before she resumed clicking on the computer. "It'll take a minute for it to print, and that will be twelve dollars for the copy."

The card printer made noises as it went to work reproducing Caroline's driver's license. Lisa snuck brief glances at Caroline and Mark as she waited for the card to emerge. Mark could see that her mind was actively trying to fill in the missing pieces of who the strange man was with her friend. He pulled out his wallet and handed Lisa the correct change. Thanking him, she slipped the bills into a drawer, her eyes again bouncing between the two.

"Here you go! It's still warm!" Lisa giggled handing the card to Caroline. "How's it look?"

Caroline stared at the woman in the corner of the card. Mark looked over her shoulder, catching a glance of her pre-accident picture. She looked beautiful. But very made-up. And perfectly miserable! Caroline held the card out to Mark to slip into his pocket.

"Thank you, Lisa! This was a lot easier than I thought it would be!"

"Oh, you're welcome! And when you're ready to make the change, you know where we are!"

Caroline started to turn away from the counter when Lisa spoke up again.

"Oh, by the way, have you been to see your parents, Caroline? They've been asking around about how you are doing. You know, how rumors take a town! I'm sure they'd love to see you. You know, to make sure you're okay and all!" By Lisa's words, Mark immediately knew she was aware of Caroline's estrangement with her family.

"No, not yet. But I will." Caroline looked back and forced upturned lips. "Thanks for letting me know, Lisa!" As she limped towards the door, Mark stayed closed and put his hand on her lower back. An action he knew would send the women in the clerk's office into a gossip frenzy once they exited the building. And he was quietly satisfied that someone other than himself brought up the topic of Caroline's family. It gave him another avenue to approach her about the topic.

In the truck, Mark started the engine and then pulled the plastic card from his pocket, looking at the 'old Caroline.' Caroline looked over at him and shook her head disparagingly. After a quick sideways glance, Mark laughed.

"Yeah, we're going to have to do something about this picture," he said. "This is definitely not you. You left this woman on the bridge. You're much more beautiful." He shot her a smile. She sighed and shook her head in denial. Slipping the card back into his pocket, he asked, "Where to now?" He almost asked, *"your parents?"* but decided there would be a more appropriate time for that.

"Do you mind if we run to the university? My office?" Caroline's question was framed with raised brows. "My boss said she'd pull together things for me to pick up. And there are a few things in my office I'll need. That way I can start back next Monday."

"Sure," Mark agreed. "Do you think she's had enough time to get things together?"

"Oh, yeah." Caroline nodded. "There's really not much. My laptop, a catalog. Some paperwork and reference sheets. It wouldn't even fill a box!"

"Remind me," Mark glanced at Caroline. "While we're out, I need to swing by Beth's to pick up the turkey."

"Turkey?" She shot him a look, frowning.

"Yes," he glanced back at her. "Beth's got the turkey thawing in her fridge."

Caroline continued to give him a clueless look.

"For Thanksgiving…"

"Oh! I'd forgotten all about that!" She looked away in embarrassment.

"I'm on turkey and dressing duty." He spoke proudly about his contribution to the meal. "Mom used to do the turkey every Thanksgiving, and when she started getting worse, she handed the carving knife over to me. I've been cooking the turkey ever since." Then he added, "And the ham at Christmas, and the lamb at Easter."

"Lamb?" She scrunched her nose up. "You'd eat a little bitty cute lamb? Ugh! You're a monster!"

"Of course!" Mark laughed. "No more a monster than for eating a turkey. Or a piggie!"

Caroline shuddered at the thought. "Where do you have Thanksgiving? At Beth's?"

"Yep." Mark turned onto the highway towards Morehead. "The whole crew will be there. You'll meet the rest of them."

"Didn't I already meet the 'whole crew'?" Her tone was apprehensive. "There's more?"

"Yep. Larry's other two kids and their kids, and a couple of aunts and uncles." Mark shot her a grin. "If we play our cards right, we might be able to eat at the kiddie table!"

Caroline giggled, watching the farms pass the window.

"What did you do normally do for Thanksgiving?" Mark asked. "A big meal with Steven's people?"

"Oh, no. Steven's family lived up in the northeast." She replied, continuing to gaze out the window. "A few times we went to 'friends' houses, once to a neighbor. But mostly we just went out to eat."

"You never went to his parents?" Mark asked. "They never came to your place for the holidays?"

"Nope!" Caroline replied. "Never even met them. They were travelling abroad when we got married. They were always here or there. Never even talked to them. I actually joked one time with Steven that they didn't even exist. He got so mad and so hurt. I never did that again. It was a very sore subject with him."

"Maybe they didn't," Mark suggested. He didn't look at her. He didn't have to. He knew she was contemplating the comment.

CHAPTER 13 – COMMUNICATION

It had been a while since Mark was in Morehead, so once they approached campus, Caroline became navigator, guiding him to the building she worked in. She directed him to pull his truck over parking in a 'loading zone' spot behind one of the buildings. Helping her out, he walked with her to the top of an outdoor flight of stairs that tunneled between two buildings. Spying through the windows, he saw nothing but shelves and shelves of books. Mark remembered it was the library. He couldn't recall ever actually being in the place.

"Are you okay with these steps?" Mark asked, shooting her an unsure look. She simply nodded and grabbed ahold of the tube railing that divided the concrete staircase into an 'up' and 'down.' She took her time with each step, Mark at her side in case she lost balance and ready to steady her. Reaching the bottom, they emerged from the tunnel on the other side of the buildings. Instead of walls of concrete and brick, they faced lawns and large, grand leafless trees.

Caroline hobbled towards a doorway to another brick building, and Mark held the door open for her. As he stepped inside behind her, he saw a narrow flight of stairs going down and another flight of stairs going up to a landing followed by another flight of stairs. Caroline paused, taking a deep breath.

"They apparently never heard the word 'handicapped'!" Mark shook his head. "How do they get by with this?" He pictured a person in a wheelchair.

"Oh, there's an ADA entrance, but it's around the front of the building. It goes into the first floor, and you can access the elevator," she replied. Pointing up the stairs, she added, "which is right there on the landing." Pointing to the down-flight of stairs, "Or, down there! It's just as easy for us to take the stairs." Taking a couple steps up, Caroline commented, "You never truly understand what a disabled person goes through until you're in their shoes. Or *shoe!*"

Mark shook his head in disbelief, but the buildings were old. They had to be retrofitted to accommodate the laws and the needs. It wasn't an easy task. He knew for himself, having built several wheelchair ramps for customers. As Caroline held onto the railing to the left of the stairs, Mark followed her up three sections of stairs and through a heavy metal door. Caroline breathed hard as the door closed behind them. The steps were taller than conventional steps, and the three short flights also left Mark searching for air.

The hallway was not as narrow as the stairway and was lined with doors on each side. Some were open, some were closed. Halfway down the hall, Caroline stopped at an open door and leaned on the door frame. Mark stood behind her staying in the hall, giving her some space.

"Hey, Theresa!" Caroline said into the room. Mark saw a slightly heavyset woman sitting on the other side of a desk with her side to the door. She looked up from a set of computer screens.

"Caroline!" The woman turned, removing reading glasses. "O!M!G!" came from bright pink lips, as the tip of her reading glasses landed between her teeth. She looked over Caroline from head to toe, shaking her head. "Caroline, I had NO idea! When you described your injuries…Oh, my!"

"I'm actually doing a lot better than I look," Caroline replied.

Mark cleared his throat. *Not entirely true!* It earned him a quick look over Caroline's shoulder. He'd known Caroline only three weeks, and she was already giving him 'the look'! What was it with women?

"I've got this, Theresa! I am so excited to be getting back to work and doing something useful! Thank you so much for allowing me to work remotely!"

"Well, we did it during COVID, so it won't be much different." Theresa's tone was encouraging. "Are you able to use your hand at all?" She pointed to Caroline's fingers hanging out of the cast.

"Not right now." Caroline touched her lifeless fingers. "The doctor said there was some nerve damage, and it could take six months to heal. Plus, I'm not supposed to be moving my shoulder right now. Torn ligament and tendons."

"Wow!" Theresa replied. She laid her glasses on a pile of papers on her desk and rose from her chair. "Well, let's go to your office. I gathered up a bunch of stuff you might need." As she approached her office doorway, she looked at Mark, saying, "I see you brought the brawn to carry things!"

Caroline laughed, looking at Mark. "Yes! I'm sorry! This is my friend, Mark. He's the one I told you about."

Theresa stopped just outside the doorway. "Oh! You're the one!" she addressed Mark. She obviously heard the 'hero' story. She held out her hand. "Theresa Jones, Caroline's boss and confidant! Nice to meet you!" Mark shook her hand and smiled.

He followed Caroline and Theresa further down the hallway and through a zigzag in the corridor, stopping at a door located off a large open area filled with computers. Unlocking the door and flicking the light, Theresa led them into a small room. A wooden mission style desk separated the room, and a matching hutch ran along the wall. Opposite the door were two windows outfitted with mini-blinds, open to provide light to the plants that occupied the window ledge and a metal plant stand sitting beside. Someone had been watering the plants as they were alive and thriving, not shriveled from neglect. On the wall not sporting the desk hutch were three prints, each with different views: a French café, bistro, and restaurant. The motif of burgundy, blue and tan brought the three prints together, adding a splash of color to the otherwise 'beige' office. A tan area rug with hints of blue, burgundy, and brown covered the industrial tile floor. Mark had sudden insight into the old Caroline's style and taste. A cardboard banker's box with matching lid sat on top of the desk.

"I put your laptop, cords, mouse, catalog, and other things I thought you would need in here," Theresa laid her hand on the box. "Of course, you'll probably want to look around and get anything else you think you'll need. I didn't know if you'd be coming or just sending someone." She flapped her eyelashes at Mark and smiled.

Caroline limped over to the box and removed the cover. With her left hand, she began rooting through the contents, and then looked up. "Looks like everything I need is here," she said, scanning her desk and overhead shelves. "I don't have a very large work area, so I don't need a lot. Just the essentials!"

"Oh! I almost forgot!" Theresa said. "Because you are off on family leave act and doctor's orders, Human Resources will need something from your doctor stating you can return to working remote. But not in the office, driving and all."

"I can get that. I'll have the doctor's office email something to you to forward to HR," Caroline said, as if no problem. Mark wondered whether the doctor would actually release her to work at home. "Oh, crap!" Caroline blurted out, her hand landing on top of her head.

"What's wrong?" Mark and Theresa asked simultaneously, staring at Caroline's scrunched up face.

"My paycheck!" Her hand moved to her mouth. "It's still being direct deposited into our joint bank account! Oh! I've got to talk to Payroll and have them switch everything over to the credit union!"

"It'll be okay," Theresa reassured her. "Just give the Payroll Office a call. They may need you to sign something, but I am sure you can do it digitally!" Looking down at Caroline's boot, she added, "You don't need to be trekking across campus with that on, that's for sure!"

Mark picked up the banker's box from the desk as Caroline and Theresa discussed more of the remote work arrangement and then said their goodbyes. The two women shared a brief hug as they reached the door to the stairwell. Mark guessed Theresa was the hugger, as he hadn't seen Caroline freely offering hugs during the last three weeks. She sought her hugs when needed and did so cautiously. As Mark followed Caroline down the stairs, he followed with the box in hand, wondering what type of relationship existed between her and Steven. He assumed they weren't cuddly or big huggers. Steven didn't seem the type, and Mark imagined there were no outward displays of affection on a regular basis. He guessed those were only for show when they did occur.

When they got back to the truck, still parked partly on the sidewalk with the hazard lights blinking, Mark helped Caroline into the passenger seat. She was winded and breathed hard from scaling the outdoor stairway between the buildings. He placed the banker's box in the seat behind her and got settled into the driver's seat. Surrendering his cell phone to Caroline, she immediately dialed a number to remedy her paycheck issue.

"Yes, email me the authorization," Caroline said to an unheard voice on the other end. "I'll sign it and send it back. Thanks, bye." Clicking the phone off, she continued to stare at the device.

"You know, I didn't think about it until now, but I'm going to need a phone!" She looked up at Mark. "I can't keep using yours! You need it for your own business!"

Mark's eyebrows raised, but he remained silent. He waited for further instructions, but Caroline seemed lost in thought. She stared at the phone, but once again her eyes darted this way and that. Mark came to recognize this behavior as a sign that Caroline was strategizing.

"Are we stopping at the cell phone shop?" Mark broke the silence after they reached the end of the road and paused at the stoplight. Caroline looked at him with imploring eyes.

"I'd love to, but I haven't got my new debit card from the credit union yet. They said it could take a week to ten days!" Caroline sighed, looking out the window.

"I'll spot you the cash," Mark said. "You'll need it for work. We might as well stop and get it while we're out!"

"Has anyone told you that you're pretty amazing?" Caroline asked with a half-smile.

"Nope. Never." Mark's answer was in jest, but then he began

thinking about it. When was the last time someone said he was amazing? He couldn't remember. It had to have been years before his divorce. Surely Jennifer had told him that at one time. Maybe?

***

The cellphone store was busy, but Caroline and Mark found an associate as soon as they entered the shop. The associate, Danny, took them to a station on the far end of the store. The station was a raised counter with a computer and a card swipe. Caroline noticed all the stations were identical with customers clustering around them. At one station a mother debated phones with a teenage girl. The teenager had a clear vision of her needs and wasn't willing to settle for less. A younger girl stood by observing the exchange, probably taking mental notes for when she was old enough. Caroline stood as Mark began describing Caroline's phone requirements to the associate.

"She wants an android," Mark said, glancing at Caroline. "She's not an iPhone fan. And it's got to have all the bells and whistles. She'll be using it for work, so it needs plenty of data and to be able to Zoom. That sort of thing."

"Then I would recommend our latest Samsung Galaxy," Danny replied. "It's got great functionality, and I think you'll be very pleased with it." He looked at Caroline for approval.

"What's it going to cost?" Caroline asked, glancing again at Mark. Mark nodded his head toward Danny, signaling to Caroline: 'go with it.'

Danny clicked on the computer. Caroline watched as his finger struck the mouse repeatedly scrolling down. "With the plan and the cost of the phone broken down into monthly payments, you're looking at about sixty dollars a month. Of course, there'll be taxes and all the surcharges they add on."

Caroline thought for a moment. That would be her only expense, so she could afford it. But what might her other expenses be in time? Who knows? It might be a while before she got a handle on that. She looked down at her arm, and then back up at Danny.

"Okay, that sounds good. I'll do it." She needed the phone for work. Period. End of debate.

"I'll be right back with your phone!" Danny disappeared quickly into a back room.

Caroline turned to Mark, who was sneaking glances at the mother and the two girls at the nearby station. A strange look captured his face as he listened to the teenager plead her case with the mother.

"Mom! If you get me that one, then I can use it for school!"

"They don't let you have phones in class," the mother said sternly.

"But they do! That's why I need that phone!" the teen implored. "It's different in high school! They encourage us to use our phones! I'm one of the only ones without one!"

"Christa! Do you expect me to believe that they let students sit in class texting the whole time?" the mother asked.

"No, Mom! We're not allowed to text! We use the phones to look up stuff and answer questions!"

Danny returned with a box, which he began to open and unpack. A slim black phone emerged from a foam sleeve, and he used a small key-like device to pop out the slot for the SIM card. He worked quickly and with sleight of hand like a magician. Caroline wondered how many phones he handled in a day's time. Obviously, quite a few, as Caroline could not keep up with what the associate did. Once he got it physically together, he began clicking on the computer again, referring back and forth to the phone. It was lit up and active.

"You know, I'm just thirty, almost thirty-one, and I already have no clue what you're doing!" Caroline told the young man. Technology was the playground for the young. She already felt like she'd aged out of being 'in-the-know' about such things. She turned to Mark, "But, you're still really good with that type of thing!" Her compliment pulled Mark's sideways glances away from the mother and girls.

"I try to keep up," Mark said in a low voice.

"Okay, so I've got your number assigned." Danny scribbled a number on a white area of the phone box. "And I just need some personal information to activate your account and phone."

Caroline answered the young man's questions as he typed the information into the computer. When it came to the address, she turned to Mark. "What's the address of your place?"

"Huh?" Mark looked back from the conversation at the nearby station. "Oh, I'm sorry!" Mark gave Danny the address, and then indicated he would be paying the initial fee, digging out his credit card from his wallet.

As they passed back through the door of the store, returning to the cold, Caroline breathed in the cool, fresh air. Though they hadn't been in the store for more than fifteen minutes, it got warm inside with all the customers. She noticed Mark exhaled deeply, a note of relief to it. Like he was thankful to be outside. He helped Caroline into the truck and quickly jumped in beside her, cranking the engine.

"Was getting a phone that grueling?" Caroline asked Mark. "I'm paying you back, remember!"

"Huh?" Mark replied, twisting the steering wheel to back out of the parking spot. Mark seemed anxious to get on their way; however, his thoughts already traveled somewhere else entirely.

"You okay?" she asked. "You seem distracted or something."

"Uh. Yeah, I'm okay," he said, glancing in the rearview mirror. Pulling up to the road, he checked both directions before pulling out back towards Maysville.

"Well, at least I won't be bothering you for your phone all the time!" Caroline said holding her new device up. She clicked it on and began checking out its features. She laid it on her leg and used her left hand to scroll and explore. As the truck headed towards home—well, Mark's home—Caroline noticed

Mark was unusually quiet. She looked up several times and noticed he drove with his right hand while his left elbow was propped on the door and his hand was on his mouth. His fingers played with his lips. A telltale sign. He was in deep thought, contemplating.

"Are you upset that I've got a phone and am starting back to work on Monday?" she asked him, trying to poke for a cause for the sudden mood change.

Mark swung his head briefly in her direction and then back at the road. After a few seconds, he replied, "No. Not at all. I think it's great that you're trying to get back to normal."

"Yeah, whatever 'normal' is!" Caroline snorted. "I don't think 'normal' is something I am going to experience for quite some time." She watched Mark for a moment. He'd returned to his previous stature. Driving with his right, his left propped and fingers squeezing and contorting his lips. Yep. She'd let him stay in whatever world he'd plunged for a while. She went back to her phone, studying its capabilities, while semi-consciously searching for what triggered his silent disposition.

When they reached the duplex, Mark helped Caroline out of the truck in his ordinary way and got the banker's box from the back seat. As they entered the duplex, Caroline pulled off her jacket, slipping it over the phone in her hand, and leaned up against the front door to close it. Mark carried the box toward the dining room table, and then stopped and turned.

"Where do you want this?" he asked.

She looked up from hanging the jacket on the closet door handle. Mark would hang it when he hung his own. She noticed the serious expression that filled his face, was immediately struck by the thought: *Is his upset with me because I'm moving more in on him? Taking over his space?* She felt some color drain from her face.

"Um, I guess just set it on the floor for now," she mumbled. The skin between her eyes folded as her brows reached inwards. Confused. Perplexed. *Was she over-stepping?*

She and Mark hadn't ever approached the topic of her

residence there. The arrangement they had. There wasn't one. He'd initially brought her there because she was locked out of her own house. Maybe she needed to call Emily and see if it was possible for her to return to the house. To live. To give Mark's home back to him.

Mark situated the box on the floor under the stairs, out of the way, and then passed Caroline on his way to the closet. He didn't look at her but looked past her. When he finished hanging the coats, he turned and said, "I'm going out to the freezer to find something for supper."

"Okay, that sounds great." Caroline watched him head towards the kitchen as she lowered herself in one of the chairs by the fireplace. Feeling a chill in the room, she looked at the fireplace, wishing she knew how to light it. She studied the knobs but gave up the idea of experimenting. It was gas. Propane? Natural? She didn't know, but she'd leave it to Mark who knew better what to do. Instead, she pulled the throw from the back of the chair and draped it around her the best she could. Looking at the phone she saw it was almost four in the afternoon. The day was almost spent, and so was she.

Mark reappeared in the kitchen with a frozen chunk in hand. He began running water and searched in the cabinet retrieving a bowl. Waving his fingers under the water, he dropped the frozen chunk into the bowl and filled it with warm water. Caroline then watched Mark head towards the pantry and heard the rustling of a pill bottle. He turned back to the sink and scooped a handful of water to help something go down.

"Do you want something to drink?" Mark called to her. Caroline looked up and saw that Mark leaned on the bar counter facing her direction. He gazed down at the counter, waiting for her response.

"Yes, thanks!" she replied, trying to sound upbeat. "Could we have hot tea? I am feeling a chill."

"Sure." Mark nodded his head, turning towards the stove. He rattled through the cabinets for mugs and tea. "The usual?" he asked. His tone was flat. As flat as his expression.

"Whatever you are in the mood for, Mark." Caroline wondered what he would select given his abrupt change from earlier in the day. She half watched him in the kitchen and half surfed the Internet on her phone. Whatever was troubling him, he'd taken a pill. She supposed it was good that he recognized he needed something, but this only enhanced her curiosity of what set him off.

Five minutes later, Mark walked towards her with two mugs of steaming tea, one plain and one doctored with cream and sugar. He kept the plain for himself, handing her the other.

"You're cold?" he asked with raised brows. He looked from the throw to the fireplace.

"Uh-huh."

"Do you..." before he got the words out, Caroline responded.

"The fire? I would love that! You've not had it on yet!"

Mark bent down, pausing a moment before twisting a knob. After a clicking sound, flames burst up surrounding the faux logs. He adjusted the flame height and then took his tea to the chair opposite Caroline. Sampling the tea, he rested his mug on the arm of the chair and rested his eyes on Caroline.

His eyes were red. Had he been crying? When he was in the kitchen? When he was at the freezer? Caroline sipped her own tea, feeling its warmth and sweetness finding her cool spots.

"So, what are we having tonight?" Caroline asked, skirting around the questions she really wanted to ask: *Why are your eyes red? What's bothering you?*

"I pulled some tilapia fillets out."

"That sounds good." Caroline smiled at him. "How do you usually prepare it?"

Mark let out a sigh before answering. "Um, one of my favorites is with onions, tomatoes, garlic, capers, and olives."

Caroline raised her brows, "That sounds very interesting. I don't think I've ever had it that way. When I've had it, it's either been fried or baked with lemon." Then she added, "I want to help!"

Mark replied with a nod. He took another sip of his tea,

slurping it a bit. He continued to look at Caroline, but his eyes told her his thoughts were elsewhere.

"Have I upset you, Mark? With my bringing work stuff in?" She could not resist asking any longer. Caroline figured this was the best approach to decoding his mood.

"What?" He looked at her and frowned. "No. No, not at all. Like I said, it's good for you to get back to work. Why would I mind that?" His frown dissipated, leaving him straight-faced.

"Well, I am just wondering if you're upset that I'm like… taking over your space? Cluttering things up?" She gave him a tentative smile. "You know, maybe you're getting a little tired of me being here. We never actually discussed things."

"Not at all. I love you being here. Actually." He looked towards the bouncing flames. "What do you mean, 'never discussed things'?"

"Well," Caroline began. "You brought me here because I had nowhere else to go. Locked out of my house. We never discussed for how long I'd be here, or what you wanted for my staying here. I've been quite the burden to you. Taking me around and all your help."

"I don't want anything. You're not a burden," he replied looking at her. "I've told you that. I *enjoy* you being here. You can stay as long as you want and bring whatever you need."

"Thank you, Mark." She sipped her tea, looking at him over the rim of her mug. "I guess I am feeling insecure. I just need reassurance." She glanced down at her casted arm. "I've always been so independent. And learning how to do things again… well, it's shaken my confidence, I suppose."

"I completely understand," Mark said, looking at her. "I absolutely do."

***

"It's times like this that a finger of bourbon would taste really good," Mark said rinsing the tilapia. Patting them dry with paper towel, he turned and laid the fillets in the oiled pan. Caroline stood next to him, ready for instructions as he continued, "I used to enjoy a small drink as I cooked. It was relaxing. And it made me feel grown up!" He gave a laugh. "The problem is, one finger quickly turns to two fingers, and then three..." He gave her another flat look.

Caroline nodded. "Do you ever have a glass of wine?"

He looked at her and chuckled. "The problem with a glass of wine is it..."

"Becomes two glasses of wine and then the whole bottle!" Caroline finished for him.

"Similar problem?" he asked, a corner of his mouth trying to form a smile. The whitish cast to his lower face from dried salty tears made his skin taut.

Caroline smiled and shrugged. "Oh, I've exceeded my limits a few times. But every time was completely provoked!" she justified.

"The problem with any type of alcohol is it's a depressant, which defeats the purpose of taking all the medications to keep me uplifted and happy." Mark opened the jar of green olives and scooped out several onto Caroline's cutting board. He then did the same with the Kalamata olives. "These are pitted." He pointed to the Kalamatas. "Just slice them all in half."

He cut several thin slices from a red onion and then quartered them. Then he turned to the Roma tomatoes and chopped them into even-sized chunks. Caroline pressed her knife through the center of the olives, lengthwise.

"Oops!" she said, followed by a giggle. As she pressed down on one olive, it shot out from under the knife blade past Mark, hit the wall, and landed on the floor. Spreading the onions over the fillets, Mark paused and gave her a look. Still giggling, she held the knife to another olive, saying, "Too bad we don't have a miniature golf course!"

Mark leaned over to retrieve the projectile olive and tossed it into the sink, destined to become garbage disposal food.

"You're getting dangerous with that," he pointed to her knife. A partial smile peeked out.

"Hey, you've got to cut me some slack here! One-handed cutting!" Caroline paused to plop an olive in her mouth, then she held one out before Mark's lips. He took it from between her fingers with his teeth, grinning at her before it disappeared.

"So, what's next?" she asked, leaning into him and peering into the pan. Mark spread chunks of tomato evenly across the tilapia and onions.

"Olives, please?"

Caroline scooted the cutting board covered with halved olives towards the pan. Mark distributed the olives, again making sure there was even coverage. The last to go on were the capers. After a spotty layer of capers, Mark drizzled a little of the brine from the caper jar over the fillets, followed by a drizzle of olive oil.

"Is our oven at three-fifty?" he glanced at his helper. Caroline stretched to see the wall oven temperature.

"Yes, indeed, Chef!" She saluted him with her left hand. Her eagerness to help in the kitchen made him feel good. Just being in the kitchen brought him a sense of peace, and the slicing, stirring, grating, sauteing, and other cooking actions seemed to quiet undesirable thoughts. Staying busy was the secret. Cooking and creating tasty and visually pleasing meals was incomparable to anything else he did. It relaxed him. It reminded him of good times. The kitchen was the heart of the home. It was where he grew up. It was where amazing things happened.

"Well, these go in for about a half hour." Mark slid the pan on the oven rack and closed the door. "We'll check them. I like my fish done. None of that gooey white stuff."

"As do I!" she said. "You said we're having rice with the fish?" Caroline knelt to get a pan and lid from one of the lower cabinets. She pulled out the pan and reached it up, setting it on the counter, then grabbed the counter to pull herself back up. Instead, she flopped back on her bottom. "Ugh!"

Mark looked at her from the pantry, a plastic container of

rice in his hand. He shook his head. "You really are a danger in the kitchen..." His voice trailed off as he put the container on the counter, and helped her up. He tugged her off the floor back to a standing position. As she regained her balance, he continued to clutch her hand and stepped towards her, pulling her close to him.

Pausing a moment, Mark looked into her eyes. "Thank you, Caroline." She started to speak, but he covered her mouth with his, kissing her. Letting go of her hand, his hands landed on her hips, pulling her towards him until she pressed against his body. She returned his kiss eagerly and wrapped her small hand wrapped around his neck, gently assuring his lips didn't leave hers. He grasped her tighter, his hands finding the soft tender skin of her sides. Without thinking, his hand slid up under her shirt and found her breast. He felt her body tense, and she kissed him more vigorously. Realizing where his hand was, he felt himself flush and abruptly moved his hands away. To her backside. As their kiss slowed and their lips parted, Mark's mouth lingered near Caroline's.

He whispered, "I'm sorry..." He was already beating himself up for touching her.

She looked into his eyes, seeing them fill with guilt, and whispered, "I'm not."

CHAPTER 14 – THANKSGIVING

Caroline was apprehensive about the whole Thanksgiving celebration. While she'd not voiced it to Mark, she hadn't felt entirely comfortable at the family Sunday dinner. Of course, tensions were high for everyone that day. Mark was anxious about telling his family the truth about the money. On top of that, he'd brought her, a stranger, to dinner and to witness his confession about personal family matters. Sure, they had regarded her with caution. That was a normal reaction. But Dennis Meadows' discussion about Mark had not set well with her. She planned to keep her distance as much as possible from the man, never mind be left alone with him.

Slipping into her lounge pants, she thought about what she would wear to Thanksgiving dinner. The lounge pants were fine for right then, but judging how everyone dressed for the Sunday dinner, she assumed they would all be more formally dressed for the Thanksgiving occasion. She had nothing dressy to wear. What could she possible squeeze into with two casts? Glancing in the dresser mirror, she paused looking at herself.

She ran her fingers through her angry curls, calming them down. And then studied her breasts. They weren't huge, thank heavens, but they were big enough to be noticed for what they were. Her youth still on her side, she was able to wear the t-shirt and other tops without fear of them sagging to her belly button. She still felt the warmth of Mark's hand as he had touched her breast. She assumed he'd done it inadvertently, but once his palm made contact, it was as though he'd pushed a button that set off an explosion of feelings and emotions inside her. It had taken her breath yet breathed life into her just the same. She couldn't recall her body ever responding like that to Steven. Not ever. Straightening the bottom edge of the t-shirt over the lounge pants, she nodded at the woman in the mirror and exited the room to make her slow decent down the stairs.

The smell of butter hit her first. Then the coffee. Followed by the savory fragrances of sage, thyme, rosemary, and garlic. Her stomach instantly growled. As she reached the floor, she let go of the railing and headed with her signature limp towards the kitchen. After a few weeks practice with the booted foot, her balance was much better, so she'd abandoned the cane.

A cup of coffee sat on the bar counter. A sliver of steam rose indicating it was freshly poured. Mark's back was to her as he stirred something sizzling in a pan. Tapping the wooden spoon on the side of the skillet to knock food particles off, he propped the spoon on the rim of the pan.

"Good morning!" she called as she entered the kitchen area. She reached for a mug and poured some of her own steaming brew. "Where's the birdie?" She looked around the kitchen for the turkey.

"In the oven."

"But you're just making the dressing..." Her frown announced her confusion. She went to the refrigerator for the cream. "Aren't you going to stuff the turkey?"

"It is stuffed." Mark's mouth formed a smirk as he reached for his coffee. "Just not with dressing."

She squinted her eyes at him, opening drawers looking for a spoon. She'd been there for weeks, and she still couldn't remember which drawer held the flatware. Adding two dollops of sugar after the cream, she stirred her mixture.

"Chunks of apples, onions, and butternut squash with spices."

"Huh?" She sipped her coffee, the creases still riding between her eyes.

"That's what I put in the turkey. My family seems to have this notion that the dressing from inside a turkey will cause sudden death if eaten. Arsenic. So, I bake dressing balls instead, and fill the cavity of the turkey with things that give off moisture and flavor to keep the bird moist."

"Oh." She took another sip, thinking. It seemed wasteful.

"Do you do anything with the apples and stuff?" Waste was unlike Mark.

"That will become a tasty apple squash bisque topped with nutmeg and chopped nuts for us for Friday evening." Mark replied proudly.

"Gotcha!" His creativity brought a smile to her face. She loved a winter squash soup, and one with apples had to be tasty. "Because the family wouldn't eat a soup made from anything inside the bird?"

"Exactly."

"My mom always stuffed the turkey." Caroline peered into the bowl of bread crumbs and then the pan of vegetables sauteing with the herbs and butter she smelled. "It was never dry. But she always made a cornbread dressing with sausage in it. And chopped apples and veggies. It was a meal in itself." She gave a quick laugh. "Isn't if funny how everyone had their own thing?"

Mark studied her for a moment, then turned to give the vegetables another stir. "Do you miss it?" he asked.

"What?" Caroline sipped her coffee again. "My mom's turkey?" She frowned again, thinking about it. Then looked at him, saying, "Yeah. I guess I do." Then adding, "But I am sure yours will be just as delicious! And I cannot wait for the bisque." She quickly shoved the nostalgia from her mind, smiling at Mark and watching him scrape the buttery mixture into the bowl of breadcrumbs. He first stirred the hot vegetables and spices with the wooden spoon, but then abandoned it plunging his hands in to give it a proper mix. She wondered how eager his family would be about the dressing if they knew his hands had done the mixing! But Mark was very 'hands on' with his cooking. That was one of the first things she noticed about him in the kitchen. He told her it was the only way to tell textures and consistencies. "Hands are your best tools. A spoon has no feelings, nor does it talk!" he'd said.

"Can you get out the deep baking dish from down there?" Mark asked pointed to a lower cabinet.

Caroline set her coffee next to his and proceeded to fish out his favorite ceramic dish. "Where do want this?" She held the heavy dish up.

Mark pointed to the counter next to the bowl of dressing. He scooped a handful of dressing and began to form a ball. Satisfied with its shape, he placed it in the corner of the dish. He went for another handful, and then another. Caroline leaned back against the bar counter and watched the dressing balls quickly fill the baking dish. She thought he would run out of room before he finished, but amazingly he had just the right amount of dressing to fill the dish. He sat the dish on the stove and the bowl in the sink, rinsing his hands.

"Where'd you get that dish?" Caroline asked. She noticed it didn't have any markings on it, but it seemed quite old. Mark used it frequently when he baked food.

"That I got from my mother," he said, sipping lukewarm coffee. Going to the carafe, he poured more in his cup and topped off hers. "She made it."

"She made it?" Her brows raised her words. "Like out of real clay and with her hands?"

"Yep." He slurped some dark brew. "She made quite a few things. They're scattered through the family. I've always like that. I've had it a long time."

"That's very special." Caroline had nothing of her mother's. She thought of her mother's favorite pot and pans. One was the iron skillet that had been her grandmother's. It was oddly squared in shape and black as coal from use. Caroline wondered if her mother still used it. Surely, she did.

"So, what should I wear today?" Caroline asked, changing the subject. "I gather your family will be dressing for dinner?"

"Yes, but not suits and fancy dresses," Mark said, raising his finger in the air, indicating he suddenly thought about something. "Hold on…" He disappeared into the laundry room and came out with a garment on a hanger. "In fact, Beth sent this for you. She figured you'd have a tough time getting something to go over your casts."

He turned around the garment. It was a forest green dress with long flowing sleeves. The body of the dress was entirely too large for Caroline, but the sleeves would accommodate the cast. Then he produced a scarf in fall colors.

"She thought maybe you could use this as a belt." He held the scarf against the green dress.

Caroline smiled. It was not exactly her taste, but the green was a good color for her skin and hair. She could work with it. "That was so thoughtful of her! Yes, that will be great! I might even try to fix my hair and put on some makeup!"

***

Beth's driveway was full of vehicles, indicating the house was full of people. This time, Caroline opened the front door for Mark as he carried the roasting pan with the turkey bundled inside a blanket keeping it warm. He would make a second trip for the dressing balls, also wrapped to stay warm. As Mark stepped inside the foyer, Caroline followed and closed the door. Beth scooted down the hallway towards them, stopping abruptly as two smaller children raced in front of her.

"Whoa! Whoa, y'all!" Beth yelled at the kids. "Teddy! Evie! No running in the house!" The children disappeared around a corner as Beth continued her path towards Mark and the turkey. "Here, Mark! Let me take that from you!" She practically grabbed the bundle from him, glancing at Caroline. "Why, hi, Caroline! You're getting around much better!"

Caroline smiled and nodded. "Yes, fortunately!" Mark helped her out of her coat, stashing it in the closet, before going back out to the truck for the dressing balls. Caroline's stomach rumbled, as the odor of the turkey disappeared down the hall to the kitchen. The drive to Beth's had been torture with the smells filling the truck cab. Caroline followed the fragrant path towards the kitchen, the one room she'd yet to see in the house.

Large and spacious, every wall in the kitchen was lined with counters, cabinets, and appliances. In the center of the room a long island counter was supported by more cabinets, and the top was covered with dishes and pans of food, except for a spot reserved for the turkey and the dressing. Beth slipped the turkey in its spot and began unwrapping the blanket from the foil-covered roasting pan. Lynn and Becky, wearing aprons over their dresses, gathered on either side of Beth as she lifted off the aluminum foil. A puff of steam rose in their faces, and in unison they sang, "Mm!"

"You're lucky there's still a turkey left!" Caroline said catching their expressions as she entered the room. "If I could have, I would have climbed over the seat to get at it!"

"Oh, it's so pretty!" Beth admired the turkey, her eyes smiling. "It's a shame Mark's gonna have to carve her up!" She motioned towards Lynn, "Get your phone and take a picture! That's probably Mark's best turkey!" She winked at Caroline.

"I hope it tastes as good as it looks," Becky said, inhaling another dose of the aromatic bird.

Lynn pulled her phone from the pocket of the apron and took a picture of the turkey with Beth and Becky beside it. "Oh, wait!" Lynn paused, "Caroline get on over here! You need to be in the picture!" She motioned Caroline with her hand.

"Oh, no..." Caroline tried to decline the photo opportunity, but the women urged her forward, "Come on, come on!" Caroline limped over to the other two. Beth traded places with her, putting Caroline between her and Becky. A bright flash immortalized the three and the bird.

"Now, Caroline, you're just going to put that camera shyness aside!" Lynn said, as Mark entered the kitchen with the dish of dressing balls. "Isn't that right, Mark?"

Mark looked at the phone in her hand and then at the women dispersing from their pose around the turkey. He shook his head. "I should have warned you," he addressed Caroline. "These crazy women have this thing about taking a picture with every turkey!" As the words came out of his mouth, Lynn spun around and snapped a shot of Mark walking and talking with the dressing. "Geez, Lynn!" She snapped two more shots. There was no way Mark could shield himself, short of dropping the dish.

"That's what you get for calling your sisters crazy!" Beth laughed. "And your…" She looked at Caroline, not sure what to refer to her as.

"Friend," Mark finished for her. He slid the dish of dressing balls next to the turkey.

"Oh, Caroline, you look so good in that dress!" Beth suddenly realized Caroline was swathed in the green garment. "You might as well keep that! I'll never look that good in it!"

Caroline looked down at the outfit she'd fashioned with the help of Mark. He had gotten creative with tying the scarf around her waist, forming pleats in the skirt portion.

"Thank you, Beth. It was so kind of you to think of me!" Caroline reached over and touched Beth's arm. Caroline had instantly felt comfortable around Beth, but she still had some warming up to do with Lynn and Becky. Especially after how they had acted towards Mark the last time.

"Come on, Caroline," Mark said, putting his arm around her and guiding her away from the other women. "I want you to meet some of the others. You know all you need to know about these girls!" All three women scowled at him at the same time. Well-rehearsed and choreographed.

As Mark led Caroline into the family room, the two little ones called Teddy and Evie made another mad dash through the room. At this point, Caroline wasn't sure who was chasing whom and had the idea they didn't either. Their giggles and squeals trailed behind them, as they ignored the adults' admonishments.

Mark pointed to a woman sitting on the sofa patting an infant on her shoulder. "Laura," Mark said, getting her attention, "I'd like you to meet Caroline." Turning to Caroline, he explained Laura was Larry's eldest daughter and the baby was Katie, who just finished her 'Thanksgiving bottle' and was being burped. In the next chair was Tad, Laura's husband, whose words went unheeded by the racers. Jessica half-heartedly chased after the lively ones and was Lawrence's wife. Evie belonged to her and Lawrence, Larry's son. Teddy hailed from Laura and Tad, though the child acted like he had no clue who they were!

Kevin sat with a dark-haired girl closer to the fireplace, and they seemed to have created a force field around them shielding their conversation from the commotion in the house. Caroline wondered if this was the girl Kevin had insisted was 'just a friend.' Lizzie passed through the room, glancing at the love-birds by the fire with a smirk on her face, and gave those in the rest of the room an 'I told you so' look. She was on the way to the kitchen, having heard her name being called by her mother. Larry and Dennis Meadows were nowhere to be seen.

"Where's Larry and Dad?" Mark asked.

"They're getting folding chairs from the garage." Laura replied.

"I'll go help them," Mark turned, stopping to check with Caroline, "Will you be alright?"

"Of course!" she replied, her smile earning a quick peck on the cheek. As Mark headed for the garage, Caroline instinctively touched the spot his lips landed. For a couple of seconds, she was lost in her thoughts.

"So, you're the one Uncle Mark rescued," Laura said.

"Huh? Oh, yes!" Caroline's face flushed. "He rescued me and continues to rescue me!"

"Well," Laura began. "He's totally into you! I've never seen him like that before. Not even with Aunt Jennifer!"

Caroline felt the heat from the flush growing. "He's been very good to me," she said.

"Laura! You're totally embarrassing the girl!" Jessica said from her post between the two rooms. Caroline glanced towards the young mother who stood at alert for the racers and smiled. She called Caroline a 'girl'! Despite the warm flush on her cheeks, Caroline stood a little taller for being recognized for her youth, though it was slipping away quicker than

Caroline liked.

"How old is your baby?" Caroline asked Laura, as the mother lowered the infant from her shoulder.

"Katie is seven months old as of yesterday!" Laura titled her head to look at the blue-eye babe. Katie wore a dress way too long for her with a matching headband and a flouncy bow. Katies tiny red lips poked out from between two chubby cheeks and a face that screamed adorable! "Do you want to hold her?" Laura asked with raised brows.

"Sure!" Caroline replied energetically. "I'd better sit down where I've just got the one arm! Don't want to drop her!" Caroline lowered herself in one of the chairs, and Laura stepped over and laid a content Katie in Caroline's curved left arm. As soon as the infant sank into her arm, and Caroline's hand cupped around Katie's diapered bottom, she fell in love. The little blue eyes looked at Caroline with wonder and the tiny red lips sprouted into a smile with a miniature squeal. Her one hand flopped around until it found it's mate, and then Katie became intrigued with her own fingers. Caroline marveled over the little body and the warmth that emanated. The smell of 'baby' enveloped her and held her mesmerized. Before she knew, Caroline started a conversation with the infant, introducing herself and telling Katie insignificant things about herself. Katie stared at Caroline with animated eyes, taking in every word.

"Well, if that isn't the most beautiful sight!" Mark's voice came from the opening between the family room and living room, where Jessica had stood. "Laura, you may not get Katie back…" he continued.

"Oh, Uncle Mark, I'm not worried," she laughed and flopped her hand. "At this point, I'll give her to anyone who will hold her!"

"Oh, she's just precious!" Caroline's eye grew wide, as she told Katie, "Yes, you are just the most precious baby I've ever laid eyes on! I'll just take you home with me! Would you like that?" She smiled at Katie, who instantly smiled back and reached for Caroline's nose. Suddenly the tiny red mouth opened revealing a dark cavern and a huge yawn came flying out.

"Oops! Someone's getting sleepy!" Caroline said in a softer voice.

"Yeah, it's about time for her to go down," Laura rose to fetch the bundle from Caroline, and took Katie to the Pack-n-Play, situating her on her back and handing her a fluffy toy. "At least I'll be able to eat in semi-peace!" Then she turned, saying, "Where'd Jessica go? Teddy!" She floated off in search of her other offspring.

Caroline looked up at Mark. He leaned against the doorway, with his arms crossed, watching Caroline with a smile on his face. His head nodded slightly, confirming something in his thoughts. His demeanor was still on the quiet-side, and had been all week, but at least he was curving his mouth into smiles. He sauntered towards Caroline headed for the chair next to her but stopped in mid-sit when his name sounded from the other side of the room.

"Mark!" Beth's voice boomed. "You're up! Time to carve the bird!"

Mark's smile disappeared, and his mouth dropped with a sigh. He stood straight and gave his sister a look. "Okay! Okay!" Turning to Caroline, he said, "I'll be back."

Caroline sat for a minute, awkwardly listening to the ongoing conversation between Lawrence and Tad. While adults with professional jobs and both fathers, their discussion surrounded some sort of game they both played online. She'd never heard of it and understood zero of their conversation. She decided to give them space and headed toward the kitchen.

A quick look in the doorway revealed the kitchen was full. Mark sharpened the carving knife while Beth, Becky and Lynn arranged food on the island. Larry and Dennis poked around peaking under lids and raising corners of foil coverings, getting a hand slapped here and there. Caroline kept moving and ended up at the doorway to Mark's mother's room. Opening the French door covered with lace curtains, she stepped inside the room with windows all around. Mark's mother laid in the bed, her eyes open and staring straight up at the ceiling made of wooden slats painted blue. The color must have been a carry-over from the room's porch days.

Growing up, Caroline had begged her father to paint the ceiling of their porch blue. Several of the neighbors had blue porch ceilings, and they had explained that the blue kept bad spirits and evil forces from entering the house, blessing the home with good luck. Caroline knew her family needed all the luck and blessings they could get, so Caroline had repeated this to her father, imploring him that their luck would change.

"Hog wash!" Jimmy Reeves had told her. "I ain't wastin' no money on foolish things like blue paint!" Adding, "If there's any paintin' to be done, it'll be them sides of the house! That'll change yer luck!" And so, Caroline, Adam, and Tory spent a good part of that summer slapping the clapboards with white paint that had been thinned down to make it go farther. Adam and Tory cursed her every chance they got, when their mother and father were out of earshot.

Caroline moved towards Joy Meadows and stood next to her bed. She seemed completely at peace, her breaths evenly spaced and a slight smile on her lips. Her face had several creases but none of them held stress or tension in their folds. Completely relaxed. Caroline herself exhaled stale air, drawing in fresh brightened by the light and flowers scattered about the room. Caroline reached for Joy Meadows hand that rested on the quilt, taking it in her own, and began their conversation.

"Hello, Mrs. Meadows! It's me, Caroline. Mark's friend!" The older woman's eyes fluttered slightly. "Everyone is here today for Thanksgiving. I don't know if you can smell the food, but everything looks wonderful. There's more food that I've ever seen in my life!" Slowly, Mark's mother's eyes turned toward Caroline. Caroline smiled and continued. "And you should see the turkey that Mark cooked! It's huge and is the most appetizing turkey I've ever seen. He told me you taught him the secrets for cooking a perfect turkey. And this one sure looks perfect!" Caroline nodded her head. "Of course, he made the dressing separate, and he formed them into little balls that he baked in his favorite dish. You know, the long tan square one with the scalloped edges? He told me you made it with your own hands. Such talent! He just cherishes that dish. Earlier this week he made this phenomenal baked tilapia in it!" *Did Caroline feel a slight squeeze of her fingers?* She smiled again at the woman, wondering how much she understood. "Mark used your recipe for the dressing. It smelled heavenly as it was baking! I told Mark, my own mom always stuffed her turkey. She always made a cornbread dressing with sausage in it, but I am so anxious to try your recipe!" Caroline heard something move behind her and glanced over her shoulder. Mark stood with the door partway open. Caroline winked at him, and then turned back to his mother. "Mark just got done carving the turkey. I avoided the kitchen because your kids acted like a bunch of hungry buzzards circling the island. Yep, that's how good everything looks and smells. I'm so sorry that you can't join us at the table. But I'll make sure everyone behaves themselves, okay? Mark will be in after a while to see you. I'm sure he'll tell you all about it. You rest." Caroline slowly let go of Joy Meadows' thin fingers letting them rest again on the quilt. The woman's gaze returned to the blue ceiling.

Caroline stepped towards Mark as he held the door open, and then he shut it after she returned to the living room. Mark put his hand on her shoulder, looking at her a moment. Then his hand moved to her chin, and he bent to kiss her. When their lips parted, he said softly, "That was really remarkable of you. Thank you." He drew her to him in a hug. She hugged back with her arm. Embraced, they heard Larry blessing the meal. They either didn't know Mark and Caroline were missing or were too hungry to wait. Mark and Caroline didn't care. Reaching up, Caroline kissed Mark back, this time longer and deeper, and he held her tighter. They hungered also, but not necessarily for turkey.

***

Mark crawled across the bed with his knees and situated himself on his side with his head resting on a pillow folded over. Caroline was already twenty minutes into a Christmas movie and brought him up to speed with the part he missed while showering. Her left hand searched out his head and his hair, as his hand rested on her leg. He'd gone to the barber the day before, so he towel-dried his hair. Her fingers touched the moist spikes of hair, felt around his head, and instead of twirling and playing with his curling hair as she usually did, she withdrew her hand. Mark glanced at her, seeing her mouth flattened in disappointment.

"What's wrong?" Mark asked.

"The curls. They're gone," she sighed.

"Well, you can still rub and play with it." He seemed disappointed as well, a slight pout on his face.

"It's too short. Nothing to grab," she replied. "It's going to have to grow some."

"But I like the feel of your fingers in my hair," he protested.

"You! You are getting spoiled!" she said, looking at him with narrow eyes. "Besides, I'm miserable."

"Miserable? Why?" Mark raised up on his arm.

"I ate too much!" she moaned. "Look at me!" She smoothed the covers over her protruding full belly. "I look pregnant I'm so full! No food for me for the next three days!"

Mark laughed, putting his head back on the pillow. "Yes. You do!" Then he added, "It's a good look on you!"

"What?" she snapped back. "Being fat as a pig?"

"No." He chuckled under his breath. "Looking pregnant." He had memorized the sight of Caroline holding Katie earlier that day. The way she'd cooed and talked to the baby. Caroline's face was the happiest he'd even seen. "You'd be a natural."

"A natural what?" Caroline scooted up on her stack of

pillows. She frowned and studied the back of Mark's head. He didn't respond. She reached over and grabbed a spike of hair and gave a tug.

"Hey!" Mark looked up.

"A natural what?" she repeated.

"Mother!" His mouth curled up as he spoke. "Didn't you and Steven ever talk about kids? It seemed like you were pretty keen on Katie."

"Oh, God no!" A look of fear flooded Caroline's face. "No. Steven forbid even the discussion of children. I mean, we discussed it once...well...he did. No children. He was decided. But after that, it wasn't to be mentioned."

"And you went along with that?" Mark asked squinting his eyes. "What a jerk."

"Well, I had to!" she shrugged. "But, you know, I've thought about it since the accident and everything that's happened, and I am glad...no...ecstatic that we never had children. Not with him! I'd never be rid of him!" She sighed, "It's bad enough I've got to wait until next Friday to be finally free of him!" She grew quiet. The talking of the movies characters filled the room.

Mark glanced at her, as she stared at the television, but she didn't notice. Her own thoughts were off somewhere. He took another look at her tiny belly mounded under the comforter and shook his head. Now in addition to the picture of her holding Katie, he had the vision of a Caroline with a growing belly. He felt light-headed for a moment, then realized he'd held his breath. He slowly exhaled. While the thought of having another child had occurred to him, it didn't feel truly real until earlier that afternoon. Then, all through dinner, the rest of the evening, and while showering, the thought kept coming back to him. It stirred urges inside him. He refrained from looking at Caroline again, for fear he'd lose control and do something to make that happen. But he couldn't. There were still too many things in the way. Too many unknowns. Both for him and for Caroline. He wasn't ready, and he needed to get a better sense of where she stood.

CHAPTER 15 – THINGS ARE MOVING

"Rise and shine, sleepy head!" Mark's voice boomed and bounced off the walls of the bedroom. There was way too much energy in his voice.

Caroline stirred under the covers, groaned, and grasped the corner of the comforter, drawing it over her head. Before she knew what happened, Mark flung the covers back, a rush of cold air hitting her. She yelped.

"Hey!" She rebuked. "That's not nice!" She tried to re-gain control of the covers, but Mark held them away.

"Nor is sleeping all morning!" he replied. A mischievous grin filled his face, and he'd somehow dressed without waking her.

Caroline looked at the alarm clock. It's red glow told her it was seven-fifteen.

"It's still the middle of the night!" she protested, pulling a pillow over her face. "And it's Saturday!" She felt the covers drop on her feet, and then a tug at the pillow. Mark's face peeped closely to hers. "Ugh!"

"Come on! Get up!" he said in a normal tone. "We've got a lot to do today!"

"Like what?" she asked. She could feel his breath on her chest as he huddled close to her.

Pushing the pillow completely off her head, he moved his lips close to her ear and whispered, "It's moving day!"

"Huh?" She looked at him. His face was so close, she barely was able to focus. Though some of that had to do with still being half asleep. "Moving day?"

"Yep, Jared and his wife are coming to help," Mark took ahold of her by the shoulders and began pulling her upright.

"Hey, hey! Still a little sore there!" she said. "Who's Jared?"

"You know, the guy that works for me. I told you about him," Mark eased up his hold on her shoulders, but didn't let go. He was intent on keeping her upright. "He and his wife, Shelly, are going to help us go get your things!"

Suddenly fully awake, Caroline put up her hand. "Oh no! No, no, no!" Swallowing hard, she continued, "I'm not ready..."

"You'll never be ready." Mark was being insistent. He'd hinted a few times over the past week that he was going to arrange for help, but she hadn't taken him seriously. "Come on! Get dressed so you can get some coffee. They'll be here at eight!" Letting go of her shoulders, he gave her a hopeful look with eye brows raised.

Caroline groaned again, slowly swinging her legs over the edge of the bed. "I don't want to..." As Mark helped her stand, she told him, "There's really nothing there I want."

"You've got clothes and shoes and personal items!" Mark led her to the dresser. "You can't wear sweats for the rest of your life. You'll eventually need your clothes!"

"Those were the 'old' Caroline's clothes!" Her words sounded like a pouty teenager. Like the girl in the cellphone store. Caroline immediately straightened up. "Okay. I guess if we have to..." she drew out her pouty words.

"Yes, and I promise you'll be glad you did. We'll go get your things, that way come Friday, when you go before the judge, everything will truly be final!" He pulled clothes out of the dresser. "You'll already have all your stuff and can come straight home. You'll be done!"

She held onto Mark's shoulder as he helped her step into a pair of sweatpants. Then she held her left foot out for him to work a sock on. She mulled over what he said. *Be done. Final.* There would only be the issue of selling the house. The lawyers would work out splitting everything up. She wouldn't have to think about Steven again. *EVER!* Then it occurred to her Mark had used the word 'home'! *She could come straight home*! Did he honestly think of his home as her home? Was he thinking she'd stay? She looked around the room. The place did feel more like home than any place she'd ever been...

"You know, my right foot is not hardly hurting at all now," she said with her full weight on it.

"That's good." Mark grabbed the boot and began fastening it on her casted foot. "But you still need this. I've seen you sneaking around walking on the cast!" He looked at her with a raised brow.

Caroline picked up the hoodie, pulling it over her head as Mark fastened the last of the boot straps. She got her one arm through without a problem, but the cast always grabbed the material of any shirt she wore. Mark worked the sleeve up the cast until it was in place.

"There."

"I bet you'll be so happy when you don't have to help dress me anymore."

"As long as I still get to help undress you, I'll be happy!" he teased.

Caroline slipped on her athletic shoe on her left foot and stood. "Here I was thinking how sweet and honorable you are! 'Oh, he's not your typical male,' I told myself..." She laughed taking a couple of steps towards the door.

"I'm not." Mark defended, a mischievous smile capturing his mouth. "If I was, I would be doing more than undressing you and helping you get ready for a shower!"

"Good point!" She'd give him that. He'd not made any sort of move towards intimacy except for the kisses. And those, well, they absolutely left her weak-kneed. But he never took the kisses any further. Well, except for his hand... She headed towards the stairs. "If we're doing this, I need coffee." She took two steps down, hearing Mark right behind her. "And I've got to call that deputy or whoever to let them know I'm going over there."

"Already done," Mark said, placing his hand on her shoulder. Caroline glanced behind her. "I called yesterday. I figured they'd want a little advance notice."

"Probably so." She bounced her head from side to side, steadying herself with the railing as she clomped down the remaining steps. "You think of everything!"

"Eh. Well, I didn't exactly want us getting arrested for

trespassing. Or worse: shot by Steven!"

"Oh, I doubt Steven is even there anymore," Caroline said. She watched Mark descend the last two steps. "I'm sure he's shacked up with Brandia now! Besides, I think he's too much of a wimp to use a gun. When we've gone target practicing, his hand always shook. Never hit the target!"

"Did you hit the target?" Mark took a step closer to her, their noses almost touching, his hands touching her arms.

"Of course!" Caroline gave him a sly look, and traced a heart with her finger on his shirt right where his heart was. "Every time!" The she looked down at her cast, adding, "Probably never will again…"

She turned and headed for the coffee pot. *Coffee. Had to have it.* She wondered if there was still coffee in her house. Or food. She shivered as she poured cups for her and Mark.

"Are you cold?" Mark asked as she handed him a mug.

"No. Just thinking about what's in the house." She swallowed hard. "I'm really not looking forward to this. My heart is already starting to race."

"Well, remember, Jared, Shelly, and I are going to be the to do the heavy lifting," Mark gave her a consoling look. "Your job is to supervise and tell us what goes."

Caroline lifted the mug to her lips, pausing to see her coffee was still black, and took a sip anyway. She needed all the courage and energy she could muster. She limped towards a bar chair to sit. Mark leaned against the counter, nursing his coffee, and watched Caroline. He saw her anxiety was slowly and steadily rising. Her hand shook slightly as she raised her mug.

"That's the reason I didn't say anything yesterday," Mark said motioning towards her mug as she attempted a sip of the jiggling liquid. "I knew you'd get anxious. You wouldn't have slept all night worrying about it."

Caroline shifted her mouth sideways, a dimple forming in her cheek. "True." She nodded her head. How did this man know her so well in such short time? Steven was never that tuned into her. Steven was only tuned into himself. *Ugh! The thought of him!* What would she do if he was at the house? *No, he wouldn't be.* Even if he was still living there, the deputy would make him leave. This idea eased her mind. Slightly.

A knock at the door sent Mark into action. He dashed across the living to the front door. A man and woman stood bundled in coats and hoods, each holding matching stainless travel coffee cups.

"We're here!" the woman's voice rang out. "Mark Meadows you'd better have more coffee! You know I don't get up this early on Saturdays!"

Mark stepped aside for the man and woman to enter. They obviously had been to Mark's before as they both marched through the living room towards the kitchen, Jared hanging back with Mark. The men did a fist-bump routine. *A sort of secret handshake?*

"My, man!" Jared said. "How you doin'?"

"Good." Mark did not waste words. "Shelly, help yourself to a refill." His offer was almost after-the-fact as the woman already poured steaming coffee into her cup. As she slipped the carafe back in place and twisted her lid on, her eyes landed on Caroline seated at the bar sipping from her mug.

"Oh, my goodness!" Shelly's voice went up an octave. "You are Caroline!" The woman came around the bar and plopped in the other bar chair. "Mark has told Jared all about you! Which is the same as telling me! Jared and I have no secrets!"

Caroline wished she could say the same, having only heard the woman's name less than a half hour before. "It is so nice to finally meet you and Jared!" she said told Shelly, extending her left hand for a handshake. Shelly looked at it a moment, confused, and then saw the sling and casted arm. She grasped Caroline's extended hand with her right hand and gave a squeeze.

"Wow!" Shelly's eyes went back to Caroline's cast. "You got messed up bad! Does it go all the way up?" Shelly's face became animated, and her blue eyes grew wide. Wisps of dirty blond hair hung out of the coat hood, which she still had on.

"Yes, and I've got one on my foot also. It's not as bad." Caroline lifted the boot for Shelly to see.

As Jared joined them, checking out Caroline's infirmities, Mark took Jared's stainless travel cup to refill. Jared stood shaking his head, his hands on the sides of his coat. His dark brown eyes seeped sympathy.

"She was lucky," Mark said, handing the travel cup to his friend. "Blessed actually."

"I'd say!" Shelly replied. "Oh, could you imagine if, like, your face got all mangled? Oh, that would have been the worst! I'm surprised the air bag didn't do a number on you!"

"The airbag never went off," Mark said sipping from his mug.

"I don't know if that was a good thing or a bad thing…" Jared replied.

"Oh, I just feel so bad for you!" Shelly added. "But we're here to help! We're yours all day! My mom has got the kids, and she's keeping them the night!" Shelly winked at her husband.

"Thank you, both," Caroline looked from Shelly's pale face to Jared's dark face. His hood had slipped down, revealing black hair growing close to his scalp. Caroline wondered if the handsome man usually kept it shaved. "Mark, do we have travel cups?" She held up her mug.

"We do!" He took her mug and went into the kitchen to prepare travel cups.

***

Mark remembered the way to Caroline's house. The deputy was already parked along the curb in front of the house as the mini caravan pulled into the driveway. Caroline descended from the truck with Mark's assistance, and she shed her coat throwing it back into the truck seat. It was added bulk, and she already felt constricted enough. Jared and Shelly joined them, their travel cups in hand, as Caroline fumbled in the pocket of her hoodie for the piece of paper with the keypad code for the house.

"Good morning," the deputy said approaching them. He wore khaki-colored pants, and a heavy coat with the Sheriff's office logo. His badge hung on his belt just below a dark brown jersey shirt with its ends tucked in. A bulge in his coat indicated he also wore his service pistol on his side.

"Good morning, officer," Mark replied reaching out his hand, which the deputy shook. "So sorry for bringing you out so early on a cold morning." After their hands separated, Mark continued, "I'm Mark Meadows, a friend of Caroline's."

Caroline shoved the paper back into her pocket and held out her left hand "Caroline Reeves-White, owner of the house! These are my friends here to help me!" She looked down at her arm and foot. "Obviously, I'm not doing the heavy lifting today!"

"Deputy Mason." He reached for her hand while surveying her casted body parts. "Looks like you've had quite the time."

"Yes, sir. I have," Caroline mashed her lips together. The deputy's demeanor was completely formal.

"Well, I am here just to make sure nothing goes awry. You're aware that you are limited to taking your personal effects only, correct?" Deputy Mason looked from her to the others. Heads nodded.

"Yes, I am." Caroline looked towards the house and back at the deputy. "Umm…could you tell me…Steven's not here, is he?" She scrunched her face in apprehension.

"You mean, Mr. White?" Deputy Mason confirmed. "No, he was instructed to stay away from the premises for 24 hours while you acquire your belongings. But I don't believe he has been staying here."

"Okay, thanks!" Caroline exhaled relief, knowing she wasn't facing any confrontations. Had she heard a similar release of air from Mark?

Mark, Jared and Shelly stood back as Caroline punched the number on the folded paper into the keypad. The deputy stood at the edge of the porch. A low beeping sound indicated the code took, and Caroline pressed the brass latch pushing the front door open.

They stepped into a foyer with a wide stairway leading to the second floor. The ceiling was high with a chandelier supporting countless crystals. The walnut-stained wooden floors flowed throughout the house and sported a skim of dust. Caroline's helpers waited in the foyer, as she limped towards the room to the left. The living room. It was as untouched since the day the couches were brought in and the other furnishings were put in place. No one ever used the room. In fact, Steven had thrown a fit one time when he found her in one of the chairs reading a book.

She then moved to the kitchen. The coffee pot still contained the coffee, plus some fuzzy growth, from her last morning in the house. She spun around on her booted foot and headed for Steven's office. Standing in the doorway, she scanned the room. Empty. The desk, chairs, and shelving was all gone. Every shred of paper and every dust particle had been removed. She figured as much. Steven had used the company's funds to outfit the home office. Unfortunately, any evidence of her assertion was also gone. She let out a sigh and turned back towards the kitchen.

Stopping again near the island, she looked over the cabinets and thought about the contents of the kitchen. The cabinets and drawers contained the best of the best in terms of dishware, glassware, cooking utensils, gadgets, pots, and pans. Did she want any of it? No. Not really. Where would she put it? Perhaps the new owners would relish having a well-appointed kitchen. Or perhaps there was something Shelly would like?

She limped back to the foyer where the others waited for instructions. Shelly shed her coat, and Caroline saw that she had long wavy dirty blond hair with highlights of a lighter blond and caramel. Caroline smiled at the group. As her anxiety about being in the house diminished, dread for the task ahead crept in taking its place.

Mark reached out to her as she approached, putting his hand on her bad shoulder. "Are you okay?"

She thought about his question a minute. Caroline knew he was worried about her reaction to being back in the house. She looked around the foyer, beyond the individuals waiting to get busy, and glanced back in the living room. The house felt foreign to her. It didn't feel like a home, much less like her home. They might as well have been standing in a model home. Really, that's what it had always been. The only rooms she'd been allowed any freedom to be herself had been the bedroom and the master bathroom. She used the word 'freedom' lightly, as Steven's rules had still applied to those areas. The rules were just relaxed a bit.

"I'm doing wonderfully!" she looked up at Mark. "Where's the deputy?"

"He's on the porch" Shelly replied, looking in the direction of the door.

"Oh, that's crazy! He'll freeze to death out there!" Caroline said motioning to Jared. "Tell him to come on in and make himself comfortable in the living room!" Then she turned to Shelly.

"I don't know if you're interested, but there is nothing I want from the kitchen," Caroline pointed towards the bright white room at the back of the house "I've no place for any of it, so browse around in there. If there's anything you want or can use, it's yours!"

"Really? Are you sure?" Shelly scratched her temple, a perplexed look on her face.

Caroline looked at Mark. He shrugged, adding, "My cabinets are full. All you could do is put it in a box for who knows when." He looked at Shelly saying, "We've got plenty of boxes!"

"Cool!" Shelly's face brightened. "I'll check it out. It might be nice to eat off real plates rather than plastic ones! The kids are getting big enough now!" She headed towards the kitchen, saying joyously, "It feels like Christmas! Early!"

Jared held the door open for the deputy who gladly took up

the offer. Deputy Mason stood awkwardly in the foyer, as Jared went out to get the boxes stacked flat in Shelly's Tahoe.

"Deputy Mason. Feel free to make yourself at home." Caroline pointed towards the living room. "And if you want some coffee, we can make some in the kitchen, though the pot needs a cleaning. Help yourself!" She motioned towards the kitchen.

"Coffee sounds really good!" the deputy said heading that way.

When Jared returned with tape and several flattened boxes, he and Mark went to work taping boxes together, as Caroline went upstairs to get an idea of what items go with her. Halfway up the steps, she heard Shelly and Deputy Mason discussing the condition of the coffee pot, and Shelly offered to clean it, while the deputy searched out the coffee supplies. Caroline laughed to herself. *This was the most life this house has ever seen!*

At the top of the stairs, Caroline ran her left hand along the polished walnut railing. A coating of dust collected on her hand. It was the dirtiest the house had ever been! Stepping into the master bedroom, the first thing she saw was the massive king bed. A spontaneous shiver ran through her. To think she'd share that bed with 'him.' She shook her head and went to the chest of drawers that had been Steven's. Opening one of the middle drawers, she found it empty. A musty cedar smell met her nose.

She turned and went to Steven's closet. As her hand clutched the brass knob, she knew what she'd see before she even opened the door. Not a hanger, not a shoe remained. He was gone. Closing the door, she surveyed the room. It was as foreign to her as the rest of the house. It might as well be someone else's, except she knew where everything was. Going to the dresser, she reached for the handle to pull the middle drawer open. As she did, she caught herself reflection of the mirror. Her plain skin and curly mass of dark hair didn't belong in this room. Looking down at the contents of the drawer, she felt nauseous. Inside was the collection of lingerie

Steven had bought and made her parade around in. She pulled out the drawers to each side. Lacy bras and panties were in one, and the other was empty. It used to contain the other items Steven had purchased for their pleasure-making. Or, rather, *his*. He had taken them. Caroline felt the bile rising and limped hurriedly towards the bathroom, her hand on her mouth to keep the contents of her stomach from spewing everywhere.

Confident no more was to come out, Caroline collected herself from the floor, flushed the toilet and made her way to 'her' sink. She quickly scooped handfuls of water into her mouth rinsing away the nasty aftertaste. Drying her mouth, she dropped the hand towel on the counter and opened 'her' drawers in the vanity. Various cosmetics, creams, lotions, and hair implements filled them. She figured she'd just empty the contents into a box and could sort through them later. Same thing with the items under the sink. Going to the closet, she found the stores of toilet paper, tissues, towels, and sanitary supplies. Again, some of those could go into a box for future use. No point leaving behind anything that could eventually be used.

Coming out of the bathroom, she practically ran into Mark.

"Whoa!" His hands caught her by the shoulders, dropping the boxes on the carpeted floor. "Caroline, you're pale as a ghost! What happened?"

"Oh, the coffee didn't sit so well on my stomach," she said, shielding her mouth with her hand. "I should be fine now." She glanced at the open drawers on the dresser, adding, "I think I'm going to need a few garbage bags as well. There are some in the kitchen."

Mark looked questioningly at her. "Okay, I'll go get some." Turning, he passed the dresser to exit the room. Caroline knew he'd taken a long look at the contents. Her paleness quickly replaced with a flush of embarrassment.

Picking up one of the boxes, she sat it on the top of the dresser and began taking handfuls of the bras and panties, dumping them in the bottom of the box. These she could still wear, though she had an idea Mark wouldn't be exactly crazy about the idea. He was all about practicality. Closing that drawer, she went to the one below and packed socks and more articles of clothing on top of the underwear. When that box was full, she grabbed another, letting it sit on the floor. She knelt and pulled sweaters out, starting to be more discriminating with what found the box and what found the floor.

When Mark returned with the box of garbage bags, he pulled one out and shook it open. "I think we're going to end up hauling off more for Shelly, than for you! She's having a hay day in that kitchen! Jared just keeps taking her boxes!" His face flushed briefly. "Uh…you wouldn't be opposed to us taking the block of knives home, would you? They're Wusthofs…" He tried to tone down his excitement at the find.

"I'm glad she's finding things she can use," Caroline said placing another top in the floor pile. "Someone might as well get use from them!" She didn't directly address his last comment.

"What do you want in the bag?" Mark asked, eying the open top drawer. "This?"

"Yes, please." Caroline replied putting a couple articles of clothing in the box. She glanced up at Mark. He held up one of the outfits inspecting it. He shook his head slightly, then quickly shoved it in the bag when he realized she had seen him.

"Okay, that takes care of those!" he said, after the drawer was cleared. "Is this box ready?" He motioned to the one on the dresser.

"Yes, and this one is about to be."

Mark picked up the one box, telling Caroline he'd return with more empties.

"Oh, when you're downstairs, let Shelly know I've got some clothes up here I don't want." Caroline pointed to the growing pile on the floor. "I think she's about my size. Maybe just a little taller.

While Mark was gone, Caroline finished going through the

drawers of the dresser, filling all but one box. The clothes on the floor was an ample mound, destined for other bodies. Caroline took the remaining box into the bathroom and moved make-up and creams from the drawers to the box, a handful at a time. She offered no care to the items, dropping each handful in. She took everything, not wanting to take the time to sort it, but knew she'd probably not use half of it. The rest would be thrown away.

When Mark returned with more boxes, Shelly was on his heels. Caroline heard her squeal.

"Seriously? She doesn't want any of this?" Shelly's voice carried into the bathroom. Mark appeared in the doorway with an empty box, trading it for the one Caroline had already filled.

"You're going to town!" he laughed. "At this rate, we'll be out of here by noon!" Glancing back towards Shelly on the floor next to the pile, he conditioned, "That is if we can get Shelly out of here!" This brought a smile to Caroline's face. It felt good to smile. She was glad that someone was getting a little joy out of the experience. She tried to keep her mind blank and deliberately thought of other things. As a memory began floating through, she forced herself to switch thoughts. At one point she recited the alphabet, under her breath. She put herself on autopilot, going through motions. That wasn't very difficult as she no longer felt a connection with most of what went into boxes.

Caroline finished emptying the remaining items from under the sink and went for the closet. She needed another box for those things. *Geez, how does a person collect so many things?* As she went through the past ten years of her life, items came to surface that she'd forgotten she had.

"Um, Caroline?" Shelly asked as she peered into the bag of lingerie. "Are you planning on taking these?"

Caroline picked up a larger box, saying, "Absolutely not. They are yours if you want them!"

She watched Shelly raise her eyebrows several times, obviously making plans for Jared.

"Caroline!" Mark's voice called from downstairs. "There's someone here!"

Caroline froze, that sickish feeling returning. *Who could be here?* She gave a pensive look at Shelly and started moving towards the door. "Seriously, Shelly, take anything you want. Anything left is going to the clothes bank!"

"Caroline, you are seriously my new best friend!" Shelly said, dropping the bag on the new pile she had created on the floor.

Caroline scooted along the landing to the stairs, trying to figure who knew she was here. She'd told no one. She didn't even know she was going to the house until Mark sprung the news on her. Grabbing the railing along the wall, she took each step down with care. Rounding the curve in the stairs, Mark came into view. He stood with his hands on his hips, and Deputy Mason was right behind him. Jared came through the foyer with a box loaded with kitchen items. Otherwise, Caroline saw no one. Mark opened the door for Jared, and then looked up at Caroline.

"Who's here?" Caroline asked.

"She'll be back in a min," Mark replied. "She staking the sign."

"What sign?" she asked reaching the bottom step. As she did, the door opened, but it was not Jared who entered. Caroline looked at the woman wearing the full-length red wool coat, and oversized scarf, and rubber boots. The woman looked from Mark to Caroline, and a warm smile spread across her face.

"Mindy!" Caroline recognized the woman from the hair salon. "What brings..." *Sign.* It hit Caroline. She was the realtor for the house. Mindy was her stylist but also sold real estate on the side.

"Hi Caroline!" The woman came toward Caroline, pausing to study the sling and protruding cast, but gave her a light hug anyway. "Good heavens, girl! They said you got banged up, but that is beyond!" She took a step back, studying the boot and cast on Caroline's foot. "But I love the hair!" She smiled broadly again. "That's a great look on you!"

"Thanks, Mindy!" Caroline smiled humbly. "Yeah, I've reverted to the natural look. I can't do much one-handed!"

"It suits you." Mindy's tone was sincere. "So, yes, I was selected by the lawyers as the realtor for the property, and I've just put out the 'For Sale' sign; however, I don't expect it to be up for very long!" Her eyes widened and her neatly scribed brows raised.

"What do you mean?" Caroline asked. She looked from Mindy to Mark and back.

"Caroline, I've already got three offers well above market price for the house. It seems that this baby is a hot commodity!"

"Really?" Caroline's surprise filled her face. "Before you even got the sign out?"

"Yes!" Mindy nodded. "Well, as you can imagine, word is out all over town about…well, the divorce… and other things. I guess these people were just sitting and waiting until they heard it was going to be listed. I got all three calls within a half-hour!" Taking a breath, she added, "And no telling what other offers might come in now that the property is actually listed!"

"Well, that's really wonderful!" Caroline smiled tentatively. "The quicker this place goes, the quicker I can get on with life and breathe a little easier."

"I expect we'll have a bidding war over this one!" Mindy said. "Do you mind if I just move around the house to get myself familiar with it? There's going to be an open house here tomorrow!"

"No, of course. Look at whatever you need to." Caroline motioned her hand at the surrounding rooms. "We're just getting some of my personal things. We should be out of here pretty quickly."

Mindy surveyed the living room without stepping into it. "Wow! I don't need to do any staging here at all. Is everything here staying for tomorrow?"

"Oh, yes." Caroline nodded. "I'm not taking any of the

furniture or décor. As far as I'm concerned, it can go with the house."

"Well, good! This is just beautiful!" she said, moving toward the kitchen. Stepping a few paces in she looked left and right. "This is immaculate! I see you're clearing a few things out here." Turning towards Caroline, she asked, "Can you leave a few of the cute decorative kitchen items?"

"Sure. Just take your time checking things out." Caroline turned to head back upstairs. "We'll make sure the house is presentable when we leave. I've got to get back upstairs to doing some packing!" Pausing, she added, "Just let me know if you have any questions."

Caroline rubbed her head with wonderment as she headed for the stairs. Deputy Mason took it upon himself to follow the realtor from room to room. Caroline wasn't so sure if his attention was out of duty or more that he might be looking for an opportunity to approach the attractive and divorced hair stylist/realtor. He seemed unusually interested.

Mark followed close behind Caroline on the stairs in his usual manner. He was there to prevent any falls, but with more boxes in hand. Returning to the master bedroom, she pointed to the other boxes ready for loading.

"What are we going to do with the items going to the clothes bank?" Mark asked. While Shelly had rummaged through the main pile, it was still sizable. "Garbage bags or boxes."

"Let's see how the boxes hold out." Caroline approached her closet with a sick look on her face. "Shelly will need a few boxes for her stuff, then if we run out, we can bag things."

Caroline opened the door and flicked on the light exposing a small room outfitted with a closet system. The clothes hung by colors and shade. Shoes were neatly stashed in a series of cubbies that circled the room at the floor. She looked around and sighed. At the back of the room were more drawers with shelves above and below.

"Shelly, bring me a smaller box," Caroline said going towards the drawers. Each drawer was lined with an opulent blue velvet and was full of jewelry. Gold, silver, a few diamonds, other gem stones, most of it only worn to dinners and other important events. She was surprised it was still in the drawers. She half-expected Steven would have taken it to present here and there as gifts to Brandia. No matter, Caroline was happy to dump it all in a box. Later she would visit a jeweler or pawn shop to be shed of it. After she emptied those drawers, she gathered some of her costume jewelry worn daily, dropping handfuls on top of the gems.

"Shelly, since you're *my new best friend*, I want you to know that I'll be going through all of this in the next couple weeks to see what I want to keep. Whatever I don't want, you can go through and be yours!" Caroline handed her the box. "Tell Mark to put this in the front seat." Then she turned towards the racks of clothes. One by one she pulled them off the rack. The article either went in a box or she handed it to Shelly. Shelly looked each item over and decided whether it went in one of her boxes or on the bed, which collected the hanging discards. Mark and Jared stayed busy shuttling boxes out of the house with instructions for where each box went.

"Babe," Jared stopped to get Shelly's attention. "There's no way we got room for all of this in our garage. Some of this got to go to your mom's."

"I know, sweetie!" Shelly gave her husband a sweet smile.

Caroline looked at Mark, who stood in the background surveying the boxes and the piles. She knew he was thinking the same thing. That was why very few items made the cut for her own boxes. She boxed only those things she knew she'd wear and would be functional and easy to get on, especially with a dysfunction arm.

CHAPTER 16 – MIXED MESSAGES

"I'm getting mixed messages." She raised her cup to sip, looking at him over the rim. She tried to read him, but he presented a blank face.

"Mixed messages? How?" Mark asked.

"Well, last Monday when we got my things from work, and stopped and got the phone…well, your mood changed. You became exceptionally quiet." Caroline tried to be diplomatic with her words but to the point. "You were quiet all week. Even before Thanksgiving. And after Saturday and the trip to the house, you've been super quiet."

"I had something on my mind." Mark stretched his neck and head while looking at Caroline.

"You know, you can talk to me. I'm a good listener." Caroline flattened her mouth. "I know something's bothering you. Is it me? Are you upset that I've taken over your garage?"

"No, Caroline, it's not you. And it's not your stuff. It's just me." Mark glanced at the flames rolling through the faux logs. "I get like this. Especially when I've been around my family. It always reminds me of what I lost. Once you're around for a while, you'll get used to it."

"What if I don't want to get used to it?" Caroline asked bluntly. "What if I don't want to see you get this way?" He looked abruptly at her. She continued, "I know something triggered your mood change."

"'Triggered my mood change'?" Mark laughed, defensively. "You sound like my father."

Caroline sighed, her shoulders slumping. "I'm sorry." She took a few seconds to collect her words. "You haven't asked, and the subject hasn't come up, but I have training in counseling. That was the emphasis area for my master's degree. I use it in my advising and working with students. So, I have a pretty good foundation in…you know…things."

Mark looked away from her and raised his left hand to his mouth, thinking. "So, you've been psychoanalyzing me this whole time?" Again, his tone was defensive.

"Not at all!" Caroline reached forward and put her mug on the coffee table. As she did, her phone slid off the throw on her lap to the floor. She attempted to squat down to reach for it, but before she could it was in Mark's hand. As he handed it to her, she looked up. Mark's face was just inches from her own. He paused, looking into her eyes. Caroline saw pain in his. She knew something happened when they were out that Monday. That's when his mood changed. But what? And why?

She reached to put the phone on the table next to her mug and let her body sink to the floor. The throw pooled around her as she sat on the area rug in front of the fire, her legs to her side. The soothing heat of the fire engulfed her, reaching through to the center of her bones. She looked up to see Mark's face hovering just above hers. He studied her. An indecisive look took his face.

"Mark. I care. I don't want to see you in pain."

Mark lowered himself to the floor next to her, extending one of his legs, and bending the other so he could lean on it. He continued looking at her, sizing her up. An awkward feeling reached for Caroline from Mark's intent gaze. Finally, she had to looked away. Towards the fire. And then he spoke.

"It was Jennifer."

Caroline looked back at him. His hands wrapped around his upright leg, and his chin rested on his knee. He looked like he'd aged in the past week. It occurred to her: *she had no idea of his age. Late thirties? Early forties?*

"Jennifer?" she asked.

"My ex-wife." He glanced sideways at Caroline, then back at the fire. "She was there."

"There where?" Caroline thought of all the places they had been during the last week.

"At the cell phone store."

"Your ex-wife was in the store when we were!?" Caroline's

tone was incredulous. Her eyes grew wide. "You're kidding!?" She knew his mood change had been triggered on Monday.

"No. I'm not kidding." Mark glanced briefly again. He swallowed hard.

Caroline thought for a moment, trying to remember the various face in the store, but the only ones she could picture were a couple of men and the backsides of the mother with the two girls. Caroline never saw their faces. Then she remembered how Mark stole glances towards them during their loud conversation. Caroline's mouth hung open.

"You mean the woman with the two…"

Mark nodded.

"Those were your…"

"Girls." Mark said. "They even looked our direction at one point. The girls did. Not Jennifer. She was too absorbed." Mark's eyes turned glossy as he stared at the flames. "Christa looked once, but Brittany kept looking our direction. I think she was looking at your boot. Neither of them recognized me." The last of his words were a whisper.

Caroline put her hand on Mark's shoulder and leaned her face down towards his. "Mark, I had no idea. I can't even imagine…I'm so sorry!" Her face scrunched as she tried to understand how he felt. Rejection. Let-down. "Did Jennifer see you?"

Mark shook his head. "No. I don't think so."

"Oh, God!" Caroline rubbed his shoulder. "How did your girls not recognize their own father?" She shook her head. This was a new kind of disbelief.

"It's been four years. I saw them four years ago at Christmas. But that was just briefly. It's more like six years since I *really* saw them," Mark replied. His nodding rocked his body slightly.

Six years? Caroline asked, "How long ago did you get divorced?"

"Six years ago."

"What about the photo in your wallet? You said that was taken *last* Christmas."

"It was. It was given to me by Beth."

"So, you basically haven't seen your children since your *divorce*?" Caroline shook her head again. "How is that even possible? Didn't you get visitation?"

Mark turned towards Caroline, resting head on his knee. "Yes, I got visitation. First it was joint custody. Then, a couple years later it was supervised visits with Jennifer having sole custody. But Christa and Brittany didn't want to do the visits. They didn't want to see me, so I never saw them."

"Why supervised? And sole custody?" Caroline's mind worked to tether together the bits and pieces coming towards her. "Did something happen?"

"I happened." A tear ran down the side of Mark's cheek.

"You? What do you mean?" she asked. Her hand stopped a moment but then resumed the consoling rubs. "You still had visitation though, right? Didn't they *have* to come see you?"

"Jennifer made it so that the girls wanted nothing to do with me. She made them afraid of me. Told them I was crazy. Unpredictable. Violent." He sighed. A couple more tears slid down his cheek. "Unfortunately, the court agreed. Thus, supervised visits. Christa and Brittany were too young to understand what really went on. I wasn't going to force them to spend time with someone they were afraid of."

"You're not crazy!" Caroline laughed at this. "Or, violent and unpredictable! From what I've seen, you're the most predictable person I've ever met. Painfully predictable, actually!"

Mark raised his head slightly and looked at the flames. "It didn't help matters that I spent eight weeks in the hospital. And in a psychiatric ward."

Caroline said nothing. Her brows fretted as she shook her head. *Hospital? Psychiatric ward?* She continued the circling rubs.

"I was pretty upset over the divorce," Mark began. His eyes grew vacant. "I didn't want it. Jennifer did. She'd been seeing someone. I had no clue. One day, she woke up, rolled over in bed towards me, and said she wanted a divorce. She loved someone else. Just like that. No warning." Mark raised his head, but still hugged his knee. "It hit me hard. It was a very dark time." His voice was shaky.

Caroline held her breath as his words came out. Her heart felt his pain. Her heart felt her own pain, hit by a replay of the words she'd heard in the hallway.

"She moved out that day," his face scrunched with the memories. "She packed up. Her and the girls and left. Just like that. It was like a bad dream. One minute the house was full of little voices. She told the girls, 'Tell Daddy goodbye'! Then nothing. Quiet. Empty. I couldn't handle it. After a few months it finally got to me."

"Geez!" Caroline couldn't believe her ears. "What did the girls do?"

"They hugged me and told me goodbye."

"Just like that? How old were they?" Caroline tried to subtract six years from the girls she saw in the cell phone store.

"Brittany was five and Christa was eight," Mark replied snuffling. "After the divorce became final, I found out from friends that Jennifer had been seeing the guy for almost two years. Then I found out that the girls even knew him. They'd gone places with him. As soon as they moved in, they were already calling him 'daddy'!"

"That's just cruel!" Caroline was shocked. "What mother does that to her *children*?!" Then she went back to something he'd said, "How did you end up in the hospital?" She already had an idea.

"Well, when a person no longer has anything to live for…has lost everything that meant anything to them…and the court sides with the wrong doer…what do they do?" Mark's head bobbed, and his eyes looked distant.

"What did you…do?" Caroline knew the common methods men used. A gun. Hanging. *Jumping*.

"Blew up the house. That empty damn house. With me in it."

"What?!" Her words escaped involuntary. Had she heard

correctly? "Wha…?"

Mark nodded his head and caught her eyes. His looked tired. "Yep. Turned on the gas stove wide open. Left for a while. Then came back and struck a match. I didn't feel a thing."

"Mark!" Caroline grabbed him with her arm. "Oh my God!" Her own tears swelled inside, as she watched tears sprout from Mark's eyes. He leaned forward and buried his head in the crook of her neck, and his arms grabbed around her. His tears turned to soft sobs. She held onto him best as she could while his arms remained clamped around her, hugging her tightly. Her own tears rolled down her face, down her neck, and mingled with his. She tried to make sense of it.

She understood a spontaneous decision…an impulsive action…brought about but a sudden discovery, the shock of it preventing coherent thinking. An emotive reaction. Like hers. Turning onto the bridge. A mindless action. But, turning on the gas and waiting? What had gone through his mind? What went through his mind now?

***

She wrung out the wash cloth as best as she could with her left hand, then bent to rub down her legs. 'Bird baths' her mother had called them. Caroline had taken many of them. Hundreds. Maybe thousands. Taking a bath or shower had not been a nightly luxury when she was growing up. With a twenty-gallon water heater and three kids and two adults, the members of her family rotated taking a shower. The rest of the time, a sponge bath kept the dirt and grime at bay. The only difference was, her mother handed her a basin of water, and she retreated to the room she shared with Tory to bathe. That and she had two hands to wring out the wet cloth. It was okay. She was doing alright, everything considered.

Caroline's mind kept returning to Mark's break down and recount about his worst moment. She tried to put herself in his place, to comprehend the intense feelings and thoughts that led him to trying to take his life. *And in that manner!* She tried to remember her feelings the moment she made the abrupt and unplanned turn onto the bridge. A spontaneous decision. The bridge called her. Brightly lit, it drew her like a bug. And the darkness that flowed under the bridge was just as appealing. The bridge provided her opportunity. Opportunity to end the painful emptiness the words left behind. Opportunity to thwart Steven's 'options,' giving her the last word. Opportunity to prevent him from celebrating her demise with insurance proceeds. Wrapped in grief, driving off the bridge seemed perfectly reasonable at the time. In retrospect, she realized how silly it had been. Especially, if she had been successful. But she hadn't.

Just like Mark hadn't. Not on the bridge. Not in the house. It was so dramatic! He'd obviously put a lot of thought into his method. His plan. Unusual, but consistent with what a man would choose. Extreme. Was his depression that severe? Had he been taking his medications at the time? And the fact that he'd survived! How? How did he survive the force of a blast? Surely, he had injuries! God had to have intervened. Just like on the bridge.

Which raised another question: *how could Mark conceive another attempt to end his life after the house incident?* She fully grasped now why it was so important to Mark that they had consistent 'stories' about what happened on the bridge. He'd spent time in a psychiatric setting and didn't want another stay. And his father being a psychiatrist probably made things worse. And a minister for a brother. People offering constant reminders. No, Mark didn't need his past mistakes continually thrust into his face. That was as unhealthy as the disorder!

Over dinner, she was tempted to ask if he had injuries from the blast but decided it best to let the topic lag. His face was already swollen from the crying, and she assumed his ego was also. Their cooking together in the kitchen rejuvenated him slightly, but his mood was still quite flat. If he wanted to tell her details, he would in his own time. She knew what it was like to be hounded, pressured to tell something she wasn't ready to discuss. Steven had done it all the time. All that resulted was her increased resentment for his lack of respect for her. She certainly didn't want Mark resenting her.

She needed him. And not because of her injuries. With each day, and every morsel she learned about him, their bond grew. They became more and more tangled like roots of a tree, or like the tentacles of a nerve. She couldn't shake the notion they were deliberately brought together.

She let the murky water out of the sink, swishing her cloth around to rinse the sink. Squeezing the cloth again, she left it hanging on the side of the sink. After she slipped into her underwear, she struggled to pull on a white t-shirt, and began adjusting her sling over her shoulder and around her cast.

Mark appeared in the doorway of the bathroom just in time to help her with the strap. His eyes were still puffy, even after flushing them with cold water and resting a cold compress over them. He behaved meek and quiet. Caroline presumed he was embarrassed from crying and his emotional release. But she'd held him and cried with him. When his crying subsided, she let the conversation sit idle. They continued to sit on the floor in each other's arms, her head resting on his shoulder, and his resting on her head. The throw was scattered about them, and the soothing heat from the lapping flames dried their tears. Caroline even sprung a random tickle on Mark's side, totally inappropriate, but it got him laughing. And now Caroline knew he was hopelessly ticklish, knowledge she tucked away for another day.

Mark laid his night clothes on the counter. Without a word, she turned her back to him, and he grabbed the strap, fastening it taut, but not too tight, so her casted arm stayed in place.

"Thank you!" Caroline said, turning. She smiled. "Are you going to join me for Hallmark?"

"No..." His reply word drew out. "I think I'll turn in after my shower. It's been a long day." He reached toward her to smooth a crease in her sling, avoiding contact with her eyes.

"Okay," she replied, standing on her toes to plant a quick kiss on his stubbly cheek. "Sleep tight."

As Caroline got situated under the covers and flipped channels, she thought about Mark sleeping solo in the twin bed adorned with pink sheets and a comforter drowned in flowers. A thought popped into her head. Mark outfitted the room for his daughters yet was the only one who'd ever slept in that room. *His daughters had never seen it!* They probably didn't know it existed! No wonder he'd put her in his room! He couldn't bear anyone else sleeping in the room he hoped his daughters might one day use! *Did he somehow felt closer to them when he slept there?*

Caroline's hand went to her chest. Her heart ached for Mark! It was an ache she could only imagine. To have children and not be able to see them! It had to be worse than not having children at all. Steven had been unwavering about no children. At the time, she'd thought it an unfair condition and even had hopes of eventually wearing down his steadfast attitude. Now, she was thankful. The thought of being forever tied to Steven because of children…Ugh! She had always wanted children, but now realized—just not with him! *The good Lord really does know what we need! And what we don't!*

***

The first couple of days back to work exhausted Caroline. First it required her to dress more appropriately from the waist up. Quite a challenging task, given her cast. She settled for a cardigan over a white t-shirt with either a scarf or a chunky piece of jewelry around her neck. Then she felt compelled to add some make-up to cover the pallor. She learned there had been rumors on campus that she had died in the accident. She didn't want to look like she had! Fortunately, all the coloring, circling wordsearch words, and practice writing with her left hand increased her dexterity enough that she applied eyeshadow and mascara without looking garish or clownish.

She set up her home work space on the dining room table at the end opposite where Mark usually worked. It was odd watching him walk around on tippy toes attempting to be church-mouse quiet and stay out of the range of the camera when she was doing video conference sessions with students. The first couple of sessions were painfully long as she navigated the key board and mouse with her left hand only. She found herself apologizing to the student over and over, but they expressed being totally okay with it. Each student was happy she was back to work, even if remotely, and looked forward to her working her 'magic' with their class schedules.

Because she needed her hand to work the keyboard, she relied on her memory to make notes after each session. By the end of the day, she picked up speed with her left hand covering the entire keyboard and resorted to making notes in a Word document, typing them out. Everything would be on her laptop for future reference.

She found herself viewing her job with a new set of eyes. It was no longer 'just a job.' The old Caroline had a 'job,' which she worked in order to get the medical insurance. The old Caroline had listened over and over again as Steven had diminished her services, describing her work as putting in time, and that she was easily replaceable. The new Caroline viewed the work as her calling, answering questions and helping the students to get the right classes to stay on track towards a career that would hopefully establish them as productive and happy adults. Yes, that is what Caroline had: a career. For the past ten years, Caroline honed her skills and her knowledge. She was one of the most knowledgeable about undergraduate studies at the university. She was a professional. The Zoom conferences were evidence of the impact she made. As she ended each session, she witnessed the relief of each student and knew they would approach their world a little more confident. What could possibly be better than that? Making a difference one student at a time.

At the end of Tuesday, Caroline closed her laptop feeling

satisfied but exhausted. She was so happy she'd taken the plunge back into work. It made her feel purposeful and productive. It also gave her an outlet for her increasing anxiousness as Friday neared. *D-day. Divorce-Day!* Her excess energy from the growing worry channeled into her work. The combination, worry and work, left her drained, and her head felt like someone squeezed out everything inside. Like a juiced lemon. All that was left were the random fibers clinging to the rind.

"Are you done for the day?" Mark asked, coming home from the garage. That had become his new hang out. He claimed he was servicing some of the stored landscaping equipment, getting it ready for the new season.

"Yep." She held her head up with her left hand, which throbbed from overuse. "And I'm exhausted. Invigorated, but exhausted."

"Maybe you should pace yourself," Mark said over running water as he soaped his hands. "You've jumped in head-first. That might be too much for you. Especially, with…you know…other things going on this week!"

"Perhaps." She looked at him with tired eyes. She squinted, trying to focus on him across the room. "But I feel so guilty that these kids have been ignored for so many weeks! There's just not enough of us to help everyone on a good day. Then, take one of us out of the mix, and it's a mess!"

"Well, you can't feel responsible for other people's staffing decisions," Mark said.

"I know…"

"Speaking of which," Mark paused with the refrigerator door open, "Tomorrow, Jared's meeting me at the garage. I'll be out of your hair most of the day hopefully." He pulled vegetables out of the crisper and grabbed a bag of shrimp from the refrigerator shelf, placing them all next to the sink.

"You are not in my hair!" Caroline protested. Unconsciously, she reached for the top of her head, feeling around her curls. "What are you two going to do at the garage?"

"We need to put the plows on the trucks. We're actually behind doing this." Mark rinsed a couple of zucchinis, celery, and some cabbage. "Normally, Jared and I have the plows on by Thanksgiving, and they're calling for some snow for next week." Hunting for the carrot scrapper, he added, "You may have the house to yourself for a couple days if we get the snow they're calling for."

"I...hate...snow." Caroline emphasized each word.

"Now, see—I love it! It rings dollar signs in my eyes!" Mark winked at her. "If you weren't laid up, I'd take you along so you could shovel walkways for old people!"

"I guess God knew what he was doing by letting me break my arm!" she said with a sour expression. "Extra prayers for Him at bedtime!"

The cleaned carrot joined the other clean vegetables. Mark disappeared from view, as he rattled around in a lower cabinet. Reappearing with a colander and placing it in the sink, he asked, "Did today go any smoother than yesterday?"

Caroline struggled to get up from the table. Not because of her ailments but from sluggishness. She did her limp walk towards the kitchen. "Yes. It did. I'm finding different ways of doing things. Funny, when you have only one hand, you find yourself trying to streamline things. How's that saying go? Necessity is the mother of innovation..."

"Actually," Mark gave her a sideways glance as she joined him at the counter. "I believe the proverb actually goes: 'Necessity is the mother of invention'!"

"Invention. Innovation. It's all the same thing!" she defended, a little more energy in her voice. "I was close. No, actually, I was spot on! I am innovating! Which is a form of invention. Inventing new ways of doing things! And in the process, realizing how many unnecessary steps we take! Time wasters!" She sighed. "I just wish this week were over!"

"I know." Mark poured the shrimp into the colander.

"Not soon enough!" Caroline replied. "Why are you putting the shrimp in that?"

"To drain the excess water off the shrimp," he shook the colander and set in inside a bowl to collect any drainage. "I'm making us a stir-fry. If there's too much water in the shrimp, it takes it longer to cook, and then it gets tough."

"Oh." Caroline raised her eyebrows. "I guess you'll need some chopping done?" She looked at him hopefully. She grabbed one of the Wusthof knives from the knife block she agreed to let him bring home, when a vibrating noise caused them both to look for their phones.

"It's not mine," Mark said.

Caroline 'sprinted' to the table to answer her phone, but it quit vibrating before she was halfway there. Once she reached the phone, she went to her missed calls. "Oh…" She stared at the screen for a few seconds before looking up at Mark. He had his back to her as he rummaged around in the spice cabinet. Caroline redialed the number and walked back towards the kitchen.

"Emily, this is Caroline. I'm returning your call…" her voice trailed off.

Mark glanced over at her as she leaned against the counter with the phone to her ear.

"Caroline! I'm glad you called me back!" Emily's voice sounded pressured. "I was planning to touch base with you about Friday anyway, but there have been some developments."

"Okay…" Caroline looked at Mark who was searching the pantry for more ingredients.

"The realtor called and there are—*no joke*—five offers on the house. Each offer is well-above market value." Emily's voice was tentative.

"But?" Caroline knew a 'but' was coming.

"But, we've learned that Steven took out a second mortgage on the house and deposited those funds into a company account." Emily paused waiting for Caroline's response. "I'm assuming this is brand new information to you."

Caroline's mouth flapped, grasping for words. She made a

noise that Emily must have assumed was a 'yes.' Her knees felt weak, but she locked them to keep from going to the floor. She should have stayed near the chairs.

"Anyway, I've been in communication with Steven's lawyer and the bank. Steven will be repaying the money in the morning, so the second mortgage note is paid off. Then it will just be a matter of deciding which offer you both agree to go with."

"The...the highest one," Caroline managed to say. "What a... how could he do that without my knowledge. Without my *signature*?" She looked straight ahead at the knob of the bottom cabinet. Brushed nickel. It shined, but yet it didn't.

"Well, it looks like forgery may be added to the laundry list stacking up against him," Emily replied. "The president at the bank was, well, less than happy."

"I'd say." Caroline's anxious moved to a higher level. Her heart thumped in her chest.

"Um...there is a silver lining." Emily's tone turned optimistic. Caroline needed good news. "Steven's lawyer is dismissing the restraining order against you! That means there is no reason for you to be in court on Friday! The judge will simply sign off on the divorce!"

"Yay! I never have to see Steven again!" Caroline wanted to dance but could only make jumping motions! This earned Mark's attention. He set the bottle of soy sauce next to the sesame oil. Leaning on the counter with one hand, he put the other on his side giving full attention to Caroline's conversation.

"There's more," Emily said breaking into Caroline's version of a happy dance. "I've heard through the grapevine that the judge has signed a warrant for Steven's arrest. I'm sure that's why his lawyer dropped the restraining order. Steven's got bigger things to worry about. My sources tell me that they have evidence, a witness, and a confession from an accomplice!"

"So...my suspicions were for *real*..." Caroline's words weren't a question or a statement. They were more of a verbal pondering.

"Yes, Caroline," Emily replied. "I'm afraid so. You may be called at some point to testify, but this one's between the County Attorney and Steven and his lawyer. This is not your worry!"

"Thanks, Emily," Caroline said. "So, what do I do come Friday?"

"Whatever you want, Caroline," Emily said. "I'll get copies of the signed order sent to you. That will take a few days as it will need to be recorded by the court. But Friday, you're a *free* woman! And the timing couldn't be better."

Caroline clicked off the phone and stared at the device a moment. The dark screen screamed *end of subject!* Numbness spread through her body. It felt like her blood was freezing and turning to crystals cutting off all feeling. She shook her head.

"Good news?" Mark finally asked, giving her a few moments to digest the call.

Caroline looked at him and nodded. The dance left her body, replaced with a subdued state. She didn't know what she was feeling or why. She expected to be elated—no, euphoric—to permanently wipe Steven from her life. And on Friday, that would be the case. But there was just…nothing.

"What's wrong, Caroline?" Mark came towards her. She stared at an invisible spot on the spotless floor. He tilted her chin upward with his fingers. "Talk to me." He raised his brows expectantly.

"I'm sorry." A crooked smile tried to form along her lips. "I think it all just hit me at once. I need to sit down." She pushed herself away from the counter and began shuffling her feet toward the living room. Mark walked with her, his arm around her waist to steady her. The warmth of his arm comforted the chill that inhabited her body. As she walked, she looked up at Mark, saying, "There are five offers on the house."

"That's good!" Mark smiled.

"I don't have to go to court Friday." She eased into the chair with Mark's help.

"That's also good!" Going to the fireplace, he asked, "Do you want the fire? You seem chilled."

"I'm freezing," she replied. "My body is as numb as my arm." She reached for the throw hanging on the corner of the chair, spreading it around her. She watched Mark adjust the flame in the fireplace. "Sometime on Friday I will become Caroline Reeves again."

"That's good, too!" Mark took a seat on the end of the sofa nearest her. Sitting on the edge, he clasped his hands between his knees. "You seemed happy at the beginning of the call. What happened?"

"It really has just hit me." Caroline looked up at him. The blue of her eyes paled against the brown ring. Drained. "I'm free of him, but it's like suddenly ten years of my life have vanished. A big, black bottomless hole!"

"Caroline, that hole has been forming for quite some time. You just didn't see it. Just Like I didn't see it with Jennifer." He wet his lips. "I'm sure you and Steven had some great times together. It just didn't hold out. You grew apart. Just like Jennifer and me." He glanced at up at her. "Sometimes things end badly."

Caroline nodded. "Very badly."

"But you're already on course for a better life! You're living it!" Mark looked down as his fumbling hands. "It took me a while to get back on course. I had a hard time letting go. Don't make my mistakes. Just keep looking forward, Caroline." He gave her an earnest look.

She studied him as she inhaled his words. She felt the flickering heat from the fire. She was starting to thaw. "Can I ask you something, Mark?"

"Of course."

"Do you still love Jennifer?" Caroline cocked her head. It was a question she'd wanted to ask since his revelation.

Mark sat a little straighter, connecting with Caroline's eyes. "No." He sighed, "I did for a long time. I clung to something that was no longer there, but I finally let go." He bit his lip and asked, "Do you still have feelings for Steven?"

Caroline shook her head, keeping her eyes on Mark. "I don't have *any* feelings for Steven. Nothing. Not love, not friendship, not hate. I think you're right. That hole's been around for a while and bits and pieces have been falling in for a while. Whatever still remained, was left on the bridge. It didn't come with me." She swallowed hard. After a moment, drawing the throw closer around her, she continued.

"That day I drove around…in the Range Rover…I drove around because I was stuck. I couldn't go home because I knew home didn't exist anymore. I realized it never had. It was like someone drew open the curtains, and I finally saw things for what they were. It was all fake. The entire time I felt like I was living someone else's life. It was like I was a character in a play, and my role was re-casted." She glanced down at her arm, not intending the pun. "I was written out of the storyline. I couldn't go forward because I had nowhere to go. Steven had managed to cut me off from everyone and everything. He sucked the life out of me. Every bit of emotion. And I let it happen. I realized it that day. So, I drove around. And around. I was stuck in some sort of purgatory. I honestly don't even remember how I ended up in Maysville. My mind was somewhere else. I just drove. You know the rest."

"I'm sorry, Caroline." Mark looked away towards the flames curling around the logs. "I had no idea."

"The crazy part was waking up in the hospital and feeling the pain!" She smiled, following Mark's look to the fire. "I suddenly felt alive again! To feel something! Re-born! And I had this overwhelming feeling of peace." Caroline's eyes became fuzzy around the edges from the collecting tears. She blinked them back. "I think I understand, Mark."

"What's that?" He looked from the fire to her.

"Feeling pain is so much better than feeling nothing at all. It's like our body's survival mechanism. It tells us something's wrong and to fix it. It lets us know we're not dead yet, and we still have a chance."

CHAPTER 17 – GETTING IN THE SPIRIT

Caroline woke Saturday morning a divorced woman. Single. She expected she would feel lighter and freer, jubilant even, having the weight and burden of a bad marriage lifted from her. But she felt no different. She felt like the same Caroline that woke in the hospital. No pretenses. No 'for show.' Just Caroline. It only further confirmed her belief her that something magical happened on the bridge that night. Miraculous! Her old life and all of its concerns burned up in the flames, taking with it any shred of sorrow or guilt that might have tried to haunt her. She began her day the same way she had since she arrived at the duplex. A healthy dose of coffee, and then she got busy.

Caroline leaned over the open box and sorted through the layers. It had only been a week since she packed the boxes and brought them to Mark's garage, but she'd already forgotten what she'd packed. Inspecting the contents, she was uncertain if she even wanted what she had taken from the house. She pulled out a sweater on a hanger. She turned it around, contemplating what she would wear it with. Jeans? *Okay, it was a keeper.* Slowly she created a pile of clothes that would hang in the closet in the girls' room. The jeans were all keepers, provided she could squeeze back in them after her foot cast came off. With the delicious meals Mark cooked, she had her doubts whether some of the clothes would find their way on her body, though she had been rationing her calories during the day, saving them for the evening meal.

Mark returned to the garage for another armload of hanging items. "Wow. You're really going to town on these boxes!" He picked up the stack of jeans by the hangers, disappearing with that armload. He was getting a workout going up and down the stairs. He had already carted two boxes of shoes to the closet, but many remained in the garage. They were mostly high heels that Caroline doubted she'd be able to wear after a foot injury. Caroline found the box of jewelry and put that aside. She'd sort that on the dining room table where she could lay things out, see the pieces in the light, and make decisions. The same with the box she'd tossed the make-up and creams in. She opened the last box and found shirts, socks and of course the bras and undies. She'd have Mark carry the entire box upstairs so she could unload it directly into the dresser. Her apprehension about the lacy bras still lingered in her thoughts. What would Mark say? Would he want her wearing something she'd worn around Steven? Though these were just her everyday items. She'd purchased them for herself, so she could feel pretty in them, not for Steven's benefit. The only thing she could do is wait and see.

On Mark's next return trip, Caroline pointed to a pile of Rubbermaid tubes with lids. "Mark, what's in those plastic tubs stacked up over there?"

"Oh. Those?" Mark lifted the box to go to the bedroom, taking a quick peek at the stack. "Christmas stuff. It all came from Mom and Dad's house when they sold. There was no room at Beth's, and she had her own Christmas decorations."

"Huh." Caroline's fingers grabbed her mouth twisting her lower lip, as her mind swung into gear. "So, is that what you put up in the house? Or do you have your own Christmas tree and decorations?"

Mark turned from the doorway, the box resting on his shoulder. "I don't do trees." Then he disappeared through the door.

Caroline abandoned her own boxes and went to the Rubbermaid tubs. Prying the lid off one of the tubs, she saw a collection of glass ornaments of all sizes, shapes and colors protected by layers of tissue paper. Several were covered by designs in glitter. The oblong ornaments especially caught her attention. They were multi-colored with swirls and thin lines of glitter separating each color. *Hmm.* Mark's house needed a little color. And some twinkling lights at nighttime. It might help keep his doldrums at bay! She closed the lid and took peeks into some of the other accessible tubs. One of the larger tubs contained an artificial tree, but judging by the three-foot branch, it had to be huge. Too big for Mark's living room. *Hmm...*

"You know, I've been thinking," Mark announced on return to the garage for another load.

"What's that?" Caroline stood up right, brushing a bunch of curls behind her ear.

"What would you think about me converting the spare bedroom into a home office?" He spoke while lifting the box of undergarments.

"But that room is for your girls," Caroline replied. "I feel bad enough I'm taking the closet. Seriously, I could just hang things on a bar out here!"

Mark's mouth went flat, giving her a look. "Caroline." He sighed, adding, "The girls haven't shown yet. I seriously doubt I am at the top of their list of sights and attractions. The room might as well be used."

"What about the other room?" Caroline asked. "The unfinished room? Unless you had special plans for that?"

Mark paused before responding, heaving the box on his shoulder. "Um, no nothing really *special*. I had a few ideas what it might be used for, but the timing's not right at the moment."

Caroline frowned. *Now that was vague!* She bent down and picked up the box of make-up and toted it to the table in the dining room. She went back to get the box of jewelry. With the box on the ground, she struggled to get a hold on it with one hand. Mark returned just in time. He swooped the box from the floor and tucked it under her arm. "Huh!" she replied. She thought for sure he would be a gentleman and take it to the table for her. Nope. He was clearly still promoting her independence! "Okay!" she called going up the two steps to the kitchen. "I'll just go ahead and carry this box in. However, you've got to take me to get a tree!"

"A tree?" he called from the garage.

"Yep!" she said returning to the top of the stairs. "A Christmas tree! I'm not going through Christmas without one! The past few months have been hard enough. I need something cheery!" She smiled at him. "One of those skinny artificial trees would fit perfectly in the front corner of the living room!"

Mark shook his head, looking towards the Heavens. He knew he had no choice. He wouldn't say no to her. He looked back at her. She had her left arm crossed over her casted arm, standing her ground on the top step.

"So, what are we doing with the rest of this stuff?" He motioned to the rummaged boxes.

"Goodwill?" Caroline suggested.

"Get our jackets. I'll load these on the truck." Mark leaned to pick up a box and headed towards the garage door opener. Caroline grabbed coats from the closet and lock the front door. She then stopped at the bar to grab her wallet and phone before heading back to the garage.

"Do you have your keys and wallet?" Caroline checked before closing the door to the kitchen.

"Sure do!" He smiled. He stopped to put on his jacket, and then carried the remaining boxes to the back of the truck. "We'll stop at Goodwill first. It's on the way."

"Does that mean we're really going for a tree?" She gave Mark a hopeful look.

"Here let me help you get in!" He avoided her question. Caroline waited by the open passenger door for Mark to give her a boost into the seat and leaned over her to strap her in. As he leaned back, he stopped, touched the side of her neck with his hand, and covered her lips with his. She closed her eyes and let him kiss her, trying to memorize every moment of it. Her first kiss as a divorced woman. When he pulled back, she took a deep breath and looked into his eyes. They twinkled, and she smiled, filled with a fluttering warmth. It had been days since he last kissed her, maybe even a week. She really hadn't given it much thought, assuming he was just giving her space to deal with all the recent changes. But the feel and taste of him lingered on her lips, continuing to elicit a dreamy, tingling feeling.

The Goodwill worker rolled three bins out to capture all the boxes they unloaded. Each bin was so full that the fabric sides bulged, scraping the door jams as the worked wheeled them inside. Another worker joined them at the drop-off to inquire if they needed a receipt. Caroline just smiled and told her, "No thanks!" Just being shed of the weight of things was rewarding enough. That and thought that a customer would find one of the items she donated, thinking they had found a treasure. No, that was all she needed. That, and a Christmas tree!

Walmart was the first stop on the artificial tree search. She walked around the forest of Christmas trees on display in the Garden Center. Mark followed along with his hands tucked into the pockets of his jeans. Silent, he looked from her to a tree and back to her, trying to see her reaction. At one point, her forefinger landed between her teeth as she circled around the display a second time. She stopped here and there, pausing to inspect a particular tree. Her eyes narrowed and then grew wide again, before moving on. Then she stopped, grabbed a hold of Mark's arm, and backtracked. She positioned him just so, and then pointed. Again, her eyes narrowed, and she looked up at Mark. He too studied the tree. She could tell he was taking mental measurements and trying to visualize it in the barren corner of the living room.

She raised an eyebrow, asking, "What do you think?" She tilted her head this way and that. The tree was about seven feet tall and couldn't be more than three feet at the bottom. It was a mixture of different types of evergreens, looking quite attractive even undecorated.

"I think that if they have one of those in a box, it will be going home with us!" Mark replied, nodding his head. Caroline gave him a giddy smile, clenching her hand and shaking it happily. She was as excited about the tree as she was hearing him say the word 'home.'

***

Mark carried the boxed tree through the front door and set it down near the corner. Caroline closed the door and practically danced over to the box, trying to open it before it even hit the floor.

"Hold on now, Mrs. Clause!" Mark put his hand out. "I've got to get a utility knife to cut through this tape. He slipped off his coat and hat, handing them to Caroline to hang up, and started for the toolbox in the garage.

"Wait!" she called. He heard the ripping noise of tape. Turning, his coat and hat laid on the floor, and Caroline held a long piece of tape with parts of box stuck to it. She shrugged her shoulders and smiled at him. Shaking his head, he turned back. Approaching her, he helped her out of her coat and glove and put the outwear away.

With one hand, she pulled the three parts of the tree and the stand from the box and tried to line up the pole for the bottom section with the hole in the stand. The end swung all around the hole except into it.

"Here, here!" Mark joined her. Taking the tree piece. he inserted it into the stand. "This is easier with two hands. I'll let you fluff it out, how's that?" Eagerly, Caroline nodded, watching him slip the other two parts into the pole, creating an upright scrunched-up tree.

"Thank you!" Caroline stood on her toes, pecking his cheek. She immediately got busy pulling the branches down into place and arranging the limbs to give the tree fullness.

"I'm going to go hunt for some lights." Mark headed for the garage. "Then we can decide what will go on it!" Caroline just nodded, muttering what sounded like 'uh-huh,' with her focus totally on the tree branches.

He couldn't remember anyone else being as excited about a Christmas tree other than his mother. The Friday after Thanksgiving had always been 'the day.' His mother woke early and began rooting around in boxes in the attic, hollering for his father and Larry to help bring them down. With grim faces, Dennis and his eldest son trucked box after box to the first floor with Joy Meadows calling instructions for which room each box was to go. In short time, brown boxes were littered all over the house. Mark's earliest memories included Beth still at home, but after a few years, she escaped her mother's Christmas zeal for a home and husband of her own. The next to go was Larry, leaving Dennis and Mark to shuttle the boxes, while his mother and sister, Lynn, hung decorations on the tree, the mantel, the stairway and anywhere there was an empty space for a Christmas knickknack. Once Lynn was gone, his mother stepped down the amount of decorating in the house, but she continued to have a vigor for the perfect Christmas tree and a decked-out mantel with the Christmas stockings hanging.

Every Friday after Thanksgiving, Mark reserved the day for his mother, decorating the tree together. Even after he married Jennifer, he got up early on that Friday morning and headed to his childhood home to spend the day with his mom, the tree, and an oratory of what each ornament meant and its origin.

Sometimes Jennifer stopped by and hung a few ornaments, and after Christa and Brittany were of size, Jennifer would bring them by later in the morning. But Jennifer always had one reason or another for why she had to leave. Grocery shopping, Christmas shopping, meeting a girlfriend for lunch, which later translated into meeting her boyfriend for lunch.

The year Mark came home from the Burn Center in Cincinnati was the last Friday he and his mother put up the Christmas tree. It was a grueling effort for both of them. Mark's ability to stand and walk was limited, and the compression garments further limited his movement. Then, his mother became disturbed and upset when trying to tell the history of an ornament, failing to recall the details. She knew at that point she had Alzheimer's and was painfully aware of and distressed by her lapses in memory. At one point she broke down and cried. Mark could do nothing but hold her and cry with her. The following year, Joy Meadows barely knew what a Christmas tree was.

Mark opened lid after lid of the Rubbermaid boxes, looking for the one containing the lights. When he found the right one, he carried it into the house. Caroline was more than halfway finished arranging the branches.

"That was an excellent choice!" Mark said, admiring her handiwork. "This box has the lights, but I believe they are all colored lights."

"That's perfect!" Caroline replied, a peacefulness in her voice. "That's all we had when I grew up. I miss colored lights!"

Mark assumed Steven insisted on white lights. Surely, they had a tree. Maybe two or three. For show, of course. "I'm going to grab a few of the boxes of ornaments. It'll be easier for you to see what you want with them in here."

"And for you too!" she said, giving Mark a big smile. She pursed her lips, giving him an 'air kiss' and then returned to fluff out branches. When he came back with the two tubs of ornaments, he found her standing on one of the dining room chairs leaning precariously towards the tree arranging the last of the branches.

"Whoa! Whoa!" Mark called as soon as he saw her. She stopped in mid-fluff and looked at him, clueless to his concern. Mark set the boxes down and then grabbed her with both hands around her waist, removing her from the chair. Lowering her to the floor, he scolded, "Never, never do that again!" He moved his hands to her shoulders and looked in her frowning eyes. "We don't need you falling and getting banged up more than you are! Besides, that's what you have me for. And step ladders!" Before she had a chance to reply, he planted a kiss on her downward turned lips. Then he let her go, saying, "I'll get this last part, and then we'll string the lights on."

As the sky beyond the windows began to darken, the colored lights sent splashes of colors on the living room's grey walls. Caroline decided to use only the glass balls and more vintage ornaments on the tree. Together, they moved around and around the tree looking for vacant spots to fit one more. Then one more after that. Mark looked at the tree with concern, wondering if the branches could hold the weight of the ornaments. He took covert deep breaths each time Caroline handed him another glass ball, and he exhaled quite noticeably when she proclaimed the tree finished.

"What? I thought we were having fun!" She gave him a pained look. "Was it that awful?"

"Not at all!" Mark took her in his arms and pulled her against his body. He was used to the cast digging into his belly. "I've had the best time. I just get nervous handling all the glass."
He looked toward the well-adorned tree. It sparkled from top to bottom. He recounted to Caroline how he helped his mother decorate the tree each year. Caroline looked up at him with a smile on her face and tears in her eyes as he pointed out a couple of ornaments and told her of their story. "Mom would have loved decorating trees with you!" Mark wiped a tear of his own, and tugged Caroline closer. "I'm sorry I was resistant to the whole Christmas tree idea. But now you know why." Looking down at her, he regarded her for a moment. "Caroline, tonight you've given a little bit of my mom back to me! I hope there are many Christmas trees in our future."

***

"Yesterday you mentioned you had colored lights on your trees growing up," Mark began. He set the toast slathered in peanut butter next to Caroline's coffee. She wrote words in tiny capital letters along the blue lines. "What were your trees like?"

"Trees?" Caroline looked up from the notebook, glanced at the toast, and looked at Mark as he sat at the end of the table. His plate contained two slices of toast with slices of banana slowly sinking into the thick layer of melting peanut butter. "Thanks," she motioned to the toast. "What were whose trees like?"

"Your Christmas trees when you were a kid." Mark bit the corner off one of the toasts. Peanut butter dribbled on the plate. As he laid awake in the flowery bed the night before, he had decided that Caroline's comment about the colored lights gave him the perfect opportunity to bring up the subject of her family again. She knew so many things about him, his past and his family, but he barely knew anything about her before the accident.

"Our Christmas trees?" Caroline's expression was uncertain, and she looked away from Mark, glimpsing at the tree in the corner. "Um…" She laid the pen down and rubbed her hand on her pant leg, stalling for time. "Well…Um…When we had a tree, it was one that we cut from the woods. A lot of times it was a cedar because those didn't lose needles like other trees and there were plenty around. But they were prickly."

"Really?" Mark washed the sticky peanut butter down with a sip of coffee.

"It was usually small. Maybe four feet tall at the most." She stared down at the lines on the pad. "Sometimes, we didn't have a tree at all."

"Why was that?" Mark licked the side of his hand to keep a stream of molten peanut butter from flowing towards his wrist. He'd put entirely too much peanut butter on his toast.

"Well…our house was small. Not a lot of room." Caroline glanced at Mark as he combatted his food. "Some years not a lot of money. Mom would say, 'No point in puttin' up a tree if there ain't gonna be nothin' under it!' She thought it was too depressing." The was a note of anxiety in Caroline's voice. She took a sip of lukewarm coffee to wet her throat.

"When you did have a tree, what sorts of ornaments did you all put on it?" Mark asked.

"Oh, we had some lights of course. Colored ones. Sometimes mom got old strands off neighbors and was able to replace enough of the light bulbs, so she'd have a strand that worked." She shrugged. "Then Mom had a box of different ornaments that people gave her. Some paper ones we made at school. A few that came from Mamaw. The cedar branches wouldn't hold anything real heavy."

"I assume the trees you had with Steven were pretty elaborate," Mark said, chewing another sticky bite. A smudge of peanut butter stuck to his cheek. Caroline hadn't touched her toast yet.

"Yes." Caroline sighed. "They were 'over the top' you could say!" She rolled her eyes. "The last few years, Steven wouldn't even let me put up the trees myself. He commissioned a designer to do them."

"Commissioned a designer?" Mark shot a look at her.

"Yes, you know, those interior decorators that come in and decorate your place for the holidays or for a party?" She licked her tongue against the roof of her mouth like it had a bad taste. "He had this lady, Melissa Adams, on speed dial to come in whenever we entertained. He didn't trust me with the decorating."

"That's rude." Mark shoved back his chair and headed for the kitchen. "He didn't like the homespun look?" He returned with a couple of forks and paper towels. He laid a fork next to Caroline's toast. "Eat up!"

"I will." She watched him resume tackling his toast. She picked up her toast and took a small bite. Chewing, she looked at him. Her eyes narrowed slightly.

Mark knew she was trying to anticipate where he was going with his questioning. He had learned Caroline's pattern: she became defensive and guarded when anyone asked about her family or her childhood. She either tried to stay one-step ahead of the questions by being prepared with a vague answer, or she attempted to subtly derail the conversation, slipping into another topic. He took another forkful of his messy toast and slowly chewed, studying her. She looked away, out the window, although well aware that his eyes were fastened to her. Her own eyes indicated she was still actively on alert.

Finishing one of his toasts, Mark set his fork on his plate, and took a long drink of his coffee. He looked toward the carafe, wishing he had the power to make it come to him, and then got up to give it a nudge. Bringing it to the table, he poured more coffee in his cup and topped off Caroline's, before setting it on the table.

"So," Mark said leaning back in his chair. "How about we talk about your family. You've got me intrigued with the great mysterious origins of Caroline Reeves!"

She looked at him sideways. Then she picked up her cup and sipped, still eyeing him. She made it clear to him she didn't want to engage in the subject without saying a word.

"I have a feeling this 'new' Caroline you talk about is a lot like the pre-Steven Caroline," Mark prodded.

"The 'new' Caroline lacks the innocence and naivete of the 'pre-Steven' Caroline," she said dryly.

"What happened with you and your family?"

"Geez!" This time when she rolled her eyes, her whole body seemed to roll with them. "You just don't give up, do you?" Her tone was annoyed, but she made no effort to get up and flee the discussion. Mark sensed she needed to talk about it. It was time, but she'd suppressed it for so long, the story had to find a path out of its hiding place.

"Nope."

Caroline dropped her head in her hand, her curls falling forward covering her face. After a minute she took a deep breath and looked back up at Mark, her mouth pursed and her face red.

"We had a horrible falling out, okay?" There was a higher-than-normal pitch to her voice.

"I figured that much." Mark's tone was soft, understanding. "But why?"

"Because of Steven."

"I somehow gathered he had something to do with it," Mark added. "What happened?"

Shaking her head multiple times, she open her mouth and then snapped it shut. She took a deep breath and held it before exhaling slowly and deliberately. "You know I don't want to discuss this, right?"

"Yep." Mark reached for his cup and took a sip of coffee. He savored the taste before swallowing. They had all morning. He wasn't in a rush. He tilted his head, noticing how the morning sunlight bounced off the shiny tabletop and illuminated Caroline's face. She was in nature's spotlight. "Little bits and pieces have escaped on their own. But the big part is weighing on you. You're itching to get it in the open. Once it is, you'll finally be free."

Caroline looked at him with narrow eyes again. Her head gently nodded. She picked up her cup and took a sizeable drink. Swallowing, she set the cup before her, pushing the pad and her plate to the side.

"My dad did not like Steven from the moment he met him," she began. "I met Steven when I was in college, and Steven came to the house to pick me up for dates and when we'd go off and do things. He and dad were oil and water." She cleared her throat. "My dad was very country and on the gruff side. He was a logger and spent his time around sawmills, that sort of thing, so when Steven would show up in pressed khaki's, a nice button-down shirt, and a pair of Ray Ban's, speaking 'fancy' as Dad called it...well, Dad just dismissed him."

"Of course, my mom *just loved* Steven. Steven had that *charm* and smile that won people over. Well, most people. But Dad was outright rude when Steven came around, and would say things right in front of Steven, like 'Caroline, you're wastin' yourself on that no-good' or 'front porch is as far as that fella goes. I'll not have the like of him in my house'." Caroline sighed.

"Sadly, I should have trusted my dad. He apparently saw things that I didn't. But I didn't. My mom had always told me, 'Caroline, it's just as easy to love a man who has promise and money as a man who is going to struggle his whole life to provide for his family.' I saw how Mom had to stretch our food, sometimes rationing it. And how she had to make do during lean times. It was hard. And there were so many nights that after Adam, Tory and I went to bed, we'd hear Mom and Dad arguing in the kitchen. It was always about money and bills."

Mark sat quietly, taking an occasional sip, and listened to the words spill from Caroline's lips. "Home life got better as we got older, but my mom and dad were used to scrimping, saving, and they made sure we had what we needed, but nothing more. Steven was the opposite. He had big dreams. The sky was the limit. He constantly showered me with gifts and clothes. That didn't sit well with Dad. My dad told me once, 'You're selling your soul to the Devil!' And then when Steven and I went to tell my parent's we were getting married, Dad told me, "You are dead to us!' Those were the last words he spoke to me. He threw me out of the house. Told my mom and sister to pack my things and leave them by the gate." Caroline mashed her lips together and looked at Mark with tired eyes.

"What about your mother and your brother and sister?" Mark asked. "Didn't they keep in contact with you?"

"Nope!" Caroline took another sip and reached for the carafe. "Dad's word was law!" She poured her cup half full and offered the carafe to Mark. He poured the remains in his cup.

"Adam was working with Dad by then, so he wouldn't dare go against him. Mom…well, she stood by her husband. Just like I stood by Steven. And Tory? Well, she and I never really got along. It was like we were always in competition or something. I think she was jealous or something. Though she shouldn't have been. Truth be known, she's ten times better off than me!"

"Do you miss them?" Mark leaned forward, resting his elbows on the table and clasping his hands.

Caroline glanced at him and then stared down at the sunlight on the table. "Yeah." She sighed again. "At first it was awful. I was constantly wanting to call my mom to tell her about something that happened. It felt like a hole in my life. I actually got angry for a while. I was angry at Dad, and I was angry with Steven. But then those feelings eventually passed. It's been a long time. Oddly enough, I've never run into any of them! I guess that tells you what totally different circles we were in."

"Every family has it's dynamics," Mark said. "Look at mine! And I'm the black sheep!"

"You are not!" Caroline replied.

Mark shot her a look. "You haven't noticed how everyone tiptoes around me like I'm a stick of dynamite ready to blow? 'Be careful! You don't want to set Mark off'!"

"Well…now that you mentioned it," Caroline teased, a smile finding her face.

"You should go see them." Mark reached over and rested his hand on her slinged arm, feeling the hard cast beneath the layer of fabric.

"No, I can't." Caroline shook her head slowly.

"If the whole situation was brought about because of Steven, then this is the time. Steven's out of your life." Mark reasoned. "What's the worst that could happen?"

"My dad tell me that I'm still dead to them."

"Exactly. At least you can say you tried," Mark leaned his head to look at her downward turned face. She glanced at him from the corner of her eyes. "The rest is up to them, right?"

CHAPTER 18 – HOME

Mark pulled over into a partially graveled area just off the side of the road behind a silver Equinox. On the left side of Mark's truck, a chain link fence surrounded a modest house, the matching gate showing spots of rust. Faded white clapboards sided the house, and a black metal roof showed wear from the elements. Flecks of the black paint were missing in areas and the edges were bent from the wind and from being hammered down and hammered down again. A galvanized stove pipe rose high above the second story, indicating the use of a wood stove for heat. Large, misshapen, flat stones sunk into the grassless path leading from the gate to a small porch that ran halfway across the front of the house. A simple wooden door with two vertical window panes was tucked into the corner where the porch ended and the front of the house jutted out. The door was scratched and muddy in the lower left corner, indicating the presence of a dog. A sole window occupied the jutted section of the dwelling, and another window looked out on the porch. The house had not changed since the day Caroline left.

What had changed was the addition of a tall metal building with huge doors in the lot next to the house yard, and a singlewide trailer in the lot beside that. A worn log truck was backed to the side the metal building, and a small bulldozer sat behind that. Jimmy Reeves' green dodge pickup rested in front of one of the garage doors. It looked the same save a few extra dents. Caroline made a 'humph' noise.

"What?" Mark asked, shutting off the engine.

"Dad's finally got his equipment barn." Caroline motioned towards the metal structure. "And I bet that's where Adam lives." She pointed to the trailer. "I didn't figure he'd ever move far from home!"

"Are you ready?" Mark asked.

Caroline looked at him. She gave him the look. It said, 'do I look ready?'

"Oh, look!" Her expression changed instantly. She pointed to a dog coming around the side of the house. "I bet that's Chester! He was just a pup when I left! Maybe a year old, if that!" The beagle was heavy-set and wore a thick faded orange collar partially hidden by a fold around its neck. He moved slowly, favoring a back hip, but came forward to inspect the strangers. A low bark let his people know he was on duty.

"I guess I'm ready as I ever will be," Caroline sighed. Chester announced their presence. She couldn't sit in the truck all day contemplating what to do.

Mark came around to her side and assisted her out of the truck. She smoothed out the oversized tan sweater she wore over a pair of black leggings she'd manage to pull on over her cast. She wore the boot on her casted foot and wore one of her own boots on her left foot. Her curls hung loose about her face, and she decided to forego any makeup. She wanted to be presentable, but she didn't want to present as the 'Steven-Caroline.'

Mark eased the gate open to keep Chester from escaping but enough to allow Caroline and himself to enter. The dog attempted to jump, but his front paws barely left the ground. He barked again, and Caroline reached down to pet his head. He sniffed her hand a moment and then went to Mark, smelling around his feet and his jeans.

Caroline grabbed ahold of the rickety railing as she climbed the three steps to the porch. The porch floor was mostly bare wood, greyed from weather, except for the corners and places along the edge of the house. Remnants of a painted porch floor clung to the less-traversed wood. Mark was dutifully right behind her, ready to steady her if needed. From the steps it was three paces to the door. She paused looking around the frame of the door. On the right side were the holes from the wooden screen door that used to hang.

Caroline remembered the hot summer day the screen door

had come down. She and Adam had been nine and Tory was eight. With some neighborhood friends over, the kids had gone in and out of the front door at least fifty times, getting water, ice pops, you name it. Every time, the screen door shut with a slam. Each time, Caroline's mother, Sylvie, yelled, "Don't y'all let the door slam! Your daddy be tryin' to rest!" But none of the kids paid a bit of attention to her. The last time the screen door slammed was when Adam had used the bathroom and raced back outside. Within seconds, Jimmy Reeves appeared in the doorway and glared out at the playing children. Caroline was the first to freeze in place with wide eyes, and one by one the others realized that the stocky Jimmy Reeves was not happy. The children stood silent and motionless in the yard as Caroline's father literally ripped the hinges of the screen door out of the door frame, and then tossed the screen door into the front yard. He didn't say a word, but his look scattered the children in all directions. It was almost dark before the Reeves children cautiously found their way home. Caroline stared at the ragged holes. She'd often wondered how no one lost a finger in that door.

She stiffened up, remembering how strong her father had been and how he made tearing the door from the frame look like he was pulling off a piece of tape. She exhaled heavily and looked at Mark. Mark began to raise his fisted hand to knock on the door, looking to Caroline for approval. She nodded. Mark's wrap on the door was loud and echoed on the porch. Inside muffled voices accompanied the sound of heavy footsteps approaching the door.

The door swung open with a high-pitched squeal revealing a man well over six foot tall. With shoulders broader than Mark's, the man was muscular and thickset, with a neck as large as the trees he cut. He appeared to be in his late fifties, and a grey mustache offset thick grey eyebrows and a head of grey hair. Jimmy Reeves' face was straight and emotionless as he looked from Mark to Caroline and back to Mark.

"What's your business?" Caroline's dad asked addressing

Mark.

Mark glanced at Caroline and back at her dad. "Sir, my name is Mark Meadows, and I have brought your daughter, Caroline, to see you and your wife." Mark motioned towards Caroline, whose eyes were frozen on her dad.

In the background, a woman wearing bright blue scrubs came out of a side room and approached the door. She halted when she saw the faces at the door. She also appeared to be in her late fifties and her greying hair was pulled back pinned into a bun. Her hand flew to her lips, as she exclaimed, "Caroline!" Caroline's heart shifted into high gear as she saw her mother.

Jimmy Reeves kept his eyes on Mark. "Well, Mr. Meadows, you're mistaken. I ain't got a daughter called Caroline. Tory's the only girl I got."

"Jimmy!" Caroline's mother rushed forward taking hold of the massive arm he rested on the door frame, blocking anyone from entering or exiting. "Jimmy! It's Caroline!" Sylvie Reeves insisted. "Oh, my goodness Caroline! Oh, my poor baby!" Her slender hand with long fingers still covered her mouth in shock.

"Sylvie, don't know what you're squallin' about!" Jimmy Reeves said over his shoulder. "The only person out here is some man by the name of Meadows. A very lost man." Caroline's father turned back to Mark, avoiding any glance at Caroline, and said, "Son, I believe you've got the wrong house. Good day!" The door shut abruptly, the curtains swaying from the force.

Caroline bit on her lips. She stared a moment at the door, hearing her parents voices beyond the wood and glass. A quarrel erupted briefly inside between her parents, and her father's voice boomed, "Enough!"

Mark also stood stunned by the response, but instead of staring at the door, he looked with concern at Caroline. "Caroline..."

Caroline looked from the door to Mark, forcing her lips

corners awkwardly upward. She turned, saying, "I'm fine!" She took the three paces back to the steps and began descending the creaking steps. Mark rested his arm on her back, as Chester returned to sniff their feet. The beagle escorted them down the walk and stood back as Mark undid the latch to swing the gate open. As Caroline stepped through the gate, she heard the squeal of front door hinges. She turned to look, but Mark blocked her view as he stepped through the gate opening and relatched it. When he looked up, he stopped and stood aside, revealing Sylvie Reeves standing at the top of the steps. Sylvie's thin, bare arms were folded to ward off the cold.

Caroline locked eyes with her mother. Streams of tears flowed down her mother's cheeks, but Carolines's remained dry. She was not disappointed by her father's reaction. In fact, she'd expected it. He was not a man who embraced change.

"Caroline…" her mother called softly. "I been worried sick. We been hearin' all sorts of things! I hope you gonna be okay!" She swallowed hard, fighting back emotion. "Just give your daddy some time…he'll come around…"

Caroline nodded, the rest of her fixed to the ground. "Thanks, Mom. I'll be okay. Don't worry." Caroline turned and went around the truck. A lump grew inside her throat.

Mark lifted his hand to Caroline's mother, saying, "Nice to meet you, Mrs. Reeves." With her nod, he turned and went to assist Caroline into the truck. Once he got seated and started the truck, he again lifted his hand to the woman who shivered on the porch. In the side mirror, Caroline saw that her mother watched them until the truck disappeared out of sight.

***

Caroline did not shed a tear during the encounter with her parents or afterward. This concerned Mark. He was on heightened alert in case she had a sudden breakdown, but so far nothing. She said little, but when she spoke her tone seemed normal. On the ride home, Caroline told him she wasn't ready to talk about it. When they returned to the duplex, she asked Mark to move one of the comfy chairs close to the Christmas tree. She then selected a book from Mark's library of books upstairs and settled under the throw in the glow of colors twinkling on the tree. She told Mark there was nothing to say. He was there with her. He heard. He saw.

He did. And what he saw, what he heard disturbed him. A father not only shunning his child, their own flesh, blood, and DNA, but not even acknowledging her. Pretending she wasn't even present. Invisible to them. And a mother, hesitant to disobey her husband's decisions and proclamation to embrace her own broken child. A child she gave birth to. It was obvious to Mark that Sylvie Reeves' heart broke for her daughter. It was also obvious to Mark that Caroline was not that different from her mother. Caroline had drawn to a man just like her father.

Mark recognized that while outwardly there was a difference in education and standing, Jimmy Reeves and Steven White were at the core the same man. A man who was about himself. A man who was the center of his own world. A man who permitted people to exist in his world. They orbited around him. They illuminated him, brought attention to him, lent to his success, and made him look strong and powerful and important. If such a person failed to follow the rules and uphold the man, they were tossed aside. If such a person no longer served their useful purpose, they were expelled from his world. If a person posed a threat or tried to contest the tenets of his world, they were banished. Only those who were gullible or who conceded to the man's law remained in his world. Caroline inadvertently replaced her father with Steven. Already indoctrinated to the ways of one man with sociopathic qualities, she had no awareness she had selected the same man just in the form of a husband rather than of a father. She leaped from one man's world to the other's, and while outwardly they looked and behaved differently, they were very much the same.

Caroline couldn't exist in both worlds at the same time. The forces would not allow convergence. Thus, by accepting Steven's world, Caroline's existence in her father's world terminated, and all that circled within. At a basic, subconscious level, Mark suspected Caroline knew this. She knew the rules better than anyone else and knew the cost of rejecting those rules. Maybe this was the reason Caroline had no tears. Perhaps this was why Caroline had no words. What was left to say?

Mark periodically looked up from his computer towards Caroline and the happily lit tree. He worked on a landscaping plan for a new condominium development going in. Mark had the landscaping contract and had full creative discretion for the project, except for the budget. It would be easy: work miracles for a set amount of money. He had already researched prices of various shrubs, trees, flowers, and stones, and tried to pick as many maintenance-free options as possible. He had also landed the contract for mowing, trimming and upkeep as well as plowing. Keeping the design manageable was only in his best interest.

Glancing up again, he saw a large snowflake drift down outside the window. Looking out the window beside him, another smaller flake spiraled down from the sky. It had begun. He glanced at corner of his laptop screen. Almost three-thirty. The snow was ahead of schedule. The forecast put the storm starting well after dark. Mark made a couple of clicks on the keyboard bringing up the weather site. Waiting for it to load, he glanced again Caroline's direction.

She sat slumped in the chair, her head leaning on the arm of the chair and both legs resting on the hassock in front of the chair. The throw covered her in a chaotic manner with a corner touching the floor, and the only part of her Mark saw was the top of her head of curls. She held the paperback with her unseen left hand, and every few minutes her thumb flipped a page. Beyond her the snow was peppering down. She hadn't noticed yet, or if she had, she made no mention.

Mark's anxiety began to grow. Looking at the radar map, the storm system was moving faster than expected. Both good and bad. Good in that if the storm kept its current pace, it might dump less snow than expected. Bad in that Mark would need to leave Caroline sooner than anticipated. He hated the idea of leaving her. He had hoped it was going to be later in the evening when she would sleep through most of it. But regardless, he had a job to do, and he had to leave to do it.

Just as Mark picked up his phone to dial Jared, the phone began making noises. It was Jared.

"Hey." It was Mark's usual greeting for friends and family. Caroline twisted her head to look Mark's direction. "Yeah, it started here about ten minutes ago. It's moving quicker than they originally said."

Caroline sat up in the chair, stretching and letting out a yawn. Slowly, the white fluff out the window drew her attention. Mark listened to Jared as he watched Caroline become intrigued by the snow. Her silhouette against the large window, a curtain of falling snow, and the gentle blinking colors framed a picture-perfect scene in Mark's mind.

"Huh?" Mark responded, realizing he hadn't heard a word of what Jared said. He heard Jared laughing on the other end, giving him grief about his distraction. "Yeah, yeah!" Mark admitted guilt. "Ok, listen, I'll meet you at the garage in a half hour." Mark clicked off the phone, his eyes still trapped by Caroline's image. Getting up from the table, he began walking towards her. She stretched again, shooting her left arm straight into the air and then turned towards the footsteps.

"It's snowing!" A smile filled her face. "Did you know that I absolutely and completely detest snow?"

"No, really?" Mark was surprised by her comment, especially with the way she watched it.

"Yep. Never liked it." As she nodded her head, she straightened herself in the chair. "Mom couldn't drag me out of the house when it snowed. Adam and Tory loved it. They couldn't wait to get their boots, gloves, and hats on. But not me!" Caroline turned her head to the window again. "But for some reason, I find this absolutely beautiful! It's filling me with a happy feeling!"

Mark stood next to the back of the chair, cupping the side of her head with his hand and looking down at her gleaming face as she marveled at the flakes. Mark said, "I've always loved the snow and never could wait to get out in it! Even as an adult. It gives me an adrenaline rush or something." He brushed her hair with his fingers. "Except now…"

She looked up at him, a questioning look on her face. "Why now? What's changed?"

"You." He forced a smile. "I don't want to leave you…"

His words drew a bigger smile out of Caroline and a small chuckle. "But you have to go! People are depending on you to keep the roads clear and safe!" Then she added, "I'll be fine. And I'll be right here when you get back!" She moved away from his hand and began pushing herself out of the chair. Her first couple of steps were unsteady.

"Where are you going?" Mark asked.

"I'm going to make a nice hot pot of coffee for your thermos while you go get ready!" Caroline's steps became more stable as she headed towards the kitchen.

"Seriously?" Mark watched her move with a mission. "You're amazing!"

"No. I just don't want you freezing to death out there!" she laughed. "I kinda need you!"

By the time Mark returned downstairs with an extra layer and insulated boots on his feet, the odor of coffee permeated the downstairs. He paused a moment, taking a good whiff. It was as close to the smell of home that Mark could imagine. Perhaps that is why the drink was his favorite. And now Caroline was sending him off with a bottle full of the essence. As he pulled his coat from the closet, he watched her pour the steaming contents of the carafe into the thermos and twist the lid on tightly.

"Here you go! That was perfect timing!" Caroline said, shuffling towards him with the stainless bottle in hand. "Got your phone?" She asked, handing him the coffee.

"Yep. Right here!" Mark patted the pocket of his shirt hidden by his coat.

"Be careful!" She raised up to leave a kiss on his cheek, but Mark was quick. He caught her lips with his and gave her a real kiss. Moving his head away, he gave her a gentle nod.

***

The knock at the door couldn't have been more than five minutes after Mark pulled out of the driveway. Caroline was in the kitchen hunting around in the pantry and surveying the contents of the refrigerator to see what kind of meal she could pull together with one hand. Mark had some ground beef thawing, but she had no idea what his intentions for it had been. She closed the refrigerator door and scooted towards the front door. Without checking the peephole, she unlocked the deadbolt and opened the door.

Beth stood holding Mark's favorite dish in mittened hands. The hood of her coat was pulled over her head and the fur on the edge caught the snowflakes before they landed on her eyelashes. Behind her, a black Suburban was parked with the engine still running and it's windshield wipers clearing snowflakes before they had a chance to melt.

"Hi, Caroline!" Beth greeted before Caroline could speak. "I guess I missed Mark!"

"Beth! Yes. Only by about five minutes! He just left!" Caroline stepped back, "Come on in out of the cold!"

Beth stepped up into the house and stomped her snowy boots on the rug.

"What have you got there?" Caroline pointed to the dish.

"Oh, let me go set this down!" Beth started towards the kitchen. "I'm returning Mark's dish, and it's our tradition to not return a dish unless it full! I made a baked macaroni and cheese! One of Mark's favorites." She set the dish on the burner of the stove and pushed her hood off her head. "Phew! That thing's amazing outside but burns me up inside!"

"That was very thoughtful, Beth!" Caroline said following much slower to the kitchen.

"From what they're saying about this here storm, it sounds like Mark will be out for a good stretch." Beth tried to smooth some random hairs roused by the static electricity. "I figured this would give y'all something to nibble on. And, if I know my brother, he'll come home with an appetite! Make sure you get your share ahead of time, otherwise all you'll be left with is an empty dish!"

Caroline giggled. "Thanks for the fair warning! I was just trying to figure out what I could make, and the options are slim with on one hand to work with!" Laughing, she added, "I can't even open a can by myself!"

"Now, see? Problem solved!" Beth smiled. "All you need to do is sit back, relax, stay warm and enjoy the snow!" Beth reached and gave Caroline's shoulders a gentle squeeze. Then with raised eyebrows, she added, "And be ready to warm up my brother with some good lovin' when he comes through that door!"

"Oh, Beth!" Caroline flushed with embarrassment. "It's not like that…"

"Why sure it is, darlin'!" Beth faced her and rubbed Caroline's arm with her mittened hand. "Anyone can see the look in both of y'all's eyes and the way y'all carry on together!"

Caroline glanced at Beth and quickly looked towards the floor. "We're…uh…taking things slow. Besides, I'm not really sure he…"

"Darlin'!" Beth cut her off. "Let me tell you somethin'! Life's short. The both of you ought to know that better than anybody! What are you waitin' for? Life's already almost slipped through your fingers. Don't give it another chance to get away from you!" Beth put her arm around Caroline's shoulder and began to walk her towards the door. "Now, Mark's a bit gun-shy with all he's been through, but I can tell you I've never seen him so smitten with a woman! Not even Jennifer. Mark was never this way with her!" As they reached the door,

Beth stopped and again faced a flushed Caroline who tried to avoid her look but couldn't.

"Caroline, you've already lost enough time. You're at that place in life where you know exactly what you want! Don't be wastin' another day!" Beth tilted her head and gave Caroline a slanted smile. With a wink, the older woman hugged Caroline. "Well, I better get while the getting's still good! I got a trunk load of groceries to get to the house! Thank the Good Lord for four-wheel-drive!"

"Thanks, Beth!" Caroline smiled, opening the door. "Be careful and say hello to your dad and mom!"

As Beth stepped out into the swirling snow, she tugged her hood back over her head and waved her mittened hand creating a swirl of snowflakes. Caroline closed the door to the storm and leaned against it, contemplating the older woman's words. Beth vocalized the thoughts that swirled in Caroline's head. Looking upward, not at the ceiling or the roof or the snow that flew down from full clouds, but at something beyond, Caroline smiled. Beth brought the baked macaroni and cheese, but Caroline sensed that she delivered the message on behalf of someone higher and wiser. A warmth spread through her body. Minutes later, the tracks left by the Suburban filled with snow. As if they hadn't even been there.

***

After a small dish of the baked macaroni, which she heated in the microwave and ate standing up at the counter, Caroline returned to the chair by the tree. She flopped this way and that trying to find the comfortable position she'd had earlier, but it was gone. She managed to spread the throw and returned to her book. She read the same page four times, before setting the book face down in her lap. Between the fading light outside and a new set of thoughts left by Beth, the words simply did not register. She leaned over on her left side and propped her head with a pillow on the side of the chair. The snowflakes falling outside the windows took on the colors of the Christmas tree.

She first thought about Mark out in the cold and on the snowy roads, plowing and salting. Surely, he'd had some of the coffee she sent along. She hadn't thought to ask where he was plowing. She just knew that between the contracts he had for developments and parking lots, and clearing some of the narrower city streets, he'd been gone for the night. Depending on how long the snow kept falling, maybe even part of the next day. He'd be exhausted when he returned. She was worried about him, concerned he was safe. She had never thought about all the men, and woman too, who were out in the storm, putting their lives at potential risk, working to keep the roads safe and passable for others. Until that moment, she had totally taken this for granted. The streets just magically cleared. She had never considered the human element involved, and the families left behind with the worry.

Beth's words squirrelled right in with the snow thoughts. She told her, '...you know exactly what you want.' Did she? How did Beth see this so clearly, yet it was so hazy to Caroline? No, she didn't deny her feelings for Mark Meadows had grown tremendously and continued to gain strength in the thirty-nine days since the accident. But she was so confused on where he stood. He'd make advances and even kissed her passionately, but then he'd back off. For days there wouldn't be so much as brushing one of her strands of hair aside. He'd say things that indicated he expected her to be around long term, such as converting the girls' room to an office for her or she could store her things as long as she needed in the garage, but then the next moment he was loading the boxes for Goodwill! Granted, he wasn't much on keeping things around that were not useful. She just couldn't get a good read on him.

Perhaps, Beth was right? Maybe it was up to Caroline to be the forward one. To be the one to make that monumental step from 'a fabulous kiss' to ...? Beth had mentioned Caroline showering him with 'good lovin's' when Mark got home, but

Caroline figured he'd be tired and want nothing more than food and sleep! Or would he?

Finally, her mind drifted to their trip to her parent's house earlier that day. It warmed her heart to see Chester still at command of his little kingdom, but it saddened her that even he was feeling the effects of age. Her father hadn't changed a bit from the day she left. A few more gray hairs, of course, but Jimmy Reeves was true to himself. Once the man took a notion on something, it might have well as been set in concrete. She admitted, seeing her mother upset on the porch hit a nerve. She was so thin. The scrubs hung on her blowing in the breeze and worry and sadness filled her eyes. This disturbed Caroline. Where was the strong woman she knew as 'mother'? Caroline didn't display an emotional response to Mark, but it undeniably pecked at her heart.

However, Caroline learned it from Sylvie Reeves herself: "when you choose your bed, you gotta lie in it!" Her mother had chosen Jimmy Reeves and all that baggage he brought just the same as Caroline had accepted Steven and his ideas about things. The only difference? Caroline had an out. Steven betrayed her. Steven more than betrayed her. Where or what would Sylvie Reeves do? Then again, where or what would Caroline do if it hadn't been for Mark Meadows plopping in that chair at her bedside day after day?

***

She hadn't lied. Caroline was in the exact spot Mark had left her. When he walked in the front door and slid off his boots, his first sight was of the Caroline sleeping in the chair by the Christmas tree in the corner. Her head rested on a pillow, with her curly dark locks sprawled out. The book she had been reading was on the floor on its edge with the pages fanned out. The glare from the white outdoor on the blanket made the glass ornaments on the tree shine, throwing patches of color on Caroline's pale skin. Mark stood with one boot off, the other still on, taking in a scene that caused his heart to skip a beat.

He was worn out, barely able to lift a foot, as he dragged toward the orange door of the duplex, but once inside, the door shut, his entire body rejuvenated with the site of the woman in the chair. As a smile sprung on his face, he slipped the other boot off, his sock coming halfway off in the process. He didn't care. Unzipping his coat, he pulled his arms out of the sleeves and let it, his hat, and his gloves drop on top of his boots. Something he never did. Everything always found its place immediately. This time he found his place. Immediately.

Leaning on one knee beside the chair, Mark rested his eyes on Caroline. His sleeping beauty. All he had to do was place a kiss on her lips, and she was sure to come alive. And he did. Bending towards her, his lips still cold from the outdoors touched her warm soft red lips, and her eyes fluttered several times before opening. Pulling back, Mark saw the misty haze of sleep in her eyes as a smile gradually bloomed on her face.

"Hey there! Good morning!" She turned her head slightly toward the window. "How long have you been watching me?" she asked in a sleepy voice, followed by a yawn and a stretch of her limbs.

"Oh, a few minutes," Mark spoke softly. "Not long. I didn't want you to wake and find me. That would be creepy." He gave a slight laugh.

She attempted to sit straighter in the chair. "Yes, you're right. That would have been totally creepy! I prefer the way you did it." She stretched her neck to each side, then said, "In fact, I think your lips are cold! Perhaps they need to be warmed up?" She gave a slight smile, hinting to a mischievous side. Without comment, Mark obliged. His hands went to each side of her head, and he leaned towards her lips, kissing her like he'd been gone days.

If fact, it felt like he had been gone days. While he'd been occupied every minute driving the truck, operating the plow and spreading salt in slick areas and near stops, his thoughts were full of her. It seemed like the night was endless and the snow would never abate. When the storm finally waned to light flurries, he felt his insides start fluttering like wings of butterflies with the anticipation of returning home.

He understood now why Jared was always so anxious to get the last few streets or lots cleared. He had Shelly and the kids to return to, whereas Mark returned to either an empty house or he went to Beth's for coffee and something to eat, and inevitably crashed on her couch for a few hours of sleep. This time, he had Caroline to return to. As he finished their kiss, his lips much warmer, he wondered if she knew how much her being here meant to him.

"I may be still asleep and dreaming this, but I believe you might be glad to see me!" Caroline said, raising her hand to touch the side of Mark's face. Her slender fingers ran along his strong jawline, feeling the soft stubble that had returned with him.

Mark chuckled. "You know," he said dipping his head, "That's scary! I was just thinking if you knew how glad I was to be home with you!"

"Really?" Caroline had a dreamy look about her.

Mark nodded, as he stood, reaching for her hand to help her out of the chair. "Really. And do you know what my sore, stiff body needs?" He watched as Caroline shift her eyes around playfully. "A hug!" He drew her to him and folded his arms around her, bringing her warmth and closeness to him. He buried his nose in her hair around her neck, breathing in her smell. He decided instantly, it was a much better smell than coffee. If only he could put it in a bottle.

"I bet you're beyond tired." Caroline's words were muffled by the double layers of shirts.

"I am," he said, stray hairs sticking to his lips. Pulling away, he held her in front of him and looked at her nodding his head. "I need to get a few hours of shuteye. I'm fading fast here."

"That's perfectly understandable," she replied. "By the way, Beth brought by a baked macaroni and cheese. No cooking later!"

"Bless her heart!" Mark smiled. "Listen, if I'm not up by two, come wake me, okay?"

"Sure," she said looking around for a clock. "What time is it now?" She frowned, probably wondering how late she'd slept in.

"It's almost eleven," Mark said yawning. He reluctantly let go of her snuggly warm body, and began towards the stairs, his sock flopping as he went.

CHAPTER 19 – COMING CLEAN

Two o'clock came and went without Caroline realizing. She'd been busily working on her computer. Not doing work-work, as the university closed due to the weather. Instead, she practiced her typing with her left hand. Her fingers needed more familiarity with the key locations on the full keyboard, and she needed to gain some speed. Making notes was tedious after each Zoom advising session, yet she had to get her thoughts on each student down in a limited window of time before the next session.

In spare moments during the day and at night when watching Christmas bliss on the Hallmark channel, Caroline played with her fingers on her right hand. Each day, she woke with hopes that they would feel something or would make the slightest wiggle or motion. Each morning, she found the safety pin she'd tucked into the nightstand drawer beside her bed and gave each finger a good jab. Nothing. Well, no feeling. Each jab did yield a speck of blood. That was all. Each morning brought a disappointment that became more and more predictable. But she hid it well.

After all, what could she do? If there was permanent damage, it was done. If there was a chance that feeling and movement could return in time as nerves, ligaments, tendons, muscles, and bones healed, that was good too. That would reveal in time. She didn't know what the future held in that regard, so she resolved herself to dealing with each day. As a kid, she'd heard Mamaw Reeves' say over and over, "Today's troubles are 'nough for today. Don't ya' worry none 'bout tomorraw. It'll have worries its own!' The young Caroline took Mamaw Reeves' words as gospel, revering her grandmother for her wisdom. It wasn't until Caroline was in college that she learned Mamaw Reeves' words truly were 'Gospel' and came from Matthew 6:34. None-the-less, they were words Caroline tried to live by, and she was thankful Mamaw Reeves did also.

When the laptop came home with Caroline two weeks prior, she'd begun keeping a journal of sorts. Her typing practice entailed recording events, thoughts, feelings, observations, and anything Caroline felt relevant to her moving forward with her life. She was entirely random in her typed recordings, again putting into one-handed words what seemed significant to the moment and given day. Each day, more words joined the ones from the days before, but Caroline didn't go back and review any of them. 'Stream of thought' was her method, and she didn't want any perspectives from preceding days casting a slant on or coloring the current one. As she finished her sentence and saved her work, she looked down at the clock in the display. Two-twenty-six.

She jumped up, realizing she'd let Mark sleep longer than wanted. She went up the steps with a firm grip on the railing and went into the master bedroom. The bed was empty. She thought for sure he would have crashed on his own bed! She turned and headed into the room of lavender and flowers. It was her turn to gaze upon a sleeping soul. Mark laid on his stomach, his face bent to the side, and his arms raised above his shoulders and hidden under the pillow. Short snorting sounds came from his partially open mouth. Caroline suddenly wished she had her phone, as the picture before her was perfect for situations requiring a little 'encouragement'! She laughed quietly to herself, and then thought about Beth's words: 'Don't waste another day' and 'good lovin.'

She moved to the side of the bed Mark faced. She sat gently on the edge of the bed and rested her hand lightly on his back. She began rubbing his back slowly and within a half-minute he began to stir. She ran her hand up around his shoulders and began to rub one then the other, eliciting a moan from the partially awake Mark. His one visible eye opened and searched for her. She was almost out of range of sight.

"You keep doing that and you're headed for some trouble," Mark mumbled partially into the pillow.

Caroline slid her hand across his back and ran it over the other shoulder. "That was what I was kind of hoping for…" she said in a low voice.

Mark's arms appeared as he rolled on his side. In an instant, he grabbed her and drug her under the covers, so she laid against his front. Her head was on the pillow but facing away from his. His right arm went around her, resting on her torso just below her cast. Her left foot found his legs, while her booted foot tangled with the comforter and ended up resting on top.

Mark raised up on his left arm, and leaned over her and began showering short wet kisses on the side of her face. She tried to turn her head search his lips with hers, but Mark moved his hand, putting his forefinger in a 'shh' over her lips. He continued to work his way down her cheek the side of her jaw, then to her neck, leaving a trail of invisible kisses. While he concentrated on painting her neck with his tender lips, his hand moved back down, finding her breast rather than her cast. The instant he touched her, she felt her body stiffen in response, and feelings inside her began unleashing. Flutters. Buzzing. Pulsing. Laying against him, she was not the only one to stiffen. He continued to massage her breast through her shirt, and then his lips found their way to her lips. This time when he kissed her, his tongue dove deep into her mouth searching for hers. She totally forgot about the actions of his hand as she concentrated on the tango of their lips and tongues. Mark's kiss expressed a passion Caroline had never experienced. It took her breath and made her dizzy, but she responded with a fervor she never knew was within her. She closed her eyes and savored to the moment, wondering where had Mark Meadows been her whole life?

When their lips parted, Mark shook his head two times quickly and gasped for air. Caroline's breaths also searched to fill her lungs. Opening her eyes, Mark's stared into her with a look she'd never seen before. The look filled her, and she drank it in with her own eyes, capturing as much of it as she could.

Mark moved his hand from her breast and ran the outside of his fingers along her chin, and then smiled. His touch sent a tingle through her body.

Mark smiled. He knew exactly what he'd done. He'd brought her to a level of excitement she'd never...no...*never* experienced. Then he spoke, "Want to go see some snow?"

"What?!" She jerked her head. *Where in the world did that come from?* In the heat of the moment, he's talking snow?

"Yeah." His voice was soft. "You said you always hated snow but now thought it was beautiful. There is truly nothing more beautiful than a fresh snow." He rubbed her face again, his eyes sparking and entirely enjoying her frustration. "Except for you, that is."

"You're serious?" She wasn't sure if she was asking or making a statement. "Do I look like I am in the condition to go out in snow?"

"If you're in the truck, you do!" Mark replied sitting up. "Let's go for a ride! The sun should have most of the roads down to the pavement by now!"

Caroline looked at him with her mouth hanging open. No words. She imperceptibly shook her head in amazement. But this was his pattern. Kiss her, get her excited, then drop her cold turkey! No...frozen turkey! What was he avoiding? "Yeah. Sure. Let's go for a ride. Me, the new Caroline, loves snow. Whoopie." She sat up, swung her feet off the bed, and stood. Mark was already crawling out at the foot of the bed.

As she descend the stairs, she thought about Dennis Meadows. His diagnosis was entirely off. Mark was more ADHD and OCD than MDD!

***

Remarkably, more vehicles were on the roads than what Caroline expected. Just as Mark stated, the sun reduced any remaining snow to wet pavement, calling people to return to their usual daily activities. The parking lots around the Kroger,

Wal-Mart and Lowes were full of cars, some parked at odd angles around tall mounds of snow piled around light posts. Caroline chuckled. She imagined some mother having to lasso her child or children from wanting to climb the snow mounds.

As Mark cruised along the AA Highway, Caroline took in the views of the rolling hills blanketed with white fluff. High in the trees, groups of flakes huddled together in the cold clinging to branches and sparkling like glitter in the fading rays of light. They travelled along some back country roads, where they passed entire farms hidden beneath Nature's white wonder. Holstein cows waited for feed near barns, many of them blending into the surrounding snow.

Dogs leaped across the snow like deer as they chased and played. Children and adults speckled some of the slopes trying out sleds and discs that had been collecting dust in garages and outbuildings. The sights and scenes were Norman Rockwell paintings sprung to life.

After bouncing along the country roads, Mark headed for the heart of Maysville: the downtown and the flood wall. Caroline's mind took snapshots every direction she turned. The warmth of the red brick of buildings popped against the snow-covered roads, walks, awnings, and parked cars. Snow even clung to the Christmas wreaths and decor hanging from the tall lamps that lined the streets. Nature's magnificence. She regretted not having her phone with her but doubted photographs could come close to capturing what her eyes and heart saw. As they passed Market Street, Caroline had a sudden urge to jump out of the truck to run and play in the snow. Yeah, not a good idea with a casted foot and arm. Besides, she couldn't even form a proper snowball with one hand, and a one-winged snow angel? Caroline shook her head.

"What's wrong?" Mark asked as they passed the fountain wearing a coat of snow.

"Oh, I was just thinking about how I'd love to get out and play in the snow!" Caroline said laughing. "Isn't that crazy? A grown woman?"

"No, I don't think that's crazy at all," Mark replied stopping next to the Justice Center. Its metal railings were adorned with boughs of greenery and ribbons. The boughs bowed down with the weight of the snow, and one came loose altogether hanging down to the sidewalk. "I like to think there's a little kid left in all of us. You're seeing all of this with fresh eyes. They eyes of a kid."

"Yeah, I guess so," Caroline nodded. Her smile faded somewhat as she remembered how the kid inside the old Caroline wanted nothing to do with the snow. But the new Caroline's internal child loved the feeling of a snowflake landing on her cheek or the tip of her nose. It made her feel alive.

"I don't think it wise for you to get out," Mark added. "This is a really wet, heavy snow and it's slick."

"Oh, trust me! I'm not up for any more broken bones!" Caroline looked down at her arm. "I'm hoping to shed these casts next week! I don't want to trade them for new ones, that's for sure!"

Mark put the truck back in gear, and they began rolling down the road again, passing shops and homes. Caroline recognized that the snow so adequately covered everything that the scenes before her could well have been vintage views from fifty years ago. Who could tell what the models of the cars were? The houses and most of the buildings hadn't changed much! Funny, how something as simple as a few snowflakes stacked up could change a person's perception!

She struggled to remember why she had disliked snow so much, but her reasons evaded her, as if they too were hidden somewhere under the blanket of good and purity.

***

Caroline waited for Mark to finish in the kitchen so he could help tape her bags on for her shower. She sat on the edge of the bed as the sounds of dishes clacking against each other flowed up the stairs. The drive around town had been beautiful and relaxing. Caroline enjoyed most seeing the downtown area covered in winter. It made the approaching Christmas feel more real and joyous in her heart, reviving a little of the excitement she felt as a child. The counting down the days, the anticipation of what Santa might bring, and the candies, cookies and cakes that only appeared at that time of year all came to mind. The spirit of the season had found her for sure.

She now attached a good, tingly feeling to snow, though not exactly like the tingly feeling she felt right before Mark spontaneously suggested going for a ride. What was up with that? Laying there, things were progressing between them. The baby steps were becoming bigger steps, and Caroline was sure it was all leading to 'the moment.' But just like that—cut off! Cut short! What was Mark waiting for? She thought for a while that maybe it was because she was still legally tied to Steven, but that ended four days before. She also contemplated that maybe Mark just didn't find her appealing in that way, but then he did and said things contradictory. Also, there was the matter of the casts. Was he apprehensive about doing something that could cause her discomfort or further injury? She just couldn't figure out what was holding him back. She'd never been a 'forward' person in that way but perhaps she need to put her old ways aside and be more assertive. Maybe? She sighed and rose from the bed.

Caroline collected a clean t-shirt, underwear, and sleep shorts. The sleep shorts were a pair of Mark's boxer shorts she'd claimed. She didn't feel guilty about it. In fact, she derived comfort from wearing something of Mark's. Silly, but she felt closer to him. She'd given up on the long sleep pants as they sweated her during the night, and she'd found them comfortable for lounging around the house during the day. At least on days when they weren't going anywhere. But, depending on where they were going, she sometimes still wore them. She chuckled to herself. If Steven could only see her now —going around and out in public dressed in men's sleep pants and an oversized sweatshirt. He'd just die! Not the image he wanted portrayed to the outside world!

Caroline headed into the bathroom and set her clothes on the counter. The image in the mirror caught her attention. Glancing up, she saw a woman staring back at her with pale blue eyes edged in brown like the curls that hung to her shoulders. She reached up and tucked some of the hair behind her ear. An image of the 'old Caroline' popped in her head. It was the Caroline that drove on the bridge. That Caroline's hair had been arrow-straight thanks to a hot iron and plenty of product to tame the curls and had been pulled back from a face with even-toned skin. Eyeliner and mascara highlighted perfectly applied eyeshadow, and her small, kissable lips were plump and pink. That woman never left the bridge.

Caroline tilted her head from side to side, studying the new her. Her eyebrows were no longer trimmed and shaped, and her pale complexion hadn't seen a drop of foundation since the accident. While she'd gotten a few items of make-up at the store and from the house, applying it proved more of a challenge than Caroline had been prepared for. Her left hand lacked the dexterity needed to brush on mascara and to line her eyes and lips for shadow and lipstick. And the hair? She just didn't have the fight in her to deal with it. She combed it when wet, then the rest was up to it. The woman who looked back at Caroline smiled, letting her know it was okay to let go of the old and embrace the new.

Mark's face appeared behind the face of the woman in the mirror. His eyes searched for Caroline's, and they connected in the reflection. Her smile brought a smirk to his face as he brushed her curls away and proceeded to leave another path a wet kisses on her neck. Caroline closed her eyes, focusing on the soft lips once again painting her skin. It tickled and sent tingly sensations down her shoulder and back. Caroline turned as his lips worked their way around to the front of her neck and up, bringing the grand finale by finding her lips. When they parted, Caroline kept her eyes closed a moment longer and then exhaled, the tingles fleeing with the air.

"Ready?" Mark asked.

"Hmm?" Caroline replied, opening her eyes. *Ready for what?* Mark picked up the duct tape that laid on one of the two boxes of bags on top of the toilet tank, grabbing a smaller bag for her foot.

"Oh." She followed with, "That." Three more weeks, hopefully, for the foot. Who knew how many for the arm. A sense of disappointment seeped in.

Mark stepped back as Caroline pushed down her pants, stepping out of them as they pooled around her feet. The bulky sweatshirt still covering her, she sat on the toilet lid and held out her casted leg. Mark bent down on knee, slipped the bag over her foot and up her leg, and Caroline held the bag as Mark taped the bag opening tightly to her calf. He ran his palm around the tape, making sure there were no creases to allow water. Before rising, he landed a kiss on her knobby knee, eliciting a giggle.

"Does that tickle?" he asked with a hopeful tone.

"Not one bit!" she promptly replied. "It's just sweet!"

Rising to his feet, Mark reached behind her for the second bag. Caroline struggled with the sweatshirt, freeing her left arm, and pulled it over her head. Mark ended up helping her work the fleecy arm down over the cast, which acted like Velcro.

"Ugh! I'll be so happy..." Caroline began. She didn't have to finish her thought. Mark nodded.

"The sad part is, when that day comes, you'll no longer need me," Mark sighed.

"Well, sad for you! You're enjoying this!" Caroline teased. "You're getting a birds-eye view every other night!" She laughed and looked at Mark slowly unfolding the bag, taking short peeks at her. Having let go of her last shred of modesty, weeks before, she shook her head. *Typical male. They just can't help themselves!* He suppressed a smile as he worked the bag over her casted arm, 'accidentally' brushing her breast with his hand. Shaking her head, she chuckled. *It's how they're wired!* Again, she held the bag to her shoulder as Mark gathered the opening and applied the duct tape.

"There you go!" he said, smoothing the tape, making super sure it was sticking in the front.

Still chuckling inside, Caroline turned and started the shower, testing the water temperature. Glancing over her shoulder, she saw Mark pulling his shirt over his head. "You know," she said stepping into the water raining down. "It's ridiculous for you to get soaked helping me..." she doused her head under the water, wetting her hair. Wiping the water from her eyes, she was staring at Mark's bare chest in front of her, getting wet from the spray. His jeans laid a heap on the floor next to her sweatshirt.

"Oh..." She looked from the stray chest hairs up to Mark's face. A serious expression accompanied a twitching jaw, a sign that he was feeling uneasy about something.

"This doesn't upset you, does it?" Mark asked, brushing back wet strands of hair from her face. An uncertainty filled his eyes.

"No. Not at all." Caroline gave a quick smile as she stepped back allowing Mark access to the water. "Like I was saying... there's no sense getting your *clothes* soaked helping me." She reached for the shampoo, handing it to him, attempting a covert glance down. The shampoo bottle blocked her view as Mark squeezed out some in his hand.

"Speaking of birds..." He began rubbing and lathering up Caroline's hair with both hands. "We can clean two birds at one time this way!"

"Yes, that is true. But you might ruffle my feathers in the process!" she giggled.

As Caroline rinsed her head, the suds rolled down her body spreading the tingling sensation growing within her. She'd never showered with a man before. Certainly not Steven. He would hardly dress in front of her, never mind fully expose himself in running water. Opening her eyes, she saw the white foam covering Mark's head as he scrubbed his own hair. She stepped out of the water to give him room to rinse and took a casual peak downward, checking out Mark's other 'features.' She supposed she must be a *typical woman*. A corner of her mouth upturned as she held her scrubby towards him for a squirt of body wash. She ran the pink puff over her torso and bent to get her legs, as Mark soaped his own arms and torso. Leaning her hip against the shower wall to steady herself, she ran the scrubby over her left foot and then extended her foot into the water to rinse it. *No more soapy falls.* She glanced at Mark's feet with his cute long toe, and then began running her eyes up. Her mouth dropped open and her eyes grew wide as she put her foot down and dropped the scrubby. She grabbed for the wall and froze.

"Mark..." She wasn't sure if she thought it or spoke it. His feet and ankles were pale white, as if he wore a pair of crew socks. Right where the 'socks' ended, the skin on both of his calves was abruptly red and purplish and looked waxen. Rough. Like molten plastic. Her eyes flowed up to his knees, seeing the same melted texture and patches of purple-red scars that extended to his mid-thighs. Caroline wasn't sure what she saw. Slowly, her eyes continued up his body until they reached his eyes. Her mouth moved, but her words were silent. *Wha...?*

Mark looked back at her with a flat expression. The water rained down between them. He finally spoke, "Scars." He bent over to pick up the scrubby, then turned to squirt more body wash on it. "Let me get your back."

Caroline hesitantly turned, finding her words as she did. "What...how did you...what are they from?"

"The explosion." Mark ran the soapy scrubby over her left shoulder and down her arm. "I told you it wasn't pretty down there."

"I had no idea what you meant." She glanced over her shoulder. "I thought you were..." She winced.

"Joking?" Mark gave a laugh. "No. No joke. Second and third-degree burns."

"Mark, I'm so sorry! Are they painful?" She turned, taking the scrubby from him looking down at his legs again.

"Not really," Mark said. "Not now. Mostly itchy but there's not much feeling in the scarred areas. The nerves are gone. Numb. There's some sensation around the edges, but it's more like a tingle."

"Oh my God! I...I had no..." Caroline shook her head looking back up at Mark. A sadness claimed her, her eyebrows expressing the pain she felt for him.

"Idea?" Mark gave her a smile. "Of course not. It's not my best feature. Not something I go around talking about. Not my proudest moment." He turned, asking her, "Can you get my back?"

Nodding, she ran the scrubby along his strong shoulders, her thoughts consumed by his injuries. She stole another glance at his legs. The back of them. They were scarred just the same. "How did you not get burned everywhere? How are you still alive?"

"A neighbor was outside when the explosion happened. The house was reduced to toothpicks. He ran over and found me. Put out the flames. Just my jeans caught fire. Had on leather boots. Spared my feet."

"You were so lucky." Caroline paused the scrubby as she reached his backside. He had some scarring on his butt as well, but not like his legs. These scars were straight and deliberate. She timidly went on. "How did you not get killed in the blast?" When she pulled the scrubby away, Mark ran his back under the water and then faced her.

"Just as you said. Extremely lucky." He sighed, looking down at his own legs. "I guess God was watching over me then too. I just wasn't ready to see it, I guess." Looking back at her, he asked, "Does it disgust you?"

Caroline was briefly taken aback by his question. "The scaring? No. No." She shook her head. "I guess we all have our scars. Some are just more visible than others." She glanced at the bag on her arm. "I'm sure I'll be wearing lots of long-sleeves in my future."

"Maybe not." Mark smiled at her. "When I went through this, I thought it was going to be way worse than what it is. I thought I wasn't going to walk. The skin got real tight. Especially at the knees. But skin grafts. Physical therapy. Compression clothes for a time. Creams and ointments. No one knows the difference. Except me." He sighed deeply. "And now you."

"What about your butt?" she asked apprehensively, as Mark turned to shut the water off.

"My butt?" he asked. "Oh! That's where they got skin for the grafts. For my knees. So that area could be more flexible. Reduce the tightness so I could bend more easily."

Caroline winced and took the towel Mark handed her. As she began drying off, her eyes kept returning to Mark's legs. As she peeled the duct tape from her shoulder and pulled off the bag, attempting to crumple it into a ball, she winced as Mark ran his towel over his legs. She could tell he wiped the towel lighter there than on the rest of his body. When done, he immediately reached into the cabinet under the vanity and pulled out a bottle of lotion and massaged healthy amounts on his scarred areas. Caroline shed the bag on her foot cast and added that crumpled bag to the other in the trash.

Rubbing her hair vigorously with the towel, Caroline wondered how she was never able to tell that something had been different with Mark's legs. But she hadn't notice anything. Not until now. Maybe she was so hung up in her own injuries. She ran a comb through the tangles left by the towel.

"My biggest challenge is making sure the skin stays moist and doesn't dry out and get stiff. I've had it crack before, and that's not pleasant," Mark said grimacing slightly. He put the lotion bottle back in place. "Exercise and motion keeps the skin stretched and pliable." Then facing her, he added, "Winter's harder than the rest of the year. I'm really active except the colder months, so I have to take special care."

Caroline nodded. She didn't know what to say. She saw her

face cream on the counter. Normally, she'd slather a good layer on her face as a pre-emptive strike against wrinkles and age spots, but it seemed petty given Mark's situation. She bypassed the nightly ritual and reached for her underwear instead. Mark reached out and put his hand on her arm. She glanced at him, not expecting his touch. He shook his head and took a step closer to her, drawing her body towards him until they touched.

A tentativeness filled his eyes, but his motions were decisive. He bent down and kissed her on the lips. Briefly. When he pulled away, he raised a questioning eyebrow. She knew the question. She nodded, reaching her arm up on his bare chest. He bent slightly and with a hand around each of her thighs, lifted her and carried her towards the master bedroom.

***

Mark laid Caroline in the center of the master bed, crawling next to her. The air on her still damp skin felt cold, but it was Mark's warm body touching hers that sent shivers to her extremities.

"Um…" Caroline began, only to be silenced by Mark's finger touching her lips. Instead of his lips touching hers to quiet her, he began a trail of gentle kisses on her neck. Slowly and deliberately, he made his way down her neck to her shoulders, then her chest, and parts of her naked arm. When she made another attempt to speak, unsure of what was transpiring, he replied between gentle grazes on her body, "Shh. Just lay back and enjoy!" She awkwardly laid her head back down on the bed and closed her eyes.

She concentrated on the feeling of each wet interaction Mark's lips made with her body. Her tension began to fade in wisps like a fog in a light wind. Thoughts sprung into her mind.

His legs? Did they hurt when he laid on them? When they touched something? She focused on his kisses. When he reached her legs and feet, a calm and loftiness encircled her. A state of relaxation she couldn't imagine possible claimed her. The kisses dwindled and Mark shifted his body, covering her with his bare skin. His arms slid around her. Floating in a trance-like state, she opened her eyes finding herself staring directly into Mark's. She swore she saw a flash of light, but realized it was love flowing from his eyes to hers and back to his. He covered her budding smile with his lips and…

CHAPTER 20 – THE REAL CAROLINE

Sleep came quickly to Mark, given he'd been awake basically since the day before except for a few-hour nap, but the restorative state evaded Caroline. She laid motionless wrapped in a combination of Mark's bare torso, his arms and legs and the comforter they drew around them. Apart from Mark's soft, even breaths, the world was quiet. Shrouded in a toasty, lofty feeling, tucked into the dark room, Caroline's mind flooded with an invisible glow.

It was the part of the night when everything living thing went silent. It was her favorite time of the day, ironically the night. The span on the clock when the old Caroline relished being awake. With the world paused, painfully still and in its dark minutes just before the sun began to chase shadows again, Caroline was best able to hear her inner thoughts: the deliberations she suppressed from the outside world and dealt with in solitude. Her mind sorted through those internal issues and one-sided debates without distraction or competition from the outside world.

Except as she laid there entwined, her mind was full of distraction. It replayed every detail, every hand-stoke, every splendored moment of the previous several hours. Hours. Their lovemaking had taken them into the early hours of the next day. That's right: *lovemaking.* At one point as they rested and played between sessions, Caroline told Mark she'd never knew sex could feel like what she was experiencing. He quickly informed her that it was not 'sex' but that it was 'making love.' He looked her in the eyes and said, "I will never have 'sex' with you." Her breath stopped at his proclamation. She could only imagine the look on her face. Shock? She heard only snippets of his comment that followed—something about respect and making love. She never considered the difference before, but as Mark called her attention to the two activities, she recognized there was a clear distinction. She had sex with Steven. Or, rather, he had sex with her. What she experienced with Mark was akin to their souls rising above their bodies, dancing, intertwining, and flowing around and through each other. There was no telling where one ended and the other began. A complete feeling of togetherness and ... love.

The word had not been said. Love. She didn't need to hear it from Mark. She felt it. With Steven, she needed constant affirmation. She needed to hear it from him before they went to sleep at night, when he left in the morning, when he returned in the evening, and during every phone call. And Steven needed to hear it from her the same. With Mark, she only needed to take his hand, to feel his arm around her shoulders, or to see the way he looked at her. His every movement and action communicated the word 'love' to her. She contemplated whether he felt the same from her. He must. She decided that he wouldn't have shared his most intimate details with her if he hadn't. He wouldn't allow her to remain in his home, in his life, if he didn't share her feelings. It wasn't a pressured love. It was comfortable.

She'd wondered and worried why he had held off intimate contact with her—teased her and then let go—but she now understood why. Timing. Timing was everything. Certain facts and conditions had to be in place. Of course, he wanted to make sure she was 'healed' enough, both physically and emotionally. Plus, given the religious background of his family, Caroline was sure Mark wasn't keen on sleeping with a still married woman. With the finalizing of the divorce, came a green light. But more than anything, Caroline realized Mark needed to be sure for himself. With what he'd gone through, Caroline sensed Mark couldn't take another failed relationship. He took commitment seriously. He searched for the real thing. He sought a soulmate.

Her attraction to Mark Meadows had been instantly present. From the moment she opened her eyes and was able to focus, the man in the chair intrigued her. Though she wasn't particularly pleasant the first day or so, overly cautious about his presence, she felt herself drawn to the stranger. Curious. He kept coming back, sitting in the chair. Also, it didn't hurt her feelings one bit when he brought her real coffee. And he wasn't bad to look at, especially when he smiled. Her initial irritation dwindled, especially after Steven showed up. Caroline was grateful for Mark's presence in the chair as she confronted Steven. Oddly, Mark had been a source of strength for Caroline. And when Mark wasn't there and the chair was empty, she felt alone. Like someone had dimmed the lights and the sounds to life.

When daylight presented itself and the silence of night tucked itself away, Caroline stowed her internal conversation. After a morning greeting as they woke in the same bed, sheepish smiles communicating satisfaction from the hours before, she and Mark each rose, dressed, and attacked the coffee pot for its reviving brew.

Caroline was tickled to find that the university had 'called off' another day due to the snowy weather. She hadn't slept, and a lazy day was exceptionally appealing to her. On the other hand, Mark needed to meet Jared at the garage and check over the equipment, gas up the vehicles and get things ready for the next round of frozen precipitation that came their way.

Caroline poured the remaining contents of the carafe into the thermos, trapping the curls of steam as she screwed on the cap. Mark sat the table as he pulled on and laced his insulated boots one at a time. His Carhartt work jacket hung on the back of the chair with the knitted cap sticking out of the pocket.

"I hate to leave you," Mark said, pausing to sip the coffee in his mug on the table. Caroline set the thermos on the table so he wouldn't forget to grab it.

"I hate for you to go!" she smiled. "But I didn't sleep much last night, so I'm going to try to catch a catnap!" Then she added, "Maybe finish that book I've been reading."

"Ah, a lady of leisure!" Mark teased.

"Yeah, well the 'leisure' thing has gotten quite old," she

replied. "I'm counting the days until I am free of my bondage here." She motioned to the purple arm cast. She'd left the sling upstairs. On purpose. Tired of the confinement.

Mark must have read her mind. "Where's your sling?" he asked with a raised brow.

She sighed, giving him a look. "I'll get it if I need it." Her words were defensive. "I just need a little freedom from it. It's makes me feel so claustrophobic. Besides, I'll probably just be in the chair by the tree most of the day!" She motioned towards her new favorite spot in the house.

"Okay..." Mark replied apprehensively. Standing, he pulled the hat out of his coat pocket, and slipped it over his head. Since his haircut, the random sprigs of curled hair no longer stuck out. Caroline missed them. Turning to get his coat, he continued, "Jared and I have several things planned for this week and next week, so I'll be gone some more than usual."

"Really? What sorts of things?" Caroline tried to take interest in Mark's work whenever she could. His business actually fascinated her and made her think of the times she would help her mother and grandmother in the garden with flowers and vegetables. She loved the feel of the cool earth between her fingers and her toes and had never considered that a person could make a sustainable living playing with dirt and rocks.

"We've got meetings with several potential customers to present landscaping plans. Hopefully, they will like what we've come up with." Mark gave a half smile as he slipped his arm in his jacket. "If they decide to go with us, I'll be needing to start working on ordering materials and plants right after the first of the year." Pulling his other arm through, he added, "And I've got some new leads on jobs that Jared and I are going to go over."

"Huh." Caroline considered his schedule. "You know, I would have thought the winter was a dead time for a landscaping business, but it seems this is when all the ground work takes place!"

Mark laughed at her pun. "Did you really…"

"Totally unintended!" She laughed at herself. She reached up with her arm to give Mark a quick kiss before he departed. The quick kisses had somehow morphed into more lingering experiences in the last few days. When Mark broke away, Caroline gulped needed air, and handed him the thermos. "What time do you think you'll be back?"

"Four or five," he said walking towards the front door. Caroline stood by the open door, watching Mark climb into his truck. "Thaw something from the freezer. We'll cook together when I get back!" He flashed a smile-full of teeth.

Caroline nodded and lifted her hand in a wave. She began to close the orange door as Mark backed out of the driveway, pausing to consider that the brightly colored door needed a wreath. Immediately an idea started forming. She was sure Wal-Mart would have the items needed to make a durable but attractive decoration for the door that would also be weather tolerant. Hmm. What would Mark's reaction be to her making a subtle change to his environment? She'd find out on the next trip to the store.

So far, Caroline hadn't made many changes to the duplex. The Christmas tree. Moving the chair next to it. She wondered when Mark might move the other chair to the festive corner. Then she had taken over a couple drawers in the upstairs vanity, the dresser drawers, and of course the closet in the girls' room. Otherwise, the duplex remained Mark's castle. Minimal décor. Clean and modern. Caroline liked it. She stood in the open downstairs assessing the various areas—the couch and chair by the gas fireplace, the dining room table with basic lines, the open-tread stairway, the galley kitchen overlooking the entire area. It was functional and cozy. Despite the neutral furnishings, Mark added enough pops of color with pillows, the throw, artistic sculptures and artwork on and over the mantel. Yes, she liked it all.

Caroline retrieved her coffee from the kitchen and headed to the festive corner. Situated in the chair, Caroline sipped from her cup and admired the simply decorated tree. Relief flowed through her veins, as the warm coffee soothed her insides. While Mark had been completely favorable about her moving her things in, at the time she'd still had doubts about his level of commitment. However, the night before erased any and all lingering doubts.

As did that night. And the nights that followed.

The rest of the week and into the next, Caroline and Mark fell into the ritual of cooking and enjoying a meal together, showering, and then expressing their most intimate feelings for each other before falling asleep in each other's arms. Caroline held her Zoom conferences with students and updated notes and paperwork, while Mark slipped out to take care of work matters.

On Tuesday afternoon, Emily called to let Caroline know that she was sending documents for Caroline's signature related to the house sale. Once Caroline put her digital signature to the documents, the sale would be complete! Caroline's heart sped up inside her chest from anticipation. Not so much for the money that was resulting from the sale, but from the knowledge that the last thread that joined her to Steven would be severed! She'd be truly free to resume life as the 'new' Caroline.

Minutes later, the documents popped up in Caroline's email. Clicking on the link in the email, a document signing program installed and Caroline established her account to lay her name to the documents. Ten minutes later, she emailed Emily communicating, "Done!" *It was done.* And, once Caroline received a copy of her divorce decree, she would head to the court house to have her driver's license remade, wiping the 'White' away.

Caroline Reeves. She had come full circle. Right back where she began, trying to ascertain, who was 'Caroline Reeves'? Fortunately, this go-around, she knew clearly who 'Caroline Reeves' was not! This brought a smile to her face. Even with some unexpected modifications to her physical abilities,

Caroline was a peace with her person. She was even a bit excited to see where this Caroline was headed!

**

Mark was prepared this time. He brought his laptop to occupy his time as Caroline met with her doctor. They were pretty sure the foot cast was coming off for good but weren't certain about the arm cast. Over the last several days, Caroline had gotten slack in wearing the sling and had been using her casted arm more to brace things and hold things. She still had no feeling in her lower arm, hand or fingers and no signs of movement. It worried Mark. Half-heartedly, he reviewed the landscaping plan for the condominium project. He had a meeting with the developer after Christmas, and wanted to make sure his proposal was a good one and within the budget given. Yet, his thoughts kept going back to Caroline. Would she emerge with one cast or no casts?

After the night in the shower and the week and a half that followed, his thoughts were saturated by Caroline. As he had approached her on the bed, he practically forgot he'd been married before. His nervousness with her made him feel like it had been his first time with a woman, and in many ways it was. He was so apprehensive and wanted everything to be perfect. He placed tremendous pressure on himself that he had trembled slightly. When she had commented about never having had such great 'sex' before, he had responded, "I will never have 'sex' with you." The comment earned him a startled and confused response from Caroline as he rested on his elbows above her, looking into her eyes. He followed his confusing comment with, "I will only and always *make love to you!*"

It was just as Caroline had said. They were two stars that collided on the bridge. Magical and miraculous. He couldn't shake the feeling it had left him with. The next two nights were the same, as were the nights that followed. There was no rush. They took their time. They learned all sorts of things about each other. Heavenly. That was the proper description. Their physical union lifted them high, and they both travelled on a cloud. A smile joined his face, just thinking about it.

Lost in his thoughts as the glow of the landscape plan shined on his grinning face, the door opened, and Caroline came out escorted by the doctor. Unlike the last visit, where had the time gone?

Caroline wore her boot on her right foot, but it seemed much smaller than before, and a sock covered her toes. Also, her arm remained in the sling, but it was also less bulky than before. Caroline shot a smile at Mark as she followed the doctor to the counter. He was giving the medical assistant instructions for follow-up appointments and appointments with a physical therapist. After he left, the assistant asked Caroline questions about days and times, and then flooded her with a series of cards and papers.

Mark joined her at the counter, his laptop in his hand at his side, and he looked her over from shoulder to the floor. No casts! He understood why Caroline smiled. Beamed. The happiest he'd ever seen her. His heart swelled with warmth and positive vibes seeing her like this. So different than her last visit. Which instantly made him wonder what the prognosis was for her arm. He'd let her bring that up! Taking her cards and papers, Mark tucked them inside his laptop for safekeeping.

As they left the office, all the business done, Mark asked, "Well?" His expression was hopeful.

Caroline continued to smile. "No Casts!" she proclaimed. "You know, that saw is so intimidating! When they come at you with it, you feel for sure they're going to cut your arm or leg off or at least leave deep gashes. It's quite amazing! But I'm glad I don't have to worry about that again! Hopefully!"

"So, what did he say?" Mark asked opening the truck door and giving Caroline a boost up to the seat. "How long do you have to still wear the boot?"

"Oh, I don't!" she replied. "I'm only wearing it because I didn't think to bring a shoe! He said I could wear any flat shoe with a good rubber sole. And that I just needed to ease back into any lengthy walking, and no running for about six months. The physical therapist will tell me more."

Mark handed her the laptop as he strapped her in, and then he made his way around the truck, climbing into the driver's seat. Caroline set the laptop on the console between them and looked at him expectantly.

"What?" he asked.

"Aren't you going to ask about my arm?"

"Well, I figured I'd let you tell me when you're ready." Mark spoke cautiously, remembering her emotional upset before. She nodded, as if she were reading his thoughts.

"No cast, as you can see!" She looked upward exhaling with glee. "I can move my shoulder, obviously, but he wants me to still be cautious with it for the next six months or so. So, I don't pull the ligament or tendon loose. And I can bend it at the elbow, but it's very stiff." She looked at him with a matter-of-fact expression. "The doctor said physical therapy and the exercises they will show me should help loosen that up! He said the ligament could be causing part of that."

Mark glanced at her as he drove. "What about the lower arm." He couldn't help it. He had to ask.

"Oh, there's still no feeling and no sign of movement with my wrist, hand or fingers," her mouth went as flat as her tone. "But, again, time will tell. He said nerves could heal. Or not. The x-ray showed some healing of the bones, but where the tissue around them was so torn up... He told me to use the rest of my arm the best I can, and just see what happens with the rest. Worst scenario, at least I didn't lose my lower arm and hand. He said there's still good blood flow and told me to just watch in case it starts looking blue or purple."

Mark nodded. He was not happy with the news, but he was happy she was taking it much better. He supposed the idea of the loss of use had soaked in for Caroline, making it easier to accept the verdict. Plus, the doctor did leave her with some hope.

"So why are you still in the sling?"

"Just to support the arm until I've had a few sessions of physical therapy. You know, to make sure the weight of the lower arm doesn't pull on where they fixed the tendons and ligaments."

"Makes sense." Mark nodded.

"Yeah, I think I'll get shed of this as soon as we get to the house!" Caroline said, inspecting the sling and fumbling with the strap.

"If not before?" Mark laughed.

Sure enough, the strap came over her head, and Caroline pulled the sling loose from her arm. She placed it on top of the laptop.

***

The following day was Caroline's last day of work before the university closed for Winter Break. The students completed the semester the week before and headed home to prepare for the Holidays with their families, so Caroline's Zoom sessions became non-existent. She tidied up some remaining 'paperwork.' She wasn't quite sure why they continued to refer to it as 'paperwork,' as everything was now done electronically. Not a shred of paper was used in her job. And, she had a few Zoom sessions with her supervisor and colleagues. The rest of them gathered for a Holiday celebration, but Caroline opted to stay put in Maysville and share her well-wishes remotely. When she signed off from visiting with her co-workers, she sat in front of the darkened computer screen, playing with her lower lip. She mulled over how long Theresa would allow her to work from home.

Fortunately, her doctor had not released her for driving, a perfect excuse for delaying her return. He wanted to see how the physical therapy went before turning her loose. This was good. It gave her time to find a car, and if she eventually needed to commute to Morehead, she was going to need a gas-efficient vehicle for sure. She and Mark had discussed a couple options for vehicles, but Caroline wasn't sold on any of them. She hated to admit to herself, but she wasn't keen on getting behind a steering wheel, and being in the passenger seat presented anxiety she hadn't anticipated. So far, she'd kept these feelings to herself. She told Mark she wanted to wait and see how much money she ended up receiving from the sale of the house before she made any decisions. And there was the issue of how much she'd be able to use her right arm. That made a huge difference in vehicle choice and location of controls. There was so much to think about that Caroline previously never considered.

"Hey, there!" Mark called as he came through the front door. Instead of his Carhart coat and insulated boots, he was clad in his wool dress coat and leather boots. He caught Caroline in contemplation, playing with her lip. "What's happening?"

"Oh, not much," she replied. "Just got done with the Zoom with the office. I am officially done until January second!" She managed a smile for Mark as he slid out of his coat, hanging it on the knob of the closet door.

"I think I am also!" The soles of his boots made a slight squeaking noise on the floor as he crossed the room. "Hey, I've been meaning to ask you..." he paused, glancing at Caroline.

"What's that?" She raised her eyebrows.

"Don't you have Christmas shopping to do?" Mark headed for the refrigerator to grab a water.

Christmas shopping? Caroline's head snapped to attention. She stared off at some invisible object in the room. "Uh..." she began. "I guess I do. I completely blanked on that." Other than Mark, who did she really have to shop for? She'd pondered what to get him. "Have you been shopping?"

"Oh, I've picked up a thing here and there," he replied. "I usually start pretty early, but I've been a little distracted here lately!" He gave her a sly smile and winked at her.

"Who do you have to shop for?" she asked.

"I always try to get something for the little ones," Mark replied. Caroline assumed he was talking about the great nieces and nephews. "Then I get some knick-knack or something Christmas-y for Dad, Larry, Lynn, and Beth. An ornament. Or fruitcake, if they've pissed me off!" He said this with a laugh.

"Don't be insulting fruitcake! There are some good fruitcakes, you know!" Caroline defended. "It's not cheap either!" Caroline sighed. She thought about the fruitcake her grandmother used to make. It was time-consuming, but the result was heavenly! Then it hit her that she had siblings, but she wouldn't be handing them a gift, nor would she be showering her nieces and nephews with the magic of Santa and Christmas.

Mark continued to laugh, shaking his head. "I get the kind they sell at the dollar store that can be used as a stone in a foundation!"

"Oh, you're awful!" she replied. "I wish I had my grandmother's fruitcake recipe. I'd make them some fruitcake they'd never forget!"

"Which grandmother?" Mark asked with a raised brow.

"My Mom's mom," Caroline looked up as she shut her laptop. "She'd soak the fruit and nuts in bourbon for a week!"

"Now, that would have to be good!" Mark nodded. "Hey, do you want to go window shopping?"

"Right now?" Caroline furrowed her brows. "Where? Who has 'windows' these days?"

"Have you never been through downtown Maysville at Christmas time?"

Caroline shook her head. Really, she hadn't spent much time in Maysville until she set out on her random journey two months before.

"Oh, then we've got to go!" Mark said. "There's this one gift shop that serves hot chocolate with candy canes in it!" Mark added, "Just like in the Halmark movies!"

"You're kidding!" Caroline stated, her mouth hanging open.

"Nope. No joke!" Mark motioned to her. "Go get some shoes on! We'll go spend an hour or so bumming around downtown!"

"Okay," Caroline shrugged, rising from the chair. Now when she shrugged, both of her shoulder participated. This made her insides smile. And, as she ascended the stairs, she relished that she was going for a *pair* of boots, not the boot that kept her foot captive for six weeks!

***

Downtown Maysville was made for 'bumming.' Mark parked the truck in a community lot next to the drycleaner, and they set out on foot to explore the downtown shops and eats. As they rounded a small park with stone footpaths enclosed by a wrought iron fence, Mark pointed out a small café tucked discretely on the side of one of the historic brick buildings.

"That's the Parc Café." He pointed to a partially hidden doorway along a path through an open gate in the wrought iron. Wreaths of simple greenery with plaid bows hung on the wooden double doors among ornate trim painted a royal blue. "That place has the perfect vanilla lattes."

"Perfect?" Caroline asked. "I've never had a 'perfect' vanilla latte. What makes it 'perfect'?"

Mark glanced at his watch. They still had time. "Why don't we go find out?" With his hand touching her lower back, he guided her through the fence towards the welcoming doors. Mark held the door as Caroline stepped from the cold into the warmth of the café. Directly ahead was a wooden counter next to a glass display with the remainder of a variety of baked goods. Mark watched Caroline's eyes grow wide. She licked her lips unconsciously, tasting the sweetness that hung in the air.

"Can I help you?" A man behind the counter asked, wiping his wet hands on a towel. He glanced from Mark to Caroline, who stood peering up at the tin ceiling and the barrel lights.

"Two vanilla lattes to go." Mark held up two fingers.

The man nodded and smiled, repeating, "Two vanilla lattes to go!" Then he asked, motioning towards Caroline, "Is this her first time?" The man recognized she was a stranger to the place.

"Yes." Mark said, looking towards Caroline. Her attention was fully captured by the unique atmosphere of the café. A Christmas tree was in one corner, and a long leather sofa was positioned under a bank of windows. Another wall sported a series of built-in shelves filled with books and collectibles, and an upright piano sat opposite the sofa. Small marble-topped tables and woven chairs took up the floor space, providing intimate din-in seating. Caroline turned as the cappuccino maker steamed the milk.

"This place is so cool!" Caroline said, a look of amazement on her face.

"The food's really good also, but they're only open until one o'clock each day," Mark said. "We got in just under the wire."

Caroline smiled, as she inhaled the aroma of coffee. "I need to come back some time with my laptop or a book and just hang for a while." She scanned the room again, adding, "This place feels like the 'new' me! It calls to me…"

"Okay, here are your lattes!" The man set two tall paper cups with lids and cup sleeves on the counter. As Mark, pulled out his wallet, the man said to Caroline, "These are made with our own vanilla. We make it here!"

Caroline reached for a cup and put it to her lips as Mark exchanged a bill for his own cup. "Oh, my God!" she said, her eyes rolling up. "This really is *perfect*!" She again licked her lips, not allowing any of it to waste.

"Well, thank you so much!" the man said as he handed Mark the change. "We aim to please! Please come back to see us!"

As they started down the street again, Mark reached for Caroline's hand, but stopped. She held the latte in her only hand, preoccupied with savoring small sips. He figured she'd finish the drink quickly, and then her hand could be his. They walked casually, stopping at various store fronts, peering inside at the displayed goods. At one point, they stepped inside a boutique named Bradley's Boutique and Haberdashery and browsed the packed shelves. The shop contained an eclectic assortment of jellies, sauces, mixers, jewelry, clothing, books, and gift items. Items old and new sought refuge together on tables, along the floor, and in any once-empty spot. The sauces and jams all appeared to be locally sourced, and the jewelry was handmade, probably also by local artisans. Caroline stopped at a table filled with an assortment of decorative nightlights. One was a honeybee situated on a honeycomb. She held it up, imagining how the bee looked with the light bright behind it. As a child, she loved bees of any kind. What she would have given to have had this in her and Tory's bedroom!

Another shop they entered was a bookstore-bar-restaurant combination. Kenton's Books and Spirits. The ambiance was almost homey. The seating included a couch, chairs, coffee table as well as other tables. It felt very much like someone's home library, complete with the bourbon on the side. Caroline took the last sip of her latte, spied a trash can, and continued to peruse the titles on the shelves. Mark inspected a few books on his own, reading the book jackets, then slid them back in the empty spot on the shelf. As much as he appreciated the feel of a book in his hands, he'd given up hard copies several years before. Electronic books did not take of the space like a physical book, and Mark favored his clutter-free home. He stepped across the room to Caroline, looking over her shoulder.

"Find anything interesting?" he asked. She held a paperback, reading the backside of the book. She flipped over the book showing him the cover. Pictured was the Simon Kenton Memorial Bridge all lit up at nighttime. The title read, *The Bridge*.

"Ironic, isn't it?" Caroline said with a humph. "This is by a local author. Never heard of her before. She lives over by my parents. I'm going to look her up online." She set the book back in the display stand and turned to Mark. His continued to study the book, taking in the cover, and then looked at Caroline with a smile.

"You ready to move on?" he asked. She gave a nod, and he casually took her hand and led her towards the door.

Stepping back into the cold, a gust of wind swirled around them. Mark held Caroline's hand firmly, enjoying the smooth feel of her slender fingers. Their joined hands swung casually with their pace as they proceed to the next set of windows.

"You warm enough?" Mark asked.

"Yep." She perked her head up and turned it to feel the cold sweep on each side of her face. "The cold feels good. It makes me feel alive! Invigorating!"

Mark laughed. "Yes, it does that!"

"It doesn't hurt that I can wear my coat like a real person!" she added, looking down at her down jacket, each of her arms in a sleeve and the jacket zipped. A few days before, she would have been struggling to hold the jacket closed with her good hand.

"Yeah. I like the scaled back look!" Mark replied, still gripping her hand. He wasn't looking at her coat, but into her blue eyes. The brown ring was barely visible.

"Getting out like this has been just perfect!" Caroline smiled at him. "The only thing missing are a few flurries. That would make this picture-perfect!"

"Ha!" Mark blurted. "If there were flurries, then I'd be the one missing! I'd be getting things ready to plow!" He gently bumped her good shoulder, laughing as they reached the end of the street and turned.

CHAPTER 21 – PIECE OF CAKE

Caroline hadn't been honest with Mark. She *had* begun her Christmas shopping. In fact, she thought she finished her shopping, until Mark brought up the subject. Now she fretted over whether she should be securing gifts for Mark's family. She hadn't thought about including them in her Christmas list. She'd only seen some of them two times. Beth three times. What would she get them? She barely knew them. Besides them, who else would she buy for? Jared and Shelly? Their kids? She'd never seen their kids, had no clue their ages or names, just that there was a boy and a girl. Which one was older? No idea.

While online, she had stumbled across a jeweler who specialized in celestial-themed items. The necklace with the two stars, one yellow gold, the other white gold, caught her eye right away. The silver star was larger, and the smaller gold star was placed directly on top and affixed. Two stars collided. It was providence. The only questionable part of the necklace was the chain. It was a delicate chain, meant more for a woman or someone who was not a manual laborer. She wanted something sturdy enough that once it went on Mark's neck, it would stay. She'd emailed the jeweler to see if there was an option for a heavier chain. There was. The jeweler substituted a thicker white gold chain for the thin yellow gold chain pictured. Caroline was thrilled, and it was scheduled to arrive any day.

She had been nervous that it would be delivered the day before when they were out window-shopping. But no package sat by the orange door when they returned. She hid her sigh of relief. How would she explain the shipment to Mark? Yet, she was beginning to worry that it might get delayed and not arrive in time. She also worried that Mark might not want to wear it. She'd noticed he had several jewelry items, including a gold chain. It just laid in a small box on his chest of drawers. She hadn't seen him wear any of it. But it was all dressier. For special occasions. Her intention was that the stars would be daily wear. Wash and wear. Work and wear. Sleep and wear.

Caroline walked behind the dust mop running it over the light wood floor. The only bad part of having huge windows on the front and side of the room was that the sunlight illuminated every speck of dust that fell on the polished floors. A path ran from the front door to the kitchen and another from the kitchen to the stairs. The path was dust-free. It shined. The rest of the room had a thin layer of particles which gave the floor the look of a matte finish in the sun. Footprints led to the chair by the tree, resembling footprints in snow. It was her new favorite spot. She didn't even mind that she was on full display to the neighborhood through the wall of glass. She navigated the dustmop around the chair and around the tree, eliminating the evidence of her leisure.

She wanted to damp-mop the floor, especially the high-traffic area, but she couldn't squeeze the water from the mop. Mark was particular about not wetting the floor too much but just enough to loosen the dirt and catch residual dust. She had already dusted and cleaned the bathrooms and had two loads of laundry going. What else could she do? She needed one of those mops that wrung itself out! Aha! She'd mention to Mark she wanted one for Christmas! She hung the dust mop back in its spot after taking the microfiber sleeve off for the wash.

Returning to the kitchen she decided to heat some water for tea. Turning from the sink with the kettle, she heard the front door open. Mark struggled with several bags and gave the door a shove with his foot.

"Hey!" Caroline said, turning the heat on under the kettle. "Do you need a hand? Are there more bags?"

Mark headed for the bar counter, but not before one of the bags spit open and its contents dropped one by one from the bag. Caroline went to rescue the escaped items off the floor. She cuddled some in her right arm and carried the others in her left hand.

"What do you have here?" she asked, looking at bags of dried fruit in her hand. Apricots, prunes, and dates. The bags she clutched were walnuts and pecans. "Are we doing some holiday baking?" She pursed her lips as and frowned she approached the counter.

Mark pulled more grocery items from the bags, lining them on the counter. Caroline dumped the bags of fruit and nuts in a pile and peered into the mysterious brown sack. *Bourbon?* She reached in and removed a bottle of Buffalo Trace.

"What's the bourbon for?" she asked. "I thought you didn't drink?"

"I don't," Mark replied. "But according to your mom's recipe, you have to soak the dried fruit and nuts in bourbon for fruitcake."

His full comment didn't register with Caroline. "Fruitcake?" She turned some of the other packages, checking them out. "I thought you liked to buy the disgusting stuff for your family?"

"I did," he replied. He starting separating the items needed for the fruitcake from those that needed to be put in the pantry or refrigerator. "But after you talked about how good the ones your grandmother made were, I decided I needed to try it!"

"Well, I have no idea how she made it." Caroline pushed the pile of fruits and nuts towards him. "I wish I had the recipe. Did you find one online?"

Mark pulled off his coat and handed it to Caroline. She turned and went to the closet hanging the wool coat on a wooden hanger. The tea kettle began to whistle, signally the water was ready to brew tea. Returning to the bar counter, she watched Mark pour steaming water into the cup she had prepared. Then he prepared a cup for himself, letting both cups steep side-by-side on the counter.

"Thank you!" Caroline said, happily sliding into a bar seat. Though no longer in the sling, her injured arm hung with her elbow awkwardly bent and her forearm dangling in front of her. She still felt nothing below the elbow, so she used care when moving about to ensure she didn't accidently shut her hand or arm in a drawer or door. Her motionless hand rested in her lap.

Turning, Mark reached into his shirt pocket and pulled out a folded piece of notebook paper. He carefully opened the folds until the full size of the page was visible, and then laid it on the counter using his large hand to iron the wrinkles and creases.

"No, I did not find a recipe online," Mark said with a twinkle in his eye. His raised eyebrow and slanted smile signaled to Caroline that Mark had been up to no good. "Those could not be trusted. So, I went to the source!" His vagueness was also a clue that he'd been into mischief.

Caroline reached over and pulled the paper towards her, turning it and again flattening the creases with her hand. As her eyes ran along the words. The handwriting was familiar to her. Where had she seen it? The answer eluded her. The recipe name read, "Minnie's Fruitcake." *Minnie?* The name sounded familiar, but she couldn't place it. "What is this? Where'd you get this?" Caroline asked, turning the paper over to inspect the backside.

"Like I said," Mark picked up the two steaming mugs and set one next to Caroline and the other in front of him. He leaned with both hands on the counter. "I went to the source!" Caroline's eyebrows scrunched as she looked up at him. She shook her head to indicate her cluelessness.

"From your mother!" Mark's face brightened. "I went to the source! Got your grandmother's recipe. That's the recipe you talked about. Your mom wrote it out for me!"

Caroline's mouth dropped open as her brows parted briefly. Then they pulled together more tightly as she clamped her mouth shut and hastily looked back at the words on the paper in her hand. *Of course! It was her mother's handwriting!* She hadn't seen it in years. She looked at the perfect curves and lines and how each letter flowed into the next. *Minnie! Minnie…Thacker!* Her mother's mother! It took a minute before she remembered the last name. The grandmother who insisted on being called 'Grandma.' "Don't you be hollering 'Mamaw' at me! I'm your 'Grandma'!" she yelled at younger versions of Caroline, Adam, and Tory. "There's no such word "mamaw' in the dictionary. You go look for yourselves!" Sure enough, there wasn't.

Caroline scanned through the recipe again, practically smelling whiffs of fruit and nuts soaking up the bourbon. Her grandma would threaten to rap a wooden spoon across their fingers as she and her siblings stuck their dirty forefingers in the fermenting mixture to get a taste. It was sweet and nutty, but it had a bite. Caroline remembered the dizzy feeling she got the time she stuck her finger in one too many times. Inevitably, her grandma had to add more bourbon before the soaking time was finished. Caroline also remembered her mother standing in the background, winking at her children as they licked their fingers. She didn't say a word. She knew they'd all sleep soundly that night.

Shaking her head, her mouth opened again. Wordless at first, then a barrage of noise spilled. "You went to my *parent's house*?" Without allowing for an answer. she continued. "You saw my *mother*? And you asked her for this recipe? *Just out of the blue*? What did she say? Was my dad there? What did he say? *They actually let you in*?" This time Caroline's eyes scrunched with her eye brows. She shook her head emphatically with her mouth parted. "Without me? You went without me? *Without telling me*?" She dropped the paper on the counter next to the steaming cup. Just as Mark began to respond, she added with a little steam herself, "How *could* you?"

Mark looked like someone who just been pelted by a spray of plastic BBs, each question flying at him with a force that left a small sting. He was about to speak, to respond to the flood of questions and emotion, but the last question set him quiet. He just looked at her. He flinched and sighed deeply. Looking down at the tea, then to the paper and back at Caroline, he opened his lips but then shut them. He swallowed hard. His

Adam's apple leapt in his throat.

"What?" she asked. Her tone was a mix of hurt and anger and her expression pained. "What were you going to say?"

"Look," he began. He stared at the mug of tea. "I was trying to do something nice. I thought...I thought if you had the recipe, and if we made the fruitcake, you might feel closer to your family."

"How is fruitcake going to bring me closer to my family?" Caroline asked. Her lips were thin.

"You talked about it with such nostalgia. I thought it might, you know..." Mark glanced at her. She sat back in the bar chair, her feet propped on a rung. Her tea was untouched. She looked intently at him, adding to his discomfort. "You know, soften you up to where you might try to go talk to them again."

"Soften me up?" she asked, a laugh following. "I'm not the one who needs softening. I'm not the one who said I was 'dead' to them!" She pushed the paper away from her. "It's going to take more than fruitcake to sweeten my dear ol' Dad up! And Mom's just trapped and does what he says!" She stood abruptly. She gave Mark a long sour look, exhaled, and headed for the stairs. "I need to be alone!"

**

Sylvie Reeves had told Mark that the recipe made two good-size loaves of fruitcake, and depending on how many he intended to make, he'd need to double or triple the recipe. "It's better to have too many fruits and nuts soaked than not enough! You ain't got enough time to go back and soak more!" she'd said. Sylvie also told him, "You gotta hand-chop everythin' to get the right consistency. Can't take no shortcuts with a food processor!" Mark nodded as he folded the recipe so it fit securely in his breast pocket. He understood the recipe was to be treated with his life. "I ain't even give Adam's wife the recipe! Don't you be tellin' nobody, or we'll have an outright war goin' on!" Mark assured Caroline's mother that the recipe would go straight from his pocket to Caroline's hand. And it had.

The recipe wasn't the only valuable stowed in his pocket that day. However, he removed the small velvet box and locked it in the console of his truck. Away and safe from wandering eyes and a curious mind. He didn't want to take changes of his Christmas surprise being thwarted. But as his knife sliced through the sticky dried fruits, he contemplated if he'd thwarted the surprise himself. Shaking his head, he kept chopping and adding bits of fruit to the measuring cup until it contained the correct amount. He dumped these into a glass bowl.

Sylvie had instructed him to only use a glass bowl. "You don't want that soakin' liquor to leach out any of them metal tastes that come from them stainless bowls. Plastic's just as bad! That liquor'll pull flavors outa that plastic from six months back!" Before he'd left the Reeves home, Mark came to realize that the secrets to the fruitcake wasn't the recipe, but it was all the oral tips that came with it. These didn't make it to the paper. He continued to replay the visit in his mind to be sure he didn't forget an important step.

Chopping the nuts was another challenge. "Just use a good sharp chef's knife and your board! Those nut choppers cut them too fine and even," Sylvie had said. Mark could see how someone would be tempted to use a nut chopper. As the knife descended on the walnuts, several shot out from under the blade in various directions. It brought a smile to his face, remembering the ricocheting olives Caroline had sliced weeks before. He rounded the nuts back up and went for a second round. Again, when the measuring cup filled to the right mark, Mark poured them on top of the fruit and took a wooden spoon to mix them with the fruit.

"Now there's no measurin' the liquor. You just pour 'til them fruits and nuts are covered. Then you cover the bowl with a clean dish rag." Mark had enjoyed listening to Sylvie speak. There was a sing-song quality to her voice and words.

It reminded him in a way of his mother, though his mother's Appalachian accent wasn't quite as pronounced. "You gonna check the mix daily to make sure everythin's covered. Now don't be drinkin' down the extry liquor 'cause you may need to add more to the mix!" she had warned, adding a laugh, and looked towards Jimmy Reeves. A guilty look sat on his face below the brim of his hat. "It ain't just the children that go stickin' their fingers in the mix!" she said, eying her husband.

Mark twisted open the Buffalo Trace bottle and poured the bourbon until it just covered the contents in the bowl. Then he spread a dishtowel over the top. Sylvie made certain that he used a dishtowel and not plastic wrap or aluminum foil. "It's gonna be doin' some workin' off, you know!" Mark imagined the duplex would smell quite intoxicating in a few days.

As he cleaned the kitchen and put the last of the cooking utensils away, Mark listened for any noise from above. He hadn't heard any running water to indicate Caroline took a shower, and the television was quiet. He assumed Caroline flung herself on the bed, cried, and maybe fell asleep. Opening the refrigerator, he looked at the thawed chicken he'd planned to cook, but he wasn't certain about Caroline's appetite. His own appetite was curbed by doubting his actions and growing anxiety that he messed things up.

Going against Sylvie Reeves' advice, Mark fetched two short glasses from the cabinet and poured a shot of bourbon in each. Pushing the cork back into the bottle, he reasoned he could always get another bottle…

Caroline laid on her belly, her arms clutching a pillow and her face buried. She moved her head to the side as he entered the room. On the other side of the bed, he sat the two glasses on the nightstand. He stood gazing down on her, not sure what to say. Her exposed eye glanced up at him and then at the glasses. She remained silent.

"You still want to be alone?" Mark finally asked.

"No." Her tone was pouty and partially muffled. Mark wondered briefly if she had ever used a sulky tone with Steven.

He guessed not. Mark doubted Caroline had the privilege to express her emotions around him. As he sat on the edge of the bed, with one leg bent, Caroline rolled on her side. She studied him.

"Are you feeling better?" Mark asked, his hands nervously rubbing his jeans.

"No."

Mark reached for one of the glasses and held it towards her. She stared at the glass a few seconds and then looked at him, unsure of the offer. "For me?" she asked moving into a sitting position. She crossed her legs and then reached for the glass. Sniffing the contents, she watched as Mark picked up the other glass and swirled the liquid. He sniffed as the vapors rose from the glass. He considered the sweet, smoky smell. An oddly pleasant fragrance resembling a hint of honey and the freshness of the woods. It reminded him of being outdoors in the spring.

"I thought you don't drink," she said.

"Normally, I don't," he replied. "But I don't guess a sip or two will kill me."

He watched as Caroline raised the glass to her lips and took a healthy sip. She didn't even wince. Mark's eyebrows raised in response. As she licked and rubbed her lips, he took a sip of his own, feeling the burn. He felt every inch of its travel down towards his stomach.

"I'm sorry," he told her. "I overstepped."

"Yes, you did."

"But..." Mark countered, "In my own defense, I was just nudging the situation, just like you nudged my situation with my family."

Caroline cocked her head and frowned slightly. "How so?"

"You gave me several gentle pushes to go talk to my family about the whole money deal," Mark paused looking into his glass. "I figured your situation needed a little push."

"You already pushed when you took me there. You saw what happened." Caroline took another sip of bourbon. She swallowed it like butter. One gulp.

"Yeah, I did," Mark said nodding his head. "But afterwards I realized you weren't the one who need the pushing."

"What do you mean?" Her eyes narrowed.

"Your parents." Mark raised his glass but paused. "Not so much your mom, but your dad. He needed a 'little extra shove' to bring him around." He followed with another sip of the amber liquid. It didn't burn as much as the first.

"And how'd that 'shove' go? Did Dad come around?" Caroline asked. Skepticism ruled her face. She rested her glass on the comforter.

"I don't know," Mark replied with a perplexed look. Jimmy Reeves wasn't an easy man to 'shove.' "We talked. He was…you know…cordial enough. Your mom. She's really great. I could talk to that woman for hours."

"Cordial?" Caroline shook her head and snorted. "Not a word I would use to describe Jimmy Reeves."

Mark smiled, a low nervous laugh coming out. "No, I guess not. But I got him talking about his logging. Now, that's something he's passionate about!" Mark nodded his head. "And he's got this cut he's going to show me." Mark tilted his head, looking at a surprised Caroline. "*Tongue and groove*, he calls it. Helps control the direction of the fall better and keeps it from bumping back."

"You talked trees?" Her mouth remained open. She shook her head. "Of course, you two talked trees! I bet Dad loved that!" The sarcasm rolled off her tongue.

"Eh, he's not a bad guy," Mark shrugged. "He's on the gruff and tough side, but what logger isn't? They're out there in all kinds of weather, breathing in chainsaw fumes and saw dust. It's not the type of work for just anybody, that's for sure! I may get him and Adam to help me out sometimes when I've got a bunch of trees to be cut and stumps removed!"

"No, Dad's not a bad person," Caroline replied. "He just not a fan of me! He couldn't control me." She tilted her glass for another sip. She was glad for the bourbon. It made the conversation easier. "You met Adam?"

"Yeah, he stopped to get your dad to go look at a job. We spoke a bit. Seems nice enough." Mark downing the last of the bourbon in his glass and laughed. "Adams looks just like you except for the beard and he's twice your size." He continued to chuckle. Caroline rolled her eyes.

"Adams should look like me!" She shifted on the bed, bending one of her knees up. "We're twins. I'm the older one! By six minutes."

"No kidding!"

Caroline nodded, a faint smile rippling across her face. "So, did Mom and Dad say anything about me? Am I still banished from the family?"

Mark nodded, his upper body rocking slightly. "We discussed you. Your mother mostly. She really misses you. I told them about the accident, and how you've finally got the casts off. That you're starting physical therapy. And I told them about the divorce, but they seemed to know all about that. And Steven's issues." Mark paused, looking down at his empty glass. "But I think your dad's warming up. He didn't have a lot to say. Just sat and listened mostly. I think he feels badly about you getting banged up in the accident. Now, that's me speaking, but I can also tell he's pure ego! It might take him a while to come around. But I think he is genuinely glad you're okay."

"Huh." Caroline gave no expression. Instead, she began moving and rose from the bed. She stepped cautiously on her right foot, stretched, and then disappeared.

Mark heard her bare feet slapping the stair treads as she went down. Hearing no signs of movement from below, he looked back into his empty glass. He was startled at Caroline's lack of emotion. Empty just like his glass. And hers. He'd expected her to have a blotchy, tear-streaked face, swollen eyes, and a stuffy nose. Apparently, she'd just been thinking. Contemplating. What about, he didn't have a clue. Her parents? Him? Her new life? Mark had to wonder if they weren't moving too fast. Was she having doubts about him?

The thought panged at his insides making him sit a little straighter. Stiffer.

He'd been so diligent about not getting involved with anyone. Not getting involved equaled not getting hurt. Then Caroline charged the bridge with headlights blaring. She might as well have fallen from the sky. As the explosion landed him on top of her, he took in her beauty with his every sense. He knew instantly the woman had a place in his life going forward. By divine selection. It was as if God spoke to him. Sent him a sign. Loud and clear. Who was he to argue?

Caroline must have ascended the steps more softly than going down. Mark's thoughts were met by the spout of the bourbon bottle pouring more of the amber liquid in his glass. Startled, he put up his hand indicating *when*. Caroline also served herself another portion before setting the bottle on her nightstand.

She positioned her pillows so she could lean against them. She sat with her knees propped and took a fresh sip from her glass. "What will this do to you?"

Mark considered her question. He looked at the liquid in the glass she held and replied, "It dulls my mood some. Which isn't great when my mood is already on the dull side. And…I take all sorts of meds to keep it on the brighter side."

"Is your mood on the 'dull' side right now?"

"Yeah, a little." Mark's jaw twitched as he spoke. He knew she saw it.

"Because of me." Caroline was as hard on herself as Mark was on himself. Seeing and hearing this in her brought great awareness to his own internal beatings.

"No," instantly came from his lips, followed by a few seconds of silence as Mark found Caroline's eyes. "Yes," he admitted. "I just want to see you happy. You've been through so much. And you've lost so much. I just…I just thought if you had the support of your family, you'd feel more secure. Not so alone. I guess I screwed that up. You're unhappy with me."

"Hmm." She raised her glass but paused before sipping. "I

don't feel alone." She cleared her throat. "You haven't screwed up anything that wasn't already screwed up. I did a fine job of that on my own! I guess I feel responsible to fix it myself." She looked at Mark from her bowed head. "I'm not unhappy with you. In fact, I'm *quite* happy with you. Happier than I've ever been. And I've never felt more secure in my whole life!" She twisted her body and set the glass on the nightstand, letting out a sigh. "You know…I don't feel like I've lost a thing. If anything, I've gained." She left the cozy pillows and scooted across the bed towards Mark.

"We've *both* been through so much, and now we got each other. Don't we?" she said, settling next to him and placing her hand on his. She curled her long fingers around his palm. Mark looked at their entwined hands. Her warm hand soothed the clamminess of his. He looked at her with a frank expression. He nodded.

"Mark, I appreciate what you did. I really do." Caroline's eyes grew glossy. "No one's ever gone to battle for me. *For me!* It just shocked me!" A tear slid onto her lower lashes. Mark reached with his free hand and caught the lone tear on his forefinger. He stared at it a moment, then back at Caroline. The blotchiness crept across her face, and she sniffled. She let go of his hand and reached up towards his face.

"I love you, Mark Meadows." She whispered the words as her face moved towards him, finding his lips. Mark didn't have a chance to say a word.

CHAPTER 22 – CHRISTMAS

"They're like bricks!" Mark inspected the loaf he'd just emptied out of the bread pan. "Like lead! Look!"

Caroline peered over at the fruitcake on the cutting board. "They're supposed to be that way! But smell how good they are!"

Mark bent to get a whiff. He shrugged. "I'll trust you." He picked up the next pan to be emptied. The fruit and nuts Mark had chopped and soaked produced twelve loaves of fruitcake. "I don't know what I was thinking," Mark murmured as he freed the cooled cakes.

Caroline just smiled at him and went back to cutting ribbon. On a run to Wal-Mart, she'd found clear cellophane goodie bags large enough to accommodate the fruitcakes and ribbon to fancy them up. She fashioned bows from the ribbon to tie around the wrapped cakes. Even with one hand, the bows looked pretty good. She was able to use her right hand to hold the ribbon steady as she worked with her left. Everyone they knew now were getting fruitcake!

During the Wal-Mart trip, Caroline left Mark in the food department to get the items he needed for his part of Christmas Eve dinner. She went to round up gift wrap and gift bags, the ribbon and bags for the fruitcake, and to do a little Christmas shopping of her own. After some deliberation, she decided that she needed to get at least some token gifts for Mark's family. It looked like she might be around for a while, and she wanted at least to stay in good graces with Mark's siblings and parents.

Caroline found a nice set of earrings for each Lynn and Becky. She noticed they each had pierced ears, and that Lynn wore dangles while Becky wore studs. She then collected an assortment of hair ties and clips for Beth. Each time she had seen Beth, her long hair was pulled back, twisted or piled into a different style. Added to the cart were three different fragrances of aftershave, one each for Mark, Dennis, and Larry. The Old Spice was for Dennis. She noticed he used it generously on the two times she'd been around him. Last but not least, Caroline selected a lotion with the soothing smell of lavender for Mark's mother. She had already ordered a poster picturing a field of flowers which had arrived a day earlier, along with Mark's gift. The poster would go on the ceiling above Joy Meadow's bed. Instead of gazing at the pale blue ceiling all day, Mark's mother could look at flowers, like the ones she once tended in the garden with Mark's help. The lotion would not only calm her dry skin, but the floral smell would add to her 'garden' experience. At least Caroline hoped so.

Mark shopped on a previous trip for the nieces and nephews, having a better idea what they were into. But he wasn't sure which ones would show for Christmas Eve dinner. The gifts for those who missed the festivities would go home with the respective sibling for Christmas morning. Mark explained to Caroline that once he and his siblings were grown, they began the tradition of gathering at his parent's house for Christmas Eve dinner. As children were added to the mix, they came also. Then Christmas mornings were celebrated at each siblings' own home, opening presents with their children. Since Mark's parents moved in with Beth, that traditional Christmas Eve dinner shifted to his sister's house, just as had the Sunday dinners, where it would most likely remain after Joy and Dennis were gone.

Caroline wasn't used to the formal family dinners as there had never been anything formal about her own upbringing. Holiday meals at the Reeves household generally involved mismatched plates and flatware and food served up from the stove or the kitchen counters. Whoever got to the kitchen table first, ate there while stragglers balanced their plates on their knees either on the couch, Jimmy Reeves' recliner, or the steps leading upstairs. When she, Adam, and Tory were smaller, the stairs were their choice of dinning. They each selected one step to sit, and the step right above served as table for their plate. Less spills. Less yelling from Jimmy Reeves about the mess. For whatever reason, meals for special occasions were never held at Mamaw Reeves' house or at Grandma's. The older ladies always came to the Reeves household bringing their part of the meal, and they always had a seat at the table.

Of course, Caroline was acquainted with fine dining. Steven required it. He was always taking her to the finer dining establishments, or they hosted or attended dinner parties. The hosting always evoked a sense of panic in Caroline, calling for the aid of a nerve pill, as she pulled her event together. Steven required that everything be perfect. Inevitably, she made some unknown faux pas that Steven addressed with her after the guests left. This only added to her nervousness about the next event they hosted.

The dinner's with Mark's family weren't that formal, thank goodness. Caroline still felt out-of-her element, but she attributed that more to it being a family event, and she was not family. She still felt like she was on display with Mark's family. They were perfectly nice to her, yet she sensed they all waited to see if she was going to stick around. Each time Caroline showed up with Mark, she was greeted with an air of surprise that dissipated after a few minutes. Slowly, Caroline was getting to know all the players in Mark's family and their personalities and quirks, and more and more she was being included in conversations and plans. But, while Caroline was gradually feeling more comfortable and accepted, she much rather to escape to Joy Meadow's room for a few minutes, sit by her bedside, shares stories about her week, tell her how wonderful and thoughtful Mark was, all while rubbing the old woman's hand. Joy's eyes turned towards Caroline for the first few minutes, then they gradually returned to the endless blue above. Soon, Joy Meadows would gaze at the meadow of blooms.

"So, you haven't told me what our plans are for Christmas

morning?" Caroline asked as she affixed bows to the fruitcakes and nestled them in giftbags topped with tissue paper.

"It's a surprise!" Mark replied. He pulled out the oven rack and painted the ham with his secret glaze. The smell of sweet, salt and cloves filled the room. Caroline's stomach growled, but she was saving her appetite for later. Once again, Mark was in charge of the meat. Ham was the traditional Christmas meat. He was also preparing scalloped potatoes in a crockpot and had Brussels sprouts ready to sauté with onions in a honey mustard sauce. Caroline's contribution to the meal had been sticking the cloves into the centers of the squares Mark grooved on the ham. Mark had explained he didn't do the cherry and pineapple thing.

"Does that mean we can sleep in?" Caroline asked.

"Well of course!" Mark turned and grinned. Wide. Suspiciously devious.

"I don't think I like that look," she half-teased. "So, when do we exchange our gifts?"

"Gifts?" Mark asked, closing the oven door. "Oh, did you get me something?"

Caroline rolled her eyes at him over the sea of bags containing fruitcake. All the other gifts had been wrapped and were in the backseat of the truck ready to go.

"Didn't I mention that I don't do gifts?"

"Really?" she challenged. "Then what's in the brown box in the fridge?" She motioned her hand.

"Ingredients," Mark replied. "Secret ingredients."

"For what?" Her hand settled on her hip as she looked at him. He was laughing at her. His mouth made no noise, but the corners were upturned, and his eyes were dancing with silent laughter.

"The secret ingredients for life!" This time he let his laugh out, as he toyed.

Ugh! Shaking her head, Caroline began gathering the bag handles in her working hand and strung them along her impaired bent arm using it like a hanger. She turned to take them to the door.

"Where are you going?" he asked.

"To put these in the truck!" Her voice conveyed frustration. She really wasn't though. Her mind spun wondering what had to be refrigerated? He'd already warned her not to open the box, and it was heavily taped. There was no peaking to be done without leaving evidence of tampering. She hated surprises. Just hated them! And Mark Meadows was just full of them. From the very first split moment she laid eyes on him! Smiling to herself, she opened the door and called, "So, if you don't 'do gifts,' why is your truck full of them?"

She closed the door behind her not waiting for a reply. It was rhetorical, anyway. She loaded the fruitcakes into the backseat, sliding gifts and bags of gifts over to make room. Pausing a moment, looking at the packed back seat, she wondered where the food would go? And just how did Santa fit enough gifts for the entire planet in that one bag on his sleigh? Some things just didn't have answers. At least, not easily understood answers. One just had to believe.

***

They arrived at Beth's just before four. Lynn, Becky, and Lizzy were already in the kitchen helping to put finishing touches on the meal preparation, as Mark carried in the covered ham. Once again, the women had left a space on the counter for the meat. Mark set it on the counter and let Beth take over the unwrapping it from the blanket and layers of foil.

"Hello! Merry Christmas!" Caroline called to the ladies from the doorway of the kitchen. Her hands full of packages. "Where should these go?"

Lynn looked up from something she stirred. "Hey, Caroline!" She looked over her shoulder, saying, "Lizzy! Go show Caroline where to put the gifts!" Lizzy immediately stopped and followed Mark to the doorway. Mark winked at Caroline as he headed back towards the front door, and Lizzy led Caroline to the living room where an enormous Christmas tree sparkled in front of the bay window. The usual living room furnishings had been moved to accommodate the festive focal point.

"You can just arrange them around the bottom of the tree!" Lizzy instructed in her soft voice, as she moved her hand in a semi-circle.

Caroline looked towards the base of the tree, and her mouth dropped open. There was no base to the tree. Already the gifts were up to the bottom branches of the tree and if there was a tree skirt, it was completely hidden. "Good Lord!" Caroline wondered where she was going to put them.

"I know, right?" Lizzy nodded her head in agreement. "It's kind of wrong in a way. I'm more like Uncle Mark. I'm not so much about the materialism. I'd just rather have the people!" With that, Lizzy leaned over and gave Caroline a hug. "Merry Christmas, Aunt Caroline!"

Tears instantly sprung in Caroline's eyes. She was overcome with emotion. She sat the bags of gifts down and hugged the teen back with her good arm. "Merry Christmas, Lizzy! Best present ever!"

Lizzy smiled in returned and turned to head back to the kitchen. As she exited the living room, she met Mark carrying the crockpot. Stopping him, she placed a quick peck on his cheek and said, "Merry Christmas, Uncle Mark! I'll get that for you!" Lizzy disappeared down the hall with the scalloped potatoes.

Mark paused in the hallway looking at Caroline as she stood, wiping at her eyes. The bags of gifts at her feet and on her 'arm hanger.' She seemed oblivious to him, her focus on the tree and abundance below it.

"You okay?" Mark asked, gaining her attention.

Caroline sniffled and nodded. "Just trying to find a place for all this…" She motioned to the bags of gifts.

"Just think," Mark said. "There's more in the truck! I'll get them!"

Caroline slid her arm out of from the handles of the other

bags and took off her coat, laying it over the back of a chair. One by one she began to find a place to prop and tuck the gifts. If she put more around the base of the tree, the walking room would be taken. Instead, she began using the sill of the bay window and tucked and stacked gifts on it around and behind the tree. So, it might not look so great from the outside, but the house was far enough back from the road. Who would care? And it made for a nice picture from the front.

Mark quickly returned with the container of Brussels sprouts cradled in one arm and more bags and gifts in the other. Caroline relieved him of the gifts, letting him take the food on to the kitchen. She continued to find nooks and spots for the rest of their Christmas tidings. As Mark reappeared in the doorway, he met Larry coming in. Caroline looked up to see Larry carrying similar shopping bags full of more bags and wrapped gifts. Sniffling again, she called to the hugging brothers.

"Merry Christmas, Larry! If you want, bring those to me, and I'll find a place for them!"

Larry immediately let go of Mark to take Caroline up on her offer. He gladly handed over the bags and gave Caroline a peck on the cheek. "You are a Christmas angel!" Larry remarked, sliding out of his coat. Mark was right behind him, with a startled expression on his face. As startled as Caroline's.

"Let me take your coat Larry." Mark reached out his hand. "Dad and Kevin are in the family room involved in some debate about Christmas. They might need your expertise!" Mark chuckled.

"Always on duty!" Larry said, shaking his head. "Especially at this time of year!" As Larry disappeared through the French doors to the family room, Mark swept up Caroline's coat. "I'll hang this," he said, pausing when he saw her rubbing her cheek where Larry's greeting landed. Once again, her eyes turned glossy, and her lips trembled slightly.

"Caroline, are you okay?" Mark leaned his head to see her face. She was smiling, but a tear was getting ready to leap from her lashes. She nodded several times, sniffling again. Mark shifted Larry's coat to the other arm and pulled a handkerchief out of his back pocket. "Here." He handed her the white cloth.

Caroline dabbed at her eyes and swiped her nose. "Awe, I'm just being silly, I guess," she replied with a nasally voice. "I think I'm just struck by all of this! It's the Christmas Spirit. It's like I'm living a scene in 'It's a Wonderful Life' or something!" She motioned to everything before her. "I've never...I've never seen anything like this! It's overwhelming!" She let go of Larry's bags, letting them rest on the carpet.

Mark dropped the coats on the coffee table and stepped towards Caroline folding his arms around her. She nestled her face in the crease between Mark's coat and his pullover sweater, grasping around his waist under his coat. Mark kissed the top of her head, getting a mouthful of curls.

"Lizzy called me, 'Aunt Caroline'!" Caroline's words were muffled by Mark's coat. "I've never been called 'aunt' by anyone!" Mark could tell that her tears still flowed from the crack in her low voice and the shake in her body. Her sudden display of emotion confused him, given how flat her emotions had been earlier in the week. He'd expected a full-blown saga of tears when she found out about the recipe but was met with repressed anger. Now, as she placed gifts around the tree, she sobbed. He silently shook his head.

"Well, there's a first time for everything," Mark consoled. "And I certainly think you will hear more of such things, so let's brighten you up! Huh?" Caroline pulled her head out of Mark's coat, looked at him and nodded. He bent down, tenderly kissing her. "Besides, you don't want to go around with puffy eyes and a blotchy face, do you?"

Caroline shook her head. "I'm just being silly," she snuffed again and pulled away from Mark's warm, comforting body. "Let me get these put out!" She glanced up at him. "It'll give my face a chance to calm!"

"You sure?" Mark bent to pick up the coats.

"Yes," she snuffled again. "And see if anyone has any other

gifts that need to be put out. I'm happy to do it!" She managed a smile, as he turned from her and headed to the coat closet.

After hanging the coats, Mark paused a moment watching Caroline searching for the 'perfect' spot to place each gift. He couldn't recall ever seeing anyone place gifts under a tree with such thought and care. Having no idea of the contents or whom it was for, Caroline regarded each package individually and placed it as if it were special.

As he made his way to the kitchen, Mark contemplated how Caroline would react to his gift. He had it all planned out. But he hadn't told anyone but Beth and Caroline's parents. He trusted that Beth wouldn't accidentally slip and say something. Lynn, Larry, and his dad? Not so much. Especially Larry. Being a minister, a person would think confidentiality would be his thing, and with regard to his congregation it was. But when it came to his siblings, Larry loved to chide. Old habits were hard to break.

Mark sliced the last of the ham from the bone, adding the smaller chunks to the side of the platter. He left enough scrap meat on the bone for a good pot of pinto beans or a healthy split pea soup. The ham bone was always up for grabs among the siblings, so years before Joy Meadows had instituted the tradition of drawing straws for the hambone. As Caroline sauntered into the kitchen, she saw Lizzy clutching a grouping of straws in her hand, and Beth, Lynn, Becky and Mark surrounded her. They looked intently, almost competitively, at the straws. Caroline found the scene quite amusing and laughed.

"What's going on?" she chuckled.

Beth glanced at her with as serious a face Caroline had ever seen. "We're 'bout to find out who's gonna get the hambone!" Mark, Lynn, and Becky didn't even look up.

"Seriously?" Caroline shook her head, as Lizzy held her fist steadily out in front of her. Behind her, Larry and Dennis joined as spectators. The others had no vested interested as their turns would come in later years.

"Seriously," Dennis replied. "They draw in the order of their ages. The straws are all the same length, but one of them has a slip of paper in the end."

"Is there anything on the slip of paper?" Caroline asked.

"Ham bone." Dennis nodded his head. He was dead serious.

"Of course, it does!" Caroline shook her head again. "Why aren't you over there, Larry?" Caroline asked, as the tension mounted in the room. All eyes but Caroline's were on the clump of straws.

"Becky's my proxy," Larry replied. "She's more competitive."

"You're a sore loser, Larry!" Becky replied from the line-up.

"Okay, let's begin!" Lizzy said.

Beth was first to pull a straw from her niece's fist. One by one, the others followed, each extracting a straw, keeping the end secured and hidden in their closed palm. Once all the straws were distributed. The four opened their palms to reveal who was holding the straw with the paper. Lynn began hooping and dancing! The others wilted in their spot. Dennis just laughed.

"I got it!" she cried. "I finally got it!" She turned to Mark. "You did leave plenty of ham on it, didn't you?"

They heard moans from the family room. It was Kevin, Lynn's boy. Everyone looked his way, as he slumped on the sofa, his hand over his forehead and eyes. "Geez. We're gonna be eating beans for a week!" The rest of the cousins joined in laughter, some holding their noses. Lynn was oblivious to her son's protests as she bagged the ham bone, claiming her prize.

"Mark..." Caroline motioned him towards her. As he approached her, he reached out and rubbed her arm.

"By the way," he said before she could continue. "Did I mention how beautiful you look tonight?"

"What?" Caroline looked down at herself. She wore an oversized sweater with a Christmas scarf over a pair of plaid leggings and a pair of dressy flat-soled boots. She instantly began to blush. She managed, "Thank you!" drawing a deep breath. Mark knew it embarrassed her, but he wanted his siblings to know he was crazy about the woman before him.

"You do look wonderful, Caroline!" Beth chimed in, raising a glass of wine to her lips. Caroline nodded 'thanks' to her as well.

"What did you need?" Mark asked in a lower tone. Caroline held up a tube that looked like wrapping paper, except it was wrapped. Also, she had a bag in her hand, with green tissue paper poking out.

"I got your mom a couple of gifts," she began, pausing to wet her lips. "And I was wondering if we could go ahead and give them to her."

"Gifts? For Mom?" Mark asked. His tone was surprised. Behind him, heads turned their direction. Even Dennis and Larry took note. "Wow! I can't believe you thought to get something for Mom!" Mark paused and looked around at the others. They all were actively attending to food preparation, while casting covert glances their direction. "That's…um… so great! Um…but you do realize she doesn't know much of what's going on, right?"

Caroline felt her cheeks starting to burn from the blush. "Yes." She attempted to hide her creeping defensiveness. "That's why I took special care selecting something that would help to stimulate what recognition and senses she still has." She held up the poster. "Go ahead. Unwrap it. But be careful!"

Mark took the tube from Caroline, noting a hint of disappointment in her tone and demeanor. He gently pulled open an end and slid the tube out of the wrapping. Turning his head sideways he looked at the label that wrapped around the shrink-wrapped tube. He furrowed his brows trying to make out what it was. "A poster?"

"Yes. Open it." Caroline's directive was stilted, but her stance seemed to loosen and the flush on her face was fading.

Mark punctured the shrink-wrap and pulled the protective coating off the poster. Balling it in his hand, he tossed it on the counter beside him. Slowly, he began to unroll the poster, revealing bright splashes of colors. Caroline took ahold of one end of the poster, as Mark continued to unroll the scene. He was silent for a moment, as he took in the flowers, the different types, and the meadow. The others headed towards them to get a better look. As confusion began to form on his face, Caroline interjected.

"It's to hang on the ceiling above your mom's bed so she can see a meadow full of flowers rather than stare at the blank blue sky." Caroline held up the bag. "And I got this to go along with it." Mark was still engrossed in the poster, so Becky took the bag and pulled out the tissue paper.

"Be careful, Becky. I put pushpins in the bag to hang the poster."

Becky pulled out the bottle of lotion, looked at the label and instantly popped the lid open, taking a deep whiff. Mark glanced at the bottle, back at the poster, and then at Caroline. Now his eyes were glossy and wet.

"I was hoping you would help me hang the poster, if that's okay?" Caroline glanced at Beth. "If Beth doesn't mind a few pinholes in the wooden ceiling."

"No, not at all!" Beth wiped at her own eyes as she came over to inspect Joy Meadow's Christmas.

"I thought the lotion would not only help her dry skin, but that the fragrance might help her think she's in the meadow," Caroline explained.

Beth took ahold of the end of the poster where Mark held it and bent towards it to get a better look. Becky held the lotion to Beth's nose. Beth inhaled and closed her eyes. Mark wiped at his eyes, bit at his upper lip, then looked at Caroline, shaking his head. Looking into her eyes, he searched for words. He was numb from the shock that Caroline had not only thought of his mother but had been so thoughtful about her gift.

Caroline jumped as Dennis Meadow's placed his hand on her shoulder and sniffled behind her. Looking over her shoulder, she saw Mark's father lost the battle controlling his tears, and they flowed freely down his cheeks. He was also without words and simply nodded his head. He gave Caroline a shoulder-squeeze expressing his gratitude.

Lynn joined those clustered around the poster. She gasped, grabbing the side Caroline held. "That looks so much like the garden Mom used to keep!" She flashed a tearful smile at Caroline.

"I'll go get the step ladder!" Larry said, moving for the utility closet. "Let's go hang it!"

Mark moved around the group and took Caroline by the hand, leading her off to the side into the hallway. He embraced her and held her tightly. She didn't fight it, reciprocating the hug. At that moment the love he felt for her swelled inside him. He wanted to pull her inside his body and let the love surround her and engulf her. After a moment, he loosened his hold, bent his head and kissed her on the lips. Then he straightened his head, gently laying his lips on her forehead.

"I love you, Caroline Reeves."

She smiled at him as he let loose of her and took her hand. "Come on. Let's go hang a poster!" They followed the others through the living room to Joy Meadow's private suite, which suddenly was a flurry with action and Christmas cheer. As the others strategized positioning and pinning the poster, Caroline squirted a dab of lotion in Mark's hand and stood back, watching as he connected with his mother, bringing her eyes to his, rubbing springtime lavender on her barely mobile fingers and hand. Mark spoke to her about the poster and how they used to plant flowers together. At one point, Joy's eyes slowly returned to the ceiling. She saw the flowers her fading mind struggled to picture. She slowly breathed in the sweet smell, and her eyes smiled.

***

Caroline was not prepared for what Christmas Eve at the Meadows meant until she was emersed in the event. Halfway through the meal she realized she was participating in a marathon of sorts. Listening to the discussion around the table, it became clear that the evening had several 'courses' just like a fine meal. Caroline munched a slice of ham she'd picked up with her hand. Dinner was only the second course. The remaining events of the night laid out in casual conversation between bites and sips: storytelling, opening gifts, caroling, dessert, nightcaps to welcome the arrival of Christmas day. There was no way she and Mark were getting back to the duplex until well after midnight. No one paid attention to the ham in Caroline's fingers as the energy for the evening grew.

"Beth," Lynn addressed her older sister from across the table. "Where are we going caroling this year?" She followed her question will a forkful of scalloped potatoes. A look of ecstasy came to her face, and she looked over at Mark, pointing her fork at the potatoes.

Beth glanced at Mark as well. "I thought we would go downtown this year. We haven't caroled there for quite a while, and the buildings will block the wind." She also scooped up the potatoes but hesitated to eat them. "Better than being in a wide-open development. We almost froze last year."

"That sound lovely!" Becky remarked. "The downtown is decorated so festively this year! We will really feel the Christmas spirit!"

Caroline looked at Mark trying to hide her alarm. She had no idea they would head outside to stretch their vocal cords after the cozy, satisfying meal. "Caroling?" she asked in a low voice. "Outside?"

Mark nodded as he chewed. "We've done it since we were kids."

"It's actually a tradition Joy's family started," Dennis Meadows added. "She grew up caroling with her own family, so when we married, we joined the fun. The kids have never known a Christmas without caroling. Unfortunately, as the kids grew, we lost some of the older members of our chorus. But we've managed to keep the tradition alive." Nostalgia brought a smile to the patriarch's face. Caroline surmised the nostalgia also brought thoughts of those who'd passed and one who was no longer able to join the fun.

"That's nice really," Caroline replied. "I've only seen the caroling in Christmas movies. I never realized that people around here actually got out and caroled. I am looking forward to it!"

Beth chortled. "What Dad's not telling, Caroline, is the real tradition is returning to the house to warm up with deserts, spiked hot cocoa, and warm spirits!" Wide eyes and nods around the table agreed.

Mark's hand landed on her leg, drawing her attention. "You need to join the storytelling."

"Why is that?" she asked, glancing around the room.

"Dad does an awesome job with *'T'was the Night Before Christmas'*!" Mark replied. "And it'll get you out of clean-up! While Dad reads to the younger ones, the rest of us clear the table and clean the kitchen!"

"Thanks, Mark! Just take our help away!" Lynn barked playfully.

"No, seriously," Mark defended. "Caroline needs the full experience!"

"It's true…" Beth joined in. "By the time Dad finishes the story, we're done in the kitchen, and then we open gifts. *Then* we hit the streets!"

"Kind of like giving back for all the blessings we get," Larry added. He too held a piece of ham in his fingers. He winked at Caroline and smiled.

With the clunking of dishes in the distant background, the grandchildren and their children gathered in the living room. Dennis Meadows situated himself in a wingback chair positioned specifically for the reading, a reading light shining down on the book in his lap. The young ones sat cross-legged on the floor around his feet, while the older one's scattered in seating around the room. Mark's niece, Laura, sat on a hassock with baby Katie on her lap.

Caroline opted for the floor with the Evie and Teddy. She was surprised at their subdued state. Perhaps the meal had quieted them? Or threats of no gifts from their parents? Whatever the case, they sat patiently waiting for Dennis Meadows to begin the tale.

Dennis had the perfect voice for narrating the tale. As he read, he held the picture book towards the youngest ones, so they viewed the colorful pictures. With the glow of the color lights on the tree, the scenes on the pages took on a magical quality. Caroline enjoyed the delight and excitement that Teddy and Evie showed for the tale. Even Katie let out a squeal at one point, slapping her hands. As Caroline listened to Dennis's mesmerizing voice, she found herself drawn into the story, sharing the anticipation of the children. She found herself wondering about the taste of sugar plums.

"What happens next, Papaw D?" Teddy was up on his knees looking earnestly at his great-grandfather. Caroline snapped out of temporary dreamland. It wasn't long before the story captured her again. She was familiar with the story, having seen cartoon versions on the television, but Caroline had never seen the actual storybook, nor had she experience such an eloquent reading. In fact, she had no memory of having the story read to her or Adam and Tory. Her family simply did not read.

As Dennis drew the story to the close, Mark appeared in the doorway. From the corner of her eye, Caroline noticed Mark shaking his head. She knew it was the sight of her on the floor with the kids. Evie was snugged up next to her, and Teddy perched on his knees and heels as they intently listened as St. Nicholas made his exit.

"Papaw D?" Teddy asked as Dennis closed the book. "If that guy was St. Nik-las, where was Santa Claus? Santa s'posed to drive the reindeers!" The boy looked from Dennis around at the other adults.

"Long, long ago in the very old days," Caroline jumped in. "Santa Claus was called 'St. Nicholas.' But over time, people realized it was easier to say Santa Claus. Santa Claus became his nickname."

"It's like we call you 'Teddy,' but your actual name is 'Theodore'!" Laura added.

"Oh." Teddy sat back on his heels to think about it.

Caroline smiled as she struggled to her knees to rise from the floor. Had she asked questions like that when she was his age? As she teetered on one foot, she felt hands take ahold of her. Looking around, Mark was behind her helping to steady her as she found her feet. "Boy, that was a mistake!" she laughed, holding onto him. "Funny, but I think my 'floor days' are coming to an end! It's official! I'm not a kid anymore!" She'd completely forgotten about her bad foot and bad arm.

CHAPTER 23 – ANGELS SING

The excitement of gift opening wore the kids out. Teddy and Evie each sported a crown of bows from the packages, and dark circles under their eyes signaled needed sleep. Torn wrapping paper littered the floor, and gifts sat in piles around the room. Mark took great joy as each of his siblings revealed their fruitcakes and the leery expressions that went with the discovery.

"Mark made the fruitcake!" Caroline wanted to make sure they knew it wasn't any old ordinary fruitcake. "He used my grandmother's recipe!" The adults looked at her with surprise. "It's amazingly good!" she added, with an encouraging expression.

"Okay, this I gotta try!" Larry took their loaf out of Becky's hands, tearing into the wrapper. The rest of the family looked on skeptically as Larry broke a corner off the fruitcake. His eyebrows raised as he smelled it, and then he popped it in his mouth. As he chewed, his face remained expressionless. The room was quiet except for the parents of the little ones gathering gifts and sleepy children.

"Well?" Dennis Meadows asked. "Is it gonna kill us?"

Larry shook his head as he swallowed and licked his lips. "Well, the deadly fruitcake tradition is gone! That's the best fruitcake ever!" His words emerged as he held the loaf in his hand, regarding it as if it were a bottle of premium spirits. "Caroline, your grandmother knew her stuff!" Mark's family looked around at each other, breathing relief.

Caroline smiled. "Yes, she did! And Mark did a perfect job with her recipe!" She winked up at him as he put his arm around her. Caroline felt pleased with her role in Mark bringing pleasure to his family.

"Geez," Dennis slapped his hand playfully on the arm of the chair. "What am I going to use to bait rats now?" Everyone laughed. It must have been a standing joke.

Christmas caroling was an adult-only event. As everyone donned coats, hats, scarves, and gloves, the parents ushered sleepy kids out to vehicles and fastened them into car seats and booster seats. Beth carried an armload of caroling "books" as she climbed into the backseat of Mark's truck.

"Who's staying with Mom?" Mark asked, as his sister shut the door. Mark helped Caroline with her seatbelt. Dennis Meadows joined Larry, Becky, and Lizzy in their vehicle.

"Kevin." Lynn replied, already in the other back seat. "He said he'd rather die than be seen caroling! Teenagers!"

"We did it!" Beth laughed. Mark gave her a raised brow in the rearview mirror, reminder her how much he 'loved' caroling. "Different time and place, I guess," she added.

On the drive down the hill towards the river, random flakes of snow hit the windshield. Caroline leaned to the left to see the temperature on the dashboard. Thirty-four degrees. She decided they were crazy. Leaving a warm and cozy home to risk frostbit toes, fingers, and ears to sing Christmas songs along empty streets and dark buildings. Simply insane. But the flurries were a nice touch.

"What's wrong?" Mark asked Caroline, reaching for her hand.

"I was checking the temperature." The dash also indicated it was eight-thirty. *Wouldn't most people be in bed?* Normally, Caroline would be.

"It's cold!" Beth replied. "Cold is cold." Then she blurted, "Look! Flurries! How perfect!" Beth reached forward and patted Caroline's shoulder with her mittened hand. Caroline shot a tentative smile over her shoulder.

Both vehicles parked in the same lot as when Caroline and Mark went window shopping. As the doors of the vehicles opened, and Meadows began emerging into the shower of light snow, Beth began passing out the carol books. "We just sing them in order. That's easiest."

"Um," Caroline began, doubts claiming her. "It seems pretty

quiet down here. Are you sure this is a good idea?"

"Heaven's yes!" Beth replied. "You have no idea how many people live in apartments in these building and in the houses!" She handed a carol book to Caroline. "And there's should be several bars open! Not everyone has family to spend Christmas Eve with! Having a bunch of middle-aged teenagers strung out on fruitcake will make their day!"

"Larry's almost eaten have the loaf!" Becky told on her husband. "His singing may get pretty sloppy!"

"The bourbon was cooked, Becky!" Mark called to her. "There's just the flavor, but no potency."

"Don't tell him that!" Becky laughed joining their group. Larry was helping Dennis out of the vehicle. "He said if he gets picked up for public intoxication, a minister no less, he wants to blame the fruitcake!"

"Let's start right here on Second Street!" Beth said, handing the remaining books to Larry and her father.

As the group moved towards the street, flurries danced around their heads and landed before their feet. Caroline heard a harmonica sound. It was totally off-key, but what did she know? The group began singing the first verse of "Silent Night." Caroline didn't open her book as she was well familiar with the song. Every Christmas performance at school included "Silent Night."

Mark held his carol book open, so she stuck her book under her lame arm and slipped her gloved hand in the crook of his arm. She sang softly, not wanting to share her mediocre voice too vigorously. On the other hand, Mark had a beautiful singing voice. She looked at him with surprise as her ears enjoyed his smooth tone. The two of them strolled behind the others, with Beth and Lynn taking the lead.

While the air had a bite, Caroline found her insides warming as they strolled down the sidewalk, filling the street air with melody. Curtains and blinds in apartments above storefronts parted, and customers poured out of a local pub. The melodious Meadows paused to sing for the group. When they finished the song, the group clapped energetically, and a man holler at them.

"Come on back when you get cold! We'll give you a warm up! On the house!"

As the carolers crossed a side street, Mark motioned Caroline to the right down the side street. The continued to sing with the others until they were sufficient steps away. Mark then put his finger to his mouth, knowing Caroline was about to ask questions.

"Mark..." she whispered. He repeated the finger-to-the-mouth motion. Once they rounded the next corner, he broke the silence.

"It'll take them a while before they realize we ditched them," Mark said. Frost rose in the air as he spoke.

"What are we doing?" Caroline asked, turning partial back to the direction of the others. "Aren't we..."

"I am as eager as Kevin to go around downtown Maysville singing," he laughed. "Besides, I've something important to show you!"

"What's that?" Caroline looked around. All the shops were closed and only a few huddled people moved along the sidewalks. She wondered if they might be homeless. One figure disappeared though a doorway, the door slamming shut behind causing the light layer of powdery snow to swirl in the air.

"You'll see." Mark looked down at her and grinned.

Caroline squinted her eyes to keep the flurries out. As they made their way along the back street that paralleled the river, a large flake landed on her eyelash. She blinked thinking that would knock it loose, but it seemed to freeze there. Mark held her hand securely in his, so she leaned over and rubbed her face on his coat. Snow flake gone. Mark glanced down at her, seeming to know what she had done.

They picked up their pace. Even though Caroline's legs were long, they weren't as long as Mark Meadows, and the quick pace was causing her right foot to ache slightly. She tugged at his hand, trying to urge him to slow down.

"Mark, why are we going so fast? Why are we in such a hurry?" A cloud of frozen breath flew in her face. "My foot is starting to hurt…"

"I'm sorry!" Mark replied slowing the pace and looking down at her foot. "I didn't think this might be too much walking for you. We're just running a little behind schedule." His flattened mouth pleaded with her to try.

"Behind schedule for what?" Caroline face was full of confusion. She searched Mark's face for a clue of what they were headed for. He looked forward, intent to keep going. He finally answered her question as they rounded the corner.

"For your surprise!"

Caroline instantly recognized where they were. The fountain and tunnel under the railroad track were to the left, and the patio to the Parc Café was to the right. But they kept going.

"Surprise?" Caroline looked at him with still-squinted eyes. "I thought my surprise was in the cardboard box in the refrigerator?"

"That's one part of it," Mark replied. "For later. Tomorrow."

"Huh?" Caroline was mystified. "Okay, you've got me totally turned around. Where are we going? What's this all about?" Just as she got the words out, Mark slowed their pace and motioned in front of them.

They stood on the approach to the Simon Kenton Memorial Bridge. The lights positioned at the top of each cable light illuminated the bridge in the nighttime sky. The gently falling snow made it picturesque. Just as on the night she cruised in the Land Rover, the bridge and its lights called her. Took her breath. She looked up at Mark, shaking her head, full of questions. Mark's smile told her she'd have to wait for any answers!

"Come on!" Mark led her towards the sidewalk, and they began to walk across the bridge at a more moderate pace. Through their joined hands, she felt Mark's tension and urgency begin to slip away. "Isn't it beautiful?" he asked her as they strolled closer to the middle of the bridge.

Caroline looked around just as Mark did. The lights from the bridge reflected on the black water below. It looked like a river of ink. The further out on the bridge they moved, the breeze seemed to warm a bit. *Perhaps warmed by the water below?* Water below... A sudden flash moved before her eyes of Mark standing on the bridge illuminated by the Land Rover's headlights. The startled look of his brown eyes had reflected back at her and on instinct she swerved. She stopped walking, breaking the hold between their hands. Mark stopped a few paces ahead and turned, realizing she wasn't with him.

"Caroline, are you okay?" Mark saw she was looking at the side of the bridge and then focused on the roadway of the bridge, the pavement still darkened by the intense flames.

"This is where it happened, isn't it?" She looked up at him. She was suddenly numb, but not from the cold.

"Yes." Mark stood motionless on the sidewalk allowing Caroline to take it in. Finally, she took the several steps towards him, limping slightly.

"This is the first time I've..." her words trailed off, as she looked from the stained roadway to Mark. "What are we doing here, Mark?"

Mark swallowed hard. His scarf had fallen away from his neck in the wind. She saw the lump in his throat leap, and his jaw twitched. Mark closed the distance between them and put his arm around her shoulder. Slowly he moved her close to the railing and felt her tense. She looked up at him, a touch of fear flowing from her eyes.

"It's okay," he said calmly. "I'm not going to jump." He let out a 'humph' and shook his head. "I just want you to look out over the water, breathe, and listen."

The lights of the bridge danced on the top of the inky water. She tilted her head, looking at them a more intently. They looked like shooting stars twinkling in the night sky. The air was fresh and silent. She heard her thoughts and her heart beat. She felt the warmth of her blood flowing through her veins. The heaviness of day-to-day problems seemed to blow off her shoulders in the silent breeze. A contentedness filled her and brought a smile to her face.

Mark had mentioned several times that, even as a youngster, he had walked the bridge to clear his head. She understood this now. It gave off a rejuvenating but forgiving energy. She glanced at Mark. He stared out across the dark water, watching the 'stars.' Her eyes followed his back to the inverted sky, and then she saw it. The invisible waves caused the reflections of two of the bridge lights to floating into each other, merging into one. Two stars collided. Their eyes connected, locking onto each other's for a split second in the bright light just like the last time they were on the bridge. *Two stars collided.*

She abruptly moved from under his arm and took his hand, facing him. "I saw it. I feel it. I understand." She smiled at him. "I kept having the feeling that the old Caroline never made it off the bridge. That she burned up in the fire. When I woke, I felt nothing like her. Everything was different. Changed. And the things that used to bother me, *terrify me*, no longer had any effect on me. I felt like I'd been given a second chance. That I was an entirely new person learning how to live again. And you were there. He sent you!"

Mark nodded.

Caroline continued, "God has a way of intervening when he knows it's not your time. He did that with you and the explosion. The pain, the healing. The old Mark never left the house. The new Mark did. The pain you experienced from your injuries, was nothing compared to the pain you suffered in your old life. The healing taught you humility. As it has me."

Mark looked at her. He did not smile. He did not frown. His jaw did not twitch. He listened.

"So why did you try to do it?" she said.

"Try to do what?" Mark asked in slow words.

"To jump off the bridge?" Caroline mashed her lips together. "You were on the railing. You climbed up there for a reason.

After almost losing your life in the house explosion, what drove you to the bridge? Why would you attempt to take your life again?"

Mark sighed and looked away. He glanced down at the dark water, the water he had expected to wash him away. To wash him into non-existence. Then, he turned, leaning on the railing.

"My life still didn't have purpose," he replied. "I didn't have a reason to live. I lived through the house explosion, but I didn't find a reason to live." He swallowed hard. "I found that reason that night here on the bridge. In this spot. You were my reason. My purpose."

"Me?" Caroline put her hand on her scarf. "I was your reason?"

He nodded. "I realized something very special happened here that night. It was not coincidence. We were meant to collide and knock each other out of our current orbits."

"God?" Caroline asked.

Mark nodded. "He put us in the right place at the right time. We've put each other on a different course. Instead of orbiting other people, we're like the sun and the moon. We orbit each other."

"You're not going to…like…um…" Caroline couldn't get the words out.

"Try to kill myself again?" Mark finished her question. "No. I've no reason to. I've only got reasons to live now. That's why we're here tonight." He smiled as he stroked her face with the back of his gloved fingers.

Caroline paused, pulling a box out of her pocket. She held it towards Mark. "Thank you, Mark. Merry Christmas!" she said looking up at him and smiled.

Except Mark didn't look at her or the box. His eyes focused on something behind her. Caroline's smile faded, and she turned partially to see what captured his attention. It was his family, and they were double stepping their way towards them. Caroline's mouth dropped.

"Oh, God!" Caroline turned towards Mark, expecting to see him in a panic. She immediately thought his family must think the worst. Instead, a smile extended across his face. And being taller than Caroline, he saw something she didn't. He looked down at her and the box covered in shiny gold paper.

"Oh, God, what?" Mark asked putting a hand on each of her shoulders. He looked into her eyes. "They are coming for your surprise, Caroline! But I certainly didn't expect you to surprise me!"

"Huh?" Caroline scrunched her nose and brows. She suddenly felt cold and confused.

"With the box!" Mark pointed to the box in her hand. "I think we should wait to open that later."

"Why is everyone on the bridge?" she asked with wide eyes, as the silent carolers approached. "What surprise?"

Mark's family stepped down into the roadway to move around to the other side of Mark and Caroline. Caroline shook her head, looking at the group.

"What's going on?" She felt the shivers forming inside her body, but couldn't tell if it was from the cold, nerves, or something else. As the Meadows clustered around, Caroline's mind raced. The only coherent thought that came to her was the snowflakes looked like large specs of dandruff on their coats. Mark looked down at the golden box, but Caroline realized that his family now focused on something behind her.

Turning again, she saw another group walking towards them. She glanced back at Mark, saying "Who...?" Mark cut her off, pointing to the second group. Caroline turned again towards the newcomers and felt Mark's arm curl around her, drawing her against him.

Caroline's dropped the box as her hand flew to her mouth and her eyes grew large. A huge gulp of cold air hit her lungs causing momentary dizziness and her knees to buckle. Mark tightened his hold on her. She was grateful for his arm. She tried to look up at him but only felt his breaths on her face.

"That's....my...family..." emerged slowly from her mouth.

She looked back to see Jimmy Reeves approaching, holding Sylvie Reeve's hand. Caroline shook her head. *Had she ever seen her parent's hold hands?* It was nowhere in her memory. Behind her mother and father, was Adam and his wife, followed by Tory, her husband and both of their kids. Again, she attempted to look up at Mark, only seeing the bottom of his chin, "How…?"

"Good evening, Mr. and Mrs. Reeves." Caroline heard Mark's voice above her. It sounded confident. Mark loosen his grasp around Caroline's belly, as he reached to shake her father's hand. With still wide eyes, Caroline witnessed Mark's and Jimmy Reeves' hands clasping and her mother smiling as the men greeted each other. Caroline looked between Mark and her father, as Mark continued to speak.

"I am really glad you all could make it out on such a cold night! It means a lot!" Mark paused as Jimmy Reeves looked at Caroline. He stared at her for several seconds before swallowing hard and extending a hand towards her. Caroline stood, stunned. Looking around quickly, she hesitantly reached her good hand towards her father. As they took hands, her soft tender fingers rubbed against her father's rough, calloused hand. Before she realized what was happening, she found herself wrapped in her Jimmy's Reeves' enormous arms. She trembled, as her mind considered what he was going to do. Then she realized, her father was simply hugging her. They were making a memory. She managed to use her own arm to hug him back, as he whispered in her ear, "Love you." The words evoked a rush of water to Caroline's eyes, and as she pulled away, she saw the shine in her father's own eyes. She mouthed the words, no sound coming out, "I love you, too!" As soon as she pulled away from her father, she found herself in her mother's arms and was passed off to Adam, then Tory. Caroline looked around seeing the two family's standing on the sidewalk and in the road, shaking hands and greeting each other. It was surreal.

Dazed, Caroline made her way back to Mark, her hand

again covering her mouth, and tears flowing down her cheeks, freezing before they made it to her chin. Rejoining Mark, who had picked up the gold box, she asked, "You arranged this? Why here?"

Mark took her hand, saying, "Hold on…" He then looked at Jimmy Reeves. Caroline noticed Mark stood a little straighter, and her father puffed out his chest, as his did when he tried to assume the upper hand with someone.

"Do you have an answer for me, sir?" Mark asked.

Sighing and deflating slightly, Jimmy Reeves gave a quick nod. "You've my blessin'." Sylvie Reeves threw both hands to her mouth as tears sprouted. The look Caroline's mother gave her father reminded her of a similar look, many, many years ago. She couldn't place it.

Caroline looked from Mark to her father. Confusion filled her. Scanning the rest of the group, she noticed Mark slip the gold box in his coat pocket. As she looked around, she noticed everyone seemed to be watching with anticipation, including her own siblings. Looking back at Mark, she startled. He was gone. Then she looked down, seeing Mark kneeling, a small dark box in his hand. He looked as nervous as Caroline felt. Her face scrunched up. She tried to hide it with her hand.

Shaking, Mark flipped the top of the box open revealing a ring—two stars sitting side-by-side, one slightly covering the other, encased in diamonds. It sparkled like the stars in the sky, and the lights in the water below.

"Caroline, you are my star, my light in an otherwise dark life. You keep me steady and on keel. You remind me each waking day my life has purpose, meaning, and worth. We are two stars collided, inexplicably connected, forever changed. You are a gift from God. Will you marry me?" Despite a trembling hand, Mark's words were clear and unshaken.

Caroling just nodded her head and stuck out her hand. The word "yes" finally made it out of her lips, followed by a litany of "yes's" as Mark removed her glove and slid the ring on her finger. She continued to murmur "yes" until Mark stood, took her in his arms and kissed her.

Applause broke out all around them. As their lips parted, they noticed their audience was dispersing. Mark and Caroline stayed on the bridge as the families retreated to their vehicles. They were all headed to Beth's house to celebrate the spirit of Christmas. Dennis Meadows promised Jimmy Reeves, "There'll be plenty of spirits, my man!" Larry added, "And fruitcake!"

***

Caroline beamed as Mark tore away the gold paper. Removing the lid, his face broke into a smile bigger than the one already there. Reaching into the box, he pulled out a sturdy chain with two dangling stars, affixed to each other.

"Together we form a constellation, by which we will navigate life together!" Caroline said, as Mark fastened the chain around his neck and tucked the stars under his shirt for safekeeping. Caroline reached up, placing her hand on the side of Mark's face, and kissed him again. Taking Caroline's hand, they began walking off the bridge.

"Merry Christmas, Mark Meadows!" Caroline gave their hand a swing.

"Merry Christmas, Caroline soon-to-be-Meadows!"

Caroline was silent a moment, their footsteps making the only sound. "So, how soon are we talking?" she finally asked.

"Oh, I don't know," Mark replied, giving her hand a swing. "Why?"

Caroline pursed her lips, wiggling her head a couple of times. "Well, speaking of 'gifts from God,' we might be needing to add a star to that chain…"

About the Author

Gera Jones

Photo by Savannah Jo Photography

Gera Jones lives in Muses Mills, Kentucky on Heaven's Gait Farm with her husband, their three dogs and two cats. In her spare time, Gera farms, gardens, keeps bees (her *girls*), cans vegetables and makes homemade jellies from berries on the farm. She works full-time in higher education at a local university and is the owner of a sideline business making customized jewelry and apparel items from repurposed items. Additionally, Gera has a passion for making hand-sewn, hand-crafted journal books, also from reclaimed materials, which she also sells, but mostly gives to charitable organizations!

***

The Bridge (2023) is Gera's sixth published novel.

OTHER TITLES by Gera Jones:

Painted Windows – 2021

Dashboard Lights – 2021

Ruby Ring – 2022

The Woodsman – 2022

Fernlee -- 2022

Made in the USA
Columbia, SC
22 May 2023